THERE WILL BE BODIES

THERE WILL
BE BODIES

Lindsey Davis

HODDER &
STOUGHTON

First published in Great Britain in 2025 by Hodder & Stoughton Limited
An Hachette UK company

The authorised representative in the EEA is Hachette Ireland, 8 Castlecourt
Centre, Dublin 15, D15 XTP3, Ireland (email: info@hbgi.ie)

1

A CIP catalogue record for this title is available from the British Library

Hardback ISBN 978 1 399 71963 6
Trade Paperback ISBN 978 1 399 71965 0
ebook ISBN 978 1 399 71964 3

Typeset in Plantin Light by Hewer Text UK Ltd, Edinburgh
Printed and bound in Great Britain by Clays Ltd, Elcograf S.p.A.

Hodder & Stoughton policy is to use papers that are natural, renewable
and recyclable products and made from wood grown in sustainable
forests. The logging and manufacturing processes are expected to
conform to the environmental regulations of the country of origin.

Hodder & Stoughton Limited
Carmelite House
50 Victoria Embankment
London EC4Y 0DZ

www.hodder.co.uk

Rome, AD 90: the Bay of Neapolis area, especially Stabiae

... Where Vesuvius rears his broken summit in wrath,
*   pouring out*
Flames to rival the Sicilian fires. A marvel! Will
Future generations, when the crops have grown again and this
Wilderness greens up once more, believe that people and cities
Are buried beneath, that an ancestral countryside has
*   vanished,*
In an act of fate?

Statius, *Silvae 4*, probably published in AD 95

Campania: the Bay of Neapolis

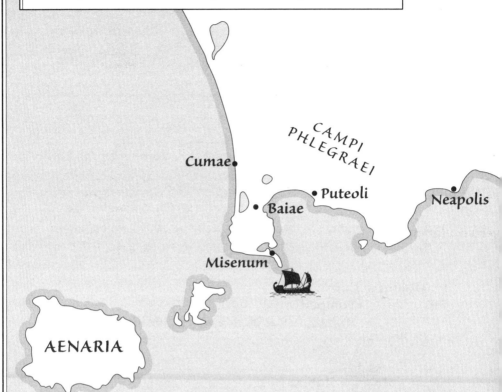

Cumae

CAMPI
PHLEGRAEI

• Puteoli

• Baiae

Neapolis

Misenum

AENARIA

PUTEOLANUS
CRATER

CAPREAE

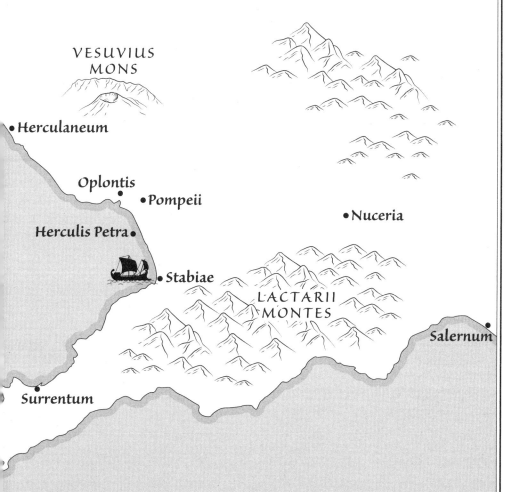

N

SPQR

VESUVIUS
MONS

•Herculaneum

Oplontis
•

•Pompeii

•Nuceria

Herculis Petra•

•Stabiae

LACTARII
MONTES

Salernum•

Surrentum

PÆSTANUS
SINUS

Characters, mainly alive

In or from Rome

Tiberius Manlius Faustus	a builder, working for nothing
Flavia Albia	a freelance investigator, comes at a price

Their household (them again): Gaius and Lucius the dear little nephews; Gratus the smooth steward; Dromo the dim slave; Paris the cheeky runabout; Fornix the celebrity chef; Suza the hopeful beautician; Glaphyra the diligent nurse; Barley the house dog
Their workmen: Larcius the clerk-of-works; Sparsus the apprentice; Serenus the old hand; Vindex and Dexter the leisure-loving painters; Drax the site watchdog; Mercury the donkey

Tullius Icilius	uncle and property impresario
Sextus Curvidius Fulvianus	his vendor, honourable, surely

The Seventh Cohort of Vigiles

Gaius Caunus	a tribune, gone on a bender
Rufeius	a cohort centurion, possibly lightweight
Milo and Hyro	porridge-eating heavyweights
Acer and Acilius	who have lost their appetites
Charis	a valiant girlfriend, with a baby

The people of Stabiae: in the town

Apuleius Innocentius	the duovir, keeping his head down
Bathyllus	a holistic herbalist
Axilius	a piecework carpenter
Septumius	in second-hand collectibles
Crispus	his nephew, shifty
Criton	a runaway, safely collected up
Dexiades	an utterly legitimate trader in art
Ergon	his driver, sinister

Docetius, Surdinius, Bitho, Acatholos	further associates
Egloge	'the jailer's beautiful daughter'
Waiters	in harbourside catering

The people of Stabiae: up on the heights

Publius Curvidius Fulvius Primus	mysteriously disappeared
Fulvia Secunda	completely absent
Blossia	her helpful slave
Tertius	curiously missing
Quartilla	keeping out of everything
Curvidia Quinctia	a priestess, packs a punch
Quinctius Polydorus	her freedman, an acolyte perforce
Publilius Gellius and Publilia Lavinia	friends of the family (they say)
Porphyrus, Endymio, Myrtale	deceased slaves, tragic
Anonymous	a child, heartbreaking
Nibble	a dead watchdog, desperate
Marius	a wandering minstrel, philosophical
Bitus	a neighbour with a hat
Favonilla and Heius	big-hearted smallholders
Pescennius Neo	a plutocrat with Roman polish

I

‘There will be bodies. It is only fair to warn you,’ my husband told his workmen. Some contractors might have kept quiet, but he liked to be open about risks. Mind you, he had brought me in on the discussion in case he needed support. I won't say the men were frightened of me, but they were generally wary.

When Tiberius Manlius took over their nearly bankrupt company, the existing team saw it as a fad. But he could recognise the right end of a chisel; they had learned that now. And for men with mortar on their boots, being employed by a toff in a laundered toga was better than losing their jobs.

Not that he was soft: 'If anyone prefers to stay behind in Rome, I won't be paying a retainer.'

'That's a joke?' Sparsus, the apprentice, was traditionally young and daft.

'Afraid not. Are you turning down a free holiday?' This really was a joke because Tiberius had explained that the project at Neapolis would be hard work. It was a favour to his uncle, a man who had grown rich through screwing his customers and who tended to view even close relatives as people to be played.

Uncle Tullius had bought a house. It was uninhabitable, but he presumed that, with a nephew in the building trade, he could have it very cheaply restored. 'No frills, just a basic clear-out. At cost, of course,' he had said airily. That meant we should not expect to make a profit.

Tiberius was humouring him. This uncle controlled the family finances: co-operation was the safest approach. Keeping him sweet applied even though the vague 'clear-out' would involve excavating volcanic material that had been dumped in and around his new property during the disastrous eruption of Mount Vesuvius. Most walls were still standing, Tullius had been assured.

'That could be a lot of pumice, Legate!' observed our clerk-of-works darkly.

Tiberius nodded. 'Larcius, it's clear how Tullius managed to nab this place at a knock-down price. All the easy-rescue projects were knocked off years ago. But we'll be fine, don't worry. I deliberately haven't told him about the sky-high billing rate we devised for "hacking out rubble" on our Eagle Building job. You know Albia had the agent paying for protective gear and specialist insurance.'

Larcius had liked that. We still had equipment from the Eagle Building job stored in the yard for future use, while the supposed insurance premium had financed an end-of-project feast.

'Helmets. First-aid supplies. Danger money . . .' I was inventing in the same merry way I had bamboozled our customer's agent. A year ago, I had known nothing about demolition and restoration, but I learn fast. Like most Roman wives I was now a lead player in the family business. Like most, I was ruthless financially.

'Custom and practice!' Tiberius winked at me. 'If we don't know what the custom is, we'll make it up as we go along.'

A year ago, *he* was a leisured playboy, until he came out of his shell when his uncle financed his election as a magistrate.

This shift into the political world was intended to raise their business profile, but Tiberius had taken the role seriously. Uncle Tullius had had a big surprise over his nephew's approach to public service. But the building trade was different: he might have another shock with his 'honest' nephew's approach to working on the new house.

My husband was a practical man, even if some people said his good sense had let him down when he married me. After six months, he was still claiming that was the best thing he had ever done; I just smiled mysteriously.

In theory, if Tiberius Manlius ever decided he had made a mistake, my own work as a private enquiry agent ought to equip me to bring about a painless divorce. I was realistic, however. Why do lawyers die without making their wills? How come doctors are killed off by coughs they have never bothered to treat? Meanwhile, informers' marriages often fall apart: the financial stress is terrible, children are permanently damaged, their dog runs away, and they certainly don't bother with any pretence that the split is so amicable they will stay friends.

Our dog could sleep soundly in her fancy kennel, I thought. Despite all I had learned from tragic clients, I envisaged Tiberius and me sticking it out, hand in hand, until we were doddery. I supported him with love and loyalty, while he showed plain determination. Marriage had been his idea, and he could always make his ideas sound reasonable. That was why most of his men agreed to travel with us to the new site. Sparsus, the excitable apprentice, even pestered us about what any corpses they uncovered might look like.

'To be honest, I don't know.' Tiberius had given it forethought. 'It's been ten years. Victims were buried deep in compacted materials that were very hot. I can't tell you whether any remains in that old crud will be decayed or preserved. We shall find out soon enough. All Tullius knows from the owner is that some people who lived in the house were never seen again. If we do come across victims, we have been asked to collect any evidence of who the poor souls were.'

Serenus, who was an experienced labourer, pulled a face. 'And what are we supposed to do with them?'

'Chip them out as best we can. Then dispose of them reverently.' It sounded as if Tiberius himself was making this rule. I suspected he had not even asked the previous owner what he wanted done. Bodies would be treated with respect, because it was the pious way to behave. I had married a good man. That was a surprise to me, just as my love of his benign character surprised him. He had feared I wanted someone rougher. 'The seller will pay for basic memorials for slaves,' Tiberius reported. 'But he did tell Uncle Tullius that he wants to hold a full funeral, in the event we are able to identify his long-lost brother.'

A long-lost brother? That was news.

Hmm. In my experience such situations are never as clean-cut as people suppose. However, tracking down a missing relative sometimes brings in business for me, so this could be welcome. 'Will the vendor give us a finder's fee?'

'I suspect not.'

Even young Sparsus, ever curious, was quick to spot the oddity: 'Chief, when fiery lava started flying around, why didn't this brother jump into some crack piece of transport and make a bolt for the hills?'

Exactly. Still, relatives can be hard to fathom. Half the time in my investigations, people who have disappeared did it to cause trouble in their family.

'Vesuvius had created utter panic.' I must have sounded sombre. I had been there afterwards. I had told them that, though so far not dwelled on it. 'What came out wasn't slowly creeping lava that people could run away from, but ferocious explosions of rock, ash, mud, gases and heat. If the brother did grab valuables and try to escape, as many people desperately did, some accident might have befallen him. Dashing off in a direction that looked passable, he could have ended up in a village where he wasn't personally known. When his lungs or heart gave out, after he'd breathed in poisonous air and dust, no one sent word to his family. But there was anarchy on the roads. He may never have reached safety. All the social rules broke down. This man could have been set upon for his "crack transport", then he was killed and dumped – one more anonymous victim beside those crowded escape routes.'

Tiberius smiled and commented, 'If you come with us, that will be something for you to investigate, Albia!'

We had already agreed that I was going with them. I cooed back, like a doe-eyed housewife, 'Thank you, darling!'

I made it sound as if I had absolutely no interest, but he knew me: I was already wondering.

2

The cut-price villa was at Stabiae, on the southern side of the Bay of Neapolis. We had been told it stood high on the cliffs above the town and port below. Such a grand position must have made a stupendous observation point when Mount Vesuvius exploded – although rather too close for comfort if you were trying to stay alive.

Stabiae and its residents had survived the first day, but as the eruption increased in violence, people either upped and fled in a hurry or they were trapped in deadly fumes. The killing waves of heat and gas that wiped out the famous towns of Pompeii and Herculaneum did reach as far as Stabiae, although with less force. Where Tullius had bought, at the eastern end, many huge, fabulous villas had been built in a tight-packed ribbon along the heights; some became smothered in volcanic debris as high as first storey ceiling level. Tiberius reckoned from advance research it could be fifty feet or so deep. Even so, Tullius had been assured that many along the Surrentum Peninsula were not buried as deeply as farms and towns closer to the volcano. Creeping back home after three days of terror, people could still see through the silence and darkness where the little town of Stabiae had been.

Elsewhere it was different. That's famous. I had gone to Campania afterwards with my father, pointlessly searching for relatives. It had a profound effect on me, which I would have to address once I was ready. Falco had known the area so he could hardly believe what we found. Herculaneum was so deeply buried it was gone for ever. At Pompeii only the very tops of the tallest buildings showed above maybe seventy feet of tephra. Occasional roof fixings hinted at monuments below, or we could sometimes decide the position of streets because lines of excavated holes showed where returning householders or thieves had already tunnelled in. A lot of property was being retrieved. Opportunists were everywhere – they must have begun scavenging while the infill was still warm. But the famous town had died. Thousands had perished. Falco and I never found the people we were looking for.

As ever, the rich had managed compensation for their grief. Like many well-off Romans, Uncle Tullius had previously owned holiday homes on the bay. Like others, he was now thinking that after ten years things ought to be improving, so that playground for the wealthy ought to become available again. Plutocrats don't accept losses easily, not even when they have to blame the gods.

In the immediate aftermath, Tullius sold his house at Neapolis to an imperial commissioner; he did so as soon as he heard how the government was providing funds to rehome refugees, and he made a packet, naturally. He had also owned a villa near the harbour at Herculaneum, but he lost that. Herculaneum's port was first smashed up by waves, then the town above was engulfed by enormous torrents of boiling mud and rock. The shape of the bay altered. Soon, nobody would even remember where Herculaneum had been.

Tullius had had to accept that his elegant holiday home, with its sunlit balcony and sweet sea breezes, must be permanently written off. He had loved that villa, or so it was said ('love' was never a word I associated with Uncle Tullius). Eventually he jumped at his accountant's suggestion that buying a new place would be good tax management. Stabiae was being recommissioned as a larger port now Pompeii had gone. Sailors could no longer land at the old Marine Gate and walk up into a racy town under the protection of the goddess Venus. Stabiae had once been smaller and staider: this minor beach and spa town was the coming place. Taking on a semi-derelict property there would make Tullius Icilius a social benefactor, giving support to the devastated community.

People did not usually see him as sentimental. Any thought of him as a benevolent old buffer would soon disperse if you met him. However, among men of the same type, he passed as canny and trustworthy – well, as much as any of them.

The family money had been made over several generations. As Rome had expanded into an aggressive empire, its citizens gained access to new provinces that either wanted what Italy produced or produced what Italy wanted. The Icilii had recognised that, but saw no reason to face the burdens of shipping and overland transport, to struggle with negotiating in trade markets, to defend against pirates and brigands, or to bribe officials. Rather than acquire a colicky mule-train or pay a dubious wagon-master of their own, they bought a warehouse in Rome for other people to hire. One building, well run and astutely priced, was soon added to until much of the Aventine Hill above the Lavernal Gate was neatly clothed in their stores.

According to Tullius, the warehouses ran themselves, although I knew he still contributed a personal input. Under a detached veneer, he worked hard, managing alone for years because he had never let his nephew be other than a cipher.

Tiberius was allowed a palaestra subscription and an account with a scroll-seller, but he was kept away from the ledgers. Tullius controlled their joint fortune.

By the time I met him, Tullius Icilius was a well-known figure on the Aventine. He was in his sixties. Wealth had made him heavy in the midriff and ponderous in manner; success let him be scathing of others. He had never married, which was for selfish reasons. Why bother? What would be the point of a wife? A woman in the home would only spend money and try to poison him off. We were sure he did not deny himself pleasure but, after all, when his only sister died she had bequeathed him a reliable adult heir in her son, Tiberius Manlius. There had been a daughter too, who also died, leaving behind three little boys, two of whom we were fostering. Tullius had no need to be disturbed by infants in his own quiet house.

He lived over by the Street of the Plane Trees, above the riverbank Emporium where his tenants would buy and sell their expensive goods. It may have felt as if he was personally supervising their safe storage, though he paid managers to do that. Yet he maintained a presence, in a large private home with understated elegance. It might have suited a senator, though such a pomposity might complain it was cramped for entertaining. Tullius only entertained if there was a business advantage. When he did, he and his guests tended to turn up unannounced and take pot-luck. Mind you, his well-organised staff always ensured that an extremely generous pot would be available, with all the trimmings, and the best fish sauce that men of business could require. His was a comfortable home, though people were lucky to be invited. It was different for us, because Tiberius had lived there for half his life so he would stroll in and out as he wanted.

The Icilii had always been plebian; Tullius saw no reason to waste money on upgrading to the next social level, though he did push his nephew into that official post last year. They had used traditional methods (dinners, favours, donations) to make Tiberius an aedile. After he startled everyone with his unexpected diligence, their standing increased until his uncle screwed his eyes into a piggy expression and grunted that he wasn't planning to do it again, but it had been worth splashing some cash.

He was less pleased when Tiberius decided to marry me. At the same time, Tiberius bought a building firm. His late father and grandfather had been successful in this line, so Tullius set aside his objections. At least he could exploit Tiberius and his men as cheap labour at Stabiae.

'The old sod seems to think we come free,' grumbled Tiberius – though he was putting up with it.

He had a vague responsibility for acquiring the villa. In some mysterious way that I never winkled out, my husband's year as a magistrate had improved his uncle's balance sheet. Out of concern for Tiberius, who was one of Rome's few honest men, I preferred not to know how his uncle had taken advantage of his stint in public service. No one but me ever seemed suspicious. Once a businessman is accepted as honest, his reputation usually carries on for life. Perhaps, since questioning appearances was part of the work I did, I was too quick here. Perhaps a completely innocent assets-review had led the uncle to purchase his supposedly desirable property at Stabiae. Especially as he believed it was a bargain.

He had snaffled it from a crony. Tullius would usually wheel and deal at bar-room lunches, where married men took refuge away from home stress, or at off-colour dinners in bachelors' houses: places where peculiar perfumes were sprinkled and foreign flute-girls poured the drinks. I had assumed all his contacts were long-term. People he had known for years, whose families he had heard about even if he had not met them. Men whose lives, wives and trading acumen he could evaluate. Those whose bankboxes his own financier sniffed out and slyly priced for him. People he called 'solid'. Perfectly safe to rely on if he was purchasing a property a hundred and fifty miles away, sight unseen.

It turned out that was not the case. Tullius knew Sextus Curvidius Fulvianus only slightly; he was the proverbial 'friend of a friend'. Tullius could barely describe the villa, let alone discuss his vendor's personal circumstances. However, to assist my husband with pre-planning the works, he invited us to dine at his house, where we could have a look at floor-plans and meet the vendor.

'See what you think, Albiola,' my husband muttered to me. I am always drawn to an enigma, but he could be even worse. He was not referring to the villa's layout. He meant *is this man a crook?*

3

M y initial thoughts were neutral.
Curvidius Fulvianus arrived slowly. His movements were stiff, but he had made it into his seventies. He
had a boyish face, despite his years. Short hair, still brown-
ish, came forwards on a domed forehead in a natural fall, not
a vanity cover-up. He was fairly tall, not gaunt but no spare
flesh.

To reach his age, his life must have been fortunate. He
might be rich, though had not acquired glittering sesterces
by heaving about big sacks and amphorae. Stronger staff,
who no doubt died younger, must have done that, while the
sheltered Fulvianus busied himself with contacts and
contracts, or flights into two-timing the Treasury.

It went without saying that everyone we ever met in the
company of Uncle Tullius finagled their fiscal affairs. Sales,
inheritance, manumissions, customs dues – and absolutely
the imperial census. They rarely boasted, but tax fiddles were
a staple of life for these men. That was the main reason
Tullius and my father had managed a meeting of minds
when Tiberius and I had announced our intended marriage.
Falco's stated profession these days was 'auctioneer', so he
was adept at massaging money in inventive ways. He
pretended he never did it; Uncle Tullius knew what that
meant so they shook hands on the wedding that neither could

avoid. They would make aloof blood-brothers, yet they could discuss a flagon of Falernian without coming to blows.

Of course, afterwards Pa would grouch that Tullius was an idiot: last night's wine had been Fundanian.

For his vendor, on our getting-to-know-you evening, Tullius served Alban. No wine buff would exclaim over that, but it would give guests a secure feeling; their host probably did not drink Alban every day (unless he was a consul). In snobbish Roman society, Alban was a compliment. It was a golden vintage, with a local terroir, a liquor of price that the best people would bring out for visitors. Slurping this, Curvidius Fulvianus would feel he had status among us, perhaps not honour, but respect. A two-pepper sauce on the entrée would reinforce his satisfaction.

Of course, if Curvidius spotted that Tullius had instructed the drinks-mixer to apply the notorious rule of 'eight parts water, one part wine', he might rethink. Still, he would have heard from fellow-traders that Tullius Icilius fell short of miserly yet was always careful. 'Careful', in business, is a synonym for mean as stink.

Watching the scene as Tiberius had urged me to, I saw Curvidius drink whatever was in his goblet. He never stretched out his arm impatiently for a refill, but he knew how to catch a slave's eye unobtrusively. Staff served him willingly; his behaviour had not caused them to look the other way, as servers in their own house will do if slighted by a boorish guest.

Tullius was barely bothering to drink. He would wait until Curvidius left, and possibly even us, his nearest relatives. Then, with his feet up in battered slippers, he would apply the other ancient adage: 'Eight parts wine for me, forget the water.' Finally on his own, he would enjoy himself.

My husband was refusing top-ups, though not from prudery. Tiberius preferred to feel sober among strangers. He liked to choose his company. Of course, if he felt comfortable, he could knock it back. Six months ago, he had managed to return alive from a stupendous bar-crawl with my father – he endured that test because Falco would not release rights in one of his daughters to a man he viewed as a wimp.

Wimpiness was not an issue. Tiberius had been pre-vetted as husband material by me, a private investigator who specialised in checking bridegrooms for nervous families. I was a widow, close to thirty and realistic. But my skills were irrelevant: Pa had enjoyed the power, putting his hopeful son-in-law through a night of stress.

On the evening at his uncle's, Tiberius viewed Curvidius Fulvianus as work, so he called the Alban 'very drinkable' yet discreetly held off. As for me, I practised the informer's trick. Falco had taught me this. I kept my nose in my bronze wine cup, gave a minute head-shake when anyone approached offering more, applied a thoughtful exterior and quietly absorbed the scene.

Uncle Tullius was expecting sharp conversation from me; he looked suspicious at my silence. Fulvianus never noticed. He must believe that the Icilius family had snared a dutiful matron who would enhance her male relatives: wear a lot of jewellery, eat a few prawn balls, look admiring when a man spoke, and otherwise behave just as authors of the duller kind tell us is traditional for Roman women.

'*Cobnuts!*' That would be my mother, Helena Justina. She had picked up the expletive from Father, but the indignation is hers. She encouraged me to shake up dinners with controversial remarks, stopping short only of anything that might cause my husband to be executed. 'Unless,' murmurs Mama,

14

'he has done something really irritating. Then you may as well let rip.'

Watching the men as they danced their dance about the villa sale, I thought Curvidius was too bland. *He* would not agitate a beetle. On one of my tetchy days, his sheer dullness would have riled me. No one should choose to be unremarkable. Would I buy a house from him? No, Legate.

Of course, it would be unfair to dismiss our uncle's vendor for keeping his own counsel. But even though the deal was already signed and stamped with their manly seal rings, I felt this fellow needed to convince us that whatever he had shifted onto Tullius was honest real estate. So far, I remained sceptical.

Tullius mostly sat out the discussion. His nephew acted as his agent. It must have been clear from his questions that if our workmen uncovered any structural flaws, my husband would take it up, even post-contract. He knew enough about buildings to judge whether failures of maintenance were responsible for problems, rather than Vesuvius. Fulvianus brushed this aside almost lazily. Like anyone Tullius knew, he had rich experience with deals. He reckoned he could negotiate his way past a tricky nephew: 'You know, we had an earthquake a few years before the eruption.'

Oh, good try, honourable vendor!

'Eight years before,' nodded Tiberius, unfazed. 'Then another, a smaller one. Recovery had been slow afterwards, according to my sources. Rebuilds had hardly got going when the fatal disaster struck. I guess repair firms had been much in demand and they were able to charge as much as they wanted.'

'Fair point,' weighed in Tullius. Uncle and nephew nodded at each other, then Tullius reapplied himself to the dessert comport. He looked surprised there were so few honeyed dates left; he could not have spotted me grazing. No platter is safe near a woman who is pretending to be a traditional matron. You cannot pick your nose (Mother again), so you have to pick at the sweetmeats.

Tiberius beat his uncle to the last apricot. 'I concede there could be earlier damage from seismic waves . . .' a thoughtful chew '. . . but when Vesuvius began its act, of course there were more earthquakes.' Everyone looked impressed. Old Grey Eyes must have drunk more of the Alban than I had realised, from the way he settled in to lecture us. 'Buildings are more easily harmed by horizontal motion than vertical. Low-frequency vibrations are the worst; the ground floor crumbles, then the upper storeys pancake down on top. We assume this doesn't apply to your property, Sextus Curvidius, my friend. But structures can be harbouring serious cracks that are a bugger to correct.' Tiberius certainly did initial research. He smiled, affable as a homing-in mosquito. 'I learned that from my grandfather. "Bugger to correct" is a technical term, he said!' Then he slid in: 'I assume you had had any earthquake damage assessed and repaired?'

Tullius began to look anxious. Clearly he had never obtained a schedule of defects before signing the purchase agreement.

Fulvianus waved it away. 'Not my responsibility. My brother was still alive.'

This introduced the brother neatly. Deflected from potential defects, Tiberius moved on to the issue of human remains. He reprised how Uncle Tullius had told him Fulvianus wished to have his sibling identified, if possible. How would we identify the brother? If our labourers were to meet any skeleton face to face, one grinning skull would look much like another.

The reply was unhelpful. Fulvianus said he had not been to Campania for many years prior to the eruption, nor had he returned there since. Before that, he and his brother had never got on. No reason was given. Tiberius shot me a glance, with the option to ask questions. I let it pass. Arguing families are the norm in my work, and if we needed to know details of a split, I might prefer to ask other people, neutral witnesses.

'We kept in touch when we had to,' Fulvianus conceded. 'Intolerable swine. I sent him a gift for his sixty-fifth birthday, never had an acknowledgement, not one word of thanks.'

'What was the gift?' I asked, pondering whether their courier had pinched it, as would be usual. 'In case we find it?'

'Bloody great vase. Some Greek with a beard, putting his spear in. Cost me a packet.'

Privately, I wondered if the recipient had felt this choice of gift was a hint: had his brother sent him a funeral urn, naughtily suggesting that sixty-five would be his last anniversary?

Tiberius double-checked: 'Even though you were at odds, you want to give your brother's soul a proper send-off?'

Bland as ever, the survivor answered, 'One has one's duties to family.'

The brother had been Publius Curvidius Fulvius Primus. He was a childless widower. As his final cognomen suggested, Primus was the first-born. Beyond that there was little to help with identification. As far as Fulvianus knew or could recall, Primus had possessed no physical peculiarities, nor had he ever experienced any broken bones. (Tiberius again caught my eye; that would have made our task too easy!) The two had been similar in height, which was a start, but colouring and other characteristics would not have survived their ten-year interment in volcanic ash. 'He let himself go. He got heavy, I believe.' Fulvianus, a trim man, seemed to enjoy this sneer.

I bestirred myself to contribute professionally: might a signet ring or other jewellery have been worn? Fulvianus raised his eyebrows at the way I joined in, but allowed himself to reply that he could not even remember what his brother's seal had been; his own secretary would have it in family records, so he would find out.

Originally the family came from Campania: to be precise, Salernum on the way to Paestum. The villa at Stabiae had been a family home, though they owned others. Fulvianus had moved to Rome many years ago to pursue business interests at the heart of things, though he still had a small clutch of relatives down south: distant connections, he implied. Once it had been determined that Primus was missing and must have perished, Fulvianus stepped up as head of the family, assuming ownership of the homestead at Stabiae. Tullius had now acquired everything within the curtilage, with an understanding that outdoor amenities that might once have existed were sadly all defunct. Behind the villa there had been gardens, a vineyard and an orchard with olive trees. They were buried by the volcano. 'Nothing that grew has survived, but I understand there are still outbuildings. You can stable your mules.'

The floor plan was brought out. Tiberius flipped the crackling skin across the serving table, but when we asked Fulvianus how rooms had been used by his family, remembrance seemed to upset him. Without pressing, Tiberius made quick descriptive notes in ink, then re-rolled the plan to take home.

We did not ask, and were not given, legal information. Curvidius Fulvianus behaved as an owner with good title; Tullius had accepted that in good faith. If Primus had ever made a will, it had vanished, like so many documents that belonged to people killed in the eruption. Fulvianus had had to guess what his brother had wanted.

It was the same for many. Family and business records perished. Only by chance were documents ever found later, usually dropped in ditches by fleeing refugees, when carrying heavy record-chests through the smog and debris became impossible. Even if old scrolls were dug out now, they would be irrecoverably damaged.

I had done research of my own kind before we came tonight. I went to the Basilica Julia to ask legal questions. I learned that attempts had been made to smooth out problem situations when landowners around Vesuvius had obviously died. Often there were no survivors to inherit. In that situation a commission appointed by the Emperor had made compulsory acquisitions. If a challenger ever did raise objections, I was told that courts had tried to find speedy, non-controversial ways to a settlement.

'Really? Didn't it lead to chancers bringing fake claims?'

My contact Honorius was an old associate of Father's, mired in Falco's cynicism. He agreed. However, as an earnest practising lawyer, he claimed that taking advantage of the catastrophe fraudulently had been viewed by judges – 'well, most judges' – as an improper use of litigation. So great was the national trauma that even those who worked in the law had reacted by being honest and helpful on land reassignment. I tried to believe that.

Conscious of libel, Honorius declined to name any property raiders – though it was clear he could have done.

'Immoral scams!' I had grumbled at him. In reply, Honorius told me the legal definition of a scam was 'an opportunity'.

I did not report this at dinner. If Tullius and Curvidius Fulvianus were mutually happy about their sale, nobody needed to cause them anxiety. To do business on a handshake was normal procedure in their world; for landed property a contract would be needed, but their spoken agreement would have been the key formality. Even Tiberius was only going to quibble if the house was really so fragile it fell down.

The servers came to carry out the table and dishes. Fulvianus took his leave.

'You'll be off, then!' exclaimed Uncle Tullius, keen to be rid of us.

Tiberius and I stayed put. We were planning to drop a surprise on him.

4

'So what are you two up to?' demanded Uncle Tullius, suspiciously.

'Just need a quick word about arrangements for our trip,' breezed Tiberius. 'Albia's the best person to explain it.' Luckily I had seen that coming.

I duly told his uncle it made sense for us both to go to Stabiae. We had recently emerged from an investigation that had involved personal danger, danger from criminals who would bear grudges; it was wise to leave town for a while. We were closing up our house in Rome. We would be taking staff south with us, I said, but not those darling infants, our two little foster sons. We felt they ought to come and stay here.

Uncle Tullius was usually astute, but I saw his jaw drop.

To explain our fears, I described going to Pompeii after the eruption. 'My father's favourite nephew was a painter in the area, so from the start we knew he and his family were likely to have perished. Falco was distraught. He set off as soon as he heard what had happened. My mother had two young children at home, and had been landed with caring for a baby; that was my brother Postumus, whom they went on to adopt. Helena Justina could not possibly accompany Father so she asked me. I was not twenty, but a serious young woman, married at the time in fact. I went, and I saw the conditions, which were unforgettable.'

I hated to talk about it, but if we were going there now, I had to. Immediately after the eruption, all of Italy was cold and dark, suffering crop failures that led to poverty and diseases. Around the volcano everything was even bleaker. The area had been blasted and remained in constant near-darkness under the ash burden that lingered in the air. We went down by sea, then found it almost impossible to get transport due to animals having been wiped out, while boats and land vehicles had been lost or destroyed. There was nowhere to stay. There was nothing to eat. Survivors were often homeless, devastated, deeply affected mentally. They had thought they were dying; they had *wanted* to die. Many people had lost everything, including their families.

Falco and I had searched for his nephew as best we could – he even dug down through the tephra in a few likely places – but we saw from the start that our task was hopeless. We asked anyone we met if they had known Larius or his young family, with no results. Father even put up notices. In the end my then husband, Lentullus, came down from Rome with a cart, found us, and drove us home. Falco and I were both depressed for a long time. I had the added burden of realising what it must have been like in Britannia, after the great tribal rebellion when I was a baby. That gave me a renewed spasm of survivor's guilt, even though I had been too young to know what happened. Dwelling on what must have happened to Larius and seeing Falco's misery, I wanted to grieve for the horrors that had over-taken my own birth family. I could not, because they were unknown to me, so for many months I suffered nightmares, low moods, insecurity and feelings of despair.

Having seen Campania's condition during my visit with Falco, I thought the area would never recover. People reck-oned things were better now, but I would have to see for myself before I could believe it. I explained to Uncle Tullius that I would not take our boys there until I was sure.

Tullius tried telling us Gaius and Lucius were tough, but I insisted they were nervous children, deeply insecure after their mother's death. They still woke up crying in the night. A disaster scene was likely to cause them deep-seated anxiety. My own mother was away on the coast, or she and Falco would have taken them. Instead, dear little Gaius and Lucius, who were, of course, great-nephews to Tullius, would love the adventure of a few weeks' staying in his lovely house.

Tiberius and I had worked out our strategy. 'You all know each other. I don't see any problem,' he said, backing me up. 'Their nurse is very experienced. Glaphyra will look after them – she is quite unflappable. Just supply her with beakers of borage tea. I could leave Dromo as extra support, if you like?'

'No, thank you!' snapped Tullius, who must have bought the young slave in the first instance. Dromo had his own style. Tullius had palmed him off on us and wasn't having him back.

I said gently, 'Don't worry, you will hardly know the boys are here.'

Tullius made a brave attempt: 'They are very young.' He meant they were noisy, snotty little tots who liked to wreck their environment.

'I can't risk them scampering around a building site,' said Tiberius, in firm mode.

'Shouldn't we keep them somewhere familiar, then? Flavia Albia should stay behind with them.'

It did make sense to pen them up at home but Tiberius rejected that. 'No, no, she is needed, Nunkle. This job of yours will have its upsetting elements. I shall be looking after the men and I'll need the support of my wife. But we shall miss our little treasures so much!' Having been a Roman magistrate, he could speak platitudes with easy sincerity. 'It will be a relief to know they are safe and happy here, while I have to be away on your behalf.'

Favours and their pay-offs are the natural medium of commercial men; Uncle Tullius was forced to swim along with this.

Tiberius reassured him that we would send our runabout, Paris, on regular visits back to Rome so if any emergency arose he could bring us word. That would have to be an emergency that could be put on hold for weeks, grumbled Tullius, more, if the damned donkey went lame. He had a businessman's grasp of logistics and a pessimist's attitude to luck.

I promised to leave Barley, my dog, so the boys would have a family pet to cuddle. Privately I was thinking that not only would I be dropping Gaius and Lucius on Tullius but I would avoid Barley jumping down any tunnels and getting stuck underground. I had been there, remember. I knew the whole area was potholed with access points dug by looters.

It made me wonder about the Curvidii: why had family survivors never yet arranged to excavate their half-buried villa, looking for their missing relative? Was he truly as unpleasant as his brother had said? The fate of a man with money normally needs to be known. In any situation, the bereaved are helped by finding answers. Or had everyone been so glad to see the back of him, nobody cared a bean what had happened to Publius Curvidius Fulvianus Primus?

Hmm! So how would people there respond, if we came looking for him now?

5

We arrived at the best maritime scene in the world. Mount Vesuvius, lording it above, had tried hard to wreck it. The surrounding landscape now comprised a bleak, black desert that we observed with sinking hearts. The Bay of Neapolis should have cheered us with its natural beauty. Instead, a local agent working for Uncle Tullius had booked us into a dank room in what we called Grumpy Goat Ginnel. It had no window, so there was no sea view.

We were too exhausted to complain. In any case, the agent never appeared in person but had sent a little slave. This sharp child was very well trained in letting his eyes glaze over as he stated that he knew nothing.

'Do we deduce our landlord is the agent's brother?'

'No. His cousin.'

Io! Friends, Romans and very tired travellers, welcome to Campania!

Soon we realised the agent's cousin aired the beds only every ten years because he was too kind-hearted to disturb any active wildlife in his mattresses.

Tiberius moved us next morning. He had found a temple where enquiries led to us renting a new townhouse; its owner was away on business but had left a key with local priests. They were keen to earn a percentage on any lettings they could organise.

Its furnishings seemed rather bright but the place had a peristyle garden, a paved street outside and a colonnade opposite where there were useful shops. A man was wandering around, trying to remember where he had left his donkey, though he seemed harmless.

Our own donkey was no longer speaking to us. Mercury had been ridden from Rome by various heavyweight workmen, her two panniers overloaded with picks and spades and not enough food in her nosebag. For all of us, getting there had had its moments. The city-based rich may convince themselves their Campanian properties are an easy three-day trip away (more likely six, let's face it), but anyone who travels down south in a rackety old building cart, while big bales of leather tents keep slumping down on them and scaffolding planks are sliding around, knows better. Drax, the site watchdog, kept wanting to lie where I was sitting. It rained; his fur smelt ghastly.

It took us over a week. We had a second cart with us that contained the rest of the workmen and a couple of our household staff (Dromo and Paris), all playing draughts and discussing charioteers. When I had come with Falco, we made part of the outward journey on a ship from Ostia. That had been gentler, even though poor old Father was so seasick, we had had to go home by road afterwards.

Ah, memories! Not as seasick as he was during our rough crossing of the Gallic Strait, when he and Helena had first brought me from Britannia. Falco was so ill that the ship's captain had wanted to put in at Insula Vectis in case his passenger was dying. Aged fourteen and never yet out of that shabby shanty town, Londinium, I had thought they were taking me to Hades.

Our journey to Stabiae was tedious, though not terrifying. A hundred and sixty unhappy miles. Our slave, Dromo, started counting milestones but forgot his tally and resorted to grizzling. We had in fact brought a ladies' carrying chair, an upright knees-up box-on-poles that would be uncomfortable after half an hour, yet a suitable conveyance for a respectable wife such as I was, supposedly. Not this wife, because the sedan was crammed to its roof with food and home comforts, like bedding. I was relieved to see parts of Campania had recovered a little from before; we were told staples were being brought in from Nola and Capua now. Yet much previously rich farming territory around the bay remained wasteland and would take decades to recover. I was glad we had brought smoked cheese from our friend Metellus and our own pillows.

After our first crotchety night, we shifted to the new accommodation. With the chair unpacked, and me scratching at my bitten wrists and ankles, Tiberius and I did not pause to evaluate why our new lodging seemed mildly exotic; we made the journey to his uncle's villa.

We travelled out through a town gate, with Paris and Dromo lugging the chair. Paris, our family runabout, had helped us change accommodation that morning. Dromo, my husband's young body slave, had stood to watch. They made hopeless bearers; I walked. After a trudge uphill onto the headland, we passed what must once have been an enormous, possibly imperial, villa. It was now buried about fifteen feet deep, though taller parts could be made out, with roofs and upper-storey windows poking through. Tiberius stopped for a look.

I gazed around. Even in its ruined state, this residence stood high, with stunning views across the bay. Surrentum lay far down the peninsula. Curving around the shore opposite there had once been towns and hamlets. Pompeii,

Oplontis and Herculaneum were gone, but across the water further along I identified smudges that must have been the bathing town of Baiae, once a fashionable spa for dissolutes; Neapolis, which served as the area capital; Misenum, where the Empire's main trireme fleet was based; Puteoli where Alexandrian grain ships had once landed until a better port at Ostia was redeveloped. Over there too, I knew, were the Phlegraean Fields, where hot fumaroles gurgled up from the earth's core and the black-ink waters of Lake Avernus poisoned birds. They were close to the Cumaean Sybil's rocky cave, supposedly an ancient access route to the Underworld.

Most prominent, of course, and visible from everywhere, was Vesuvius. My parents had seen the mountain during its days of long slumber; they liked to reminisce that they had even climbed it, some years before it vomited itself inside out. Vesuvius in their day had been taller, with a more sharply pointed profile, and richly clothed in wild vines where people said the rebel slave Spartacus had camped. Now a barren, humpbacked shell overlooked the bay, while shreds of passing cloud tugged at its dark tops. It had a permanent aura of threat.

'I can see a faint trail of smoke from the summit!'

'Don't look then,' advised Tiberius, with plebeian practicality.

'Quite right,' I said to our companions. 'We mustn't scare ourselves. The mountain is safe again. Its crater must be empty.'

'Too right. We're standing on what belched out of it!' groaned Paris, grinding his boot heels into the blackened ground. He was looking around like a city boy, as sharp as a nail, who could not believe the rural waste we'd brought him to. He shaded his eyes as if the glare off the wide sky and the Neapolis bay was hurting.

Tiberius walked across crunching tephra to the old villa. He pointed out a grand entrance to an atrium, which must have been double height. Its tall doors might have been left standing open or they had been blown in by the hot blasts from Vesuvius, but it would be a daring explorer who crawled inside, wriggling through the gap under what should have been an overhead marble lintel.

We did have an idiot with us. Gambolling around his master like a chubby, crumb-stained faun, Dromo shot away to climb up onto the roof; it protruded at no more than head-height. Calling him back, we watched him ignore us. He shot up, crablike, over the pantiles, until he was excitedly balancing right on the edge of what must be a four-sided surround to an open roof above the residence's interior.

Being Dromo, he fell in.

We could tell he was unhurt. First, he called excitedly that he could see the tops of painted frescos: half-clad figures balanced on friezes, as if they had been waiting around the past ten years for him to visit. Then it struck him that he was alone, inside a dim, deserted building, sitting high up on a deep infill of sharp-edged volcanic debris that had covered him with grazes. He had landed so far below the open roof he was now unable to climb out.

Never brave, Dromo began to scream in panic.

6

I stayed with the donkey. I know when to smile and be no trouble.

Tiberius and Paris climbed up carefully. I noticed they did this several feet apart, spreading their weight in case the ash-burdened pantiles gave way. They crawled across the roof on their bellies and were both lying down when they peered over.

'Shut up, Dromo! Dromo – *shut up!*'

The screaming stopped. 'Hello, Master,' I heard the boy saying from a distance. His particular nonchalance was unmistakable. He was but a slave; he had a master who was bound to solve this problem for him. Tiberius, considering what to do, gave him no answer.

A decision was reached. Dromo would have to stay there. We would go to the site and send rescuers with ropes.

Dromo panicked again, not wanting to be left alone. Tiberius was normally a kind-hearted master, but crossly told him to button up, sit down and keep still. Having to wait there was his punishment.

While Tiberius and Paris slid cautiously back down to ground level and were trying to brush their tunics clean, I heard a mutter of 'This is a bloody good start!' It was not from Paris.

I stroked the donkey.

★   ★   ★

In my opinion, the new villa of Uncle Tullius ought not to claim itself a fancy address above Stabiae. His vendor had thrown him some dubious dice. We seemed to wander down the headland halfway to Surrentum before we found the real location, a pleasant spot yet definitely not as described. The estate was rustic, nestling on the edge of a small plain where the soil must always have been very fertile. Clearly farming fortunes had been made here, though nothing grew now.

'Is this it? Are we sure this is it?'

The 'panoramic position' was fantasy. The most stunning prospect would have been from the cliff's edge, where the land took a sheer dive into the bay; that was where the very rich had always grabbed position. This was slightly more inland. We must have driven in from the wrong side, where the road was. But it might just about have views: if Tullius was lucky there would be visible sea in the distance, with a glimpse of Mount Vesuvius.

At least the house was not completely underground. Unlike where we had left Dromo, this villa must have stood at the outer reach of raining lapilli and ash, so the building looked only partially buried. However, it stood surrounded by a black stony waste. We were going to be here for a few months.

Tiberius assessed the situation resolutely. 'Uncle Tullius may think he could have bought better!'

Our workmen were already on site. They had pitched two ridge-pole tents, ramming pegs into hardened tephra in what would once have been a garden. Only its position told me that. The ground was inert, not a weed regaining its territory. Now, waiting for instructions, the men were squatting on their haunches, playing draughts again and this time talking about gladiators. Drax was gnawing out guy-rope pegs from the tent that was to be the site office. Sparsus threw a bucket at him. The dog picked it up in his teeth and ran about pointlessly. He thought coming on holiday was great.

Serenus and Sparsus gathered equipment and went to find Dromo, with Paris leading the way. They all seemed cheery not to have to do any hard work yet.

Tiberius had brought the floor plan. 'He loves a chart!' uttered Larcius, with no enthusiasm. Time was spent while two tetchy men tried to orientate the chart to match what they could see of the villa. Larcius said, 'We did exploratory digging before you got here, Chief. Up by the town they looked to have ten or twenty feet on top of everything but this place got off lighter. There's a bed of clinker fragments, porous pumice in different colours and sizes, with two inches of finer stuff – an ash fall? – laid down on top, like a cosy blanket. As soon as it rained, all the ash must have set solid, luckily not like concrete, not too hard to crack into. Should be feasible to clear the stuff, and it may make good hardcore afterwards. But this job is likely to cost you.'

'It's likely to cost you' is another phrase builders use. It invariably follows them realising that their tender price was far too low. Explaining the extra price of 'contingencies' to Uncle Tullius would require some skill.

Tiberius sighed. Larcius and I could see he was suffering personally. The journey from Rome had left most of us stiff and lethargic, but he had worse problems. Ever since our wedding day when, notoriously, he had been struck by lightning, he had suffered bouts of serious pain. He was forcing himself to look at the villa's plan so he could give directions as to where the men should start. But he could barely summon interest.

From Curvidius Fulvianus, we knew this had been home to farmers who had grown wealthy over several generations. One wing retained the style of the original *villa rustica*, a working country set-up that was probably a hundred years old. This oldest part had stables, workrooms and stores; the plan was marked with wine and oil presses, supposedly with rows of buried *dolia*, giant round lidded pots that were planted in the ground to keep an even temperature for their contents. It hardly mattered that they must now be completely buried. No trees had survived, so Tullius would never be harvesting olives or grapes.

A newer wing of the house must have been added when the rustic farmers started to enjoy a lifestyle of leisure, like those plutocrats on the cliff with their huge holiday homes. A columned porch had been added as an impressive entrance. Beyond that lay the best facilities.

During an initial external tour, we saw that the ground-floor rooms in the newer wing contained volcanic material but could be rescued. We peered into them through shuttered windows from an outer colonnade and saw the upper remnants of fine decoration. In this part, we came to a substantial three-sided peristyle around an interior garden that lay open towards the seaward view; it was surrounded by salon-style rooms for dining and daytime life. Further on, according to the plan, lay service areas, slave quarters and even a bathhouse.

We walked back to the centre. The men had dug out a path. We had a key, which worked. Using his substantial muscle, Larcius dragged one of the two main doors open, as he prepared to investigate the atrium. 'Looks as if nobody has been in since the mountain blew. Don't follow me if you're scared of pigeons.'

Tiberius offered me his hand. We followed cautiously, down two steps that we had to find underfoot by feel, then moving across hardened ash that sometimes became softer; where it had been protected from the weather, it gave way abruptly and landed us knee-deep. Volcanic deposits lay thicker than in enclosed rooms, because of the open roof. It was the usual arrangement: a double-height hall, its angled, plastered ceilings supported on four surviving columns with ionic pedestals. Tiberius decided the columns were brick, rendered in plaster then marked with lines to resemble white marble, handsome but at much cheaper cost. Between them, what should have been a shallow central pool was growing algae. If a statue had ever danced in the middle of this choked impluvium, somebody had stolen it.

When Larcius scraped down with a spade, making a hole through the ash to find the floor, he uncovered plain black tesserae with white dots. On the walls were friezes; they still looked good and could be salvaged if we found a touch-up painter. Doorways led off on all sides; a flight of stairs went to the upper storey. Larcius mounted carefully and called down that he had found a suite of bedrooms that looked intact. 'Clearable.' He rejoined us. 'Pictures not too rude. Nice plaster coves.'

'May as well start in the atrium,' Tiberius decided. 'Tullius will want to impress any visitors who drop in. Let's refurbish his fancy receiving room, then work outwards.'

So they started. Before the others came back with a chastened Dromo, picks, brooms and barrows were in play, while black and grey dust was flying. Tiberius gave orders to mask faces with neckerchiefs. I was dispatched to hunt for usable furniture. 'And unpack lunch.' Building-site protocol. What the owner's wife is for.

I was fairly sure that if the lost brother remained somewhere inside the house, he would not be buried in the atrium. Once lapilli had begun dropping from the sky, sometimes not pebbles but sizeable rocks, no owner would have stood, flanked by slaves holding silver titbit trays, waiting to greet visitors.

Nevertheless, the air of a friendly family home had somehow survived. Once it was fully restored, Tullius would fit in. He could show off his entrance, then might spend most of his time in those elegant, newer rooms around the peristyle.

At that point, I felt no restless ghosts watching us, only a quiet aura of the last householder's one-time presence. But I would be proved wrong.

7

The first body the workmen uncovered was that of a watchdog. Knowing my fondness, they kept the news from me as long as they could.

He – most watchdogs are male because owners want them big and fierce – had been kept in a kennel, near the tall entrance doors. When the eruption happened, he had been left beside his kennel, which was slowly buried. He was tethered by a chain from his heavy, bronze-studded collar and could not escape however he tried. And we could certainly tell that he had tried.

The men carried out parts of the kennel first. Its wood was too friable to reuse. Coming to look at the charcoal pieces, I spotted toothmarks straight away.

'Naughty dog!' Serenus tried. 'He's really chewed it.'

'Frightened,' admitted the clerk-of-works, quietly. 'Scared bloody stiff, I dare say.'

Had I not been there, who knows what they would have done? Chucked him into a rubbish skip, probably. Instead, the men muttered with Tiberius, then he and they went to clear one of the outbuildings; Tiberius had already earmarked a small building for any remains we found.

They went back into the house. As a courtesy to me and my love of dogs, the long-dead beast was lifted up on spades, placed in a hand barrow, brought out and laid in the dim shed, his remains the first to be stored. The men had named him Nibble, because he had bitten so savagely at his kennel as he struggled to escape.

Tiberius must have told the workmen that nobody must say Nibble was 'only a dog' in my hearing. They understood. None of them was meeting my eye as they put down his bones and stepped away. After one look at his broad-browed head flung back, and the scrabbling contortions of his legs, I walked off by myself.

Tiberius came after me.

'His end must have been quick, love. The poor creature was still striving to get free – you can see it – but he never knew what happened finally.' That would be right: the dog would have gone in an instant. A wave of unbearable heat had smashed across the bay unseen and unheard, until it sucked the life out of him with explosive power. Every human, every animal and bird, who had been near the volcano had died in those rolling torrents. Wherever they were, the first surge that hit them took them.

He knew. You could tell Nibble had realised a disaster was in train. He had been frightened for days by earthquakes and lightning, while equally anxious home-dwellers had left him chained. Perhaps he became so agitated that none dared approach. He had been a deterrent; he wasn't a pet. He might have had a history of going for people.

Whatever it was, those people who managed to flee had abandoned the dog. He had been left by himself, with no hope of rescue. All he had wanted was to break his chain. All he could think about was running away.

There had been times in my own life when I wanted to escape and run.

'He is free now,' Tiberius soothed me, with his resolute kindness. 'His spirit is racing for ever through the wide fields of Elysium. Ears back, tail out, teeth bared happily into the wind.'

I shoved my own emotion back into the dark. I was a woman. This is life. You have to be strong for other people. 'He was a dog, and he died ten years ago. Let's have some lunch,' I said.

Yes, Nibble was a dog – and privately I would grieve for him.

8

As we returned to the others, I did overhear Larcius grumbling to Serenus, 'If she's like this over a puppy, what if we come across people?'

I called harshly that people were dispensable.

Paris owned up that there was a dead horse too, in one of the stable buildings. He had seen its bones when he was helping me hunt for something we could sit on. We had our picnic area now. A rustic table and benches had been dragged out into what had been the orchard garden on the villa's approach, all lopsided and missing legs, but we had men with tools who could use them; miraculously, the items had been fixed up. As we perched with our bread and cheese and olives, we talked about the absence of furniture.

This house had been cleared. The empty rooms looked neat enough, not obviously ransacked by thieves; there seemed no sign of the house being hurriedly evacuated during the disaster, nor cleared recently when it was sold. Because the ash layer looked undisturbed, Tiberius and Larcius reckoned full removals had happened long ago. If the volcanic fall had ever been trampled, it might since have settled, its surface blown level by wind and draughts. Yet we could tell no one but ourselves had stepped into it.

The villa had been completely stripped. 'That would have been a big enterprise,' commented Tiberius. Nothing movable or usable had been left. We found no couches, side tables, chests or shelves, nor lamps, braziers, cushions, pictures or vases. The kitchen was empty. Fixed cupboards remained, though a couple had had their doors wrenched off. The paraphernalia of daily life had gone, apart from a couple of rickety old beds upstairs and some battered farm equipment outside. In outbuildings, the heavy stone presses for olives and grapes looked good but perhaps too heavy to move; any tools and storage jars we did find must have been condemned as past it.

From this we deduced that family members or friends of theirs had retrieved all their property – and they had done so *before* lapilli and ash started falling. People must have been extremely well prepared for the disaster, unless their leaving was a coincidence, something that would have happened anyway, without Vesuvius exploding.

I knew from my visit with Falco that in the first couple of days people had grabbed what they could carry, often not much. Some just turned the key and rushed for safety, expecting to come home again. After the eruption ended, survivors rescued what they could – where in fact there were survivors. It had happened at Pompeii, even where houses were deeply buried. Owners came back. Thieves rushed to take advantage too, of course.

At this villa, everything had been taken and, once everyone had left, the place had stood deserted for ten years. I joked that that would never have happened in Rome: opportunists would have moved in. Empty buildings were always colonised. As sophisticated urbanites, we all laughed.

After a moment, I pondered, 'Why didn't people come back and search for that missing brother's body?'

'Perhaps they thought he was somewhere else.' Tiberius was sure we, too, might find no trace of Primus. As I had first

40

speculated, he might have tried to escape and met an unknown fate while doing so. Or was his disappearance somehow connected with the thorough removal of his household property?

Dromo was bored, so decided he wanted to see the dead horse. Sparsus, the youngest on the building team, went too. They were winding each other up with suggestions of how spooky it might be, although Paris told them it was just the bones of some old beast, lying on its side in a stall under a covering of pumice and ash instead of a horse blanket. Paris stayed with us.

It was a blustery March day, with scudding clouds, but warm enough to finish a rest-break out of doors. Too tired to stir after our journey from Rome, we wrapped up in cloaks but sat on, weary and dreamy.

Dromo and Sparsus came back and complained, 'It's just old bones from a horse.'

'Told you!' jeered Paris.

Under questioning, the lads reported that the stable block still had fixed mangers, harness hooks and hitching rings, but apart from the nag's body, the stalls all had their doors open and nothing inside. 'Except a wheel.'

'What wheel?'

'Must be off a cart,' said Sparsus. 'It's got a note tied to it. Wheelwright's repair bill. Looks like the poor fellow never got paid! It's turned to charcoal so he never will be.'

A byre, also empty, might have been home to a plough ox. We hoped the absence of animals and transport meant people had managed to escape.

However, Sparsus had pulled at a plank on one shed, which was padlocked even though it had a hole in the roof and looked dilapidated. Squinting through a crack

41

into a dim interior, he thought he could see the end of a cart.

'I'll have that lock off,' Tiberius decided. None of us commented; he was famous for salvaging ironwork.

We were still sitting companionably when Drax, in the distance, began barking. Conscious that tools had been left lying around, Serenus went to check on the dog. He came back with Drax on a rope and a bent figure following: one of our neighbours had hopped in to inspect the newcomers. Larcius waited until he heard who it was, then tipped the nod to his men; they went back to their work.

'Bitus,' the rural turnip said, gazing around curiously. He wore a loose, natural-coloured tunic and an oversized country hat with a big hole. As soon as Larcius left space, he filled in on a bench as if he owned it. The hook-shouldered being was wizened and tanned. He might not have been forty yet, but looked as if he had been toiling in fields for over half a century.

He wanted to know everything about us, though intended to give nothing away himself. Tiberius went along with it. Since it would be no secret, he explained briefly that his uncle had bought the villa. 'Tullius Icilius. I am his nephew, Faustus. This is my wife, Flavia Albia.'

'Come for a look around?'

'Seeing what work needs to be done.'

'From Rome?'

'From Rome.'

Bitus deplored us as fancy folk. He waited, but we wickedly added nothing.

Dromo, whose social tact was minimal, began playing noisily with Drax, both tugging at the rope energetically while growling mock-threats at one another. Drax was slobbering; Dromo soon would be. We waved them further off. Paris remained with us, watching our performance with a faint smile.

When we had teased Bitus with enough silence, I suddenly asked whether he lived and farmed nearby. Three pairs of eyes stared him out until he felt obliged to admit it.

'Lived here all your life?' asked Paris, the city boy, amazed anyone would do so.

'Went and worked up in the mountains when I was young. Goats and sheep. Came back after my father died.'

'He died in the eruption?'

'Yes and no.' We listened expectantly. 'Took him a few years. But he had breathed in fatal dust. We call it the Vesuvius cough.'

'Lung damage?' I was remembering how people were troubled when I came with Falco. Retching up phlegm, rubbing sore, reddened eyes, scratching madly at irritated skin. Father and I must have been affected too; we felt out of sorts for a long time even after we were back in Rome. We had given up our useless search for Father's nephew Larius and we recovered, but people who lived here had to cope with permanent afflictions. Official reports, obsessed with economic damage, would never bother to record that kind of human suffering.

Bitus nodded, looking pained. Tiberius changed the subject. 'We've been wondering about the family at this villa. Did you know them?'

'My old man would have.'

'Good neighbours?'

'All right.'

'Not close?'

'Kept to themselves.' He paused. 'Not second-homers.' He implied that locals were unimpressed by all those wealthy types who wanted to own property around the bay, but who would rarely visit. When they did, it would be all lights and loud parties that frightened the fish. Such people never joined the community.

Bitus was lumping us in among that kind of folk. Tiberius must have picked up the message; he accepted the reproach but merely continued: 'Curvidius Primus, tell me, what's the story there? He disappeared, I understand?'

'I heard so.'

'Victim of the disaster?'

'Is that what they say?' Bitus sounded sceptical; I recognised wilful disinterest. He could have been any city barfly that I had to question in my work.

Tiberius stretched his arms, with linked fingers. 'He has a brother up in Rome who wants to discover what happened to him.'

'*Does* he?' asked Bitus, as if shocked.

'I gained the impression he might travel down if he was able to hold a funeral.'

'*Will* he?' Again, it had evidently caused surprise, yet the speaker gave no explanation. I could see Paris watching how Tiberius and I took note for private discussion later.

I said people seemed to have been here to clear the villa. I assumed they would have searched thoroughly for the lost master of the house.

'Well! That's the thing!' Bitus continued his annoying hints – without enlightening us.

'Do you mean there was talk?' Tiberius kept his voice level though his gaze was searching.

'Not for me to say.'

'Oh, no. You were working up in the mountains . . . Maybe your father mentioned something to you afterwards?' It seemed not. 'Well, I did promise I would try to find out. Can you suggest anyone who was living here during the disaster? Someone I could speak to about events at the time? If they don't mind remembering? I know it was all heartbreaking for those who were caught in the midst.'

'That it was!' agreed Bitus, dourly.

Now he did screw up his eyes and pull at his chin as if that helped his brain with the dangerous process of thinking. He allowed us a couple of names, with vague descriptions of where those people lived nearby. He made his information sound unreliable, but I was used to that.

We got rid of him, using the excuse that Tiberius and I had to ride back to Stabiae town. Although we left the men still digging out the atrium, they had the air of labourers who planned to stop as soon as the master left.

9

Next morning, Tiberius felt he could safely leave the site. Instead of waiting for nosy neighbours to materialise, he and I went visiting. We took our donkey down a clogged track to the next smallholding.

Heius was older than Bitus, scrawny arms and knock-kneed legs, still working the land but looking as if he could drop dead in his fields any day. He greeted us with friendly pleasure. Leaning on a scratching tool, he showed us how he was managing to grow a scatter of vegetable plants by digging holes through the rocky layer, placing seeds in dust and watering well. The soil he was creating was dry, grey and mainly composed of pebbles, but he had somehow nursed rocket and other herbs into life. He would not even try shrubs or trees. Someone had told him it might take a hundred years before natural vegetation took hold – though the land would be very fertile when it did. 'Greening had better hurry up, or I may be obliged to miss it!' he joked, openly conscious of his age.

Walking slowly, he left his patch and took us to his house. There we met his wife, Favonilla, not quite as old as him, not quite as skinny, not quite as friendly at first sight, though she brought curly little pastries as guest-greetings.

'You've seen Bitus? Didn't give much away?' A report must have flown around.

'No, he seemed more interested in us,' Tiberius confirmed.

'Oh, that's Bitus! Your uncle has bought the place,' Favonilla spelled out, as if it might be news to us. 'I expect it will be yours one day.'

We pulled faces at that idea. We saw Uncle Tullius as an unreliable prospect, not a future gold mine. Half of Rome was shamelessly sucking up to legacy donors, but we kept our self-respect in the faint hope Tullius might respect us for it. Besides, Tiberius assured the couple that his uncle still had years left in him. Accepting that with a sniff, Favonilla remarked it would be nice to have next door full of life again, 'And being looked after!'

I noted resentment about the Curvidii leaving. 'You'll be glad to know Faustus is here for renovation works. He will soon get things moving.' Having done my duty by building up my husband, I asked if they had known the previous occupants.

'No more than we had to,' Heius answered briefly.

'Any reason? You didn't like them!' I interpreted, when he only shrugged.

'My wife speaks her mind!' Tiberius put in quickly. 'A blunt Roman matron.'

Heius made no comment, though I suspected he was familiar with outspoken women.

'The owners didn't like us,' his own wife stated. 'Mind you, they never liked many people – and it cut both ways.'

Heius let her say it, then demanded curiously, 'Found anyone yet?'

'Only the watchdog.'

'That thing!' Favonilla exclaimed. 'He was a terror. Vicious mouth on him. He used to get out, then race straight here, looking for somebody to bite.'

'Either he *got* out,' added Heius darkly, 'or he was *let* out.'

'The beast went home quick enough when I hit him on the nose with a besom!' his wife remembered. They both chuckled quietly. They were a close couple, well tuned to each other's thoughts.

'Let out by whom?' I picked up.

'Who knows?' replied Heius.

'*We* know,' Favonilla corrected. 'Primus slipped the dog's chain. He did it deliberately. Who else?'

This was our first full glimpse of the Curvidii as bad neighbours, and of Primus as a special bugbear. We were rightly interested: Uncle Tullius needed to know about past tiffs over the fence. He could be gruff, but it was part of his business creed to keep people on side.

Tiberius broached a new line, saying people from our villa must have escaped when the eruption happened, so how had Heius and Favonilla managed?

Heius was the reporter. As if it was a story that he had told many times, he narrated how they had seen the high plume of debris rising straight up from Vesuvius on the first day; they felt the strong earth tremors, wondered at lightning, then opted for caution. They had friends who lived towards Surrentum, so made their way there first. Lapilli were raining down, so like other people they covered their heads with cushions and pillows as protection, even though holding them in place made it difficult to take anything else with them. When the plume collapsed and fell so that darkness rolled over the whole bay, blotting out the opposite shore, the party took a road up through the mountains to face away over the Paestanus Sinus. Debris did reach that side, but its effect was less significant. Neither they nor their friends suffered harm, though everyone was terrified.

'How soon were you able to return?' I asked.

'Not long. People made it back after a few days. We had stopped hearing explosions and the air cleared a little. It stayed murky for a long time, but we ventured home as soon as we dared. Most people who could came back, at least after a time.'

'Outsiders turned up eventually,' Tiberius presumed. 'To see what had gone on – and offer aid?'

'Not a lot of that! We all felt very much alone.'

'Really? I thought the Emperor sent commissioners. In fact, didn't Titus Caesar travel down here himself?'

'If he did, we never saw him flaunting his purple!' scoffed Favonilla. 'Let alone rolling his sleeves up in rescue work. His father would have done.'

'Ah, Vespasian!' I exclaimed. My father had worked for the old man. 'You're right – he would have been in there like a navvy, loading buckets.'

'Across the water there was aid,' interrupted Heius, sounding resentful. 'We heard that people who had lost everything were provided for in the Emperor's name. Over here, well, we didn't need it, they must have decided. We still had our houses and our town looked rebuildable so they left us to get on with it. And we were still alive, of course. What did we have to complain about? Put like that, well . . .'

'Still,' Tiberius sympathised, 'there would have been plenty you needed to do, before you could pick up normal life again?'

Heius nodded glumly. He described how, on their return, crops and animals had been wiped out. The ash-fall was like wading through snowdrifts. Everyone had urgent work dragging its weight off roofs, so buildings would not collapse. Then, after rain, the top layer of fine ash churned into thick mud and set. Roads became impassable so supplies could not be brought in. Carts and carriages overturned in the slurry; beasts fell and broke bones. Where people had had drainage, pebbles and ash blocked their sewers. Springs and wells were contaminated, likewise the aqueduct; water had to be sieved through cloth before it could be used. Vegetation died. Beasts of the field were gone. There were no fish in the bay.

'I am sorry. That must have been very hard.'

'Oh, yes! Everywhere was miserable, dark and cold. What I shall never forget,' Favonilla reminisced sadly, 'was the horrible smell. Sulphurous, someone called it. Like many baskets of bad eggs, all smashed on the same day. A foul belch from the volcano's belly, as if the deep earth was infected with disease. It clung everywhere, Albia. That smell got right in your nose, until we thought we would never be rid of it. It worked into our clothes, our tunics and cloaks. It glued itself onto your hair and your skin. I can still catch it and start hacking with phlegm again if I think about it. I'm going to remember that stench for ever, all my life.'

I told them a little about coming down south with my father, sharing my own bad memories of the disaster's impact. Eventually, it seemed polite to take our leave. We urged the pair to come over and see how we were bringing the villa back to life, although I warned them we could not be hospitable as yet. Heius obsessively wanted to show Tiberius more horticulture, so I walked with Favonilla, taking her arm as she moved even more slowly than her husband. She was flat-footed and her joints were sore. It might have been natural, but I did wonder how much the after-effects of the eruption had added to her old-age troubles.

We reached our donkey ahead of the men.

Favonilla dropped her voice. 'Now don't you go trying too hard to find that Primus. He wasn't worth it, Albia.'

'We are trying to help his brother, really. Curvidius Fulvianus seems troubled about the lack of proper burial rites.'

'Ah, well, then . . . Have you met him?'

'Yes, at our uncle's house in Rome. We discussed the villa, and Fulvianus asked Tiberius Manlius to look for his missing brother – he wants an appropriate memorial. I was not greatly impressed by him,' I volunteered, as if sharing with a grandmother. 'But that was my personal reaction, Favonilla. I saw nothing of real note to take against.'

Speaking almost in a whisper, despite the lack of witnesses, Favonilla confided, 'I thought they were all a nasty family!'

I told her how I condemned the villa's past household because of how they had left their watchdog tied up. 'Even if he was unfriendly, as you say – well, it's the same as with children. I blame the people in charge.'

Naturally the old woman asked whether I had children of my own. I decided not to go into little Gaius and Lucius living with us in Rome; there were still too many uncertainties about where that would lead. Politely, I replied that Tiberius Manlius and I had only married recently. Soon I was letting her tell me about hers – sons and daughters grown up and living away from home, no sign of grandchildren though she was hopeful, naturally . . .

'We were told Primus had been married?'

'He was, for a short time. She went to Hades ahead of him. I suppose a kind person might say his unhappiness when she passed away explained his bad attitude afterwards – although that wouldn't explain why his brother had already left for Rome in a strop and has stayed there ever since . . . The

51

marriage must have been friendly enough; her brother's children used to visit here and even came to stay. I believe they lived with Primus right up until the disaster. Of course they were family, at least through their aunt, but there was some comment about how they got their feet under the table. They were like a pair of pretty little snails, clinging to a wall, hiding under foliage so people might not realise they were there. Still, never mind them. Let's keep our fingers crossed for you, my dear!'

Our husbands were joining us. That let me out of the tricky conversation. Tiberius and I were in no hurry to produce, although more traditional people would see it as my duty to fall pregnant at the earliest opportunity. I was supposed to do that even if the dangerous process might rob him of both wife and child, depriving me of everything, including my contented life with him.

That was when I remembered I had left behind in Rome a certain casket with my prophylactic wax. It had to be kept in a locked cupboard in case the little boys who lived with us found it. With luck, my maid would realise. I hoped Suza would bring it when she and the rest of our staff came.

Tiberius put me back on our donkey with a discreet embrace. I would have to tell him marital love was banned temporarily.

I wondered if Stabiae's new town ran to an apothecary.

IO

People in the district were impatient to learn all about us, so a third neighbour had called while we were out. We found him waiting to start his interrogation. The workmen had gone off to see if they could make the kitchen area usable, but they had left him Drax for company. Tied to a bench leg, the dog was lying down asleep with his long pointy nose on crossed black paws, though he awoke with a menacing growl each time the visitor shifted. Tiberius and I were greeted with one eye open and a tail wag; our guest looked as apprehensive about us as he was about Drax.

His name was Pescennius Neo; he believed himself a cut above. He probably owned a toga, though had not worn it to meet us. Nevertheless, he was the first man we met in Campania who was clean-shaven, not stubbly, and he boasted that, although Neapolis-born, he had spent some years in Rome. Details were sparse when we forced ourselves to make the usual enquiries of where, how long for, and what doing? My father would have growled that Neo must have failed to make any impression; Falco, the great fictionaliser, would deduce this man was so much of a failure that Rome must have chewed him up and spat him out.

Now he lived in a house he described as a stylish retirement spot; I noticed he did not invite us to it. If he owned land, he had menials to farm for him; I could tell that from his neat, clean fingernails. He claimed to have returned to his roots in order to drink wine and do nothing. Again, Falco would snort that unless you are an ex-consul or a brothel pimp (or both), you need a pension in order to drink and be idle. 'Doing nothing' requires the support of serious funds.

Well, Neo had that. His money was shown by braid down his long, long-sleeved tunic (brownish-red embellishment on lichen-coloured material), plus inevitably he flashed a large agate ring, which he constantly twisted in case we had not noticed it. We were still using the trestle and benches outside as our reception area. Even in the open air, Neo removed his riding cloak specially, so we could see the teaselled nap on his well-tailored tunic. Then, throughout the ensuing conversation, we could see him looking at his cloak as if he wanted to snuggle back into it.

He knew Uncle Tullius was a businessman; he brazenly demanded what was his annual income and net worth? I flared up, but Tiberius managed to cut across me genially. 'Jupiter, don't ask about the moolah, Neo! My uncle is so close, even his banker needs a permit in triplicate before he can wield an abacus in Tullius's presence.'

I followed his lead: 'I once found his financial adviser actually throwing up, he was so nervous. The poor fellow told me he had foolishly prepared a five-year projection, forgetting how secretive Tullius is.'

Tiberius concluded, with his most winning smile, 'If Tullius was an army commander, the password would always be "We never talk about that"!'

'Settle down, darling!' I pretended to joke. 'Pescennius Neo will think we are teasing him.'

Neo felt obliged to assure us not to worry, he could take it. We both smiled at him mercilessly.

We then launched off our routine questions about the Curvidius family. He responded well, telling us that originally there had been a group of siblings; no other children played with them because they were too quarrelsome. Their scrapping had continued into adulthood. Fulvianus left Stabiae in his twenties after some spat that no one now remembered; it must have been serious to him, because he never came back, not even when he inherited.

'Did you know him in Rome, Neo? In the time you were living there yourself?'

'Oh, no! These were not people you would want to chase up socially.'

'Intriguing!' He let my hint pass unanswered.

Neo said his mother had known the wife of Primus slightly; Publilia was a mimsy little thing who would never stand up to him.

'He threw his weight about?' I asked.

'Loud mouth. Big man. Red-faced. Looked as if he had a dicky heart, but in fact he was so full of life that when he stood as a local magistrate nobody would vote for him. Normally all it takes is oodles of self-assurance plus handing out free bread. But Primus was too much even for the electorate. I heard that people went to market and put up an opinionated radish as a rival candidate. The veg beat Primus easily.'

I could warm to Pescennius after all; I had been brought up by Roman satirists. However, he spoiled it by adding, 'Primus yearned for Nero to return, of course. Everyone in Campania used to rush to his concerts and we long for those golden olden days again. Did you know he was once playing here when an earthquake struck, but he insisted the audience remain in their seats until his concert finished? Nero was so well loved, people stuck it out, only running for their lives as the theatre came down on their heels.'

I saw my husband suppress a tart reply. Tiberius Manlius did not believe in hereditary maniacs as rulers. We had one in Rome at the moment. There my role in political discussions was to prevent either my father or my husband talking too excitedly and getting us all exiled.

For a safer topic, simple women's work, I asked Pescennius Neo where best to look for new tables and couches. He recommended a trip to Nola or Capua. Timber was scarce locally because Vesuvius had denuded the area of so much forest. I played snooty, saying I might have to order fine stuff with specialist woods in Rome and have it shipped. Tiberius played henpecked, wincing at the presumed cost.

'We have to look after Uncle Tullius!' I simpered, as if we were leeches who relied on him for home comforts.

Neo asked where we were staying at the moment, since it was clear we could not be at this empty villa. We described where we were renting in Stabiae.

'Oh, you're in the *pirate*'s house!'

Excuse me?

Surprised, Tiberius said he had been told it belonged to a sea captain, a quiet man who rarely came on shore. Neo laughed, a little too drily. 'Don't buy anything off him. You won't know where it has come from – and you probably won't like the answer if you find out!'

According to him, Dexiades, the alleged pirate, still sailed in and out at will quite frequently, right under the noses of the west-coast home fleet at Misenum. Bluffing that his trade was 'general provisioning', he was a well-known colourful character. I commented that, to me, 'colourful characters' tended to be as welcome as lice.

'Then you really must meet him, Flavia Albia! We would all like to see that man de-fleaed by a strong woman armed with a nit comb.'

We were still sharing laughter when we were interrupted. Larcius, the clerk-of-works, edged into Tiberius's line of vision. He was pulling that significant builder's face: *Excuse me, Chief, you are not going to like this but we have run into a problem* ...

Tiberius stood up, apologising. I, too, jumped to my feet like a busy matron, implying that couches indoors urgently needed me to adjust their cushions. Although it had been established that we had no domestic goods, Neo was sufficiently civilised to take his leave. Maybe during his time in the city he had acquired Roman polish.

Even if the villa had been packed with furnishings for me to play with, I had never been that kind of woman. Once the visitor departed, I scurried to see why Larcius had been gesturing to Tiberius. The men put up their hands to warn me away, but that only brought me closer.

They had found the bodies of three slaves.

II

Porphyrus, Endymio, Myrtale.

We knew their names. They were scratched on a bare wall where the slaves had been left, as if the three of them, facing death, had sought to memorialise themselves. A bent nail would be found among the volcanic detritus below the uneven graffiti. Endymio also had to wear his name engraved on an iron collar: a classic 'Hold me and return me' notice, riveted around his neck. So, he had been prone to running away. Given how he had, in the end, been abandoned to die, I did not blame him.

The workmen had come across these human remains beyond the kitchen facilities, among a serious arrangement of workrooms, pantries and log stores. Space that was not needed for the householder's more important wine, vegetables, fish pickle or oil had been allowed to his slaves. We could see that most staff had occupied cubicle rooms where some organiser had labelled which shelf each could use for sleeping. Men and women were segregated. The lettering varied as if inscribed at different times; most was in the Latin alphabet though there was also Greek and even one label scratched in what I took to be the old local language of Oscan. Neither sign nor smell of the occupants remained; no frugal possessions had been left behind. When Vesuvius blew, they either ran away or must have been taken with their masters.

The three bodies Larcius showed us were in a different place from those cubicles. They occupied a mixed-material shack that was smaller, lower and darker. These three slaves were kept apart with nothing to sleep on. No escape for them: they all wore heavy ankle rings. The irons were linked together with short chains. A stretch of chain was tethered to a wall bolt. The slaves could neither move away from each other nor escape their deadly imprisonment.

What had they done to deserve that?

And how could their general behaviour have been so bad that, when others safely fled, this trio had been left behind, given up to death as mercilessly as the watchdog?

Incredible heated gas from the volcano had killed the trapped group in their cell. I hoped they never heard it coming. It had left them all with clenched fists, raised towards their faces. When I came to Neapolis with my father, we saw bodies just like this: he had reckoned the phenomenon was an involuntary spasm as sinews contracted. He knew fire-fighters who had told him it was an automatic movement, caused by extreme intense heat; the vigiles called cadavers they found like that 'boxers'.

These looked as if the final moment caught them unawares. They were all low on the floor, close together because of their chains. Endymio was squatting, head in hands, in a posture that looked like despair; Porphyrus lay on his back, stretched out at rest to await whatever befell him; Myrtale had curled up on her side, with her legs bent and an arm under her head as if she was sleeping.

We found only their skeletons. These had unusual red charring; their skulls had split with star-like patterns from breakage points. Ash had invaded the spaces inside the bone. Blood and brains must have been boiled to nothing in a flash.

59

When I covered my eyes in distress, even through the spaces between my fingers they still looked like people.

And there was worse. Larcius showed me: close to Myrtale lay a fourth small body. A child of no more than two or three years old must have been seeking refuge with his mother. With his little arms raised and hands clenched, it looked as though he was crying.

12

In some ways the prison must have helped to preserve the
slaves for us to find. It was a low-roofed place, with a heavy
door constructed of timbers that had now carbonised though
they remained intact, a door that the workmen had found
closed. It was not locked; why bother? No one could escape.
Only the child might have staggered over on his wobbly little
legs, but the door would have been too massive for him to
push open. Perhaps whoever closed it hadn't realised the
infant was inside; perhaps he was not meant to be with his
mother that day; perhaps he was hiding. At least he was not
chained like the adults.

Their place of confinement must have been pitch dark,
hot and suffocating. Flashes of lightning from Vesuvius
would not penetrate. To those inside, even loud explosions
would have sounded as only confused, muffled noises. In a
period while other people remained at the villa, no one
outside would have heard cries for help. Once these victims
thought their owner and fellow slaves had gone away, there
would be no point in shouts or screams. They were then
alone, feeling the earthquake tremors, waiting. At least the
shack being sealed so horribly meant that solid lapilli were
kept out; only very fine volcanic ash had worked its way in.
Larcius and his team had been able to follow the fixing chain
from its fastening; then careful work with picks had revealed

skeletons on the ground. The workmen had nearly missed the child altogether. It looked to me as if someone had stepped on him, crushing his bones. That was no one's fault; I knew the men were following their instruction to treat remains with dignity.

They had methodically cleared the building, coming to find Tiberius only when they knew the full extent of their discovery. Although often unsympathetic to slaves, this morning's work had sickened them.

The ten-year-old skeletons were fragile, yet not completely perished. Fused onto bones were occasional marks that must have been from clothing fibres, though flesh and material had been completely destroyed by heat. Myrtale had worn a pebble necklace, of which crude stones survived beside her skull. The child had had an amulet to protect him or her from the evil eye. When we lifted remains onto a handcart, Larcius placed the toddler's talisman among the tiny bones. Someone muttered, 'Much good it did him!'

First, Larcius had to break the chains, which he did with hard, angry blows of his pick. Then bones could be freed from their shackles and taken out, to be deposited in the store where the watchdog and horse already waited.

'How many more will there be?' wondered Serenus, a man who felt obliged to fill any silence. No one answered.

It seemed unlikely there would be others. These three had been singled out for special treatment. This was a punishment. No value had been placed on them. When the crisis came, they were abandoned like rubbish.

A villa-farm like this would have had a full staff, mostly slaves. Perhaps the occasional freedman or woman had reached the age for manumission; from what we had heard about Curvidius Primus that would only have been if they had paid him the right price to gain their liberty. But it was slaves who would make everything run smoothly. Raising water from the well, pushing wood into the furnace, heaving sacks and amphorae, harnessing and driving four-legged beasts of burden, feeding the pig, harvesting olives and grapes, answering the master's call, fulfilling whatever distasteful needs the master imposed. To do their work those workers could not normally be hampered by leg irons. Nor was it good husbandry for owners to rely on grudging, resentful souls who could not be trusted.

Most slaves had a financial worth. If people were fleeing, their slaves would be taken with them. Salvaged, with other valuables.

These three must have done something. Or they had *not* done something. Someone had called for actions or behaviour that they had not supplied. Three in a group. Perhaps plotting together. Perhaps accused of conspiracy.

Their time for blame and suffering was past. Ignorant of their crimes, we newcomers collected them up carefully, only cursing if a nugget of bone slipped through fumbling fingers. Even then, our expletives were mainly snarled against Fate and Fortune: inevitable Fate who had snuffed out their lives in terrifying circumstances, and unpredictable Fortune. We cursed *our* misfortune that we had had to find them and be saddened by these souls, souls who were now linked to us as decidedly as they had once been chained together.

'How many more?' Serenus asked again. He was consoling himself while the three slaves and the child were laid down, jumbled in a heap together because their frames fell apart.

'Now we have found some,' offered Paris, hopefully, 'I ought to run back to Rome and tell the man. Didn't you say he wants to know?' Ever the city boy, our runabout saw no point in hanging around in the country. He was homesick on principle.

Tiberius answered patiently, 'No, Paris. Now we have found some, you had better wait to see whether we find any more.'

We were all feeling grim. None of us wanted further grief.

13

The men had had enough; their energy was sapped by too much emotion, so they broke for lunch. They would talk about the people they had found, perhaps making harsh judgements. Tiberius and I decided not to listen. He left instructions about the site work then, with Paris and Dromo tagging along, we went back to our lodging at Stabiae.

Tiberius took us out to a harbour bar. Like typical eateries with a waterside view and a history, this supplied wonky benches for tired customers who wanted to gaze around. A lackadaisical server tormented our appetites as he fussed with a teensy bread basket and, of course, more wine refills than we wanted, each to be charged. When we became restive, a pot of garum sauce was plonked down with a flourish. Meanwhile, at the back, some unseen grease-monkey fried what they claimed was fish. They had no chalked menu but we made sure to ask, so the waiter had quoted an exorbitant price. His excuse was that the bay had been emptied by strange tidal movements when Vesuvius erupted.

That had been ten years ago. The Bay of Neapolis lies wide open to the Tyrrhenian Sea. For the past decade, excited fish of every kind must have rushed in over the corpses of their cousins to recolonise its warm waters. But we were strangers or, worse, tourists. We existed to be preyed upon. We knew our place: having blatant lies tossed at us like Saturnalia nuts. So we glugged down the vinegar they were passing off on us, listened to the waiter's patronising lecture on the age-old fine wines of Campania, and waited for food vacantly.

'That's a good Falernian. I know you'll like it, Legate. Have you come far?' He was a stocky lout, his uniform a buff tunic and spreading pimples, who was trying to grow a moustache that looked like a worm. Absolutely classical. He could have applied for work in any downtown thermopolium in any province of the Empire. Unless another candidate had more interesting pustules, ours would get the job.

'Rome,' we answered obediently, playing fair. He needed to know for sure that *unus,* we city sophisticates had heard of Falernian, but *duo,* no spoilsport had ever warned us that few wines served up with that label are genuine. This being the case, *tres,* the waiter could multiply his bill by *quattuor.* In Campania they were so brazen, they listed the system on caupona walls:

> **For one *as* you can drink wine**
> **For two you can drink the best**
> **For four you can drink Falernian**

The follow-on was that we would never come here again. Which would inevitably lead us to being fleeced in exactly the same way at the next bar on a harbour front we foolishly chose instead.

Take my advice. There are reasons why some women hang back and let their male associates pick the place for lunch. If there is going to be fuming you may as well prepare for it by giving him the say, so any blame will land on him.

I spoke none of this to my companions.

★   ★   ★

66

I was saying little about anything that afternoon. My heart was too full.

'You are very quiet, Flavia Albia!' exclaimed Paris. I saw Tiberius screw his eyes slightly with a tiny moue to silence him. Paris took the point and even murmured, 'Sorry!'

'What is he sorry for?' demanded Dromo, loudly. I poured the dregs out of my beaker onto the pavement and told him Paris was using tact. 'What for?' Dromo persisted. We all smiled at him.

I was feeling kinder than usual towards slaves, even this one. 'It means he realised I was upset at the way those dead people had been treated.'

Dromo thought about it.

Paris came straight out with his city prejudice: 'Rustics. Squodged in big groups in barracks while they carry out hard labour until they croak. Fed on slops. Chain gangs if they answer back.'

'Ooh!' Dromo panicked. 'I wouldn't like that. Will I ever be put into big leg rings?'

'No, you rattlebrain,' Paris reassured him. 'You are a lucky house boy. You have soft city owners. But it happens all the time in the wilds. Rural workers get used to it.'

I managed to stop the insults: 'Be tolerant of your country brothers, Paris. You were a slave once.'

'I lived in a lovely Roman home.' He brushed me aside airily. 'High class.' He sounded proud of his upscale background, with an easy-going master who had been generous and cultured. 'In our house, I was one of the family.'

'You had a very good life, Paris.' Tiberius was firm. We had known his owner before Paris was freed, a delightful man who was kind to us in our early days together. It was a short acquaintance, but we had loved him.

'Iucundus was tops,' the runabout freely agreed. 'Lovely person. I shall never forget him. But out here, slaves may as well be clods; they have no choice. They are just numbers. Numbers in anonymous battalions. We all saw the situation. Those bones came from people who were so unimportant that nobody even bothered to unfasten them when the rest rushed off to safety.' So he did understand.

Tiberius swept breadcrumbs into a little pile, which he brushed off the table with short, swift, angry movements. 'Having no choice was never their fault. In our *familia* the rule is, everyone born has a soul. That is why Flavia Albia is upset. She cannot bear that those four living souls were discarded as "unimportant".'

'But their fate has changed today,' Paris acknowledged. He had dropped the heartless act. 'Now they are important to Flavia Albia.'

'True.'

Quietly, I spelled out what I had been thinking so glumly: 'People knew they were there in that horrible place. People knew they had been chained to the wall. After all, someone at the villa had fastened the chains. People – luckier ones, who did have a choice – took a conscious decision to leave them to die.'

'We know,' said Tiberius, gently.

'You do.' I was not quarrelling.

'We are all listening, Albia.' At his master's words, even Dromo thought he had better stop kicking the table leg and look alert. Paris was drinking morosely, now affected by the chained slaves' predicament. Tiberius patted my hand. 'Tell us what is on your mind.' He realised he had better give me space to say it.

'Porphyrus, Endymio and Myrtale deserved better.' I used their names with hard determination. None of my companions would be surprised by what I said, nor by my vehemence.

'They had a value, and I don't mean what their masters could have sold them for in a slave market. They had rights, not only to be clothed and fed, but the right to humane treatment. Whoever decided to leave them there, trapped, was beyond callous. The slaves were victims – but not of the eruption. They were victims of the cruel people who owned them. I imagine you all know what I am going to say. I want to give them justice.'

Tiberius nodded, though he looked rueful. 'I don't like this any more than you do, Albia, but we must be realistic. They *were* slaves and others will simply contend that their masters had the power of life or death over them.'

'Only if any punishment was appropriate and justifiable. The law has moved on since the bad old days of Romulus.'

'I agree – but we don't know what they had done. Unless we know *why* they were chained up like that, you need to be careful, Albia.'

'Then I need to find out why.' Carefulness had never been my trademark. I was thorough, and proud of it; ditsy caution found no home with me. 'They killed the child too. Tiberius Manlius, I admire your restraint, but what capital crime could ever have been committed by that baby?'

He kept going doggedly, playing reasonable. 'People may not have known the child was there.'

'No – nor thought to wonder where he had got to. The poor toddler was even less important, being too young to do useful work. A mouth to feed. A future asset for the ledger. Somebody should have missed him.'

'Yes,' Tiberius agreed. 'He should have been picked up and held in safe arms.' I knew he was thinking about his own orphaned nephews. I remembered him bringing Gaius and Lucius to Rome, desolate after their mother had died:

69

Tiberius carrying them into our house to me, himself grieving his sister, but intent on letting her children believe all was not lost and they would be cared for.

'I am not being foolish,' I said gently. 'I do realise nobody will care enough to lay charges, even if the people responsible for those slaves could now be identified – and, of course, they may have died.'

'You hope they did!' suggested Paris.

'No. I'd like to find them still alive and I would like to make them sorry, Paris! But whose was the loss? Fulvianus, as his brother's heir and therefore the presumptive owner now? He seemed pretty cool about any lost slaves when we met him. Who was truly to blame anyway? His brother, as their owner at the time. Our vendor will excuse his brother, I am sure. That's life. In any case, Primus has gone missing; he can't be accused. So nothing will be done.'

Paris pondered: 'Suppose things were different and we even found Primus alive . . .'

I had an answer. 'Primus would pretend he knew nothing about them being left, too concerned with arrangements for his own escape. And if he used an overseer, that person will claim that, as everyone departed, the prisoners were simply forgotten.'

'Which was understandable in the chaos,' agreed Tiberius. 'We can't prove any different.'

'We don't know that. Maybe we can. I will do my level best to find out what happened.' I was so moved I had jumped to my feet. 'It was a crime!' I proclaimed. 'I am certain someone must have known they were left there. In which case, leaving them in chains – on purpose – was murder!'

14

My companions listened patiently, sitting silent. They were all used to me. I was still ranting.

The scene at our table took a new turn. Someone broke in: 'I know that voice.'

'Dear little Flavia! Our lucky day.'

Two men had paused outside. Passers-by always take notice of shouting in bars, hoping to see a fight. Definitely not locals, these were barrel-bellied, broad-faced, heavy enough to haul a long ladder up against a tall house and plant its feet on the pavement so it didn't slip. I had seen them be quick movers in an emergency, though. They looked like brothers, but were not. Over red tunics, today they wore cloaks with pointed hoods, fastened neatly down the front, like British woodland sprites.

Far from being Britons, we had been joined by two Roman firefighters. *In Stabiae?* My companions watched, even Tiberius looking bemused.

I had worked with this pair. Since I was on my feet, it enabled them to rush me and crush me in hugs. My husband, still seated, received polite salutes; our staff were granted brief nods.

The unexpected duo was marvelling at my presence there, though unsurprised by me sounding off. 'Murders again? Where do you manage to find so much foul play? Who died this time, Albia?'

'And who did the deed?'

'Just some slaves during the eruption. I don't know who is responsible – well, I don't know yet.' I stifled my stress. I could not immediately face recounting details.

I introduced the duo. 'Hyro and Milo, trusties from the Seventh Cohort but we won't blame them for that.' For vigiles they were unusual. They were as brave and well trained as those of their firemen colleagues whose only off-duty stimulations were food, drink and compliant women, but instead Milo and Hyro were addicted to theatre. Their commentaries on a bad performance were killing; their love of good stagecraft reached adoration level.

'You popping up here feels like you are my long-lost brothers in a drama,' I threw at them.

Hyro confirmed they had lost none of their wry wit: '*Dei ex machina* – descending from on high in a chariot, gripping the sides tight in case we fall out, spouting our big speech.'

'We shall put everything to rights. Not that you need help from us,' Milo hastily put in.

'We love working with Flavia Albia,' Hyro informed my companions. 'We may just have found her washed up on a rocky seashore but to us she belongs in a palace any day.'

'No, but you wouldn't take her home to meet your mother.'

'We can identify her father, though. We've seen his name written up everywhere.'

So that was still true: during the search for his nephew ten years ago, Falco had posted messages. I reminisced gloomily: 'He climbed on steps to do it, so his appeals would be too high to be washed off by Pompeian passers-by pissing on walls.'

'Well, the pleas survived. A tough family! We've even met a musician who says he is Flavia's cousin.'

That was too much. 'Cut it!' I commanded benignly. 'You are bantering like comic clowns. No cousins, please! We've left Rome to get away from the annoying chorus of relatives. Now tell me, boys, how come you two are strolling down a harbour walk in Campania?'

'Hyro fell out of a window and hurt his back.'

'Our kindly tribune put me on light duties, with Milo to look after me.'

I had met their tribune. Caunus was a no-nonsense ex-legionary, a wizened lifer of long-term centurion rank. He knew that this pair ranked among his most useful troops for controlling a blaze; however, he had no time for their constant conversation about whatever play they had seen last. Caunus had limited imagination; he distrusted culture. For Hyro and Milo, the fine points of drama were life's normal enrichment.

'Is this a rest cure? What are you really doing in Stabiae, boys?'

'It's official. Protection duty. Caunus is on a recce with the marines.'

'What recce?' scoffed Tiberius.

'Top-secret admin enquiry. Too important to tell us. We are simply to stop Caunus killing himself while he's having fun doing whatever it is.'

'Duty of the day: back-up for tribune, two-man escort, removal of drunk officer from gutter.'

Like the best mad claims, it was in part genuine. Some bureaucrat with not enough to do at the Palace had wondered to what extent Misenum or Puteoli were still receiving grain to feed Rome, so they ought to have out-stationed vigiles, like those who protected the newer imperial granaries at Ostia. Hyro and Milo explained that, having volunteered to

73

conduct an exercise, Caunus was stringing out his assignment while he 'consulted with the fleet'. Consultation meant he devoted himself to wild parties; it seemed a little out of character, though he had ordered Hyro and Milo not to cramp his style. Most of the time they shimmied off by themselves, looking for the famous Neapolis theatres.

They had found some. Those in the buried towns were gone for ever but Misenum, Puteoli, Baiae and Neapolis itself had generally survived Vesuvius. If their theatres had suffered earthquake damage, they had been patched up. Never mind rebuilding homes. Campania had its priorities.

One day in the future, when they received their certificates of release from firefighting, Hyro and Milo were bent on relocating. Drama had been endemic in this Greek-speaking area. Roman poets were born or retired there. So long as the wealthy built enormous homes in the fine climate, entertainers would come. The largest imperial villas had their own dinky stages, which still offered private performances for friends of the extremely great. The public was well served too. Until the eruption there had been regular games and festivals. Nero had played his heart out for an admiring public but before then the Isolympic Games, or Sebasta, had been initiated at Neapolis and were viewed as the most important games in the calendar.

As one-time slaves, Hyro and Milo had previously come with their old master, who had introduced them to drama. Now they were enjoying a nostalgic trip – though they had miscalculated. 'We had hopes of seeing the SameAs Games but we're two years too early.'

'SameAs two years too late.'

The Isolympics had been founded by the Emperor Augustus, much-loved in these parts. They replicated the

Greek games at Olympia exactly and the vigiles knew every detail: they were held every four years and featured equestrian events (horseback races and chariots, both two-horse bigae and four-horse quadrigae). The athletics included single- and double-length stadium races, pentathlon, wrestling, boxing, pancratium, a race while wearing armour, and acrobatics. These were followed by one more day of music and, crucially for my friends, one of drama. Domitian was keeping up the system. Our much-*un*loved current emperor had been here in person two years before but was not due again for two more.

'Bad luck! But why are you loafing around Stabiae? It's too small for a stage, surely?'

'Caunus has found himself a crony. The marines let him down – the trierarchs are too snooty, he told us. But a civilian captain carried him across from Misenum on a promise of wild days and tempestuous nights.'

'Caunus made us come with him. While he goes off on a spree, we have to wait until he reconnoitres with us at the Two Scallops. Even he admits his binge will last for days. If he kills himself carousing, let's hope Rome accepts it's not our fault.'

'Meantime, if you're solving a murder, can we help you like before?' They had once been assigned to me as bodyguards. It was the most fun they had had since *The Boasting Soldier*, the time its male lead slipped over on a cucumber and broke his hip onstage.

'I'm not hired for anything currently, I'm afraid, boys. No clients.'

'Really? Our Girl from the Aventine . . .' chortled Hyro. It was a reference to play titles, where *The Girl From . . .* (any Greek town that a Roman playwright wanted to insult) was

75

usually an actress wearing no clothes. 'Nobody wants her interfering – but, of course, she will do anyway.'

'She obviously needs looking after,' said Milo, taking comfortable charge. 'For starters, what are you doing at this crummy little bar, Albia? It's a dump.'

Hyro backed him up. 'Don't expect any grub. You'll be waiting all afternoon.'

Tiberius was nodding gloomily. 'We have been here an hour already, lads, and nothing yet.'

'Legate, you must come along with us. We've found a place that will rock off your marbles.'

It was notable that when his customers jumped up to leave for a better bar, the waiter with the worm moustache made no protest. Tiberius left coins for the cover charge. He liked to be honest. There are good people in the world.

I went along quietly. I had not dropped my wrath on behalf of the dead slaves. The vigiles had been right that nobody would want me interfering – but, as they said, that would never stop me.

15

The truth is that when people drag you off to some bar they know, that special find they claim is brilliant and unique, where the cook is a genius and the waiter treats them like his brothers, it generally turns out to be rubbish. You can wait a long time for the free drinks and garlands of roses your enthusiastic friends have promised.

The Two Scallops was about the same as the Three Clams we had just left. Hyro and Milo arrived with us just as the slipshod waiter went to lie down for a nap. The morose cook had to be fetched from lunch at his mother's to warm up the daily stew for us. The dog was asleep, although the beggar growled.

We occupied stools, made the awning hang better, ordered what they said would be fish (that stew of the day), obtained a bread basket with yesterday's rolls, and tackled another round of so-called fine local wine. There were probably people who spoke dreamily of the harbour at Stabiae with its romantic view of seawater and the brooding mountain beyond, but it was like any harbour anywhere. Ditto its bars.

While we waited for the oily cauldron to bubble back to life on a brazier, we told Hyro and Milo about the villa. They were soon demanding a chance to nose around. 'We can check for hazards and suggest fire precautions.'

'Leave off! We are not in Rome.'

'No, but you come from there,' argued Milo.

'Our duty,' said Hyro, 'requires protecting you from being foolish householders. How many fire buckets do you have at this place of yours, Aedile?'

'None.'

'Sacrilege! You need a safety inspection pronto.'

We explained that the villa was empty, no longer fitted out with furniture, or with anything else except occasional bones. Tiberius and I had to lodge at the pirate's house, an awkward distance away. Milo and Hyro decided we ought to move up to the villa; they knew where we could buy furniture. They had found a whole street of totters selling second-hand goods. 'It's ideal, if you don't object to singeing or surface damage.'

'Where does all this used property come from?' demanded Tiberius suspiciously, still clinging to his lapsed role in supervising markets.

'Don't ask!' they chorused. Tiberius flashed me a glance. *Dug up from dead victims' buried homes . . .* 'Only slightly used, we promise. Listen – they have fine bronze beds – the frames at least – and marble lamp tables – beautiful workmanship, just a bit of funny colouring where the heat got at them.'

'As for oil lamps and billy cans, we never saw so many baskets, hardly spoiled at all. We can have a good rummage and find you some gorgeous doings. Leave us your man.' That was Paris. He looked willing, prepared to go anywhere that wasn't a building site. 'Then he can fix the stallholders, saying you're good for payment. Once we've found a cart, he can show us the way and we'll bring stuff along.'

There was no stopping this pair. We thanked them weakly.

'Can I come?' asked Dromo.

'No,' said Paris.

Hyro shared an aside with Milo, then dropped his voice: 'If we visit your place, we can do something for you.'

'Hyro?'

'Milo and me, we've got the expertise. We could dismantle that shack where those poor slaves died.'

It made sense. Neither Uncle Tullius nor anyone else would ever want to use the prison again. Larcius and the men had enough to do. The vigiles were strong and trained for pulling down walls and ceilings when buildings became unstable or a firebreak was needed.

'Got any grapplers?' demanded Milo, remembering our lack of fire buckets.

'Yes,' replied Tiberius, only a little stiffly. 'My clerk-of-works has grapplers.'

'Done,' snapped the eager vigiles. While their tribune was being sick as a dog over a fan dancer, they would take a little holiday to enjoy what they were good at.

Just as in the previous bar, a pot of fish-pickle sauce had been placed with a flourish, though we were still awaiting food. When I mentioned that I wanted to find an apothecary, Hyro and Milo told me of one who had sold them a good liniment for Hyro's sprained back. Milo had rubbed on the embrocation for him, a thought I quickly passed over.

I said I might as well trot there now, while the fish stew was still in its 'Coming, coming, Legate!' stage. They would have escorted me, but I mouthed, 'Women's troubles,' so was waved off alone.

The herbalist obviously aimed his cures at rich visitors; he sat on display in his open street-side shop, surrounded by glass bottles and well-made wooden boxes with efficient sliding lids. No customers were there, but he had mastered looking busy. He was a short strip of wind in a long green tunic. Like all such, he had sour breath, pallid skin and depression. I wanted to recommend a regime of fresh air and healthy exercise.

His name was Bathyllus. I learned this from a neat wall poster: *The Best Bunion Balm from Bathyllus.* Also *Purge Your Phlegm with My Perfect Panacea* and *Non-Exotic Elixirs for Every Ailment.*

'Non-Exotic?' I queried, in puzzlement. Preference was usually given to the strange and faraway. Anything that had come such a distance it went rotten on the journey was a thrice-the-price commodity.

I introduced myself as a housewife seeking comestibles for my new kitchen cupboard. Hardly bothering to note that, Bathyllus launched into a diatribe against rare ingredients from India and Arabia whereas similar domestic herbs could be had from any local kitchen garden, often plucked for free. He pictured a local contest between hook-nosed quacks in pointed slippers who sold foreign junk to the gullible, as opposed to his own honest Mediterranean folklore recipes. Apparently the Seplasia, a forum at Capua where perfumiers sold their wares, was a sinkhole of vice. I suppressed a merry quip about rushing there to explore. This man had no time for jokes.

'I come from Britain,' I threw in. 'Often I keep that private, but if patients can tell you about their anal fissures, I assume you will be discreet about my end-of-the-Empire origins. It's not as bad there as people think. My province has a massive need for eye ointments – medics bring them in from Gaul – but our native *Britannica* is a wonderful cure-all for diseases of malnourishment. They say Germanicus Caesar swigged it all the time to prevent scurvy.'

Bathyllus narrowed his gaze. 'What's in this jollop? Nothing exotic?'

'Cheap as a chuckle. You would love it. They make it from dock-leaves.'

Finally, he looked impressed. As he climbed down from complaining, I steeled myself to ask about alum supposito- ries to use during intercourse. He reeled back in pantomime horror, thinking I meant abortion. 'I would not kill a child, Bathyllus, but I would rather not carry one until I am ready for it. Avoidance is legal, I believe.' These wise words hardly improved his attitude.

'Who told you alum will work?'

'My mother.'

'Yet she had you!' he countered in triumph.

'I am adopted,' I returned calmly.

'From Britain? She must have been desperate. Well, I am fresh out of alum.'

I nagged him for possible alternatives. He offered me a mad notion that the female partner should insert the bladder of a goat to receive her man without any dread of conse- quences. I scoffed that it sounded as useless as violent jump- ing in the air and kicking your heels back to shake out his seed. 'My family went to Egypt once. There, they recom- mend crocodile dung, moistened with sour milk, but my father said he would give away my mother to a temple if she tried it. Meanwhile my dear husband has read in an encyclo- paedia – by a writer he normally respects – that an amulet made from the insides of hairy spiders will protect. I hope,' I said drily, 'you are fresh out of spiders too, Bathyllus.'

'A placebo!' sneered the herbalist. 'If that rubbish was written by Plinius, he should have checked his sources. He died on the beach here during the eruption, you know. They blamed his asthma. If he had come to me for a linctus, he might still be alive today.' At least he felt forced to concede in my case: 'For your requirements, I recommend the seeds and rind of pomegranates.'

'Out of season, I suspect?'

'Unfortunately.'

'And don't tell me to swallow silphium once a month; I know it's extinct. What can I do, Bathyllus?'

'Warn your husband to be less demanding.'

'I would hold him off, but what about *my* needs? Anyway, I love him. We lead a full marital life.'

'Not been together long?' Bathyllus sniffed. Finally, he agreed he could make me a concoction of Cimolian earth and cedar oil, sweetening it with frankincense. Cimolian earths, whether white or purple, are baked clay and very drying, so I begged for a compromise and he quoted olive oil. Double oils would be doubly slippery. I was fearful how Manlius Faustus would manage, so an adjustment was agreed: cedar resin and honey, a mix that would be stiffer. Bathyllus wrote 'for coughs' in Greek on the label, to protect himself from prosecution.

μίγμα βήχα

Before I left, I asked for some poppy juice to ease Tiberius if he was suffering bad pain. He had brought none with him, since he was trying to stop using it. Once Bathyllus could accept that 'prolonged effects of being struck by lightning' was not my cover for witchcraft, he discussed the problem sensibly. 'Nerve damage. He was lucky he could walk away. His problems may recede in time, but he is correct to exercise caution, Domina. Opiates are highly addictive.'

'Yes, that worries him. I won't tell him I have bought a supply. The man tries to be brave, and I think he is improving, but I shall feel happier if have something to help him if ever he is desperate.'

'Better to try seeds of black henbane or white mandrake root,' Bathyllus recommended. 'Slightly less powerful. But analgesics all have the same dangerous properties. Even the correct dose has side-effects: dry mouth, itching, stool and urine retention, restlessness, poor sleep. Too little and they don't work. Too much and they kill the patient. Anyway, I am doubtful whether I should prescribe for a man I have not personally met.'

'You suspect me of wishing to do away with him?' I demanded in annoyance.

'Such things have been known.'

'Don't even think it, Bathyllus!' It did not help that I knew from my work that innocence is more difficult to prove than guilt. 'I would never give anything to him on the sly. I have too much respect for him. My husband is a reputable man from Rome, a recent aedile, Manlius Faustus.'

Eyebrows shot up (exuding dandruff). Initially, Bathyllus must have assumed I was a chicken-plucker's doxy. I had not dressed as the wife of a magistrate. For that I would need strappy shoes and three more necklaces. (Suza, a fashion idealist, would be bringing those from Rome for me, unasked.)

I smoothed out my Latin vowels, though only slightly since, if Bathyllus had bothered to remember, he already knew I was British. 'Trust me. Faustus's accident was reported in the *Acta Diurna*, should you wish to check our credentials. We are here because his uncle, another pillar of the Rome community, has bought the villa that used to be owned by the Curvidius family.'

Bathyllus suddenly came alive. 'Oh! I used to send supplies up there.'

'Often?'

With a wink, 'Masses.'

I hid my excitement, merely acting nosy. 'We have been wondering about the people who lived there before, Bathyllus. I always think past occupants become part of a house's character, so I would love to know more about them.'

The possibility of gossip washed over us like a balm. I had moved into working-informer mode. Bathyllus became Cimolian clay in my hands. He told me all I wanted. When I left his shop, I possessed vital new knowledge about our vendor's elder brother.

The villa's past owners, said the apothecary, were a herbalist's dream: hypochondriacs with cash. 'Slow to pay bills but, of course, in my trade the next bout of pain speeds up that process!' They had regularly ordered anti-inflammation potions, in particular a mix of resins, cinnamon and cassia, brightened with an expensive stir of myrrh. Sometimes, too, there was an urgent demand for a hemp bolus which, they had always claimed, was for 'earache'. But a key element in their history had been constant calls for gout and hangover cures. There could be no doubt what that meant: Publius Curvidius Fulvius Primus had a drink problem.

I feigned shock. 'When he went missing, do you think he wandered off somewhere, perhaps confused by the eruption, then simply couldn't remember where he'd come from?'

'Needing *that* amount of ground-cabbage purge,' Bathyllus replied, with a smirk, 'on most days Curvidius Primus probably had no idea who he even was!'

16

By the time I returned to the Two Scallops, the others had cleared the cauldron, so I ate only bread and olives, aiming to survive on cheese at the pirate's house. The holiday squits floored my party later. Tiberius uttered the immortal words, 'I shall be fine', followed next morning by the traditional 'Just leave me alone!'

While he was feeling sorry for himself, I had to find my own occupation. On previous evenings we had spent together-time in the peristyle garden. It had topiary tubs, three stone dining couches and some large lumps that I, as an auctioneer's daughter, deduced were sack-wrapped statues. I refrained from peeking because of the pirate's taste: he already owned a classic *Emperor Augustus Looking Imperial* with a ridiculously muscled breastplate, frothy epaulettes and an insufferable pose as a peace-bringer. *First Among Equals* (someone jests?) looked as if he had been lifted from a minor town's forum – and they would not ask for him back. He now stood in this garden, bringing peace to the plants. His long staff of office was missing, so we had put a broom in his hand.

An evening alone suited me, though I needed to stop thinking about those dead slaves. Being realistic, there was nothing I could do for them. Instead, after our talk of furniture that afternoon, I wandered around the pirate's house, assessing what kind of interior design was considered suave in Stabiae.

Quite nice. Much the same as in Rome. The frescos were as new as the house which was built in a restored part of town. To fill it, I reckoned Dexiades had taken advantage of the ghoulish local trade in fixtures. He owned some flash bronzework, for example. Suspiciously post-Vesuvian. A decent craftsman had tarted up the frames of antique metal beds and couches with good upholstery. With goat-legged marble-topped wine tables and an elegant five-foot-high candelabrum, they smacked of fast work plundering the ruins.

Pa and I had seen thieves in action at Pompeii. 'Liberators' was my father's word. He had left them to it, saying ghosts would never feel the pain of loss, and somebody had to fuel the second-hand market.

Through that market, the pirate's house had been dressed with glamour. He also owned vivid cushion covers with artisan embroidery that must reflect his origins; maybe his granny donated them. The total effect was cosmopolitan, similar to what we were aiming at for Uncle Tullius in his villa. Our landlord could show off his status like any high-brow citizen of Rome. Why he needed to rent his place to us or to anyone else was a puzzle.

I did wonder. Surely these choice chattels were not proceeds from what was officially a dead-end career these days? Piracy had been stopped in the Mediterranean. That was the official line. Various Roman generals had claimed cachet because 'clearing the seas of pirates' was a fast route to a gold wreath. Was Dexiades still at it, though?

Tiberius had been assured by the priest who arranged our tenancy that Dexiades was a normal trader, beyond reproach.

He had never been a wild eastern corsair. He simply came from Sardinia. That was positively Italian. It sounded safe, as if it described a hard-working fisherman. The realtor priest, a master of smooth talk, had derided any myth that island bandits still seized victims, terrified souls who were hauled off ships and held to ransom. Rich merchants and sons of senators sailed happily between Italy and Spain, didn't they? And no abductions had been reported for, ooh, absolutely ages.

Cynically, I thought that could be because silence was imposed as a condition of ransom.

People safe in soft beds in Rome were fascinated. Kidnapped on his way to Rhodes, Julius Caesar went back later and slaughtered his captors, but he had been an exception. Anyway, his pirates were Cilician. They were the most notorious. My father once helped a 'retired' Cilician pirate write his memoirs. In the course of this murky commission, Falco met other pirates, all of whom lied through the remaining stumps of their teeth, claiming they were retired too. He loathed them all. Heartless and murderous, they took pleasure in harming the innocent. Falco had compiled numbers, dates and locations of his client's past activities in a long appendix; he said the collaborative memoir could have been a bestseller, except that details of raids, rapes, amputations, disembowellings and throwings-overboard were too bloody even for a de-sensitised modern readership.

Was Dexiades currently away from home while he boosted his income like that? If so, we would be wise to move up to the villa before he came home. Bringing his trade to the mainland would entail risk, but when did danger deter a feisty pirate? I thought the idea was fanciful, yet if he really was still in business, lashing out on a month-long tenancy might have made Tiberius and me look like potential victims . . .

I thought some more about the slaves at the villa, then went to bed, under a vivid Sardinian coverlet. My husband slept fitfully on his own side of the mattress, groaning once or twice. I had wild cheese dreams, but simply turned over and went back to sleep. Of course the after-effects of the Two Scallops' food meant no testing that night of my cedar resin and honey 'cough mixture'.

Next morning Tiberius had improved, but still felt sluggish. Paris also looked green. He had intended to meet Hyro and Milo to look for furniture and fittings, but instead he chose to stay at the house to help Tiberius through his morning routine. That ought to have been Dromo's job, although most days Tiberius washed, cleaned his teeth, combed his hair, picked out tunics and sometimes even shaved himself. The boy just hung around watching. Today, having eaten more of the Two Scallops' stew than anyone, Dromo was too ill. When Paris and Tiberius felt better, *they* would probably have to wash *him*, clean his teeth and comb his hair. The thought gave Paris the runs again. Tiberius was holding on stoically.

I said, 'My parents would say this is a routine joy of travel.'

'Then I want to go home!' muttered Paris.

With my men indisposed, it fell to me to accompany the vigiles. When they picked me up, my old friends Hyro and Milo were not suffering. They must have been used to insanitary bars, bars that served the vigiles' end-of-duty breakfasts from thick-rimmed pots that had stood lukewarm on a griddle all night.

They took me to a short, sad street where there were dark shops, haphazard stalls and even cloths on the ground where bric-a-brac was laid out, much of it broken, some so weird the objects' purpose was undecipherable. I felt at home; it was like crawling around at dawn to preview a very bad auction in the Saepta Julia. Ragged men and women oversaw the booty, some scurrying up to us on our arrival, others so despondent they hung back from selling even after we tried to approach them and buy. Any real bargains would have been snapped up years before but a few fine goods were still being dug out from buried places. Grey material clung to some, a tragic provenance.

'Don't buy anything without consulting us,' Hyro and Milo warned me, in their paternal style.

'Auctioneer's daughter. Don't *you* buy anything without asking *me!*' I retaliated. They gave me well-choreographed mock salutes.

I set off ahead of them briskly. I had been trained as a sharp punter, not to be lured into daft buys. I walked around, skimming the stock, decided what I wanted, uncovered hidden treasures by instinct, then smiled like a nervous old lady – and haggled without shame. I never even noticed how ruthlessly I rejected duds or how hard I was bargaining, but the sellers were soon muttering.

His villa had been sold as unfurnished so Uncle Tullius would be sending furniture. I could not visualise him touring fine craftsmen; he intended to raid warehouses where his tenants had left property in store for too long, despite default notices. I suspected this would be property they did not want – and neither would we.

Tiberius and I had been granted approval to make start-up purchases locally. Tullius had even assigned us a budget, which, surprisingly, was not even mean. This fitted my theory that, despite his reputation, he looked after himself.

Top of the list were beds; I rooted some out, making sure all the frame parts were present. Hyro and Milo discovered a man who strung webbing and a family who stuffed new mattresses and cushions. We arranged for the best bed to be made good immediately, so Tiberius and I could have that. Tullius might want to choose his own. Others, more utilitarian, could follow; we would pay on completion, which should speed things up. Next, I hunted down a pleasant reading couch, with ivory panels that looked surprisingly unharmed, although one dropped off into my hand.

'Bit of fish glue will soon fix that, Domina.'

'Knock off a sestertius?'

'Quarter?'

'Half, then.'

'Shake.'

I bought cupboards, but only if they came with doors and shelves, although our men could mend minor defects. 'Missing knobs? I'll find you some.'

'Give me a full set so they'll match.'

'You want things perfect?'

'Well, why not?'

Three-legged side-buffets, low serving tables, several varieties of seating, then basketfuls of household goods were assembled. My steward and cook would be bringing our own kitchen- and dinner-wares but I unearthed a usable water heater. Its seller thought my interest meant he could overcharge, but I used the rule that when they sniff, 'Take it or leave it,' and you snap back, 'I'll leave it, then,' they will come crawling. He knew he had met bargaining talent. I snapped it up.

The last item was even more unusual. At the far end of the street I had come across a huge barn, filled to the rafters with big old junk; most punters just walked away, daunted. I wriggled in. It looked to have nothing decent – yet shoved right towards the back was a treasure. The man in charge seemed reluctant to disturb his personal truss (which he told me about shyly). I said not to bother: there was no chance I would buy it. Despite his hernia he insisted; he got Hyro and Milo to drag out the mighty piece of metal with a rope. They stationed the piece in front of his building, then we all stared.

The seller claimed this went back to his father's time. His father had passed away, so apparently there was no known history and, our man admitted openly, few hopes he could ever sell it. I accepted the story. My father reckons to know by instinct when a provenance is weak, but I simply thought the item must have been dragged out of a house where the owner had died. Along with so much else, it was Vesuvian loot.

The man's name was Septumius. I had thought it polite to ask, after he had almost been prepared to rupture himself. He must have known I was the worst kind of customer, merely curious. 'Thank you very much!' I was going to walk away . . . No, I wasn't.

It was a bathtub.

You see plunge baths in commercial premises, with blotchy old invalids seated there on marble steps and overfed regulars, who are known for assaulting younger men and boys, then blustering that they were confused by a fug of steam. Since the Empire was stuffed with public baths, even in its bleaker provinces, not many people wanted their own tub, yet a few who could afford it would have one installed. They would need a large income. Even single-person baths need many pails of hot water, brought by many grumbling slaves.

'Lovely piece, pure bronze,' Septumius claimed. 'Bit of private luxury.'

'An eyesore, you mean?'

'I think you'll find some decent scrollwork on the side.' Septumius was wrong. I wasn't an investigator for nothing: I had looked. No clawed feet, although it had ring handles on the side.

This bath had seen better days, but basically it was fine. It was plain, rectangular and deep, with a flat integral surround that could sit on a support unit if you had one. Really, the bath was meant to be freestanding; while you relaxed, you would use the surround to stand oil lamps, unguent bottles, or even your wine goblet. A key feature was an undamaged plughole to empty your water after you climbed out all pink and relaxed.

Yes, I had examined this piece quite thoroughly.

'No plug?' I know how to quibble.

'I doubt we ever had it. People are useless when they bring things in to us.'

We could improvise.

Septumius kept talking, not pushily. The bath was heavy, too much for the cart my helpers had hired, so he would happily bring it to the villa himself on his ox-cart. For nothing. His nephew would help him to load and unload it. 'Choose a position and we'll heave it right there for you. But no steps or narrow doorways, please.'

'Mulsum all round and a cinnamon cake when you finish?' He looked offended, as is normal when a customer is flippant during serious negotiations. He did say, as a one-time special offer, he would throw in a basket of free sea-sponges.

Hyro could see how much I was tempted. 'Is there a private bathhouse at your place, Flavia Albia?'

'Supposedly.'

'With a furnace?' Milo lured me some more.

'Not yet tested – but the plans do show one.'

'Water supply?'

'Condition of purchase. The villa has a pipe to the Stabian aqueduct.'

'That's up and running,' Septumius quickly assured me. While I brooded, he began pushing harder. He needed to stop me walking away as just another time-waster. I was on the verge of sensibly leaving. Septumius kept talking: '*Aqua Augusta Campaniae.* Properly famous. Marcus Agrippa built the mother-feed to serve them over the bay, and the fleet of course, but we have our own on this side. One branch is routed down to the port, and another goes out towards Surrentum. Your place will link into that one. Everything was clogged up in the eruption but has been cleaned and repaired. All you need is to pay your civic dues for using it.'

'Think!' the lads kept slyly pressuring me. 'A warm soak, Flavia Albia –'

'At the end of a long day –'

'Soft clean towels, slippers, perfumes, someone reading you a nice poem while your cousin the flautist plays his double aulos.'

'What cousin? And stop whiffling about slippers. Don't tempt me, you blighters!'

'No need to despise it as luxury –'

'Call it medicinal –'

'Oh, stop it!'

There was no escape. I wanted it. I bought it.

17

My new bath had more history than anybody realised. Its true past would emerge slowly, like an arthritic bather climbing out with careful steps, so as not to let a wobbly foot slide fatally on a marble floor.

How its last owner actually passed away had been nothing to do with a fall – although once I unearthed the story it would explain why the bath had been taken out and sold. Brought away from the sad street where I found it, the big beast looked in need of a clean and its plughole was full of spiders' webs. But when my innocent purchase first arrived, there were no clues to anyone's suspicious fate. We found no odd stains on the dulled surface and a few light dents were only to be expected in second-hand metal that dated to a time before earthquakes and volcanic eruption.

The day it arrived was already busy. Tiberius and I had returned to the villa. Paris had gone from the pirate's house down to the harbour where, as we had hoped, he found a ship unloading our expected goods and people from Rome: Gratus our steward, Suza my maid, and Fornix our cook, plus two slaves from the Tullius household that nobody had told us were coming. All were crotchety from travelling. Out from the ship's hold had swung a load of bulky luggage. Paris returned to the villa with most of our staff, bringing the first load of furniture (for which no places were ready yet), and a borrowed donkey, its panniers laden with enough crockery, cookware and cutlery to adorn a banquet, had we yet possessed a working kitchen. Fornix marched straight off to look. Stomping back, he announced that nothing at this godforsaken villa met his standards as a one-time gourmet chef at the immortal Fabulo's. Unless something was done, he was going home.

'Is it a promise?' snarled my steward, not quite under his breath.

'Wouldn't that suit your majesty?'

Gratus and Fornix had a mild feud, which worsened when either was stressed. It had been a bad idea to have them travelling together. Suza, who came with them, now walked off, close to crying. She was a tough young girlie normally; that gave me a clue as to how much spiky temperament she must have witnessed on the journey.

'Don't fight a man who habitually handles cleavers,' I advised Gratus. Calming the household was supposed to be his job. 'Fornix, we'll put your precious pans somewhere for the time being, then find me a bucket and I myself will wash down the worktops for you.'

'You mean there is water?' enquired the chef, snootily.

'We found a well, and Larcius has had the slime cleared out. But once Tiberius Manlius contacts the authorities—'

'What?' interjected Tiberius, pretending to blink like a duffer. 'I have to do something?'

'Fix us up with a connection. I believe there is a pipe to an aqueduct. I am offering a prize to the first person who finds our end of the pipe.'

Dromo popped up. 'What prize? If I find it, can I have a cake?' He loped off in his ungainly way.

Milo and Hyro chose the same time to roll up with everything I had bought in Stabiae. There was nowhere clean for that to be unloaded either. They began nosing about the villa.

Immediately behind them, my bath arrived.

Septumius had brought it as promised, on a flatbed cart pulled by a mournful old ox which was yelled at by his nephew – a tall, staring, off-putting boy – and his nephew's older, even taller, much surlier best friend. They pulled up in front of the entrance porch, whipped off a dirty cover and began unloading my purchase as if they already knew where they had to stow the mighty lump of bronze.

Heaving the tub off the cart to ground level was a dangerous strain. Our workmen strolled up to watch but did not help. Inspecting my purchase, they chorused, 'Bull's bollocks, Flavia Albia! What kind of crazy woman are you?'

Now I was stuck. I could see it would have taken hours for Septumius and his helpers to lug this monster all the way uphill from Stabiae, then over horrible roads to reach our villa. They must have started in the dark. Now they had dropped the bath with a loud metallic clang, they were look-ing to me expectantly, like Hercules delivering the stolen red cattle of Geryon after dragging the herd across half of Europe. The moment had mythical status.

I could not make them take it back. Not even when my husband strolled up, took in the situation and addressed me frankly: 'Tiddles, whatever were you thinking of?'

However much I loved him, at that moment my passion diminished – and not because he had used a family nick-name I had banned. His men saw an opening, so repeated to him their crazy-woman theory, adding, 'It's horrible. However much do you think she paid for it?'

Too much, I thought, not saying so.

'Too much', we eventually learned, was correct, though not for any reason I had guessed.

On hearing our excited voices, Serenus joined the gathering, with Milo and Hyro tailing him. They all stood around, staring at the bronze tub. Now we had a group of men in rough brown tunics, some leaning on picks, all dismissing my bath as an enormous mistake. I wished I had bought a loom. At least I could have sat by myself in the atrium, peacefully weaving like a good Roman matron. Well, a good Roman matron who was mentally plotting plague and riot.

Our clerk-of-works scuttled up, looking businesslike with his folding rule at the ready. Immediately he applied himself to measuring the flat surround on the tub, comparing notes with some details he had already scribbled on a piece of tile.

'What about it, Larcius?' Serenus asked.

Milo did not wait for the official verdict from Larcius. 'Just about right, I'd say.'

'Close enough,' Hyro agreed sagely.

Ignoring them, Larcius gave the official verdict: 'Spot on! Could have been made for us.'

Larcius, a sensible man, then looked at Tiberius and me, prior to reporting: 'I just checked the bathhouse. The rooms need a deep clean and Jupiter knows what has been happening in your drains, but the furnace outside still looks viable. You will need new mangers,' he complained, as if stowing clothes was the key requirement of a bathhouse. 'The woodwork on the old ones is completely shot – it just falls apart. Only to be expected, mind. It shouldn't be a big job, though we haven't brought a carpenter.' Our building firm used one in Rome but he had refused to come. 'But she'll go in all right.' Larcius was nodding at my bath. 'We worked out where she must have been sat before. She'll slot straight back in place again, sweet as you like!'

Septumius had a big wide grin, even though Larcius had given his game away. Now this honest-seeming man was showing his true flag: he was a fleece-anyone-from-Rome, shameless Campanian wide boy. Slowly it dawned: ages before this, his father had been paid by one party to purchase this very bath from the Curvidius villa; after storing it patiently for year after year, Septumius had been paid again by a second party – me – to return the bathtub to its original home.

'Exquisite. Your father would be delighted!' I growled. He rendered me the wry smile and slow nod of a man admitting how his late father had assured him fools would pay good money for this if they waited long enough.

'Good to bring the old girl home again!' uttered the honest-seeming Septumius.

18

If you are ever having a bath fitted, I advise you to go out that day. Visit an aunt, one who chats at length so you are late home. While we had extra people on site, we used them; the tub was carried to the bathhouse. Manoeuvring a bathtub is viewed by men as a specialist task. The one who wants to keep secret that he has a hernia gets panicky, and metal corners are bound to damage pillars in your peristyle. Helpers moving a heavy load would prefer you not to witness that and shriek at them.

Bearers lined up on either side, as if an unusual funeral bier was being taken in procession to a necropolis. I followed, feeling as unwanted as a widow, while single-minded male associates were hogging all the formal rites due to their paternal authority. There must be a section on furniture-moving in the Twelve Tables of Roman Law.

I managed not to say, 'Oh, please be careful!' more than once.

They had to transport their big bronze burden quite a long way: through the new villa wing, past the service areas and right to the far end. When that part of the house was designed, this would have been deliberate planning to position the furnace, flues and heated hypocausts where they posed least risk of fire. Milo and Hyro wanted to give us a safety lecture, but the overweight drama-groupies were too puffed after carrying the tub.

Tullius had acquired neat private bathing facilities, it seemed: an undressing nook with one marble bench and those broken clothes-mangers that Larcius had bemoaned, then a simple suite of small decorated rooms, hot and cold, then a steam room with seats, plus a private extra cubbyhole where previously a medicinal bath – this very model – had stood and now had returned.

They dumped it down with relief. We could see where it went because one of the stone drain covers in the floor, which had quatrefoil decoration like its brothers in other washing rooms, would be directly beneath it. That would accept the flow when water was let out through the hole in a corner of the bath. The friend of Septumius's nephew clambered over some lava, reached across the rectangular space where the tub was to stand, put one hand into a niche designed for a very small statue (now missing), and brought out a bronze plug.

'*Io!* Well done, Criton!'

Everyone cheered. Men poked out spiders and set the plug in place. It fitted. They were all delighted. I stared at the nephew's friend thoughtfully.

The lanky Criton looked away, writhing uneasily. He had not said much since he came. I put him at about ten years older than the nephew. The young pals were similar types physically, tall and thin; despite quite an age difference, they went around as a pair, but this one gave the impression he was holding something back and might be unreliable. It was a well-known look at one level of society. Not only was Criton shifty, I was beginning to guess why. At some point in his childhood, he had been a slave. I started to think I might know where that had been.

★   ★   ★

Gratus, my excellent steward, had become more himself since his flustered arrival. He took advantage of the extra hands. He chivvied all the men into going back outside to help him sort the other deliveries. While furniture was being unloaded from carts, with anxious cries of 'To you!' and 'That's torn it!', Suza and I managed to dash around the atrium with wet sponges and cloths to lay any loose dust where hardened tufa had been chipped out. Things would be stored in this entrance space until we were ready to place them around the house. Most Roman furniture is portable. You choose where to have it according to the event involved.

Light items were brought indoors first. We seemed to have a lot of footstools. Only the couch and beds posed problems. Whenever beds are delivered in pieces, men feel compelled to reassemble them. They set to at once, competing as eagerly as if showing off their masculinity at a palaestra; they snatch at parts but never consider the right sequence to combine them, so the task always takes longer and involves more cursing than it should. According to ours, vital pieces were missing; according to me, the sets had all been complete when I checked; according to Milo and Hyro, they had lost nothing while transporting the load.

Heifers in Hades. I left them all to it.

Gratus, a man of intelligence and order, lost patience with how stupidly the bed sets were being put together so he came to help in the atrium. 'Domina, you have assembled a bunch of idiots!'

Arranging bales and baskets neatly on our cleaned floor, my refined factotum gazed around. 'This will be all right, Flavia Albia.' He spoke as if soothing an agitated home-owner, though in fact I was calm. Anyone who has assisted at an auction knows that order can rise out of chaos.

I needed no convincing about the place or its decor. This would be a good house again soon.

After they found the supposedly lost parts, the completed couch and beds were carried indoors, filling up the atrium. The villa's shell now seemed transformed back into a liveable habitation. It actually sounded different, less echoey. Normality cheered everyone. People felt more comfortable, even with furniture gathered in an untidy group, much of it wrapped in covers. Suza and I pulled out chairs and deliberately sat beside the dry impluvium. Gratus joined us. We agreed that all we needed was a platter of frosted dates and a waiter bringing spiced mulsum. 'I shall ask Fornix!' teased Gratus, though he had more sense than to do it.

Once they brought the beds, our train of unloaders had dwindled in energy. Then, voices from outside changed in tenor. We went out to investigate.

Various carts stood empty now. The old ox had been put back under his yoke; he was stomping restlessly. Septumius and his helpers, with Milo and Hyro, and even Paris, who had left goods on the harbourside, were all going back down into Stabiae. Before they dispersed, Tiberius had arranged that Septumius could take with him any unwanted old farm equipment left behind by the Curvidii, plus some materials from the shack that Hyro and Milo had now dismantled for us. 'But not the roof tiles – nor the big door.' A broken plough and half a grindstone were among other things on the ox-cart, so now the prison's old bricks and building framework would not fit.

A serious male discussion occurred, concerning transport. Septumius needed help but his options were diminishing. Hyro and Milo waved goodbye and rattled off in a hurry; they had to return their hired cart before sunset or pay double next day if it was unavailable for market. Paris was resistant too; he reckoned he must hasten to the harbour, with no time to divert to the bric-a-brac street, or people would help themselves to the goods he had left behind. He said two men sent by Uncle Tullius had been left on guard, but the quayside was full of rural clowns on the lookout for things to pinch from us. This, at least, was the opinion of city-boy Paris. 'Tullius has sent us a damned pair of Gauls,' he explained in disgust.

'Oh,' I cried. 'Northerners! Of course, they will be easily distracted and our property stolen.' People told me to calm down. They stepped away while they said it.

Tiberius mentioned the locked shed where what looked like an old cart had been spotted. 'The horse died – we found his poor old bones. But if it really is a cart, Septumius, and if it's still usable, we can lend you our donkey. You can oversee the load down to Stabiae – one of your boys had better drive – but my lad Dromo can come, then bring the cart back empty.'

'I don't know the way!' wailed Dromo.

'Trot along to the harbour, daftie, and I'll bring you,' scolded Paris. He must be thinking Dromo could help him with his own load, but was too wise to say so in advance.

All they had to do now was unlock the store to retrieve the old cart.

They held a conversation about locks.

Suza rolled her eyes. I kept my face straight while I advised they should smash their way into the store with a lump hammer. We had plenty of those. Tiberius winced as if I wanted to desecrate a temple. Other male persons followed his lead. Clearly women are airheads who know nothing about the proper use of tools.

Undeterred, I turned to Criton, the friend of Septumius's nephew. 'All right, Criton. Do your stuff, will you?' The young man play-acted bafflement. 'It's late. Don't mess us around, laddie. You knew where the bath plug used to be kept, so I reckon you lived here in the past. Better not deny it. Where did the family hide the key to this beaten-up store-room? I don't see a flower urn to tuck it under.'

Criton began to display strange behaviour. 'What's up with you?' Tiberius spoke to him quite kindly.

Criton yelled. 'I don't know where it is!' Then he turned tail and ran off towards the garden area, highly agitated.

Raising his eyebrows, Tiberius stopped the others chasing him in a mob; he told the nephew to go after him quietly. 'No need to get hysterical. He won't be in trouble. Calm him down, please, and bring him back as soon as possible.' As the nephew followed, Tiberius then tackled Septumius. 'Is my wife correct? Did Criton once live here?'

'He may have done.'

'*May* have? All right. How do you know him?' I pressed. The man still seemed reluctant. 'Is he a runaway?' Since I had guessed, Septumius slowly nodded. 'He was one of their slaves? He made an escape during the eruption?' I demanded.

'Around then.' Septumius still played vague. 'He was distressed. My father took him in. Looked after him discreetly until nobody would turn up wanting him back. My brother raised him as a playmate for Crispus – that's my nephew. Crispus was a child, around six or so. He had lost his younger brother and his mother to illness. He was feeling it. He needed someone.'

'Criton must be older,' Tiberius said.

'Yes, by a few years, but they always got on.'

I reassured him: 'Criton is safe. None of us will tell on him. If he was a slave, we have seen how slaves were treated on this estate. But when he quietens down, I do need to talk to him.'

'Another day,' wheedled Septumius.

I agreed.

While they waited for Crispus and Criton to reappear, the others made their decision about the storehouse. They took a lump hammer to the lock. Surprise!

Wide doors to allow vehicles to pass in and out let a degree of light creep inside. From the threshold, we all peered into the murk. Big huddles of amphorae, no stoppers, were standing all along the walls, askew now and half buried in volcanic material that must have poured through a hole in the roof. One or two were broken. From their shapes, they looked like commercial oil and fish jars, but with a telling predominance of used wine containers. I remembered my conversation with the apothecary about Curvidius Primus needing hangover potions.

In the middle, covered with fine ash, we could make out a four-wheeled flatbed cart. Its low backboard was down, at the end nearest to us. The cart was lurching sideways on a block, with one wheel off. That explained why it had not been taken in the exodus when the volcano erupted, or used to move possessions afterwards. We had already found a wheel, carbonised but with signs of mending, in the stable.

Larcius hurried in and felt his way through the gloom down the side where the vehicle was supported. He could see nothing wrong with the axle, so called that his men would be able put the wheel back. They all braced to manhandle the cart out of doors. 'Hold on!' Larcius stopped them. He had seen something else. 'Someone's here on it, having a kip!'

Tiberius hauled a big door further open to let in more light. Lying on the cart, face up under a blanket of ash, we made out the shape of another body.

19

'Who is that?' demanded Dromo. As usual with his pointless questions, nobody bothered to reply. 'Master, *who?*'

At my side, Tiberius dropped an arm around my waist. We would be thinking the same: as far as we could see, this person was unencumbered, with no leg chains. It was a different situation from when we found the trapped slaves.

Larcius squeezed out of the store again, shaking his head. After a moment of shock all round, Tiberius told the rest to stay outside. He and I went in together to look.

He was carrying the lump hammer, so he knocked it against the cart to shake the material layer loose. He stopped when the cart itself began to dematerialise. The body had been there long enough to decay completely. Through a light covering of debris, we could see that a skeleton was stretched full length, arms alongside, head towards the doors, skull leaning slightly one way, as they tend to.

Larcius brought a stumpy hand brush. It had lost more bristles than it retained, but he leaned over and began gently clearing the bones so we could inspect in more detail. The skeleton was hanging together so far, though the chunky limbs might break apart if we tried to move it – as we would have to.

Not only were there no chains this time, but when Larcius cleaned away unwanted material, the neck wore no runaway-slave collar.

'Looks male, heavy joints,' Tiberius commented, in a low voice, to me.

'I think that's a masculine pelvis. He was certainly not pregnant!'

Tiberius and I continued our discussion in low voices, standing close to each other. 'Taller than average.'

'Good diet?'

'Probably.'

'Are we both thinking, never been a slave?'

He nodded. 'Hid in the store while the crap was falling, went to sleep, taken by a surge of heat, died there without knowing anything about it?'

Larcius put in, 'I can't see any twisted limbs.'

Tiberius stepped in to examine the corpse more closely, even touching it with his index finger. 'You're right. No signs of healed wounds from the past, no cuts or breaks in the long bones.'

'Not been a soldier?' I murmured, moving nearer. 'No bar fights, no agricultural accidents? He is not bow-legged from rickets or hard manual labour.' I knew about rickets from my own struggling childhood in Britain.

Back in Britain I had once seen a skeleton unearthed. It was some ancient person buried with different rites than were used now, lying straight, surrounded by funeral goods: bowls that had contained fruits and grains, beakers, gaming tokens, a dagger, beads . . . The people I had lived with as a child had dug out the corpse, looking for weaponry and jewels.

I remembered how I had stood by that uncovered grave, scared stiff as I gazed at the other skeleton. I was no longer afraid, but other feelings were the same: sadness, curiosity, even wanting to communicate with the lost soul, needing to hear his story.

'Perhaps he sheltered here for safety, waiting for the lapilli and ash showers to stop?' I felt troubled, unconvinced. 'Something about his position seems odd. Perhaps he was asleep. If so, he slept very neatly and formally. He looks more like a corpse laid out on a bier for public viewing.'

Tiberius agreed. 'I think you are right about him being a corpse. Covered with ash? Either he died almost as soon as the eruption started – or I'd say he was laid here before anything happened.'

I thought about it. 'People fleeing the crisis would not have wanted to take a dead body.'

'No, but they could have come back for him afterwards.'

'It's very odd that they didn't . . . If we were right that the house had already been cleared of furniture, to abandon a corpse during that process becomes even odder.'

'Maybe his dying was *why* people had cleared the house?' Tiberius turned and was looking at me in sudden surmise. 'Was it his house, then? The master, alone here by himself. Stretched out in state . . . Can it possibly be . . .?'

'Publius Curvidius Fulvius Primus?' I suggested.

If that was right, we had found the missing brother.

'Whoever it is, it's time he stopped lying around here.' Larcius started rolling up his sleeves. 'This old blighter will have to shift himself – the scrap merchant needs his cart!'

20

By now the workmen knew what to do with bones. Tiberius made them collect this set into a dust cloth we had unwound from furniture. If it truly was Primus, he could be kept separate. That was not out of respect for lofty sensibilities: I felt his slaves and even the watchdog deserved segregation from him. My husband thought as I did. To Tiberius and me, it seemed wrong to tumble this man's remains among those he had abused. Besides, we might despise him but we had made promises to his brother. Primus would have a full funeral.

'We'll take him off first,' Serenus told me, as they began collecting him up. 'Before we move the wagon. We don't want him dropping all over the place while we're hauling it out.'

They were all unsentimental. Think about that at times when you are imagining how people will speak of you reverently once you are gone. Some who believe in an afterlife are convinced that ghosts cannot hear what is said on earth, but suppose dwellers among the shades can answer back. *At last they've gone!* mutter the spouses of the predeceased. *Oh, I haven't finished with you yet,* returns a witter from the Underworld . . .

It was definitely Primus. That was corroborated by the workmen when something rolled out from among the small finger bones during collection. Serenus caught it. He handed the object to me. 'You're not squeamish, Flavia Albia.'

It was nothing to excite the nervous, just a big signet ring, a man's, almost certainly gold. I spat on the intaglio, which was typical carnelian. Rubbed clean, its oval shield showed a deity leaning on a rudder.

'Oh, dear me!' Gratus, my steward, surprised us. 'I am sorry – there has not been a moment to tell you, madam and sir. I bring messages from Tullius Icilius. He said to pass on that Curvidius Fulvianus has reported that his brother's seal was the goddess Fortune. Thinking about questions you asked when you met him, he has also remembered that his brother had several teeth damaged in his youth.' I wondered who Primus had been fighting with.

The seal was right: Fortuna Redux, overseeing safe returns from journeys. On one arm she held her long slim cornucopia; her other hand rested on a ship's steering oar, and a globe stood by her foot. This ring was, my father would have said, a natty example of gemstone carving. Done up, and perhaps found a showy box, it would be very saleable. To us, its value was irrelevant. I would have to preserve the heavy carnelian keepsake for Curvidius Fulvianus.

'Catch!' Larcius tossed the owner's skull to Tiberius; it was badly aimed but fortunately his receiver had good eyesight. Tiberius lunged to field the head one-handed. As he straightened, men applauded. Suza, who had joined us full of curiosity, squealed in horror.

Tiberius played along with his men's nonchalant approach. He pretended to brush hair straight. He examined the jaw, which still hung on the skull, then pronounced, laconicly, 'Three teeth are reduced to stumps. Must have been painful. Yes, this will be Primus.'

Serenus and Sparsus were carrying away the bones, holding the cloth by bunched corners, one at each end, like helpers removing someone who had been hurt in an accident. For a moment I thought Tiberius would toss in the skull. He saw me catch my breath; he placed the dead man's head gently at one end of the bones. 'Hail and farewell, Primus ... You can stick him in the shed with the others, lads, but leave his shroud tucked around him. Let's preserve him tidily for now. I must write to ask his brother's intentions.'

'Does this mean I am going back to Rome?' squawked our runabout.

'Give it a rest, Paris!' people chorused. He looked wounded.

Almost before the stretcher party had walked off with the body, the cart that had served as a bier for ten years was being drawn out for remedial works. In fact the wheel from the stables was never fetched; it obviously belonged but the vehicle was too fragile to use. Heat had so badly affected the woodwork that both cart and wheel were equally unusable. The cart collapsed when half pulled outside, only its metal fitments remaining intact.

Paris fetched our donkey, fixed panniers, and the men loaded them instead. Dromo was being given instructions. 'Listen to me. Don't forget!'

'Forget what?'

'What I just told you. Unload the panniers for Septumius, then come to the port.'

'What for?'

'To find me on the quay!'

I saw that Septumius's nephew had brought back his friend. They were looking subdued and stood as far away from the opened store and collapsed cart as they could manage without it being obvious. I marched up. 'One question right now, Criton!'

He wanted to reject me, but I could see he had an eye on Septumius. He, a man of quiet reactions, only pursed his lips at the young man.

'Criton, tell me the truth. Did you know the body of Curvidius Primus was inside there?'

Criton became agitated again. Crispus moved closer to him, protectively. Septumius approached. 'He was young. He doesn't remember much about that time.'

I said, kindly enough, that I would drop the subject for now. Next time I came down into Stabiae I would want to talk to Criton. He had better be there, and prepared for a conversation, or I really would set up a hue and cry. But if he talked to me as I wanted, he would have support. 'I have no intention of disrupting the life he leads with his new family. It's up to him, Septumius, to show he is a responsible member of the community. He can be reflecting on that.'

I was too tired by then to force the situation. I gave Septumius a hard stare, hoping he would be sensible in advising Criton. He nodded slightly. As soon as they could, they set off quickly. Septumius drove the ox, the two youngsters followed on foot, along with Dromo riding our donkey. I had seen Tiberius speaking to him, possibly saying he should listen to the others' conversation. I had not suggested it myself; Dromo would either give himself away or get the wrong end of the stick.

In fact, when he came back, Dromo said the others had hardly spoken.

Workmen and household staff began drifting indoors. Too weary to give orders about anything, I left them to organise an evening meal. I walked off by myself. Although Fornix had cursed the poor kitchen facilities, I had a good idea he would be unloading food hampers. Refreshments would be set out on the newly delivered furniture. Perhaps people would even find bowls and beakers, after which, if good manners applied, they would wait for me to appear. If I was away long enough, someone might even think of washing the unpacked bowls . . .

I wanted space for reflection.

I walked back down the length of the villa, into the bath-house, and took one more look at my bath. *Flavia Albia, what kind of crazy woman are you?* A satisfied one. Not caring what any of them said. I liked my purchase.

I felt like a fifteen-year-old who had finally won through and acquired the coveted snake bracelet.

I patted the rim. The bronze metal was cold and the tub looked filthy. I decided this woman was not sufficiently crazy to climb in tonight and try it.

I walked through the suite of bathing rooms, into the small changing space. I brushed off a place on the marble bench. There I sat, by myself, facing up to the mystery today had brought.

Soon, I heard footsteps. Tiberius found me, putting his head around the doorway. We smiled, but said nothing. Between us, there was never any need for hysterical cries of *We've been looking everywhere for you! Whatever are you doing here?* He would know.

He came and sat beside me, taking my hand. For a short while we were companionable in our own way, taking time to rest and restore our spirits while we were away from the others.

'New bed!' he murmured seductively. 'We should test it, in case it needs to go back for adjustment.'

'Are you sure? You had a busy day.'

'I paced myself.'

'Then I am a lucky wife.'

'I hope to make you think so.'

We turned together and kissed quietly, in anticipation. It was soft and appreciative, remembering other moments, moments with greater passion, moments we might yet reproduce. Neither of us mentioned our love for each other. We had no need to.

'So! What are you sitting here bothering about, Albiola?'

I did not answer immediately. I had watched him at the scene, so was sure he had been pondering the same puzzles that had struck me.

Eventually I addressed it. 'Something very peculiar seems to have happened. Primus was dead inside a storeroom – a building that somebody unknown had locked.'

Tiberius was with me, as I expected. 'Yes. I checked before I came to find you. The lock mechanism only worked from the outside, which is normal. The key is missing. Someone turned it and took it. There's no other possibility. It's a tumbler lock, a good one, though not impossible to break in an emergency – we proved that today. Anyone desperate to escape could probably have managed it. There was no sign on the inside of the store that the man had tried. At least it convinces me he was already dead.'

Tiberius having investigated came as no surprise. Talking quietly, we shared our doubts. Why was the previous owner of this villa abandoned there? Just suppose we were wrong, and he was alive: in the rush to escape, did nobody look for him? Of course there must have been chaos. A villa like this would have had a large staff, so did everyone suppose he had gone ahead, among a different group?

Agree that he was already dead. Was the store locked accidentally, or on purpose to keep the corpse safe? Tiberius said locks had been affixed everywhere else, as if the owners had been obsessed with security. Apart from the main entrance door, everywhere had been left accessible. Uncle Tullius had been supplied with only one key, to the entrance. That was a normal contract formality. Lacking other keys would be inconvenient; we would have to call in a locksmith.

We were out in open country. The house had possessed a watchdog. I thought the number of locks could have meant Primus did not trust his own slaves. Tiberius and I did consider briefly whether somebody had locked in Primus while he was still alive. That would have made his death not an accident of the eruption but deliberate murder. So why, when and by whom would Curvidius Primus have been imprisoned in a locked room?

He couldn't have been. It failed to fit the way in which he had been lying at rest on the cart.

He wasn't young. We knew he had passed his sixty-fifth birthday; his brother had sent him a gift then. It was perfectly acceptable that he had died of natural causes. Had he been ill, known it, and cleared out his home? If his death happened after his house clearance – perhaps even because of the stress that caused him – there might have been nothing suitable on which to lay him in state in his atrium as was normal for respected persons. I conceded that. But did any staff just stuff his body into a store, without planning proper rites of burial? Then why, after the eruption, was Primus still there years later, dead under his blanket of ash, and never removed for a decent funeral?

The biggest conundrum was why his family had been told he had 'gone missing', even though people must have known what had happened and where the body was. Who was in charge? And why did they intend the world to think the man had died during the eruption? What real fate did somebody want to cover up?

21

When, as promised, I went down into Stabiae next day, I spoke to Septumius first. He had his nephew and Criton moving items for him inside his big storage barn. He had to leave them to it, due to his hernia. Before I let him call them, I quizzed him. 'Tell me, when the eruption occurred, I understand this town was destroyed. Where were you and your family?'

'We felt the tremors, we saw fires on the mountain. My father was a cautious man, and able to make fast decisions. He didn't wait to wonder what was happening. We all took off. Whatever was going to happen, he wanted us out of the way.'

I kept up the pressure: 'How did you escape? In what direction?'

'Down to Nuceria. It was the quickest route out of here and, if we had to, we could keep going south. The road was chock-a-block later, but we pushed through early. We must have been ahead of the crush from Pompeii and other places. We soon had pumice raining down on us but at first you could just about see where you were going.'

'Who was escaping? Your father, your brother and nephew – and you?'

'That would be right.'

'Criton?' I could see he had realised the trick in my question. I watched him wondering how to worm his way out.

'Septumius, everyone who lived up on the heights seems to have made a dash for safety towards Surrentum – down the peninsula the other way.'

He pressed his lips together, then took the intelligent decision. 'All right. If you are asking how come, when Criton ran away from the villa, he ended up with us—'

'Yes, I am. You implied before that he ran away when the eruption began.'

'I may not have said exactly that.'

'No – because from the villa he would have been running straight into the falling lapilli and ash. For him to flee *towards* the disaster would not make sense.'

'Does it matter? What's your point?' asked Septumius stubbornly.

'When I talk to him, I have to be sure he is telling me the truth.'

'Don't torture him!'

He knew torture was the routine way to question slaves. But I shook my head. 'I never believe in that. Suspects just croak out whatever they think you want to hear. I prefer to rely on good preparation and that's why I am asking you first. So! When the volcano blew, I reckon this lad was already living with your family. Am I right?'

Septumius caved in. He confessed: Criton really escaped from the villa in the period before the eruption; Vesuvius was coincidental. By the time the mountain exploded, the family in Stabiae were already giving the lad sanctuary, so they took him with them to Nuceria.

'Now you are making sense! In that case, what had caused him to run away?'

'Badly treated,' replied Septumius baldly. I remembered those chained slaves. It seemed entirely believable.

Septumius said his father used to go up regularly to see if the villa people were throwing out any items he could take and sell. He had already encountered the boy, Criton. He was no pretty child, offering slices of melon on glass dishes to leisured owners, but had to carry water and heavy loads like logs, as if he were an adult. 'An overseer would often tell him to help my father load his ox-cart. The Curvidii were always changing their possessions. Furniture and equipment they threw out made good pickings for the second-hand market.'

I smiled, playing the matron. 'I believe some women cannot go into a dining room without deciding they must have all new couch cushions.'

'That's what it was like. My pa loved going up there. The old man didn't just collect old junk. He wanted what would be saleable.'

'Eventually they conducted a full house clearance? We can tell the villa was empty when the volcano erupted.'

'So my father said. He thought they were planning on moving.'

'Why, Septumius?'

'No idea.'

'Was this when they discarded their bathtub? The one I just bought?'

'Correct.'

'Well, what about Criton?'

'While my father was fetching the bath and some other furniture, he saw Criton skulking around as if he was terrified. He looked tear-stained and dirty too. There was no need for that. The old man was quite a character and he hated cruelty, so he tipped the wink. Criton crawled onto his cart behind the bathtub, and that was how he came down here to live in peace with us.'

'Taking him away was a brave thing for your papa to do. The Curvidii could have charged him with theft of their slave.'

'My father was fearless. If they took him to court over it, he would have come right out and told the judge why he was sympathetic towards Criton.'

'And how was that?'

'Once before, when Father was up there, Criton had been ordered to go onto a roof where some tiles had slipped. He must have been only around ten at that time, so he weighed light. But he was scared and had no idea what he was doing. He fell off the roof. His collarbone was dislocated. Nobody did anything to help; he was screaming in agony but every-one else just walked off. It was my father who went to him, pulled hard on his little arm and luckily put the bone back into its socket. I suppose that was why, afterwards, Criton trusted him.'

'Was the place with slipped tiles the shed where we found Primus?'

'Could be.'

I reminded Septumius I wanted to interview Criton because of how we had found his old master's remains at the villa. I hoped Criton could tell me what had happened. Septumius denied that Criton knew anything; I accepted he might not, if he had run away before Primus died. All Septumius could tell me was the dubious story that after the eruption it had been known Primus had disappeared. Naturally, everyone supposed it was due to Vesuvius. Plenty had been lost in that way. No previous occupants ever came back to live at the villa, so talk about them dwindled. Locals lost interest.

I said that, from all I was hearing, the Curvidii were unpleasant neighbours. Septumius replied with force that his father could have told me some ripe stories. I would have liked to hear them, but the son was either too discreet or truly could no longer remember. However, I felt readied to interview Criton. He was called outside. I sat on a piece of old stone, he squatted on his heels. Septumius and his nephew hovered protectively within earshot. If I upset Criton, they were ready to intervene.

I looked at the young man more keenly. He wore the same kind of itchy homespun tunic as his friend Crispus. He had a longer body than most locals, with a matching long face. He must be in his middle twenties now, but gangly and immature. As Septumius had said, he would have been an ordinary child, not the pretty cup-bearer type. Never one to be cherished by a master because of sweet looks. Since then he had become an ordinary young man, giving an impression that, left to himself, he might slouch about and perhaps even get into trouble. Septumius gave him plenty to do and seemed able to supervise him, which I guessed his father had done before.

This group were all thin, though I had the impression they were not starving, just poor folk who did hard physical work at the rough end of society. Crispus and Criton went everywhere together, like a boy and his dog, though I saw no distinction between which was the owner and which the pet.

'Criton,' I reminded him, 'my name is Flavia Albia. I have come down to Stabiae to talk to you.' He made no reply.

I did my best. Mostly Criton gave up nothing, but only muttered, 'Can't remember.' Even though I knew about his shoulder injury, he would discuss no details, nor talk about bad treatment by his owner, nor even tell me what had made him so frightened he had eventually chosen to escape, with all its dangers.

'Did anyone come down here from the villa trying to find you?'

Septumius called that, if so, his father had seen them off. I supposed that if Primus died around that time, people at the villa had had other things to think about.

'Criton, there was a slave called Endymio, who wore a collar that called him a runaway. We know, because we found his remains, chained with some others in a cell. If that was how people were treated, living there as a lad must have been very worrying for you. Did you know Endymio?'

'Sometimes I had to help him with his work.'

'Do you know why he and the others were chained?'

'No.' Criton was hanging his head. I could see him starting to feel awkward. Something bothered him, but too much pressure was about to make him clam up.

'All right. Then let's discuss things more generally. When you lived at his villa, the master was Curvidius Primus. I have the impression he was difficult to deal with. Even his own brother never got along with him. Did you ever hear about that, Criton? I met him. He is called Curvidius Fulvianus.'

'I don't know anything about him.'

'Well, he left and went away to Rome – it must have been before you were born. Were you born at the villa? What they call *verna*?'

'I don't know.'

'*Verna* means a slave born into the household, not bought from a dealer outside. Anyone born in might be favoured, or treated with special affection. Almost a member of the family . . .' I thought sadly of Criton being left without medical attention when he fell off the roof, and changed the subject: 'Curvidius Primus was once married, but had no

123

children, I believe? Or none with his wife.' I might have been hinting that Primus fathered Criton, though he gave no sign of recognising that possibility.

'Did you see a lot of him?'

'Can't remember.'

'Oh, come!'

'Not really.'

'That's a shame! I would have liked to hear more about him. After his wife died, is it right that Primus lived by himself?'

'People were there sometimes.'

'Oh? Relatives?' Fulvianus had told us of a distant circle, relations he still kept in touch with.

'I think he had relatives. I don't know.'

I kept testing his own position in the household. 'So would you say, Criton, that the treatment you received was the same as Primus gave to everyone?' A brief nod. 'No favourites?' For once, he showed animation, letting out a slight, derisive laugh as if Primus had never liked anyone and was famous for it. 'Special *victims*, then? I am still wondering,' I threw in abruptly. 'Why were Porphyrus, Endymio and Myrtale chained up?'

I had touched a nerve. I felt Criton knew the answer, but he would not say. It had been evident that he was a damaged soul. I recognised from my own experience the wounds of childhood pain.

For an informer this is the most maddening aspect of interviewing witnesses. You have to learn when to stop. If you apply harder pressure, you will only build greater resistance. They close up completely. You can see you won't break their silence. Better back off.

'All right,' I said gently. 'I will not force you to say.' There was no way I could use force, in fact. Yet I achieved

something. 'Look, Criton: Primus, your old master, supposedly went missing, but that was certainly his body we found
in the store. Someone knows how it got there. I want to find
out what happened when he passed away.'

'I don't know!'

'We do think there must be people who knew he was there.
Did you know?'

'No.'

'Really? I thought you might. I'm saying that because you
were so upset yesterday when we began breaking in. You ran
off when I asked you about the key, and when Crispus
brought you back after we found the skeleton, you didn't
want to be anywhere near it.'

Criton suddenly stood up. In the background I glimpsed
Crispus and Septumius tensing.

'Primus!' Criton shouted. 'I can tell you about Primus.
Primus was a horrid brute! If Primus is dead, I am glad of it.
Everyone who ever knew him must be glad that he is gone!'

The young man had become so disturbed, his friend
Crispus had rushed to him. Septumius watched them
together, but just muttered, 'Give it a rest, Flavia Albia!'

Not even promising another attempt later, I made a two-
handed gesture of pacification and left.

22

I had come down from the villa on Mercury. I rode her from the street of second-hand stuff to our lodging at the pirate's house, where I organised more of our food items and small possessions, ready to stow in her two panniers.

I felt shaken by Criton's violent outburst. With no other appointments, I walked out into the internal garden to breathe and readjust. I thought of those bones lying quietly on the cart, as peacefully as if the man was asleep under a pine tree on a summer's day. Now I had glimpsed for myself the antagonism Primus had aroused. I had often met people I took a dislike to, but the slave's intensity troubled me.

As I turned to leave, I noticed that the big, wrapped lumps I had identified as statues had all gone. The pirate was entitled to remove his own property, and since we were obviously going our ways as tenants, there was no requirement for him to warn us. But I was startled to see *Augustus Looking Imperial* had been carried off too; only the broom we had given him was there, leaning on a pillar.

At the moment no statuary remained, a complete dearth. That was unusual in a well-dressed Roman house. It gave me a sense of how Dexiades must use the place: less his personal living space, more a walk-in showroom for items he was trading. Was the harbour town of Stabiae now one mighty hub of entrepreneurship? I wondered, with my parents' cynical training, how much of that was legitimate? I imagined any customs officers who patrolled these ports on the bay would have their work cut out.

Silly girl, Albia! Of course officials' lives were relaxed. They would be kept sweet by traders in the oldest way. Each officer probably had a scroll nailed to a doorpost in his office, listing the regular tariff for bribes.

Outside, a group of local lads was looking at my donkey as if wondering whether to steal her. As I filled the panniers, I gave them a warning stare; they whistled at me cheekily.

I took Merky on a detour to the harbour. Ever the madcap, I ventured to the Two Scallops. There, as I had hoped, I found Hyro and Milo. They were checking for their tribune; Caunus had still not reappeared. More free time for them. They were happy dogs.

They had persuaded the waiter to make them some kind of granular porridge. I had seen them before, packing their solid bodies with fuel. Today even these trenchermen must have over-ordered. When I declined to help out, they gave their unwanted portion to the donkey. Merky seemed quite taken; as she slopped around greedily, I could only hope the porridge was less lethal than the fish stew. A large beast with a churning stomach can be horrific.

The vigiles had palled up with another customer. He was a regular, a small, wiry man who wore the apron and tool belt of a carpenter. Hyro and Milo had, as they saw it, brought him out of himself; they had got him talking and had pretty well hired him for work we needed at the villa. I knew enough of site procedures to joke, 'Hold on! He might not be any good!' The lads, and he, looked surprised by this fatalism.

Taking control, I said affably that if the man wanted to come up to the villa, my husband and his clerk-of-works would certainly talk to him. I decided not to mention that we were second-homers from Rome, but, curses, my two vigiles had already done that. They had also revealed Tiberius Manlius had been a magistrate, which in street parlance meant he was made of money, dim and a complete pushover.

Backtracking, I warned it was a trek uphill. This failed to deter the carpenter. He knew where the villa was; he had worked there in the past. My heart dropped further. My father has a rule never to take on inherited tradesmen: they will only repeat the very mistakes that are why you now need remedial work in your creaky, leaky home . . . Tiberius would say the only thing more stupid is hiring someone in a bar, especially when you have only just met him.

I would have to ride this out. Clearly, there was no chance of obtaining alternative quotes. Milo and Hyro, born disrupters, had appointed themselves our agents in any area of life. There was probably a very funny play called *The Building Contract* but, if so, the kings of drama cannot have seen it.

Slumping into a daydream about this hypothetical comedy, I imagined a 'clever slave' tells an audience long-winded jokes about carpentry until the scenery collapses (to reveal a couple of lovers *in flagrante*). Reaching out an arm to take charge of the general snack saucer, I picked at an olive. In our desert here, they must be imported; the squashed bits had been in the amphora too long. I suspected a damaged stopper.

It takes devoted husbandry to produce black olives with no trace of oil. Chewing dismally, I managed to interrogate the carpenter while he finished his drink. His name was Axilius.

I did a better job on Axilius than I had on Criton. Details concerning the villa's former occupants were few, but the man spoke lovingly of expensive citron-wood doorframes, which told me the house's owner had had expensive taste. Axilius complained that bills were rarely paid on time. 'Some old boy used to complain for years about that lot. He mended a wheel for them, took it up there, never got his money.' This showed Primus was mean and thoughtless, though it only made him the usual kind of swine. Social selfishness was familiar to me, since I often worked for the same kind of people. Some demand service but think it clever to acquire your work for nothing, people who have never known an empty table or the anxiety that comes with it.

As I sympathised, I tried to elicit more about Primus, but it seemed he rarely made an appearance. Criton had said he was aloof with slaves; apparently, the same applied to employed craftsmen. Work was carried out for him, and word would come if he was displeased by the results, but Axilius had hardly met him. What did he know about the man's character? Was it true that he drank? Was he a hypochondriac? Was he violent? Axilius could not say.

'I heard he was married at one time. Did you ever meet the wife?'

'She had died. I believe she was very submissive,' Axilius said. So someone else had chucked out furniture, not her. Primus himself? I didn't feel that fitted.

I asked whether Axilius knew that Primus was supposed to have disappeared ten years ago, and whether it surprised him that we had just found his body. He shrugged again, more deeply. I said it was assumed Primus had been a victim of Vesuvius, although I found it odd that when the house was cleared, no one had taken away the corpse for burial. Was that a sign of how much he had been disliked?

That was when Axilius asked in return, 'Well, what does the sister have to say about it?'

23

The sister?

What sister was this? How could people talking about occupants never have mentioned that a sister existed? According to Axilius, not only had she grown up at the villa but as an adult she had returned to live there. 'What does the sister say?' had a ring, as if all the world knew about her. I might even deduce she was a force to be reckoned with.

I reprised my ever-more-relevant joke, about women who regularly change their household goods: 'At least this explains who might have demanded new fixings all the time. Perhaps it was this sister who laid down the law that they no longer needed their bronze bath!'

'Oh, that bath!' exclaimed Axilius. It sounded as if it was a noble object, famed in legend. He told me it had been used by Curvidius Primus; it caused a commotion every time, because of problems filling it. Primus never felt he needed to pre-warn his staff, so hot water might not be available. If he suddenly demanded a soak, he would be roaring for the bucket slaves. 'Some were mere lads, and he had no compunction about beating them. Half the time, they ended up in tears.' Criton? I wondered. 'Then Primus would bellow for attention whenever he wanted to climb in, or climb out – he needed people to steady him because he was so overweight and doddery – or he'd scream if he took against the bath oil

131

they had put out, or his water had gone cold while he drowsed.'

So, he and his sister were both picky.

'She was a widow,' Axilius said, as if that explained it.

'I have been a widow. That never made me difficult.'

Milo and Hyro had been listening quietly. They both sniggered. 'What did he die of, Albia?' Milo asked me pointedly. 'Your husband who croaked?'

'An accident. The poor mite was watching a public-statue installation. A huge horse's leg fell off and crushed him.'

'Well, that's a tragedy!' commented Hyro. 'You don't have much luck with men.'

'Or it's her men who have no luck!' Milo chipped in. 'Someone should warn Manlius Faustus.'

'He knows,' I said.

'Oh, yes!' Still chortling, Milo regaled Axilius with how my current husband had been struck by lightning.

I would like to believe these revelations caused new respect for me, as a woman who had been brave in tragedy. On the other hand, I am a realist.

I returned my thoughts to my puzzle. If a sister lived at the villa, she might have had direct knowledge of whatever happened to Primus. Hell, she must have done. Hadn't she and Fulvianus conferred about their elder brother's loss at least by letter? Surely it must have been his sister who told him their brother had disappeared? If 'disappeared' was her word, didn't she know his remains were lying on a cart in a storehouse?

'Was she there during the house clearance?'

'She must have been. She lived there.'

'Does that mean it was the sister who ordered the house to be emptied?'

132

'Not for me to say,' said Axilius.

Would she want to attend any funeral if one was held now, I wondered. But why ever did she never organise burial rites ten years ago? This woman had a lot to answer for.

All the family seemed peculiar. Consider the reticence of Curvidius Fulvianus. All he had implied when we dined with Uncle Tullius was that he possessed distant relatives, who sounded as if they lived in other towns, with whom he barely communicated. He spoke as if they included no one closer than those the inheritance laws call cognates and agnates.

My father would say, 'Avoid agnates!'

'Hey-ho,' my mother would mutter. 'Can agnates be worse than siblings?' By which she generally meant Father's sisters, although her own brothers could both be a handful.

My brother was twelve. Adopted at birth, he was a child who called for a lot of explaining. It's true I might not mention him to strangers. But my sisters were unforgettable. They were vivid, talented, lovable spirits whom nobody could hold down. I felt sure that if ever I disappeared, a sudden absence might not immediately strike Julia and Favonia – because all their concentration was locked onto fashion – yet once they spotted that I'd gone, both would create a lively fuss. I belonged in their lives. They would never let me vanish without explanation.

Not so the Curvidius sister. My companions listened thoughtfully as I expressed my feelings. I was annoyed about this woman. She had lived in the villa. What kind of washed-out character could she be to ignore such a curious disposal of her brother Primus? Or had it been her idea? Abandoned among his empty amphorae: was that some kind of apt punishment for antisocial drinking habits? Was she so exasperated by his behaviour, she gave up on him and dumped him in a store with his empties?

'She must be an old lady nowadays. What is her name, Axilius?' The carpenter supposed a name might have been mentioned – but he had never dealt with her in person and now could not remember. Nor could he help me on whether the anonymous one was still alive or where she lived these days. I ground my teeth. If she had been an exotic timber, he would have known.

So where had she gone? When Curvidius Fulvianus assumed the role of heir to his brother's estate, what did he feel about their sister having emptied the villa? Did he refuse to allow her use of the old family home? Such behaviour happened. Women were often provided for fairly, but sometimes they were pushed aside. If so, there was very little they could do. Roman law was written by men who needed women to provide male heirs, but not a lot else.

Was the sister evicted, or had she thought that would happen if Fulvianus heard their brother had passed away? Indeed, was that why she had had the place emptied of everything movable? Had she sold the goods and pinched the money? That, too, would not have been unknown. But Fulvianus had not muttered to us about it.

I needed to find her. Hyro and Milo offered to make enquiries while they were waiting around for their tribune. I replied that, so long as no locals complained about them, they could use their free time as they liked. However, asking questions for me could not be official because no one had commissioned me. We were in a strange district; we had to respect local sensibilities.

'She is the sister of a man who lives in Rome,' asserted Hyro. 'Blast the locals. This is Campania so they are all bound to be crooks. Our tribune hates how problems are always covered up out in the country. On the way down from Rome, he was ranting about it. If he knew about this, he would order us to find her and report to her Rome brother.'

I stopped him. 'If we track the sister down, leave me to do any reporting, please.'

I saw no point in staying at a bar where I distrusted the food and drink. I pulled the porridge bowl away from Mercury, hopped onto her, kicked until she deigned to move, and waved goodbye.

24

By the time I reached our villa I was calmer, though still frustrated. It soon evaporated. Tiberius had better news. He already knew about the invisible sister.

'Damn! I wanted to surprise you.'

'Oh, you do that often enough!' he commented obscurely.

He said our neighbours, Heius and Favonilla, had come over to return our visit politely. They had brought fresh flatbreads, baked by her. Fortunately, the recent arrival of Fornix meant Tiberius could be hospitable even when his feckless wife had gone gadding. Suitable dainties had been offered; Tiberius had also parted with the gift of a smoked cheese. When Fornix brought a handsome snacks tray, grumbling about our kitchen facilities, Heius had promised to send a cartload of logs so the oven could be fired up. Fornix rewarded him with another platter of treats.

The doughty pair was suspicious of gourmet Roman food, but while they nibbled cautiously, they provided extra gossip. Heius had not much to say on the subject, but having met her, I was not surprised to hear Favonilla was a woman who brooded in a manner I approved of. She had told Tiberius she had been thinking we might not know that Primus had given houseroom to his sister, after she found living alone too hard. When she was widowed, she came home. Even though her brother was difficult to deal with, from all appearances they had rubbed along.

'Perhaps he was never difficult with her,' Tiberius suggested to me, ever fair.

I snorted. 'Or stroppiness runs in the family. Perhaps she was even worse than him!'

Her name was Fulvia Secunda, born a year after Primus. As an adult she had been married to man called Gabius, who owned a substantial vineyard close to Surrentum. They had no children, or none living. Nor did the Curvidius parents remain alive, so with Gabius gone, Secunda was stuck. Rome does not allow women to float around unattached in case they enjoy themselves too freely. Once Fulvia Secunda lost her husband, her elder brother had to assume a role as her head of household; Primus acquired a duty to protect and supervise her, while she might have felt she could not refuse to be absorbed into his establishment. Our villa was where Secunda had grown up, so she would have been no stranger. No longer running her own home, perhaps she was expected to run his for him; Favonilla said he, too, lost his spouse around the same time.

Some sisters would not mind being hauled in to help out; some might even welcome it. Not all! I thought. (Not me, I meant.) I had a brief horrible vision – suppose that one day I lost Tiberius and was forced to become a surrogate home-maker for my brother, Postumus. It would drive both of us mad. Even at twelve he was unhealthily fascinated by the idea that he might own parochial powers. His glee as he plotted future tyranny was unnerving. 'I would be your head of household, Albia!'

'Drop it, sprog!'

That, legally, is the Roman rule, however. Of course, plenty of Roman women reckon that men's rules exist to be chucked overboard. There may even be men who cannot stand the idea of cohabiting with their sisters.

The Curvidii did rebond. Our neighbour, Favonilla, was basically a nice woman, an older woman with traditional attitudes; she assured Tiberius the new arrangements had worked well. She thought this natural. I had my doubts. My position was that if Curvidius Fulvianus had never got on with his awkward brother, why would anyone expect that their sister could tolerate Primus any better? Nor was it likely that either brother would be fond of their sister. That might explain why Fulvianus had left her out of our discussion in Rome.

At least we now knew where the villa's people had escaped to when the eruption began. Heius and Favonilla said Fulvia Secunda and her brother's household had made their way to safety at her late husband's vineyard. She still owned it, and the estate included a fine sea-view mansion.

Secunda had lived out the immediate Vesuvian crisis there. Her home, further west than her brother's villa, was barely affected by eruption damage. The Surrentum district had rich, sun-baked soil that produced wonderful wines. The vineyard had always been highly profitable, which gave her a future income. With Primus gone, she decided to stay there instead of returning to Stabiae.

'To a house that had been emptied,' I reminded Tiberius. 'As she must have known – especially if it was Secunda who made the arrangements. Even without the eruption, it looks as if she was planning to move away from here.'

There was an interesting wrinkle: Tiberius had learned that in the past there had been occasional gossip about the vineyard. Perhaps Primus had been creaming off its profits after his sister's husband died. I jumped. 'Bad feeling?'

'Our neighbours were surprisingly frank. They felt Primus might have been a little too happy to suck his sister into his control and cream off her wealth.'

'Did she raise objections?'

'Not easy to do,' Tiberius demurred. 'It would have been explained away. Nobody would quibble if Primus said he was using the money for their joint benefit, while Secunda was living with him. Happens all the time.' I wondered whether my husband was thinking of how Uncle Tullius had swung all their family collateral into one set of bank chests – his own. But Tiberius went on, 'I did quiz, but they were sure: people in the district had no serious sense of wrong being done, even though some thought it a possibility.'

'They certainly wouldn't have bearded Primus about it! What was said when Secunda returned to her own home?'

'It seemed a natural move after her brother had disappeared and his villa looked derelict. Stabiae had been shaken by earthquakes and covered with tephra, whereas her own house and the vineyard had escaped.'

'Hmm! And from then on Secunda could fully enjoy what was hers! . . . Is she still alive?' I asked.

'Heius and Favonilla believe so.'

'Would you mind if I borrowed the donkey tomorrow and rode down the headland to look for her?'

'I am a reasonable husband.'

'You mean you can't stop me!'

'My darling, you never decline sensible advice. I am a blessed man.'

I teased him. 'You mean you want to come too?'

'No, I'd best stay on site.'

I was a little disappointed. 'This could be a nice tour of vineyards.'

Tiberius smiled sadly in return. 'If men sporting vine leaves in their hats offer you free wine samples, tell them you want to bring the pitcher home to share with your husband.'

'I could simply say, "No thanks, get lost, you creep."'

Tiberius winced. 'Keep in with them if you can. Tullius will need a local wine supplier.'

'Oh, I see. Do you think he would welcome me being sent out as bait?'

'Tullius thinks you can look after yourself,' returned his nephew, as if he thought the same. 'Don't come home drunk!'

Well, there was still plenty of work needed at the villa so I bore the fact that he ought to stay here. I remembered that Hyro and Milo had arranged for their carpenter to visit, though I omitted that news. If the man arrived, well and good.

However, Tiberius said, 'I may go down to the town. If I can find a local magistrate, I shall talk it out – I mean the peculiar way we discovered Primus and whether there might have been foul play.'

'They will say it happened ten years ago, love, and blame the volcano.'

'They will,' he agreed, smiling. He knew I was thinking that if an ex-aedile from Rome appeared with penetrating questions, anyone in authority there was bound to resent him. On the other hand, a magistrate from Rome would have had contact with the Emperor during his term of office. Locals would be mindful that Manlius Faustus might have political influence ... Any wise magistrate would give him the usual excuses – yet quietly check that nothing suspicious had been missed.

25

Tiberius wanted me to take Paris as an escort. Paris could be useful on site, so I opted for my young maid Suza. Instead of doubling up on the donkey, we were allowed a cart. Though not nippy, it was manoeuvrable while the flat-bed was empty. I drove. Suza was always torn between pretending she was haring a chariot around the spina in the Circus Maximus or feeling terrified that she would meet an ox-cart coming the other way.

She was a nervous passenger too. 'This is not going to be like when you took me to that woman's house in Rome, is it?' Suza had been dragged along as my chaperone during a previous case, which was still giving her nightmares for reasons we never talked about. She was a chubby, good-natured teen, whose normal dreams were of transparent Coan silks, gold platform shoes and wired-up imperial hair-styles. Tough luck for her to be stuck with me as a model. Today I was in a sombre brown tunic and a plain bun stuck with two bone pins. She had brought a stole with a heavy fringe for me, but I had wrapped it around my waist; she said I looked like a shrimp-seller.

'It's just an exploratory trip. I don't know what to expect, Suza, but I believe we are going to visit a sweet old duck, who should be harmless.'

'That sounds like one of your fibs, Flavia Albia.'

Suza decided Secunda would be a mad-eyed fury who lashed virgins with a seven-tongued whip. Though that seemed unlikely, I worried her by pretending the old duck was famous for wild actions with her walking-stick.

We went along the Via Minerva, a road that ran west behind the back of the clifftop villas. They all had narrow service tracks to it. Once or twice, there was a route leading off the other way, towards the uplands of the Lactarii Mountains where cattle, sheep and goats were pastured, famous for fine milk that supposedly cured invalids. Not long after we started, the road dropped down to run closer to the coast.

Working our way out along the promontory towards Surrentum, I understood why this area had always been so attractive to busy city types who could afford extra homes. On one side were steep hills, on the other the sea. It all reeked of nature. The area's deep tranquillity was as different as possible from the bustle and clamour of Rome, so cosmo-politans could convince themselves they were at one with the environment. It did make me wonder why our vendor, Fulvianus, rejected this soul-soothing peacefulness, let alone why he had abandoned his place of birth for good.

Although it was March, that day the sun was shining. Locals stayed bundled up with superstitious caution, while anyone from Britain brightened and threw off their cloak. I was struck by the silence. We hardly ever saw anyone. All I could hear was birdsong: a constant background of cheeps and whistles from shyly hidden chickadees in the brush-wood, sometimes broken by a blackbird's territorial warble or a crow's caw. Sounds carried a long way. From what seemed to be the far distance would come a cockerel or a dog barking, yet there was no visible human presence.

'Where are the people, Albia?'

'We may not be seeing anyone,' I warned Suza, 'but someone will be making a note of us at every farm we pass.'

'Ooh, I don't like that!'

There were plenty of those farms, occupying small fertile plains between the mountain ridges that rolled seawards. If we really were observed, it could have been by many eyes.

'At least if a big ox-cart shoves us off the road, people will know.'

Suza did not like that either. 'Scary! How long are we going to have to stay in the country?'

'Tiberius Manlius will say as long as his project takes.'

'It's all right for him. He *likes* the country.'

'He was born on an estate. To him, this is normal.'

'Where were you born, Albia?'

'You know. I was born in Britannia.'

To Suza, that was scariest of all. Sometimes, when I woke from too deep a sleep and could not remember where I was, the thought it might be Londinium made even me feel anxious.

When our way to Surrentum hugged the shore, we had to make short detours around rugged inlets. The Via Minerva was a difficult road, winding and not wide, a local route and nothing like a military highway. I imagined it must have been problematic, in near darkness, when clogged with hysterical people fleeing from Mount Vesuvius. The steep heights must have offered some protection. Soon after we started out, signs of volcanic deposits lessened and then ended, so in this part market gardens and orchards flourished as they must once have done everywhere; we had left behind the barren, clogged landscape around the inner curve of the great bay.

We had come at the magical moment of springtime when everything returned to life. Once we began to pass orchards, many vines were still bare but those that were sufficiently sheltered already showed their first bright green summer shoots. Soon the long perennial stems would be weighing down the rows of strings where they were firmly tied in. Among them, fruit and nut trees stood, gorgeous with blossom. Herbs looked bushy and we even saw pots overflowing with tiny strawberries. Vegetables like runner beans, peas and fennel were far ahead of those in other places; sometimes we saw a morning stall where locals were selling cooked baby artichokes to customers who came along, obviously aware this treat would be at the roadside. The sellers nodded at us, yet never engaged us in conversation and took our passing for granted. Strangers came and went here; it was neighbours they relied on for regular sales and society.

Once I felt we had driven far enough, I began to ask anyone we passed about Secunda's estate. We were told to look out for a signboard for the Gabius vineyard. After passing neat orchards and vegetables in tidy enclosures, we started to ride through vines on either side of the road. Eventually, we found the family name faintly inscribed beside a worn stone herm, where a track left the road between wonky old gateposts. We had to make our way up a longer driveway than any we had passed before. There was topiary. It was established, green and neatly clipped.

'I told you,' Suza muttered. 'Your old duck is rich. You ought to have worn a gold necklace and the Etruscan earrings, Albia. How are you going to screw secrets out of anyone here if they think you're a travelling lupin-seller?'

I specialised in collecting outspoken staff.

'Suza, my father has made a lifetime career out of knocking on doors, pretending he can fix water fountains or offering to buy cranky old Greek vases.'

'Your father,' said Suza, with the frankness of the young, 'only has to use that grin of his, then apply his trust-me-I-am-honest-Falco voice. You sound too cultured to be sent around to the housekeeper, but too foreign to be let in through the main door.'

I sniffed. I do *not* sound foreign. My Latin is clear-cut though not aggressive; even my Greek will buy me an onion at a fair price at any agora. Well, maybe not Athens. 'Suza, I don't know how I managed before I had you to give me careers advice!'

'Hide your shoes!' Suza retorted.

'Nothing wrong with these.' I moved my feet nervously as we emerged through the last ornamental trees and could see the entrance porch. Its columns were about two feet higher than they needed to be. 'They will see I have the best-groomed maid ever, so they will scurry for a silver salver for me to leave my introduction scroll. You'll see.'

That failed to happen. As I had no letter of introduction, it was just as well.

No one was about. It happens in the country, where people have work to do – or, in the case of the pig-boy, a sty to snooze in. Without benefit of an ostler, we hitched our cart to a garden obelisk and put a nosebag on the mule ourselves.

'I am dying for a flatbread!'

'I am dying for a pee . . .'

At last, a pudding-faced female slave answered our hammering on their door. Whether or not she noticed that I wore hefty walking shoes, with studs, while Suza had spent two hours plaiting her hair like a princess seemed to make no difference. I had been to homes where they sent me away because I had no appointment; at other places porters were trained to be obnoxious on principle, or they took it upon themselves to say, 'Get lost,' because they reckoned women do not tip. This body seemed pleasant enough. She simply straightened the folds of her homespun gown and told us that Fulvia Secunda never saw people these days. She was a very old lady, not up to visitors.

I felt depressed. We had probably not travelled as far that morning as it felt, but I hated to turn around straight away with no results.

Suza screwed up her face. She deplored incompetence, mine in this case. 'I say!'

The woman who came to the door backed down a little and applied her respectful tone. 'Yes?'

I stood and observed while the two minions drew apart from me to conduct their own negotiations.

Enunciating painfully, as if I had forced her to take elocution lessons, Suza spelled out, 'I do think you should tell your mistress that my lady is a significant person in Rome, which is where we live normally, by the way. Flavia Albia's husband is called Manlius Faustus. He has been a city magistrate, and he has sent her today on his behalf, even though out of her perfect good manners she has not mentioned his high position. The business that brings us concerns Fulvia Secunda's brother, the one in Rome, who wants some particular questions answered, and Flavia Albia does have to tell your mistress about a curious situation we have discovered at the villa, which is the villa where your people used to live.'

'Is it important?' the slave murmured back to Suza.

'I would say it is,' Suza half whispered.

'What do you think I should do?'

'Let her in would be best.'

'I don't know . . .'

Suza firmly took a hand: 'Is there anybody else she can see, who can speak for the old lady if she's past it?'

'She is not completely gone!'

'Well, good-oh. Can she answer for herself?'

'No. She can be asked as much as you like, but she lives in her own world and will never reply.'

'Then who does the talking around here?' Suza demanded. She had a no-nonsense grasp of domestic life. 'Somebody has to.'

She was right. It turned out that if we were dead-set on meaningful conversation, Gellius and Lavinia were the people to see. And, yes, I could be led to them.

Suza triumphantly gestured that *she* had obtained this favour, while she made a swishing movement with one hand, instructing me to use the hem of my gown to hide my unsuitable shoes. First, though, she performed a mime of leg-crossing. 'We had quite a long journey. Is it possible,' she mouthed to her new crony, 'we might avail ourselves of your facilities, before we are taken in and introduced to the people of the house?'

I dreamed of the days when I used to work alone. I had loved my independence. But there were advantages in a chaperone whose boldness of character and blatant cheek could always be relied upon.

26

Gellius and Lavinia were persons of leisure. From their ages, and the way they were relaxing on that sunlit morning, I might have assumed they were Secunda's adult children, but our neighbours had said she had none. Otherwise, they would have seemed like feckless offspring who refused to leave home for year after year, even when marriages and careers were suggested by parents.

Whatever their official role, both were very well dressed and groomed as they lazed in the sun beside a long, cana-lised water feature in a terraced garden. Portable long chairs had been set out for them. They must have been relaxed here for a while. On a side-table they had finished drinks on a tray, scatters of nuts in near-emptied bowls, and half-unrolled scrolls to read. Swallows were so at ease with their presence, the birds swooped and dipped over the canal in the search for insects. Sometimes a long-tailed hunter crashed right under the water surface before soaring away gracefully with whatever it had scooped up.

I put them in their early thirties. Not much older than me. We would see whether we had anything else in common.

They reclined quietly beside the water feature: people who often spent time together, people who knew each other well. They had dark hair and eyes, with squarish faces, as if they derived from the same tribe. He was clean-shaven; she had improved fine-line eyebrows. Neither was speaking. He appeared to be absorbed in whatever he was reading, while she had a scroll in her lap but was lying with her eyes closed, enjoying the warm weather. They gave the impression that nothing had been said between them for a long period. They personified the Roman ideal of *otium*, leisure for the non-working wealthy.

He was a half-bald mid-lifer, in a long beige tunic, who would have looked like an off-duty clerk if his tunic had been less well laundered. Maybe a senator who had never yet spoken in the Curia. Or a successful burglar, living off years of loot. If he had ever been married, I could imagine him as an undiscovered bigamist, though from his state of complete passivity it seemed unlikely he would put any effort into subterfuge. He had walnut brown stripes from his tunic shoulders, leather wrist-protectors that hinted at athletic pretensions, but a slight paunch and thin legs.

She had her hair in an updo that an attendant must have created, though not overly fanciful; when she went to bed that evening, she would be able to dismantle the gem-topped pins and hot-rodded curls herself. She wore a blue stole over a yellow gown, and several bangles on one forearm. Her shoes were off and lay neatly against her long couch.

'There they are!' the house slave announced to Suza, before turning away and leaving. Her sandals, originally made for someone else, flapped flat-footedly as she made off at speed. Perhaps she was afraid of recriminations for allowing us entry, though I saw no sign of annoyance when the couple responded to our arrival. They twisted and swung sideways on their couches, almost together. If they had been a touch more synchronised, it might have been sinister.

Lavinia poked her feet back into her shoes. Suza would have judged them more proper than mine. Hers had strappy uppers and were so tight to reinstate I guessed they cut into her feet. Still, there was no sign she intended to walk anywhere.

'Oh, hello,' she said. He let her do the talking. She had a high, soft voice, with a good accent. 'We were not expecting visitors.'

'I hope this is not an intrusion.' I implied that even if it was, Suza and I were not intending to leave.

'It's simply that we don't see many people.'

'Your lucky day!' I now gave them my special, gentle smile: the one that says to watch out because the Fates might plan on playing them up. I supplied my name, not bothering to adorn it with impressive male connections. 'Flavia Albia. Relatives have bought a villa near Stabiae from Curvidius Fulvianus.' Perhaps they blinked; neither asked who my relatives with the property portfolio might be. I was starting to view them as intelligent, though not dangerously sharp. 'I was hoping to meet his sister.' Gellius and Lavinia exchanged glances; neither responded.

I carried on, deliberately normal: 'I gather Fulvia Secunda is a frail old thing these days. I wouldn't want to be a trouble, but she might like news from her brother in Rome. Are you able to accommodate this? Forgive me, I am not sure of your position here.'

Nuts to forgiveness: I meant to have the facts. With no way out, the fellow took over and introduced them; his voice was stronger than his sister's though his drowsy manner was the same. Their names were Publilius Gellius and Publilia Lavinia; he called them 'friends of the family'. He then said they were specifically friends of Curvidius Primus. They were children of his late wife's brother. One of our neighbours had called that wife 'a mimsy little thing'; the reliable

Favonilla had said this niece and nephew used to visit Primus even after his wife died. I had to presume they were friends of his sister too, since they now lived in her house.

'It sounds as if you can help me. I am so glad!'

Suza lost interest and wandered off on her own, but I marched around the canal's perimeter and stationed myself close to the couple in an upright wicker chair. It was a little shaky, as they tend to be if left out of doors, but it had cushions. For a moment I lifted my face to the sun, giving a short laugh and explaining that I had a bleak British background. After that basic softening up, I set to.

I kept the tone conversational. I never said I was an informer. I played the scene as if I only wanted to know more about the estate Uncle Tullius had bought. In this mild charade, I started out as an inquisitive neighbour making a social call.

Gellius and Lavinia reacted well enough, even though I blatantly wanted to pry. They painted a picture of past family life, when they had begun visiting the villa while their aunt still lived, then later went to live there because Primus needed support.

'Support?'

'He drank,' advised Lavinia openly. 'He liked his wine, liked it a bit too much. It was rather unfortunate.'

'It happens.' I accepted her comment. Then I tossed in matter-of-factly, 'Did the drink kill him?'

There was a very slight pause, almost as if an answer needed to be decided between them.

Lavinia left it to Gellius. 'It never helps, does it?' he dodged. 'Life at the villa grew rather chaotic. Fortunately, my sister and I were staying there when difficulties arose, doing all we could to hold things together.'

'As friends of the family?' It might have sounded sarcastic, but I kept it pleasant.

'Exactly that.'

'You were on good terms with Primus, you say, as well as your aunt?'

'Very good.'

'Oh, you liked him?' I mentioned frankly how several people had spoken of him as an awkward character.

'My brother and he were particular friends,' said Lavinia. 'They originally used to meet up at a spa Primus attended for his aches and pains. In Stabiae. There used to be both hot and cold mineral springs, running like rivers all over the place, near the old port. I believe someone once counted nearly thirty. One had been turned into a massive nymphaeum, built in the time of the Emperor Claudius, I think. It was where Curvidius Primus often went.' Perhaps she could tell I thought this heritage information amounted to stalling. She ended swiftly, 'And after our aunt passed away, we tried to look after his interests.'

'Didn't his sister live with him?'

'By the time she came to join the household, we were there, caring for him. She could not be much use anyway. Losing her husband had left her with a nervous disposition. Besides, her brother would never listen to anything she said.'

'If his sister owned a vineyard, as I believe Secunda does, reforming him must have been a hopeless task,' I suggested. 'There would never be any problem with supply?'

'No!' Gellius seemed surprised by the idea. 'You are right. There never was!'

'But you two were there, luckily for him, trying to hide the amphorae and persuading the slaves to secretly add more water to his goblets . . .'

'We were there,' Lavinia stated firmly, neither contesting nor agreeing with my details. 'You have to do what you can, don't you?' After I let a moment pass for everyone to sigh at this truism, she added, 'He was grateful.'

And again, Gellius murmured, 'Always grateful.'

I wondered. No drunk I ever met was happy to be kept short of his alcohol.

'I know that somebody there got through a great many amphorae.' I kept my tone cheerful. 'We have found the evidence – so many empties, lined up in the storehouse. Quite a collection!'

I watched carefully: would they make the store connection? The couple were expressionless. Nobody would have known from them that those amphorae not only bore witness to Primus having over-indulged but had stood sentinel for the past ten years around his body.

Nobody would have known it from me either, at that point. I withheld my revelation of his odd circumstances a little longer.

'Naturally,' I said, lowering my voice as if to show discretion, 'we have wondered why such a beautiful estate fell into disuse. While my husband's workmen are removing the tephra infill, we cannot help thinking about the terrible event that destroyed so much.' I lifted my face again, savouring the peaceful atmosphere. 'On a day like today when all is bright and magical, it's hard to imagine Vesuvius in spate: the shock of sudden darkness, fire, smoke, and aggressive noise, filling this whole area.'

'It was horrible,' Lavinia agreed.

'But you all managed to escape safely?'

'We were safe here.'

'Someone,' I suggested, 'must have gone back later for furniture and so forth?' Neither corrected me on 'later'. 'Part of the agreement Tullius Icilius made with his vendor was that the house would be standing empty; Curvidius Fulvianus declared it had already been cleared. Not that we ever thought he had been to do the work himself.'

'We brought what Secunda wanted,' Gellius agreed. 'She was entitled to family things, of course. Everything else was disposed of.'

'Even the bathtub!' I giggled. As before, I fancied that a look passed between them, though they said nothing. 'I happened to find that bath down in the town.' For some reason it felt too personal to mention that I myself had bought it. 'A man called Septumius had it for resale. Do you know him? He told me where it had come from.' No response from Lavinia or Gellius.

I drew myself up in the wicker chair as if coming to the crux of the visit.

I breathed. 'Look, this is rather difficult. The fact is I came to see Fulvia Secunda particularly. I have some tragic news to give her.'

Gellius leaned forward, one elbow on his knee. He assumed an earnest expression. It made him look unreliable, although the way he controlled this conversation, one I had initiated, verged on bullying. 'Let me help you, Flavia Albia. I can guess what this must be. Are you saying that you have found something to do with her brother?'

He appeared to think he was giving sympathetic guidance to a weak woman who had no clue how to break bad news. He could not know I did this all the time.

'Yes, we "found something",' I answered bluntly. 'We found him!'

27

When you announce a death, there are two possible outcomes. Either people are expecting bad news and jump in with their exclamations of grief almost before you finish speaking, or it is a complete shock, which they don't want to believe.

This was curious. Gellius himself had suggested they had guessed why I had come, yet when I produced the fact, there were no exclamations. He and his sister received my words as calmly as if I had announced that morning's bread delivery.

I was now certain they had known Primus had been lying dead at his villa. I told them outright that their lack of surprise was evident. 'I see you knew about the body.' To this they nodded, though maintaining their reserve. 'Tullius Icilius is having the property made good; finding any remains was inevitable. So, what happened? What can you tell me about when Primus died?'

'What has it to do with you?' Lavinia posed the question like a perplexed schoolgirl.

'My husband, acting for his uncle in the renovation, has a commission from Fulvianus.'

'We had no idea he meant to sell up.' If they had known, I wondered, would they have removed the corpse?

'Well, Fulvianus held title to the estate. He could have sold it at any time.' I was ready for them to raise issues about him

155

claiming possession as his brother's heir, but they made no attempt. 'He may have done nothing with the place for ten years, but clearly the time has come. He has disposed of the property. I am sorry if he never told his sister. Perhaps, in light of her frailty, he thought there was no point.'

'She will take no interest,' Gellius confirmed.

'Then at least it won't distress her.' I saw little reason to be sympathetic. It was not as if Fulvia Secunda would be plunged into poverty by the sale. 'Since my husband was coming to work on the place, Fulvianus charged Faustus with trying to identify anyone we might find. He appeared to think his brother was "missing", fate unknown. He wishes to hold a full funeral. Once we send word, I imagine he will come to officiate.'

'Oh, he has no need to come!' Gellius broke in quickly.

'From what he told us, he will want to,' I insisted, immediately suspicious.

'No, no . . . Better get it over quickly and discreetly.' Gellius writhed, clearly troubled by this situation. 'In any case, are you certain you have found *Primus*?'

I was having none of that. 'If you want the tragic details, what we found is his skeleton.'

'Bones? That could be anyone. How can you be sure?'

'We have details his brother supplied. We identified a signet ring – carnelian, picturing Fortuna Redux. Perhaps you saw it in the past?'

'Yes, that was what he used—' Lavinia began.

Her brother cut across her: 'May not be his. Or anyone could have put it there.'

I said firmly, 'Trust me. It was on his finger.' That was an exaggeration; I remembered how the ring had rolled away unexpectedly and Serenus caught it. But this wide-eyed pair were being awkward; I meant to stop them disputing sensible deductions. 'Also, the skull has several broken teeth. That damage, which looks old, matches what his brother told us to look for. Is there a problem?' I sternly demanded.

Gellius was backing down, but his sister intervened anyway. 'We just want to be sure there is no mistake – for Fulvia Secunda.'

'That is why I came today,' I smacked back. 'I want to tell her in person that her elder brother's body has been found. She should know that their other brother will be visiting Campania. But from what you have said, it troubles me that this old lady may find the news difficult?'

'We can tell her the situation,' Lavinia assured me. 'Of course we must. I don't think she will comprehend.'

'A funeral will provide a chance for her to see Fulvianus.'

'Neither of them will be interested in that,' said Gellius.

I raised my eyebrows. 'Why not?'

'They haven't met for years,' explained Lavinia. 'They never correspond. They will be strangers.'

'Did they quarrel?'

'Nothing like that. Secunda is an extremely sweet old lady.'

I suggested carefully, 'If Secunda is becoming very frail, wouldn't it be good for Fulvianus to see her, and for her to see him – while they still can?'

'Of course.' Gellius seemed to drop all his resistance. With a sigh, he stood up, saying he would go into the house to speak to Fulvia Secunda. It was made clear that he was going alone; he would not allow me to accompany him.

I was left in Lavinia's custody. For a short time, I remained silent, allowing her to absorb what had been discussed. Some young women cannot bear to remain silent, yet she seemed content with her thoughts. Eventually I looked around, admiring the garden. 'This is a lovely place. Do I gather you are free to be here? Nothing else claims you? Your brother doesn't work?'

'He was a government administrator. He supervised the spa at Stabiae that I mentioned. He gave it up when we went to care for Primus. Later, we were left some money of our own.'

I was itching to ask what the legacy was, but I had not come here to investigate this pair, however intrigued I felt. Those chosen to be 'friends of the family' are often a puzzle. Relationships develop over time until people forget how it happened, yet feel nothing can now be questioned.

'From our aunt.' Lavinia answered the question for me.

I nodded. 'That was nice . . . I meant to ask, have you any keys to the villa?' I made the change of subject a simple housekeeping request. 'Most of the doors seem to have locks, but we were only given the main entrance key. I suspect the rest must have been taken away in the house clearance.'

'I think there may be a bunch. We can look.'

'Thank you. It would be helpful.' I let her see my speculation. I had decided to tackle her, sneakily hoping she might be more compliant on her own than with her brother. 'There was one lock where the key had been turned. Just the one. Maybe you know something about that?'

Lavinia looked vague. Her eyes tracked in the direction Gellius had gone.

I continued: 'Honestly, I am concerned about where we found Primus. We came upon him in a storehouse – which seems very peculiar. You knew he was at the villa. Did you know where?'

Lavinia shook her head. She managed to seem curious about what I was saying, though not curious enough. More had to be said, so she made herself speculate: 'Maybe he was sheltering?'

I pretended to accept the idea. 'During the eruption? Could be. Or people might suppose that gases from the volcano gave him some kind of sudden seizure . . . I do not think so! Why would he have been locked in?' I finished quietly, laying on emphasis.

Lavinia was making no contribution, so after a pause I went on, 'When you and the rest left the villa, did nobody look around and miss Primus?'

'Gellius and I were looking after Fulvia Secunda. There were quite a lot of people from the house with us.'

'I understand. Everyone must have assumed Primus was travelling in a different group . . . Unless, of course, everyone knew he was already dead. Is there anyone I can speak to about this? A slave, perhaps?'

'No, they were all elderly,' Lavinia said smoothly. 'They have all passed away now.' Seeing my expression, she quickly thought to add, 'The volcano affected many people afterwards. They thought they were safe, but many died before their time.'

'Then what about retrieving the body, Lavinia?'

'What do you mean?'

'Did none of you think to return to take him from the store?' Apparently not.

'Should someone have gone to look for him? What do you think, Flavia Albia?'

My moment came. 'I think it's the same as the three slaves.' She assumed a puzzled look. I swung into my second reveal: 'Porphyrus, Endymio and Myrtale. Do they mean anything to you?'

Lavinia hardly paused. 'The names sound somewhat familiar, though I am afraid I cannot picture them.' She was shrugging. A tinselly whisper came from her fine necklaces. I suspected she was tenser than she looked. 'I was quite young.' At the time of the eruption, she must have been around twenty, not much older. Still, that made her an adult. 'It was a long time ago.'

'But you lived in that house. A "friend of the family" supposedly looking after the master's interests, supposedly holding some authority?'

'Only a kind of visitor.'

'You must have known the other occupants.'

'There were a lot of slaves.'

'A small child was with the people we found chained.'

'Oh, no! That's horrible.' She applied a suitably distressed look.

I could not imagine her dealing with children. Nor could I believe she really felt anything for that two-year-old.

'Yes, horrible.' I was still angry. My tone must have been hard as I revisited my outrage. 'But you and the rest of the household had already gone, hadn't you? The slaves were bolted to a wall. Left behind, deliberately left to starve and die there!'

She flinched. It looked genuine, or at least, personal criticism came as a surprise. Publilia Lavinia led a pampered life – I felt even her early years must have been free of restraint. No one had ever checked her.

'Let's put it in context with the eruption,' I said. 'When activity on the mountain became a dangerous threat, everyone in the district left if they could. Those three slaves had been abandoned, and afterwards no one bothered to discover their fate, let alone recover them.' Lavinia began wearing a chastened face, as if she had to accept my reprimand, even though she found it unfair. 'If the slaves were in disgrace, do you know why? No idea? And if Primus had died, why was he stuffed into a store and left there to rot?' Another head-shake. 'Well, young woman!' I made my tone even chillier. 'My husband and I have reached very bleak conclusions about events at that villa. Blaming the volcano seems to be a wilful cover-up.'

Lavinia had presumably never faced an interrogation before. Even so, she did not weep or protest. She led a relaxed, comfortable life. Plainly feeling entitled to it, she and her brother shared a kind of self-satisfied strength. If they were suspects, it made them difficult to interview. She complained, 'You seem rather annoyed, Flavia Albia. You are making horrible remarks, like accusations.'

'Regarding the slaves,' I answered coolly, 'I can make no accusation. I simply express my moral outrage. Whoever owned them and decided to leave them will be answerable to the gods of justice – if you believe in judgement after death.'

Lavinia ignored that. 'And Primus?' she was quick to demand.

I gave her a long look. 'I was present when his body was found.' As with Serenus capturing the signet ring, I remembered how we had clustered in the poorly lit store while Larcius made short stabbing movements with his brush. I imagined him cleaning off the debris that we found: debris lying *on* the corpse. Lavinia waited until I spelled it out: 'His bones were underneath volcanic material. A covering of ash.'

'What does that mean?'

I reprised for her what Tiberius and I had discussed; I deliberately made it vivid: 'There was a hole in the roof and material entered. Imagine it. Stretched on his back, Primus was not lying like a man who was asleep. He must have stayed prone in the same position all the time Vesuvius was throwing clouds of material over Stabiae. Before the final killing heat waves struck, there was a steady fall of ash. The storehouse was somewhat dilapidated. Volcanic material worked its way in, through the roof and loose planking, while he lay on the cart where we found him. Ash outlined his head and limbs, ash dropped onto his eyelids, ash filtered into his nostrils. If he had breathed, ash would have choked him. It means,' I explained, 'when somebody laid out his body on the cart, Curvidius Primus was already dead. It was before the eruption. The story his brother has been told, that Primus went missing when Vesuvius exploded, is a complete fabrication.'

28

If Lavinia gasped, I never heard it. She did put fingertips to her lips abruptly in a gesture of shock. However, her gaze went past me.

Our scenario was changing. Out from the house came the slave who had admitted us, accompanied by Gellius and my young Suza. She had perhaps gone to wander into the kitchen, to beg for refreshments. The party was approaching us, very, very slowly. Gellius was acting as escort, with a shawl or blanket folded over one arm. Between Suza and the slave, patiently supported by them, one foot at a time as if terrified of stumbling, they were bringing a thin, grey-haired old lady.

'That's timely!' I murmured to Lavinia, who looked upset. I was implying she was relieved at the interruption.

I jumped up from my seat so the wavering senior could be installed in what must have been her own wicker chair. Suza and the slave fussed around, settling her. She let it happen. After a quick signal, Lavinia and Gellius walked away to a colonnade. I saw her bend close and say something to her brother. Not looking my way, he replied briefly, then patted her shoulder. I was sure she must be telling him what I had said about the death of Primus. When they rejoined us, Gellius alleged he had decided it would be simpler if I saw for myself the condition of Fulvia Secunda.

I hope never to be as she was. Still, she seemed happy. She had a round, pale face that was reminiscent of a child who had been damaged at birth. Her eyes were watery and probably half blind. Her skin had thinned to wrinkled parchment, like a fowl being prepared for roasting. There was hardly any weight on her: knobbly, painful-looking bones showed at every joint and her hands rested in an inwardly curved position. She looked around as if unsure why she was here with us, then accepted the situation. Although she produced a series of vague smiles, she had no idea who anybody was, not even those who lived with her.

I went close, kneeling down, so I could greet her gently. She smiled, this time at me, as if I were a granddaughter she ought to recognise. My words found no real reception.

'She will never speak,' the slave said brusquely. Secunda looked up at her, hearing her voice, but gave no sign of understanding. The woman brought out a handkerchief, no doubt carried for the purpose as it looked fresh and clean; she wiped the old lady's teary eyes with a practised gesture.

I regained my feet. 'You told her?' I asked Gellius.

'I did. I shall repeat your news from time to time, but as you see, it will be useless.'

I could only sigh.

Even if Fulvia Secunda knew, there was no way she would ever enlighten me as to what had happened to her brother. Come to that, even if one day I learned what had befallen Primus, there was no possibility I could inform her.

29

Of course I had intended to shake the Publilii into telling me what they must know, but this experience only caused me discomfiture. My pity and concern must have been visible. They remained impossible to fathom.

I was encouraged to depart from the property as soon as they could dispatch us. Lavinia found a large bunch of rusty keys for the villa, which she brought out to me surprisingly quickly. After they were handed over, her brother formally pronounced their statement on the death of Primus. He showed he was peeved by my suggestion that someone was covering up foul play: 'We were entirely unaware of his fate. We had no idea where or how he had ended up, and never saw him after we had come back with Secunda to her estate.'

I saw no point in arguing. I was ready to leave, though I promised them that if anything untoward had occurred, I would uncover the facts. If and when I did, I would return to address issues. 'If you really cared for Primus, and if you care about his poor sister, you ought to want the truth.'

When we left, I drove as if I was hurling a chariot around the Circus. Suza squeaked once, then kept any protest to herself.

I rattled our mule cart back down the coast road towards Stabiae. At first there was no other traffic. For a while we went in silence. I was not only disappointed, but livid. We were being palmed off with nonsense. Informers encounter this all the time, but today's blatant evasion enraged me.

I made that mule gallop so fast sparks flew when our wheels struck kerbstones. Then, as were rounding one of the sudden bends, where the road took a hairpin because of an ocean inlet, we met a fast two-wheeled carriage coming the other way, head on.

We avoided a crash.

The other driver must have known what he was doing. He had an expensive equipage and was probably a professional. Our mule skidded into a slowdown, emitting a peevish bray. They just about managed to skate around us. I heard curses from the driver and saw his passenger's head, as he leaned out of a window and looked back at us. He was bearded, and dressed in dark clothing, roguishly turbaned. Perhaps he was making sure no one had come to grief, though more likely he was expressing a raw opinion of mad woman drivers. He did not order his man to stop. They carried straight on, almost without slowing.

I had shot a straight arm sideways in front of Suza, to ensure she was not thrown out. The gesture reminded me of my father, driving the family on some trip, in a tetchy day of family chaos; after some hideous jerk, my mother would wax poetical about Falco's courtesy to passengers and his driving skills – by which she meant he was a thoughtless boy-racer who was liable to kill us all. Falco would then meander through stories of Helena's own risky exploits when allowed charge of vehicles. Between them, that irresponsible pair had taught me to drive.

I hauled the mule to the side of the road and stopped completely. I calmed down.

'Bit close!' Suza had grown up in a shellfish factory. Ever since we rescued her from picking out the mucus glands of murex sea snails, she had been placid. Nothing could ever be as terrible as her early life.

'You're all right!' I chided, battening down my guilt.

'Thank you, Flavia Albia. I expect the bruises will soon fade.'

The mule looked around over one shoulder at us, humphed in disgust, then began munching rank grass from the verge.

I let out a huge pessimistic sigh. 'I apologise. I just hated that smooth-tongued prevaricator and his secretive, smarming sister. They claim they know nothing about Primus dying, but they must do.'

'Mmm,' Suza agreed. She folded her hands over the big set of keys in her lap. It was a significant gesture. I was meant to feel intrigue. 'I suppose I had better tell you, Flavia Albia, what I found out when I went into the house.'

I breathed. The sun appeared to brighten. I told her she was a good girl, and I must have trained her well.

30

I leaned behind me and fetched out our picnic basket. We had not bothered with it earlier because we knew what to expect: the usual fare supplied by the kitchen when you set out very early on a trip. Even Fornix had absorbed the myth that hard-boiled eggs are perfect for travellers because they will not break. Because gourmet chefs insist that no one should ever question their seasoning, he had not sent salt, let alone a little jar of salad dressing. His other items were as bad. In some countries, yesterday's bread rolls will crack enamel off your teeth. In Campania we just had to chew them patiently. The Publilius siblings had not given us a sample of the Gabius vintage. But we had water in a goat-skin; only part had leaked out, so we managed to wet our lips.

Suza passed judgement: 'The words "a packed lunch" are the worst in Latin.'

'*Cibus in canistro* . . . It will be as bad in Greek.' I decided against attempting a translation. I can read a Hellenic menu board or ask the way to the acropolis but anything beyond that finds my vocabulary faulty. I was not even sure the phrase I used to deter perverts really meant what I intended. Greek perverts, who come in a wide variety, had given me some very odd looks. It could not all have been because they believe young women only exist to be frantically pawed, so those I met were outraged when I fought back.

168

'You have had a picnic in Greece?' demanded Suza, keen to expand horizons.

'Yes, the water was wine dark – full of boggy bits. Once, I even tried snacking beside a papyrus bog in Greek-speaking Egypt. Same thing. The water there was tepid and gritty, the flatbread was tough, and pharaohs do not like their hard-boiled eggs to contain any flavour.'

'I bet they eat them with a really beautiful enamel spoon, though,' Suza comforted herself. She was a dreamer; she wanted to imagine the world was exotic.

We relaxed in the current scenery, between the stinging blue sea and the stark mountain crags. Birds sang, from avian enthusiasm, not for us. Whether it's a sodden British forest or a baked Italian promontory, the countryside belongs to other creatures. Humans must venture there politely, allowed among the boscage only on sufferance.

I started to muse on equivalent alienation when you step into a city backstreet. It took me too close to homesickness. I was turning into Falco, who could never be away from Rome without yearning to be insulted, arrested and mugged. When we came to Campania that time, my mother advised me to soothe him by saying the dung you step in accidentally has the same smell anywhere.

'Now, Suza. Stop mucking about and tell me. What happened, then, when you flittered off by yourself?'

Suza was an amiable lass. Dark-haired, less bouncy than she used to be but still a clumsy lump, she had more front than an imperial monument. It was hard work teaching her to stop speaking her mind without forethought, but I would never fault her passion for learning. In or out of the house, she absorbed almost too much of what other people were saying. Whenever I took her with me on an assignment, she reckoned it was her job to burrow where I could not go. In her opinion, what she weeded out would have more value than any banal facts I extracted through standard procedure.

'There were other people there, but I thought I ought to find Blossia.'

Blossia, I gathered, was the female slave who had let us in. I felt some shame that I had not bothered to enquire her name, whereas my little maid had done it instinctively. Suza had palled up with Blossia so much she had initially been offered a tour of the house.

'Did you go?'

'Not to all of it.'

'That's investigating! Back a bit then: who were the other people you saw? Staff? Other slaves?'

'I never talked to them.'

'All right, but how were they behaving? Moving around, doing jobs they were supposed to, or taking their ease and taking advantage?'

'They must have been doing their proper jobs. They had bedcovers hung up airing. Lunch was being set in a dining room. A boy was washing a dog in a fountain. It escaped and ran around shaking water off its fur. That was why Blossia had to give up on showing me the rooms, because she mopped the floor in the colonnade, so nobody slipped on the water. We lost time over that, so she took me to see the old lady.'

'Who never speaks?'

Suza confirmed that Secunda only sat in silence. She had been positioned in front of a large picture window, where she could look out at a pleasing view. Blossia had said she liked that. Cushions were packed at her back and shawls wound around her. A young man with long hair was playing a flute. 'As soon as we came to be with her, he thought he could trot off. He said he was going to practise his music, but Blossia told me he would be having a kip.'

'Typical!'

'He looked a bit of all right.'

'You're too young for him.'

'You don't know how old he was.'

'I don't have to be told, Suza. Any layabout with a flute is bad news.'

'He could play it quite nicely.'

'I bet he could! And you wanted to experience his fingering.'

'I did not!'

Left to her own devices Secunda would sit there all day, quite happily, according to Blossia, whose main work in the house comprised looking after her mistress. This task had fallen to her since everyone had returned to the vineyard estate in the year of Vesuvius. Before that she had been a general-duties attendant. Blossia had been born in the Gabius house and never went to the Stabiae villa. That meant she had no knowledge of Primus or his fate. Nor, Blossia had told Suza, had Secunda ever mentioned her brother once she came home again. All the other slaves from Stabiae had either died or been dispersed.

'Sold off?'

'Yes, or given away to other people.'

'Friends or relatives?'

'She never said.'

'And does Blossia think that was unusual?'

'No. Secunda had ended up with too many. The ones she had had with her old husband took precedence when the rest were thinned out. The ones from Stabiae were brought with her, but they expected to be ditched.'

'Botheration . . . What had the husband been like?'

'Nothing special, but Blossia said there were no complaints.'

'What about Gellius and Lavinia? They will have turned up at Secunda's estate, firmly established as people in control. Was Secunda already confused and silent then?'

'Blossia says she seemed to be terrified out of her wits,' confirmed Suza. 'It's destroyed her. Ever since the volcano, she cannot stand loud noises or people shouting. Any fright makes her start trembling.'

'*Was* it the volcano?'

'Everyone assumes so. Gellius and his sister explained to everyone that she had been in decline before they brought her back, but fear finished her off. She'd already been jumpy. Then the world seemed to be ending . . . All her life she was easily agitated and could even become violent. Nowadays everyone looks after her and keeps her quiet. She spends her days very peacefully.'

Suza looked at me. She pursed her lips. I gazed back, so she nodded. 'Oh?' I queried, keeping it light.

'Blossia whispered to me, "Of course, they have to give her a little bit of help, but they make sure of it." Like a hint.'

'A hint?'

Suza was disapproving. She described the scene when Gellius came in from the garden to fetch Secunda. 'I'm there watching carefully, but saying nowt. It goes like this, Albia. He says to us he has come to fetch the old lady because there is somebody she has to meet. I realise it must be you. He goes up to the old duck. "Medicine time, I think!" he cries. He fetches out a little bottle from behind a statuette, where I could tell they always keep it. He pours her some drops on a spoonie. She laps it up as if she likes it, and he licks the spoon clean afterwards.'

'Goodness!'

'You can bet I was cursing him. When the old lady was taken outside to you, I thought I could have lingered behind secretly, so I could grab a quick taste of it.'

'Suza! For heaven's sake! You don't know what it was.'

'Wrong! I did know,' Suza claimed, with her legendary confidence. This was a high point in her narrative. She was queening it. 'The old lady's medicine looked – and, pooh, it smelt – just like that poppy-juice linctus Tiberius Manlius has to take, when his pains from the lightning grow agonising. If that annoying fellow Gellius hadn't sucked the spoon like a hungry dog, I could easily have tested whether the poor duckie's juice had the same flavour as the aedile's.'

I decided not to ask how Suza would have recognised a likeness to my husband's opioid. Tiberius either measured it out himself, or I would fetch it for him. With small boys in the house at home, we kept strong medicines secure in a cupboard. I had one key on my chatelaine; Gratus kept a duplicate. No one else should have been sampling.

Mind you, let's be realistic. I had a lockable jewellery box, yet that never deterred Suza when she wanted to spend an afternoon trying on my earrings.

The key question now was: if the Publilius siblings were giving Secunda strong drugs, had they done the same to Primus? If so, had they one day, on purpose or by accident, given him an overdose?

31

We rushed home to the villa. Our mule, a beast that was supposedly intelligent and cautious by nature, had developed a liking for speed. Suza and I pretended we were in charge; steerage was now out of our hands. On arrival, we drew up beside an empty building cart and an unattended litter.

'Whoa there, ladies!' It is guaranteed that when you are wrestling with a frisky beast, there will be masculine spectators. 'Left a bit, straighten up . . . Do you want us to park it for you?'

'Get lost!' shouted Suza, to spare me the bother as I leaned back with the reins.

All building sites contain groups of men doing nothing. The carpenter, Axilius, must have come to court Tiberius with his knowledge of dovetail joints. Instead of begging for employment, he regally gave me his driving expertise. To do this, he was sitting at the outdoor table with the two slaves Uncle Tullius had sent us, who looked on admiringly at the way Axilius annoyed me. They were all drinking mulsum from our second-best beakers, the ones I had brought for more important visitors.

Axilius was so at home, he even introduced the slaves, although I knew exactly who they were. 'These are Vindex and Dexter. Tullius Icilius acquired them in payment for a debt.'

I would have rejected them and forgotten the debt. This pair tended to turn up at our house in Rome, in patched tunics and a layer of grime, pretending to be painters we had hired for frescos we knew nothing about. His uncle must dispatch them to Tiberius whenever they ran out of work at his own house. It was too late to ask whether they could, in fact, paint. Still, that is a question you might ask of so many workers in skilled trades.

They were tall and big-boned, one blond, one ginger, both reticent. Never talking was how they got away with being accepted, as they wandered around people's homes as if they were following mysterious instructions. I knew a clerk once who gave me that advice: tired of your desk? Pick up a scroll and walk about. People will let you go anywhere.

Axilius had been telling them how they looked like Britons, although everyone told him they were Gauls. They listened, impassive. One scratched his ear, the other lightly belched.

'Germans!' I corrected coldly. Celt-differentiation was a talent I possessed. In Londinium I had sometimes needed to be sure whose shins I was kicking.

'I never knew that Germans could do frescos.'

'Oh, they just like playing with paint, Axilius.'

We had a wall at home where Vindex and Dexter had put up colour swabs, not for our consideration as customers but simply to see what happened when they mixed ingredients for fun. This had encouraged little Gaius and Lucius to draw a dado full of stick-men gladiators. Dromo had added a cartoon lion.

'Your husband's uncle had them sent down from Rome, in case any scenes here need touching up.'

'Surprisingly, I guessed as much.'

I had an idea Dexter and Vindex intended to sit on their well-padded backsides, claiming that any task with a broom, barrow or pickaxe wasn't their job. Tiberius and Larcius would turn to supervising them eventually, so I would not interfere. However, I was the beady-eyed matriarch, one of those Roman women who keep so many family firms solvent; I knew the score in this dice game. Since they had arrived on site, they had done nothing. Keyed up to avoid work experience, as soon as they reached Campania this pair embraced *otium* as heartily as the super-rich; they were ready to communicate with the natural world, absorb the balm of sea and sun, and leave behind their daily cares . . .

I was egalitarian. I would allow a love of leisure to all grades of society, the lowest as well as the high – that meant slaves too. However, not on my budget, babies!

They looked at me with their inscrutable blue eyes, fully aware of what I was thinking. In Rome I had simply put up with them. Could they tell they were encountering a tricky new regime? I collected up their beakers as if setting a full stop on idle time. The one who was probably Vindex, the ginger, instinctively put out a hand to keep his drink. He had second thoughts. I silently indicated, 'Good choice!'

Axilius, a well-baked piece of marching-biscuit, murmured to himself, 'Mummy's home . . .' He tidied his bag of wood-working tools with the innocent air of a man who had been leaving anyway.

'Not so fast! Mummy hasn't said you can go out to play. Have you talked to Larcius, Axilius?'

'Your clerk-of-works? Yes, he kindly gave me some of his time. Nice fellow. He reckons he can find me a few bits and bobs, piece work. I was just waiting to be introduced to the aedile after he finishes up . . .'

I handed the beakers to Suza, after which I kicked my skirt hems straight as a proper matriarch does. Then I went to find out what Tiberius was finishing.

A second knot of men on site was inspecting scenes connected with our finding of Primus. It looked intensive work, with much discussion. Nobody was taking notes in a site diary, but I could see gesticulation.

This group comprised Tiberius and Larcius, with our workmen, plus a stranger. Two attendants or bearers must belong with him; they came in different sizes but matching tunics. They stood close to each other, bored. In another direction, Dromo was loafing on his own, as if he could not understand the fuss, whatever it was.

'What are you up to, laddie?'

'I want to win the prize for finding the water pipe.'

'You'll stand more chance if you start looking for it, then. Hang on a minute – what's the game over there, Dromo?'

He told me Tiberius had gone into Stabiae, asked at the temple, found a priest who had sent him to a man, who was the man I could see over there. Dromo seemed envious that this man had not one but two public slaves attached to him, which meant they shared any work he ordered.

'I expect they share any complaints from him too, Dromo. Rank?'

'Town councillor.'

I sighed. Stabiae presumably had *duoviri*, two men with an ambition to serve (or a love of pomp), who administered justice, finance and the election of their planned successors. (You think democracy is based on choice? Has no one ever explained to you how voting works?) As well as duovirs, Stabiae might have aediles, who would inspect streets and

177

check market weights, not bothering about administering justice in case they copped for anything difficult.

An official who could be prevailed upon to take an interest made a change. I had been sure of a classic brush-off. Either this one was very bored at home, or my husband had been brutally insistent.

Although Tiberius Manlius had no truck with the chicanery that generally happened, from the way they were talking together it looked as if today he had bonded. With him, this did not always follow. He liked imposing standards. In Rome, he had ignored the entrenched system of inefficiency and fraud, while he ran his patch properly. It had caused a stir at first, although people soon grew used to him. After all, they only had to endure his propriety for a year, then normal business would resume.

I marched over to join in. Once again, gold earrings would have helped. It was definitely a good idea *not* to be carrying a tray of used beakers; I would need to establish I was more than the building site's mulsum wench.

Tiberius greeted me with a smile that clinched it. He performed introductions. 'My soul-mate! Here she is. Albia, this is Apuleius Innocentius.'

I had encountered magistrates who were thin, hollow-cheeked men with rich wives they dared not divorce, plus transparently dangerous politics. They spoke of the sacred past as if it governed their actions, while imposing wreckage and bankruptcy on the future. This happy, roly-poly roust-about must have become a town councillor because he hoped it would bring some benefit to him. Well, that made him no worse than the others.

Apuleius looked and spoke as if he had a heart of gold. I feared he wasn't very bright. Still, towns have to have some mutt to blame when their drains are clogged.

178

I gathered that everyone had already been inside the shed where we kept excavated bones. The bundle we had designated as Curvidius Primus had been unwrapped and the duovir told me his reaction with sweet, uncomfortable honesty: 'It's very odd to look at a skull you can remember with all its flesh and life.'

He was happier now he was being shown what remained of the cart. He inspected the shattered fragments, fitments and the wonky wheel. Then Tiberius led him deeper into the store. 'Come inside my cupboard of collectibles. After you, Duovir.'

As they burrowed, Tiberius threw back at me, 'They left behind a lumpy statue at the back, looks like a water feature. *Drunken Bacchus.*'

'Appropriate!' I chortled.

Apuleius shot me a glance, then began inspecting the rows of amphorae. Checking trade vessels was his kind of work. He admitted he was obsessive, which people groaned about, although he boasted that had never stopped him. He took delight in big foodstuff jars.

While we tactfully smothered our own groans, he pointed out that only one or two containers in our store had labels on their necks for the Gabius estate; the rest came from a wide range of places and were dated over many years. He spoke with joy of stamps impressed onto the handles, rims or necks of amphorae before firing, to show the ceramic pots' origins; he was fascinated by the various painted inscriptions later added around the handles, white rectangles with red letters that told of contents, origins, producers' names and customs data. 'I love to find a good customs mark.'

I broke in on his delicious pleasure to say I would have expected Primus to be supplied by his sister's vineyard.

Apuleius took my interruption in good part; he explained that the Gabius vintage was excellent. 'Always reliable. Most of theirs goes up to Rome. Always has. A shipper comes across from Puteoli – he looks dubious, but no one has ever managed to charge him with anything. I've tried, believe me. He was blood brothers with Gabius, so he's done business there for years. He always transports the bulk of their wine north for them. I dare say they pass it off as Falernian, because that's such a known name.'

Tiberius politely suggested that Surrentum was fine enough to hold its own. Genuinely touched, Apuleius made a shy confession that he himself owned a few vines further up the coast. These 'few' had presumably paid for his election campaign. 'Let me send you an amphora, Aedile!' Tiberius tried to put him off, thinking the offer was his initiation into local bribery. He soon stopped trying. He might be a man of rectitude, but he liked Campanian wines.

I still wondered whether, or why, Fulvia Secunda had refused to supply her brother. 'Wouldn't he expect a share of her vintage, at mate's rates, minimum?'

'Free, you mean?' Apuleius shook his head. He said the Gabii had their traditional markets firmly in place and Primus was such a famously bad payer he had ended up having to shop around. Even his sister had refused to be fleeced.

'Yes, I have been told she never listened to him.'

'Two of a kind. Neither ever listened to anyone. Secunda could be outspoken, and everyone knew she took no nonsense from her brother. When he snarled, she snarled right back. If there was one person he was afraid of, it would have been her.'

Privately, I thought it doubly sad that she was now reduced to a vague old lady who wouldn't bat away a buzzing fly. 'I've met her. She seems very timid.'

'Something must have happened to her, then!' Apuleius had known Primus at one time. They had met on a few occasions at the Claudian spa near the port. 'I only went occasionally. Too busy. Too many show-offs. I decided I liked a hot spring where you can soak quietly on your own and think. Even better, soak quietly and *not* have to think.'

This was surprisingly philosophical. While he pottered away again along the containers, I drew Tiberius aside. 'Have you asked him to stay to dinner?'

'No, he's a bonehead.'

'Oh, he's not that bad! I'll invite him. I'll need you to grit your teeth and pass the olives nicely.' I wanted to quiz the man further about Primus. I sent Dromo to warn Fornix we would be entertaining. Soon my chef would be in a royal tizz, citing lack of time, lack of assistance, and a dearth of good ingredients. At least that meant my steward was happy, gloating.

Entertaining the magistrate turned into a good move. From him, we learned more about Curvidius Primus, with confirmation he had been a loud, aggressive character, tricky to deal with and disliked in the neighbourhood. Apuleius said his own father had attended a day school with the Curvidius siblings, until the teacher kicked them out because they kept fighting. 'Girls as well as boys. In fact, Pater said the girls were more dangerous.'

I asked about the younger associates I had just encountered: how had the Publilius brother and sister forged such a close relationship with Primus? Apuleius himself had observed the friendship developing. 'Gellius worked at the nymphaeum.'

'He implied to me he ran the spa. His sister called him the supervisor.'

Apuleius scoffed. 'If that means cleaning oil slime off the floor! He could just about pass himself off as a manager. They take your admission money, then they are the men to kick if your clothes get stolen . . . Which tunics often were. Mind you, I had no reason to believe Gellius pinched them. He was too scared of being found out, like all those who call themselves respectable.'

'Were they? Respectable?'

'Just about. A grandfather was a melon millionaire, known as Melopepo. His descendants dropped the cognomen and tried to forget they owed their loot to fruit. Their aunt had married well enough with Primus, but their father was a deadbeat who ran through all his money.'

'Gambling?'

'Fancy tastes. Enjoyed the high life. Spent all the cash, then dropped dead on them. His children were left not quite destitute, but they hungered for better. Once he had gone, they set out to improve their lifestyle.'

'They seduced their aunt and Primus into providing for them?'

Apuleius shook his head. 'Not real seduction. In fairness, I'd say it was above board. The aunt liked the niece and welcomed having another woman in the house. Gellius and Primus were proper friends, I cannot say otherwise. They looked an odd pairing, yet they matched up somehow. It can happen. They genuinely enjoyed talking to one another – they played board games for hours, hunched over the counters.'

'And they drank together?' I hinted.

'Not particularly. Gellius is rather prim.' That, I thought privately, did not fit a man who would dose an old lady with jollop until she was comatose – then himself lick the spoon.

'Was there ever any suggestion that Primus was being wrongfully given opiates?'

'No! He liked his wine and, I would have thought, wasn't a man to stand for bad treatment from others.' Apuleius continued reminiscing. 'Primus went into his decline quite late in life. Before that he was simply boorish.'

'Lavinia told me his wife, their aunt, left the young couple money when she died.'

'Did she?' Apuleius winked. 'That would have been a thrill. Those two would love a bequest. No need to wash floors any more. Up they went where the toffs have their holiday villas. Good views, good living, and all found. They accustomed themselves to fine clothes and a comfortable lifestyle. But I do believe it suited everyone. Even after the aunt had gone to the gods, it didn't end. The word was, Primus himself generously welcomed them staying.'

Tiberius shifted on his elbow as we ate on our newly installed couches. 'I thought Primus was tight?'

'Yes – odd that, isn't it?' agreed the duovir. His grin was telling.

'They had Primus under the thumb?' I quizzed, frowning.

'Well, he was going to pieces, which was clear from the donkey-loads of medicaments everyone knew were going up the hill. Gellius and the girl were soon running his place for him. He seemed to accept he needed help. I expect they called it charity. He will have been too woozy to call it anything.'

'And his sister?' I asked. 'Secunda arrived when she lost her husband?'

'Yes, things were then fiery, by all accounts. Primus yelled at her a lot, but she still had guts. I believe she was not infrequently heard to yell back at him!'

At that, my husband asked how Gellius and Lavinia reacted. Then Tiberius came right out and wondered whether they might have engineered a premature death. 'Has it ever been suggested they could have finished Primus off, hoping to inherit his wealth?' Apuleius, more of an innocent than he sometimes seemed, was shocked.

'Friends of the family!' I spelled out, then told him the wise adage that if you were murdered you were most likely to be killed by someone close to you.

Recovering his poise, Apuleius joked back, 'So presumably if someone you know croaks unexpectedly, they have been done in by you!' We all laughed.

'But there was never suspicious talk about how Primus died?' Tiberius pressed.

'None, really, Faustus.'

The local verdict when Primus disappeared, we were told, was that his addiction to wine had finally finished off his liver. Whether the eruption played a direct part was unknown, but no one thought twice about it. So many people had disappeared. In poor health, Primus had had ailments that had troubled him for years; he was known to be deteriorating, so could have passed away naturally at any time.

Apuleius then held up a hand, overdramatically, like a bad orator. Lawyers who take too long a lunch do this in afternoon court sessions. '*Io!* There is something I find ugly.'

'What's that?' Tiberius, chewing, broke into the significant pause.

The duovir had been thinking more than he had so far shown. Before he had come up here today, Tiberius must have revealed our doubts. Now Apuleius claimed those suspicions as his own. 'Laid out neatly on a cart, with ash on top of him? *Locked in?* Nobody looked for him, nobody retrieved the corpse? Hold on! You were absolutely correct, coming to me to discuss this, Aedile. Even at such a very late stage, these anomalies demand consideration. Of course, it may all be innocent . . .' Tiberius and I were silent, waiting for the usual rationale. Like my cook, Apuleius would have well-honed excuses. Lack of time, lack of expertise, lack of manpower, and the old clincher, lack of significant evidence to justify an inquiry. 'But if I ignore the issues, will I be remiss?' he wondered portentously.

'Well, you came today and had a look,' I comforted him.

We were all thinking it was more than most officials would have done. Tiberius had dragged Apuleius up here, but now seemed to accept the inevitable. 'Don't worry. I imagine the public will be satisfied that you have used due diligence.'

'Thank you. But, Faustus and Flavia Albia, I have a role that carries big responsibilities. I do not want people to criti-cise. You alerted me to your concerns, which I find valid. Now the big question is, do I feel this can be ignored?'

That was when Apuleius Innocentius surprised us. We were wrong to have dismissed him as a small-town, small-minded magistrate. This one liked to stir the crud with a stick as much as we did. Either that or he thought my husband, an ex-Roman official, was a good person to keep sweet while he tried to climb the ladder of success.

Apuleius said the victim – if victim he was – had been a man of substance. That counted. There had to be a rule of law: persons with social standing could not vanish in murky circumstances. A volcano had erupted, yes, but that should not be used as cover for illegal activities.

Then what should a worthy duovir do? Any examination of facts would have to be informal and low-profile so as not to offend the family. But a fresh assessment by an outsider, someone who was uncontaminated by local preconceptions, would be useful: results would carry weight in the community. He knew I was an investigator (he explained that Tiberius had told him so, proudly listing my successes). 'I don't want to touch this too obviously myself,' he said. 'I need someone to act for me, at a stage removed. I have no prejudice against women. In this part of the world, female entrepreneurs are common. Those who do good in the community have their statues in the forum.' That would be rich ones, I supposed. Rich ones who had spent money on very visible public benefits.

Apuleius said he was prepared to authorise reasonable expenditure in the name of public interest. He would, therefore, commission me to take our legitimate concerns to the next stage.

32

That was a surprise. The puzzle would have niggled at me so much anyway that I was bound to have gone further, so I welcomed a formal right to investigate. An official role would give me a warrant.

We agreed a one-off fee for a basic probe. I outlined my rates for extras. The matter was left with me.

Apuleius went back to Stabiae, borrowing a lantern for his litter-bearers. He now had a clear conscience. By the time his head hit the swansdown pillow, he would have forgotten any fear of being blamed for negligent administration. He could safely dream of the true burdens of his office: having to interpret sacrificial pigs' livers for omens or drinking too much at guild dinners, then falling on his face on shiny marble.

Next morning, a heavy haze hid our view of Vesuvius. All the coastline opposite was a grey blur as far as Neapolis and on to Puteoli and Misenum. I was bright. Good shoes, neat tunic, straight belt, clean teeth. A good informer ignores second thoughts. Having no idea where to start gives you free rein.

It might not be easy. Ten years after the event, with no one admitting they witnessed a thing? Slaves now all dead – or so said the smooth-talking Lavinia. All the locals wanted to believe the man's death was a natural accident, so the authorities would not come asking questions? The complication of a frail old sister, who might become distressed; if I upset poor Secunda, it would incur adverse comment, especially if it turned out that in truth nothing unusual had happened . . . Apuleius had been frank: the main thing he wanted was to avoid criticism – especially from relatives.

'The brother in Rome needs a warning,' growled Tiberius. 'I've sent one. Let him cope!'

He had instructed Paris to take a letter to Curvidius Fulvianus, not merely to say we had found the corpse but describing the odd circumstances. Apuleius had been unusually helpful; he had straight away produced a pass for the official post. He never normally had much chance to use his imperial allocation, so was very keen, otherwise his prized diploma's validity would expire. Setting off yesterday, with permits to use fast horses as a courier, our runabout would be in Rome today.

'That will please Paris!'

'He won't like it that he has to check in with Uncle Tullius, visit Curvidius, gather up any letters from them, then gallop down the Via Appia straight back here.'

'You are a cruel master.'

'Paris has an easy life. It's good to shake him up.'

'Well, he will enjoy riding like fury.'

'At state expense!' gleamed Tiberius.

I saw one potential disadvantage. From his courier system, the Emperor might learn that the demise of a rich Stabian resident was being questioned, with the use of an informer. Informers had a bad name (although most emperors used them). Domitian was obsessive: he liked to study official documents right down to the most basic level, to keep absolutist control. He could well spend long dark nights perusing the chits that covered postal relays.

My family had an old feud with him too; we did not want it reactivated. 'Tiberius, I hope the words "I am hiring Falco's daughter" do not feature.'

'No. Apuleius filled in the diploma "on advice from an ex-aedile, Faustus" – though that may not be any better for us!' He liked to keep his head down almost as much as my publicity-shy family.

I considered whether we should go home to Rome, to ready ourselves for when soldiers knocked on our door at midnight. Co-operation is the last hope sometimes – well, it sounds a good theory. Another idea is that you can counter an oppressive secret service by submitting so much information it can only be filed away, unread by security minions and unseen by the dark lord.

As we brooded, something happened. Outside arose a loud clamour that spoke of catastrophe.

Together Tiberius and I ran towards the sudden noise. Shouts were coming from along the villa's newer wing. At its furthermost end we met the problem, stepping right into it. Water was flowing everywhere. We had to wade through expanding muddy floods to reach the cause.

Outside the bathhouse lay an exterior space that housed woodsheds, the furnace and, at one time, a planted area. A statue base could well be for the reclining *Drunken Bacchus* we had found abandoned in the storehouse. That could easily have been a fountain: someone had exposed a substantial lead pipe, previously covered by tiles for protection. There were also signs that someone had recently been hacking at the plinth.

The pipe had – or had had – a cylindrical collection tank, from which ran three separate, smaller-volume pipes, each with a metal stop valve. These were above ground, presumably for access. 'Hades, a triple distributor!' Tiberius marvelled to Larcius.

Larcius was in no mood for hydrological brilliance. The clerk-of-works was tearing out his hair, as he strode around in helpless consternation. His brown tunic looked wet to the waist so he must have been swooshing through the floods for half an hour now. Someone – 'Some idiot, let me just get my hands on him' – had put a pickaxe into the collection tank. From the resultant flood, it must have happened a while ago, maybe even yesterday. Whoever did it had wisely run away.

The stop valves were all situated on the wrong side of the breach to be of any use; they must have been turned off while the villa stood empty and might well have seized up with calcification anyway. Before the triple division, a water supply would have come hurtling into the collection tank with really good pressure, pressure that was now being released in one big cascade through the idiot's ragged pickaxe hole.

By my guess the three pipes served the bathhouse, the kitchen and a water feature system. It would be lovely to get them working . . . 'This must be our feed coming in from the municipal aqueduct.' We were currently spreading the contents of the Aqua Augusta Campaniae all over our estate. We owned the best pressurised jet I had ever seen. Public fountains in Surrentum must be running low. Give it three days, and a very pompous water-board official would be calling on us.

'Brilliant. The flow has nowhere to go but everywhere!' Larcius included a copulatory adjective before 'flow', 'go' and 'everywhere'. As a term it was not truly technical, though no one could blame him.

Tiberius looked around and deduced, 'It must have been spurting high and wild all night.' He even used the same non-technical adjective before 'night'.

Serenus was making half-hearted passes with a broom. It only caused water to move around pointlessly, entering previously dry areas with glee. Then Sparsus, the apprentice, let out a spiteful cry of 'None of us would be so stupid. So here's the question: where is Dromo?'

33

Water kept rushing wherever it could. It had pushed across what must have been a kitchen garden, its clean waves churning into knee-deep mud with the enthusiasm of a two-year-old child who has found a pile of dung to play in. It continued on, dashing inside any building it hit. A colonnade became an exciting racetrack for torrents. The bathhouse had satisfying waterproof floors and walls that soon filled, turning its rooms into plunge baths. The plunge pool itself had disappeared. It lay in wait secretly for anyone who ventured to wade into it.

Men who claimed expert knowledge discussed clamping the burst. Their pooled wisdom acknowledged that even if we had sheet lead and solder, a ladle, heat and a moleskin cloth for wiping, there was no possibility of putting on a patch while this lively water was spewing. Repairs needed to be done dry. 'Oh, cheer us up!' somebody scoffed. To ensure complete depression, another bright soul covered the topic of how lead can 'blow' if weakened by time or shaken up by building work . . .

Tiberius announced there must be a master tap. It would be at the point where we connected to the aqueduct – if anyone could find that. The aqueduct was thought to run underground, so would not be obvious.

To find it, they decided Serenus should start digging a trench. He must track all along our access pipe, taking care not to cause any more damage. How far, he asked sarcastically, did we think he had to go to the boundary? How long was this going to take him and would his back hold out?

It was me who peeled off to fetch the floor plan; my beloved had been keeping it in our bedroom, in case he was struck by some urgent thought during the night. Some might call ours an unusual marriage. Fortunately, I liked eccentricity: his quirks allowed me a right to be myself.

The plan showed the entire estate curtilage. After bringing it out into daylight and pelting back to the burst, I discerned a faded red-ink star, drawn beside the road that passed our boundary. There seemed no other reason for the mark, not unless a great-grandfather had been buried there and had imposed tomb regulations on his plot.

Tiberius and Larcius strode away to look. 'We don't need the chart,' Tiberius called back, sounding frazzled. 'Name of the gods, put it somewhere dry, Albia.'

Serenus, a happy soul, sent a shout after him: 'Don't break the tap!'

'If you can find it,' added Sparsus (under his breath).

My husband had already set off on his mission, so his reply was inaudible.

While they were seeking out the aqueduct, I took myself away from the spreading water gardens to look for Dromo.

He was hiding. Being Dromo, he had chosen a place I could easily guess: the kitchen. As soon as I appeared in the doorway Fornix looked up from shaping a pie-case and pointed. 'He's behind the brooms in the alcove. What has he done this time?'

'Bought himself an early ticket across the Styx to the Underworld.'

'He looks wrecked.'

'He soon will be. Dromo, you really are in trouble. Even your master is furious with you. Come out and explain yourself to me, in case you can be saved.'

'Can I have a cake if I tell you?' begged a small voice from behind a clutch of besoms.

Fornix and I looked at one another. We had learned to judge levels of guilt with Dromo. This lacked the ring of totality. 'I'll give him a small almond biscuit, Flavia Albia, if he confesses to you properly,' my cook declaimed. The big-bellied professional could be dangerous with sharp knives but was at heart a kindly man.

Dromo slunk out. He was covered from head to foot in dirt. His face was badly bleeding, almost as if his nose was broken.

'Dromo, you're too old to be playing with mud pies. What's your excuse for this?'

'Fell over.'

As we expected, he knew about the breeched pipe and the floodwater. Of course he said it wasn't caused by him.

34

'Get a grip, you lunatic!' I poked him with a finger, though I did it cautiously. He was never a lad I wanted to touch too closely. 'If not you, who was it?'

'Ghosts,' said Dromo.

He had to be lying.

35

'Ghosts?'

By Dromo's standards of fantasy this was mild. I had known him a year, approximately. Tiberius had already had him as a body slave, though I never worked out quite how long they had been yoked together. Dromo must have been a child in the beginning and had barely matured since.

'Don't play up, boy!' Fornix wanted us out of his kitchen so he could fill his pie in peace.

I was equally firm. 'Ghosts do not exist, Dromo.'

'They had one at Falco's house. *Whoo-hoo.*'

'Last Saturnalia? He was a man, acting. No ghoul, Dromo, even if they were real, would bring his own pickaxe to smash into a water supply.'

'It was *our* pickaxe,' he mumbled sulkily.

'In your hands?' I had a vision of him wildly swinging the tool, breaking a hole in the tank, then falling over in the momentum of his own swing. 'Dromo, if you broke the pipe, own up, please.'

'Three ghosts!' he wailed. 'Three ghosts, gibbering, all in black. I saw them. They were trying to dig out the fountain base.'

'Whatever for?'

'To put a fountain on it?'

'What fountain?'

'I don't know.'

I made a grab for a broom. I had never beaten Dromo – I had never beaten any slave. Nor did I intend to. All the same, he jumped behind the cook, who was twice as large. 'Don't hurt me!' he screamed, clinging to Fornix around his substantial waist.

'Jupiter, Albia!' observed Fornix, not known for referring matters to the gods. His cookery was divine but he took full credit himself. 'Do you have to put the wind up him when I'm trying to brush on a milk wash?' They did not even know I had a violent past, I thought. Fornix extended his pastry brush towards me. 'Three gibbering creeps in black all sounds very specific, Albia.' Noble peace-makers are rarely portrayed winking, but my cook did it. He shimmied to shake Dromo off. 'Suppose you leave the lad with me – put your bum on that stool and behave yourself, Dromo. I'll have a little chat with him.'

The chef's offer would solve my dilemma over corporal punishment. I lowered the broom while I mimed thinking.

As I peered at his pie, which appeared to be mixed fish in an egg and nutmeg sauce, Fornix slid in a plea of his own. 'Is there any chance the men can fix the damage, to give me water here?'

'Only if I can persuade a bunch of sea nymphs to materialise and work magic with pipe sealant, Fornix. Don't plan on washing any leeks yet.'

I left him to deal with Dromo.

Back at the scene the jet had sunk to half its original height. With a few spurting coughs, the high pressure began fading. A subtle diminution signalled that somebody somewhere had arrested the flow. Slowly the force of water declined until it became a residual trickle. Serenus and Sparsus set off to tell Tiberius and Larcius they had succeeded.

I might have found myself a quiet spot to enjoy some chewy figs and professional contemplation. No chance. As I was wading through a colonnade, I heard wheels. When I went to investigate, visitors had turned up: the Publilius siblings, fully cloaked for travel in toning shades of pistachio green. They had big expensive shoulder brooches holding together the eau-de-Nil. A factotum or several must have spent hours on their fold work.

I took note of the conveyance. 'Interesting!' It was the carriage Suza and I had encountered on the road back from Surrentum, the one we had nearly crashed into. Its driver, still surly-looking, was stationing it in our cart park; he remained seated as if wary of vehicle theft. I noticed he was dressed in black, as had been his passenger yesterday.

'A friend lent us his carriage so we could come and speak to you,' the siblings informed me. I wondered who that would be. The carriage-owner? Was he specifically close to Gellius and Lavinia, or would he, too, be generically classed as a 'friend of the family'? Either way, just how friendly was he?

Tiberius and workmen arrived along the track from the road. Turning away from me, Gellius immediately set upon Larcius, who was stomping at the front. Gellius was asking whether any white plaster plaques had been found. A number had been left behind, stored under a staircase; he was claiming them as the property of the previous owners. He did not say the artwork was valuable, though we all deduced it.

'Not seen any stored materials,' Larcius maintained, in his thoughtful way. 'If plaques are here, I believe they must be firmly attached.'

Tiberius part-raised an eyebrow to me, implying, *They will be!* Still wet and dressed as a labourer, he had been ignored by the siblings. 'What's on the plaques? Warriors? Floating demigods?'

'Not at all. Primus had chosen them and they meant a lot to him. That is why I am asking. He had roared at the stucco artist, "None of your Bacchus finding bloody Ariadne, I want beef!" Labours of Hercules.'

'Stolen cattle. Should be beefy enough!' Even though Tiberius knew his myths and had a cultured accent, the visitors had not placed him.

'Would it be possible to look around?' persisted Gellius, still pressurising Larcius rather than Tiberius. 'I would recognise them for what they are, assuming they may have been overlooked . . .'

'Sorry, Legate, love to give you a guided tour, but not possible today. We've had a flooding incident and there's too much cleaning up to do.' When Larcius was boot-faced, he resembled the impervious wall of the Capitol. It would take a determined marauder to climb over his negativity. 'The house is a building site,' he continued stubbornly. 'We have to store our tools in the atrium from now on. Intruders got in last night. They pinched tools and I've just noticed that a statue has been moved. Luckily, we have a lethal watchdog.' He meant that, apparently. 'Drax is a killer.'

Drax, famously, would run up to intruders wagging his tail. He would then fetch a nice selection of tools he thought visitors might like.

'Another time, perhaps.' I stepped in to deal with the siblings. I, too, felt reluctant to let people who had once lived here come inside the property. Partly, I wanted to establish that it now belonged to Tullius. 'Our uncle will never agree to anything being pulled off a wall, you know. The terms of his sale included all remaining fixtures.'

'Is there something special about these items?' Larcius asked slyly. Gellius could not bring himself to admit the plaques had commercial value. 'They were new and unused,' he quavered feebly.

Larcius pulled a tough-luck face, the one that had been developed over centuries by clerks-of-works to show owners, employees, architects or idiot site visitors how much they are despised.

Tiberius stepped in and sent the men to begin their clear-up. While the Publilius siblings adjusted their view of his importance, he and I led them to the usual outside wooden table and seats. He hauled off his work tunic, still soaked; I took it and spread it on the table where it might dry. Our mutual respect must have become more meaningful. So did our status, when Suza rushed up, bringing a dry over-tunic for Tiberius and a cloak in which she wrapped me. After peering at our soaked feet, she hurried away again, returning later with dry shoes.

I noticed that when I introduced my husband, the couple exchanged one of their glances. These were perfectly visible and were starting to annoy me. I like discretion in conspirators. Why they seemed apprehensive became clear: although I had only introduced him by his name, they knew this man Faustus had been an aedile. In the short time since I met them, someone had told them I was a neighbour of consequence, married to a magistrate from Rome. It did not matter that his term of office had expired; its clout would linger.

There was more. Gellius and Lavinia had learned that Tiberius and I had been asking questions about Primus down in Stabiae. I knew there had been no time for them to travel to the port, so their discovery was fast work. They could have heard it from a commodity supplier who routinely visited their house or from the man with the carriage. What mattered to me was that they must have been quizzing people. Who I was and my interest in the Curvidius family had caused a reaction: this visit. I even wondered if news had leaked that a messenger had been sent flying up to Rome, using an official courier permit.

I made my position clear. 'I have experience as a private investigator, a specialist in family work. I have been asked by the authorities to look again at the demise of Curvidius Primus. How we found him is of concern. I did ask you what had happened. Now the official view, which my husband and I share, is that there are gaps and inconsistencies in your story.'

'Oh!' gasped Lavinia.

Nevertheless, her controlling brother had planned a rebuttal: 'The purpose of our visit is to amend what we told you,' he admitted. 'To avoid misunderstanding.'

That was a very old term for 'we know we have been found out'. I maintained a neutral aspect, mirrored by Tiberius. If I'd had my work satchel with me, I would have produced a note-tablet. He sucked the end of one index finger, as if thoughtfully chewing a stylus. His grey eyes rested on them in a way that made them uncomfortable. I hid a smile; he always provided good support for me. We waited.

Although Gellius had begun as their spokesman, Lavinia piped up next: 'Would you be able to explain to us what the "inconsistencies" are supposed to be?'

I tried not to show annoyance. 'I did outline the problematic facts for you, Publilia Lavinia.'

'The first issue that strikes me,' Tiberius intervened, in his measured way, 'is how Primus was said to be "missing". The man was never lost. Everyone in his household must have known where his body was. An impression has put about that his death happened during the eruption of Mount Vesuvius but that is plainly incorrect. Someone is being dishonest.'

Lavinia gulped. 'Oh!' I was starting to object to her little cries of shock. We had laid truth in front of her, not some nasty piece of roadkill. 'What are you saying, Aedile?'

'What I am saying ought to be clear. Primus was already dead when the eruption started. Of that,' stated Tiberius, as if startling jurors who were falling asleep, 'there can be no doubt! He was lying on a cart in a store when the ash cloud fell upon Stabiae. He lay in a peaceful position, not struggling – and, inexplicably, he was naked.'

Everyone stared. That was a new point, even to me.

Tiberius turned to me with a slight apologetic hand sign. 'Fabric has not survived the intense heat, although metal remains. We found his signet ring. However, there were no signs of clothing, no shoelace eyelets or tangs, no belt buckle, no shoulder brooches. If he ever wore jewellery – a chain, a bangle – there was nothing like that.'

'His body had been stripped, then?' I asked, addressing him directly as if he and I were debating in private. 'Any jewellery must have been stolen?'

'That is possible. Or else he was naked voluntarily.'

'Though why, love?'

'Unclear – well, so far.'

'And his ring?'

'Some people do keep them on all the time, or his signet may have become so tight he could never remove it. Was that so?' Tiberius abruptly asked the Publilii, who both jumped. 'Do you remember?'

Neither spoke although they nodded weakly.

'So,' I mused, still looking at my husband, 'we must determine not only how the man died but also, if it was natural causes, why his naked corpse was shoved into a store?'

'Why was his fate blotted from memory? Only one alternative,' Tiberius answered himself. 'True details of his death are being concealed.'

Lavinia kept up her pose of childlike innocence. I could not decide whether her brother agreed with her taking the lead sometimes or whether he wished her to keep quiet. If I was him, I would have thrown a cloak over her head to keep her out of this. 'What does he mean, Flavia Albia, "concealed"?'

'It probably means he was murdered.' I watched for any recoil, though the couple managed to avoid it.

'Goodness!'

'Goodness had nothing to do with it.'

'What if that is true?'

'There will be clues. They have never been detected before, presumably because no one ever looked.' I decided to discuss the issues, with options. 'Foul play would be very serious and, for his brother's sake, I hope it did not happen. Perhaps Primus was only "encouraged" on his way to the Styx. In life, he is said to have drunk a lot. I shall want to know, was he plied with excess wine deliberately, until his organs failed?'

'Is that murder?' Gellius asked. Was he hoping it might be a technicality?

'I would say so,' Tiberius decreed. 'I would argue that before a judge.'

The siblings shook their heads as if what we suggested was insane.

I kept going. 'Or was it even more deliberate? Did somebody make him drowsy with too many brimming goblets, then, while he was incapable of resistance, an assailant or assailants physically beat him to death?'

'There were no signs of him having been beaten, love,' Tiberius corrected me fairly.

'But we accept the concept that he was good and dead when deposited in the store.' I rammed it home. 'So who placed his corpse like that?' Time to attack. 'You two so-called friends lived here. Recipients of ample generosity. Possibly hoping for more. You have to be suspects.'

'We *were* his friends!' Gellius at once responded indignantly. 'We gained nothing from his death.'

'That can be checked,' I warned, unmoved. 'His brother stepped in as his executor after his alleged disappearance. Incidentally, was it you who devised the story that Vesuvius had caused his death? If so, all the more reason for Fulvianus to demand what happened financially after Primus died.'

'Nothing untoward,' Gellius maintained. 'For being helpful to him during his life, Primus always showed his gratitude.'

'Shouldn't *you* have been grateful to *him*?' Tiberius put in quickly, openly sceptical. 'Did he ever write a will – and, if so, did someone guide his hand, I wonder?'

'He may have said he was grateful,' I added insistently, 'but did he formally specify gifts? If you are going to claim that a legacy was left to you, there needs to be proof any document is legitimate. I shall formally question the parties who witnessed it. They will have to be found, then describe how and when it was signed.'

'No coercion and fraud,' emphasised Tiberius.

'That is slander!'

'*Oh!*'

Publilius Gellius took a look at his sister, rose to his feet, then threw out his chest to make a disputation. 'We deny these accusations. We always acted from complete disinterest. All our acts towards Primus were kindly. We treated him as gently as we treat his sister. There was no foul play.'

'Did you encourage his drinking?' I asked.

'No, we tried to stop him.'

'Did you ever give him poppy-juice medication?'

'Never.'

'Did *you* place his body in the store?'

Gellius took a deep breath. Lavinia clasped her hands as if she knew what was coming. 'Primus had died, you are correct,' said Gellius stiffly. 'Fulvia Secunda reacted very strongly. In fact, she was hysterical. Nothing would settle her. She was so distressed by losing him, we took her away. It was the only thing to do. She could not bear to remain in the house where her brother had died.'

'Do you confirm you had left for the Gabius estate before the eruption even started?' I questioned. 'You had emptied the house and you took the household?'

'It seemed for the best. Secunda was in a terrible state, which was when she stopped communicating.'

'And Primus?'

'Not being relatives, Lavinia and I did not know what we ought to do about her brother's body. He was placed carefully where nothing would harm him then we left him behind.'

'Later,' Lavinia added quickly, 'Secunda still became uncontrollably anxious if we mentioned a funeral, so nothing more was ever organised. We needed her agreement, and she never would discuss it.'

'After the eruption,' continued Gellius, 'we heard that the villa had been at least partially buried. I suppose we assumed the body would have been covered over and lost.'

Tiberius stated, sombre as a post-prandial judge, that all this had changed. We had found the body. A funeral would be held. Curvidius Fulvianus would come to officiate. To this Lavinia burbled, in the hurried way she had, that it would be so much easier on everyone if a rapid interment was quietly arranged. 'Afraid not!' answered Tiberius, baldly.

Gellius stood there, a picture of aggrieved innocence. When Vesuvius blew, he was probably thinner, but now he was thickening into middle age. He must be heavier, his cheeks fuller; his hair though still dark was less bushy. He was managing to portray himself as honest. 'So that is the real story,' he pronounced.

I managed not to scoff at his declaration, though to me it was obviously untrue. 'You mentioned that you want to rephrase your statement of yesterday. This would be the moment. Primus had died. We agree that – but still lack an explanation. Tell me, please. How did it happen?'

'Primus died of natural causes.'

'Good.'

'Not good for his friends. Sad for us. Very sad.'

'Tragic! What natural causes?'

'He died!'

'That we know. Too much wine?'

'Age.'

'He would have been just over sixty-five?' His brother had told us Primus had had that birthday. 'Not young, yet not decrepit . . . That was all?'

'Ailments. Years of suffering with pains.'

'Where did he die?' I insisted. 'What time of day? Who found him?'

Lavinia had been growing tense as I battered her brother with my questions. Now she joined in with a new edge in her tone: 'He died in the hour before dinner. His slaves found him. That was why he had no clothes on. He was a large man, sometimes unstable, often clumsy. He must have slipped over. It was an accident.' I gazed at her, uncomprehending. 'He drowned,' said Lavinia.

'He *drowned*? In the ocean?'

'No. At home here. He drowned in his bathtub.'

36

Oh, spit! I could not help considering that the bathtub Primus had drowned in was mine. Did I ever want to use it now?

Tiberius may have sensed my abstraction. 'What was wrong with the bath?' he intervened. 'Was it dangerous?'

'It was deep.' Lavinia sounded over-confident, as if supplying a list of prepared excuses. 'It was made of bronze, with smooth surfaces. He always called for the slaves to bring more hot water. Then he liked to use calamus in olive oil, sometimes a special mix that was made for him, with honey added. He wanted its pain-relieving properties, but the texture was very slippery. The slaves used to moan about having to clean the bath with dry cloths, every time he had used it. Perhaps on the day he passed away the surface was worse than usual. Perhaps, if he had already taken wine that day, he was wobbly so he knocked over the oil bottle or dropped it and spilled it.'

I took her up on that. 'Was a bottle found?'

'I don't remember. In the chaos no one could be expected to look. The unguents were always in little green glass flasks with stoppers. They came up from an apothecary in Stabiae . . .'

'Bathyllus.' They looked surprised; I chose not to explain. *The Best Bunion Balm from Bathyllus* . . . Let them think I was all-knowing.

Tiberius ignored the perfumier talk. 'The bathtub in question has been taken out of a salvage yard and will be available for inspection in the light of your new witness statement.' It looked as if they had not realised our conversation was formal. 'Flavia Albia will give consideration to how an accident might have occurred. Of course we can draw on the advice of specialists.'

Specialists, darling? What a wily investigator he could be! To dodge any awkward questions, I seized the baton from him: 'You said Primus might have taken wine that day. Do you know for sure?'

'Almost certainly he did,' nodded Gellius.

'Whatever the time of day, he would have done, you mean?'

'Even in the morning. However, as my sister said, he died in the lead-up to dinner.'

'Yes, an aperitif would be usual,' I conceded. 'Talk to me about your friend Primus and his habits, please.'

'Wine was one of the ways he sought refuge from his pain.' I raised my eyebrows. Gellius elaborated: 'Agony from muscles and joints. He had suffered for years. He devoted his life to hopeless attempts to stem his physical misery.'

'Muscles, joints – and headaches from wine?' suggested Tiberius, unusually jocular.

'Headaches were one symptom he was spared.' Gellius either had no sense of humour or he thought the circumstances inappropriate. If the latter, he had failed to grasp how seriously we always took foul play. Tiberius would certainly not be smiling when we came to impose justice, as I hoped would happen.

'What kind of drunkard are we talking about?' I probed bluntly. 'Maudlin? Belligerent? Hopelessly slurred, with uncontrolled gestures? Or the other type: some addicts become so accustomed to wine, it hardly shows. They imbibe extraordinary amounts yet seem to lead normal lives. Strangers would never suspect they had a problem. People around them find it hard to believe these habitual drinkers bounce back on a daily basis, brighter than you or I could ever be. Would that describe Primus?'

'That was him.'

I jumped on it. 'Yet he drowned in his bath? Had he fallen? Was he subject to falls?'

'Not really . . .'

'So, he was stable on his feet. I want to picture what you are saying. Do you mean he was trying to climb out and slipped? Or did he find it impossible to raise himself because he was a big man and the tub, made slithery with calamus oil, was too long and deep?'

'That must have been it,' Lavinia decided. 'He found himself trapped. The water was too deep. He couldn't get out.'

'We don't know for sure,' argued her brother, ever cautious. 'He may have fallen asleep and slid under the water. Perhaps he had a seizure first.'

'Had he experienced seizures?'

'Not that we knew.'

'You lived with him, so you ought to have known . . . Was a great deal of water found spilled on the floor around the bathtub?' I asked. 'Sloshed out as if he had struggled?'

'I believe so.' Lavinia sounded uncertain, perhaps even nervous.

Gellius was firmer. 'There must have been. Of course water spread everywhere while people were trying to lift him out, after he was found. He was heavy. The area became extremely messy, especially with everyone panicking.'

'Everyone? Who found him?' I rapped.

'The slaves who attended him.'

'Slaves who always attended when he took a bath?'

'Correct.'

I hate that 'correct'; it is patronising and, trust me, Legate, it's so often a lie. 'What tasks did they perform?'

'Normal ones. Bringing hot water. Providing unguent flasks and sponges when he wanted them. Helping to steady him when he climbed in and out. Having towels ready. Positioning his slippers.'

This reminded me of the alluring scene Milo and Hyro had painted for me. 'Did he ever dismiss them to spend time lying in a private soak? Was he alone then?'

'Usually.'

'No poems were read or music played?' From their expressions, I gathered such things would have been too cultured. His sister Secunda had a flautist for relaxing music, I recalled. Presumably no one read aloud to her; words would mean nothing in her present state, even though the human voice can be soothing. 'But,' I murmured, 'while the master was dreaming away in his warm bath, these slaves you mention would remain on call nearby?'

'They had to. They would wait in the changing room,' Lavinia supplied. 'Primus had a lusty voice. When he wanted to shout for attention, there was no mistaking it. He would shout, then expect them to come scampering immediately.'

I noticed her brother looked more wary, as if he thought she was supplying information too easily. These people gave the impression they were close, yet not chummy. I wondered if today they had argued over something before coming here. Had there been a dispute about what they were going to say?

'How many? How many slaves were in attendance on him that day?'

'Two or three would have been usual. Young men, of course. An extra boy sometimes helped carry water buckets. Someone regularly cleared up the wet floor.'

'One of them?' She shrugged. 'Tell me their names?'

Lavinia put her hands up to her cheeks in a fluttery movement. She looked trapped. 'Oh, I couldn't say!'

'How would we know?' her brother reinforced it. 'They were not *our* slaves. We were only staying in the house. We were like lodgers.'

I smiled. 'Friendly ones!'

'Friends of the family.' Lavinia nervously reiterated.

I stared at them openly, while I absorbed this.

Tiberius stirred. 'Let me put a point to you: might the slaves who attended on Primus have been named Endymio and Porphyrus?'

This time the consultation between brother and sister was deliberately mannered. Gellius turned back to us with a stagey shrug. 'Those names do sound familiar.'

'Thank you!' returned Tiberius, as if reserving a note for use later. I pursed my lips, without comment.

Lavinia piped up, 'Are you suspicious that his slaves might have attacked him?'

'That's a thought!' Tiberius gave her a slow, sad smile.

'They might have had a motive!' Gellius jumped on the idea. 'If their master had previously behaved sternly towards them.'

'He has been described as something of a domestic tyrant,' agreed Tiberius, though he sounded dour.

'Faustus mentioned those names,' I explained, 'because Endymio and Porphyrus, with a female called Myrtale, were very severely punished for something. I told you that before. They were imprisoned and it appears they subsequently died in the eruption. We found their bodies.'

Neither witness asked for further details. When the couple remained silent, Tiberius changed tack. 'By the way, who else was in the bath suite at the time Primus met his death?'

'It was before dinner,' Gellius replied. 'Only family used the baths during that period.'

'You two?' I suggested.

'We certainly could, and we often did – though we were not there when the accident happened.'

I did not take him up on still calling it an accident. 'Were there any other visitors at the villa at the time? Anyone coming to dinner?'

'No one.' Gellius stared at us, perhaps too directly. 'Primus was hostile to visitors.'

'Really?' I felt sceptical. 'What about his sister? Where was Fulvia Secunda?'

'Bathing. She was still in the steam room,' said Lavinia. 'Her dresser was looking after her. That I do remember.'

'Myrtale?'

'That might have been her name.'

'I suppose when Primus was discovered by his own slaves, a loud commotion happened? Did Fulvia Secunda come running?' To press the point, I elaborated: 'Bursting onto the scene, flushed and sweating, barefoot and wrapped only in her towel, feeling vulnerable, perhaps, if she was modest?'

'Myrtale ran after her with a cover-up,' Lavinia interjected quickly.

I let the slip pass momentarily. 'Secunda actually witnessed her brother dying?'

'He was dead. She saw he was past help.' Gellius was sombre. 'What she witnessed that day is the root cause of her pitiful condition ever since. Such a terrible shock for her. Finding him naked and dead among other people shouting and panicking in a small space – it shattered her. People hauling him about as they tried to revive him ... She has never recovered.'

'Understandable distress,' commented Tiberius. 'I am seeing it – water, slippery floors, frightened slaves, at the centre the naked body ... Horrific.'

'An awful fuss,' Lavinia carried on, unhappily shuddering. 'Nothing could be done for Primus, so everyone had to try to calm Secunda. She kept screaming, I can still hear her, and throwing herself about in all directions.'

'If you heard her, then you *were* there?' I challenged, jumping in swiftly this time. 'And I suppose that was how you know Myrtale provided a robe?'

'Oh! I see what you mean. Well, of course we had heard troubled noises and rushed to investigate.'

Her brother then almost enjoyed dramatising the scene. 'A balmy evening. We had been enjoying olives and light reading, in a peristyle outside the summer triclinium, prior to dinner. Sounds reached us. The timbre was desperate, we could tell at once. We hastened there in trepidation and found our poor dear friend lying shiny and wet on the tiles. People were screaming and shouting to revive him, but he had gone. He looked like a beached porpoise after a wild night of storms.'

Gellius! Such colourful embroidery. 'Did you beat Secunda to it?'

'You know, I really do not remember.'

'People did try to revive Primus?'

'Yes, he was rather manhandled. I myself checked him as best I could,' stated Gellius. 'I had some idea of what is needed, from when I was at the warm springs in Stabiae.'

'Ah! People drowned regularly in the Claudian nymphaeum?' Tiberius queried, in a dry voice.

'Well, not in my experience,' Gellius replied stiffly. He seriously disliked being teased. 'But we were all aware that it might happen one day, because many of the clientele were elderly or unfit. Those of us in a management position had discussed the possibility. It was natural to wonder what emergency measures we might need to apply if some wheezing patriarch with too big a lunch in his belly ever collapsed.'

'Commendable forethought.'

'My brother is very public-spirited,' Lavinia assured us. I gazed at her. 'He was extremely fond of Primus. He would have saved him if he could.'

37

Soon afterwards the Publilii claimed they needed to return home to Fulvia Secunda. My suspicions remained. If Primus really had had a heart attack or similar and died in his bath – *my* bath, I reminisced again bitterly – I still found their story suspect. Tiberius made a barbed remark to Gellius, saying that Curvidius Fulvianus would have the most personal interest, but he himself would look into legal remedies when disrespect had been shown to a corpse.

We walked them right to their carriage. I noticed Publilia Lavinia called the driver Ergon. He snarled, 'Are we off, then?' in a jarringly familiar way.

They drove away. We did not wave goodbye.

'We shall see them again,' I told Tiberius.

'And will still disbelieve their patter!'

'Embroidery can always be unpicked.'

He had noticed Sparsus, the apprentice, sitting on a pile of excavated lava, cleaning his teeth with a fingernail, then cleaning his nails between his teeth. Sparsus told us he had been assigned to watch the driver, after Ergon was spotted poking around. Larcius had sent him smartly back to his vehicle; he thought the man must have been looking for the Hercules plaques. 'He gave us a mouthful. Luckily it was all foreign. Larcius just answered back, "Yes, it looks like rain tomorrow." The blighter spat, though not straight at him.'

Tiberius worried, 'That driver looked as if he could handle himself.'

'Fear not, Chief. Larcius would have laid him out in a minute.'

Tiberius was not reassured. 'I don't want fights. Have you found those damned plaques they want, Sparsus?'

'No, but we discovered where they must have been. Larcius picked up a broken corner, and the floor is covered with fine white dust under a staircase, just as the people said.'

'Larcius made a mention of intruders and lost tools,' Tiberius remembered with a frown. 'I didn't want to discuss it with him in front of the visitors.'

'We were going to tell you. Someone must have been here last night, Chief. That old fountain – the fellow with the wineskin – that was in the amphora store, it's been moved, as if someone was trying to pinch it. And a pickaxe has gone missing. Must be Dromo's ghosts!' giggled Sparsus.

Ghosts or not, Tiberius was bothered. 'We will have to set a night watchman . . . What about Drax? Did he have nothing to say for himself?'

'Oh, the woof was barking,' agreed Sparsus complaisantly. 'We had him shut in the stable because he keeps trying to get at the bones. None of us took any notice of him baying. We all thought he's missing Trypho.' Trypho normally guarded our sites overnight, while the dog guarded him. Trypho had refused to come south with the group; the others had amused themselves with various colourful reasons. The man had excused himself with a plea of travel sickness, but I thought he had been scared when Tiberius warned the men there would be bodies. We had dug out human remains in the past; Trypho never liked it.

★   ★   ★

We all returned to the house.

In the atrium we found Vindex and Dexter. They had taken my hint and were working. We watched them for a moment.

The atrium walls were composed of delicate, white-painted panels, with divisions formed from tall, narrow candelabra of fanciful design; these trailed grey-green leaves on which balanced tiny figures that pointed booted toes as they danced in the air. Lower regions of the panels had been buried; Tullius's two men now gently cleaned the once-glossy painted surface, half-inches at a time, gently picking away attached material, using small scrapers and brushes.

They seemed to know what they were doing. Occasionally they even nudged loose a recalcitrant knobble with a tooth-pick. In the main the task was easier. The grey infill that had built up from the eruption was dry and crumbly, quite soft to pull away. A beautiful frieze was emerging, with rows and squares of golden patterning that showed little damage.

On the opposite side of the atrium the workmen had stored tools for safety. Since this meant the interior could be claimed as theirs, they had brought in a bench, where I could see mess-tins and beakers neatly positioned alongside a cloth-covered basket. From now on, if we wanted to impress visitors with flirty canapés in our elegant entrance hall, the entertainment would be a row of chomping labourers in one-sleeved tunics.

'I see you are abandoning life in a tent,' Tiberius grumbled, mildly because at least their presence would protect the rest of us from intruders.

'Excellent idea of yours, Aedile,' smirked Sparsus.

I went to the kitchen. Dromo would have known I might come back so he had scrammed. Fornix said he had washed off blood from his battered face; he thought the lad's nose was not actually broken, though he feared infection. 'Someone threw a big punch at him, Albia. I don't reckon that fist was ectoplasm.'

'No, there really were thieves on the premises last night. Did you squeeze any more out of Dromo?'

'Not much. He was woken early by the dog barking. Instead of telling someone, he toddled off on his own little mission to find the water pipe – apparently you had offered a prize?'

'Oh, yes, blame me!'

'This is it. Dromo blithely walked in on the so-called ghosts when the trespassers were apparently trying to remove a fountain plinth by the bathhouse. He yelled, so instead they gave up and smashed a pipe. He heard one say, "Something else to think about, nosy Romans!" In Latin, incidentally. Dromo quaintly fancied they might acquire the pipe prize, so he ran at them, protesting. They let out shouts in some foreign language, and one went for him, hit him in the face, made him fall over. They ordered him to say he saw nothing, then disappeared, laughing.'

'Taking our pickaxe!'

Fornix groaned. 'Yes. Larcius is in a bate over that. He says it was his favourite – he made it himself. I had to brew up a pannikin of fresh mulsum to stop him creating.'

'Thanks for that. Everyone is on edge today . . . The thieves really scared Dromo?'

'They did, Albia. He slunk off to lick his wounds, saying he didn't want to talk about it.'

Suza found him later. Dromo was playing with a piece of dark cloth the intruders had dropped. He was wrapping it around his own head, covering his face, then murmuring, '*Whoo-hoo*,' through it.

Real bruises had come out where he had been thumped. The cut on his face was deep and ugly. Fornix was right. An all-too human fist had caused that. The black cloth turban was not ectoplasm either.

38

The Publilius siblings must have thrown on their coordinated green travelwear at dawn. Such an early getaway told me that cloaks had been waiting, ready brushed, and Ergon must have been stabling the carriage at Secunda's home. Did it mean the visitor I had glimpsed on the road stayed the night? So once more: who was he?

It seemed a good day for chivvying witnesses. The grey haze had blown away on the far side of the bay. There, Vesuvius reared with a pretence of innocence, although at its new summit the crater had captured a thin wisp of cloud that again looked like a trail of smoke. Campania lay in a patchwork, either inert black that would last for years or, where there was topsoil outside the volcanic plume's area, bountifully burgeoning. Perhaps life was faintly returning around the mountain, but for miles around, desert predominated. It was still too soon for even the most basic scrub and maquis to have snatched a toehold.

I paused again in the atrium to watch Vindex and Dexter picking off tephra. They did so with silent intensity, fascinated as they slowly revealed pictures and patterns from the past. They had a holy reverence for bringing back the wonderful designs that had probably been chosen by several generations. Uncovering them made me feel close to those previous people who had never planned to leave but would not pass this way again.

I found myself thinking about my father's nephew, a painter who was lost in the eruption with his wife and several young children. Larius had been trained at Stabiae. I could even have been looking at a fresco he had worked on.

'Good work, lads!' Fighting the lump in my throat, I practised my role as a domestic matron. It failed to convince. Vindex and Dexter had seen the scatty way I ran things at home. They stared.

'Can you give us some space, Flavia Albia? This is a specialist job. We need to concentrate.'

Fine.

I was waiting for my husband. Tiberius first had to agree a procedure for clearing the flood that was settled in huge pools out of doors, then for cleaning and drying interiors. After that, he wanted to go down to Stabiae, on the hunt for a fabricating plumber. Our men were capable of basic leadwork but he had decided against patching up: he glumly feared another leak if the job wasn't done properly. Looking ahead, he muttered that the damage would be all the worse if Uncle Tullius was in Rome at the time, so nobody noticed the problem. 'A new dispersal tank would be safest. Three tight junctions.'

Larcius and Serenus deployed colourful curses, but pretended to agree he was right. Now that the aqueduct link had been turned off, they managed to remove the holed contraption, which they carried to a cart for him. Somewhere on the Bay of Neapolis, Tiberius Manlius believed, there would be a specialist fitment-maker who could duplicate it. Originally the whole bay had been lined with luxury villas, until it seemed like a single linked city. That would have called for big quantities of prime sanitary ware. New properties were being built nowadays even on top of rocky debris

222

and mud. Wealthy homes in Pompeii, Herculaneum, Surrentum and right here at Stabiae would have been fitted with the best pipework accessories, which must have been made by somebody with skills. He meant to find that man.

I went with him. I had no interest in being dragged around yards and forges, but he was driving a cart down; a good informer grabs any available transport to save energy and, more important, boot leather. I could peel off for my own purposes. I felt bright with ideas about potential witnesses, but pulled a veil over my head to play the loyal wife.

'What are you up to?' he asked me, never fooled.

He dropped me at the apothecary's, claiming he would be back in an hour. I thought, Call that three ... We arranged that whoever finished first would wait at the Two Scallops. It would be a chance to catch up with Milo and Hyro, if their tribune still had them on standby.

Visiting the apothecary was to double-check on what he used to supply to the Curvidii, but I also enquired about an ointment against infection on Dromo's battered nose; he had never been known for keeping his face clean. Bathyllus, ever a natural therapist, told me the best thing was to hang up an old cheese in a barn, then scrape off its green growth and smooth that on the wound.

Don't blame me for insensitively testing this premise on a slave. I had heard the same folksy notion before. It came with provenance. The only problem was our love of cheese: in our house very little was ever left over to grow mould.

Regarding my case, I told Bathyllus we were being spun a flimsy tale that Primus died of natural causes, drowning in his bath. 'Could that easily happen?'

Bathyllus smirked. 'It could happen. Not easily.'

'If he had swallowed too many potions?'

The apothecary reprised that he had often sent anti-inflammation mixtures to Primus, any one of which could have made him woozy when mixed with too much wine. Primus also liked a hemp bolus, which was supposedly for 'earache'; if that ache had been vertigo, perhaps he keeled over because of it, off balance. 'He tried all the hardline pain-killers, henbane, mandrake, or sometimes the serious forms of poppy juice. He didn't take to that: he complained it made him constipated. I had warned him! He had fads. None of them lasted. At least that prevented addiction.'

Bathyllus confirmed there had been purchases of cala-mus oil for the bathhouse. He sneered that this was much used in Egypt. People supposed any unguent must be made from delightful flowers; calamus was a nasty kind of river sedge.

'Slippery?'

'Lethal. I mix it with olive or almond oil to make it usable.'

'Why did you supply that to a suspected drunk?'

'One of his house-guests had worked at the hot springs. They ought to have known what they were doing. I can issue warnings – which I would swear in court I did – but people do have to take responsibility for their decisions.'

I said not to worry. I thought it unlikely anyone would sue Bathyllus if Primus had slipped over on his bath lotion. 'Tell me, then, you supplied Primus. Do you still send opiate mixtures to his sister?'

For the first time, I thought Bathyllus looked shifty. 'Never since she went away. At least, never directly, as far as I know. Of course, if a third party buys drugs without saying who they are for, I am none the wiser.'

'By "third party" do you mean Gellius or Lavinia?'

'Oh, I haven't seen either of them since they went off with Fulvia Secunda . . . Why? Are you suspicious of them?'

'They are stalling. They gave me a version of events for when Primus died, but I still think there is more to it.'

'No witnesses?' Bathyllus asked hopefully.

'None I would trust.'

There might have been one. If that was right, I was on his trail.

I went next to the second-hand furniture store. Unluckily the man in charge, Septumius, was absent; Criton, the ex-slave, was out with him. I was told this by the nephew, Crispus. I felt annoyed, because I suspected Criton might have seen the so-called accident. I wondered whether he had not only been badly treated, but the death scene had made him so frightened, it explained why he ran away.

'I'm sorry to miss him. I want to ask if he used to carry water for Curvidius Primus to bathe. Has he ever told you about that? I believe the man died in some sort of mishap at home. It involved the tub I bought.'

Crispus had mastered the art of looking vague.

'All right, I shall have to ask Criton later.' I reminded Crispus his uncle had already told me the bath had belonged to the villa originally. Perhaps people had taken against it after the drowning fatality. Crispus agreed that sounded reasonable. 'They were selling off all sorts around that time – legendary!'

'I know there was a full house clearance. Were Gellius and Lavinia giving the instructions?'

'I believe so. It took a lot of trips to bring it all. I was only a child but there was so much going on I still remember the event. My grandpa did really well out of that sale.'

225

'They cleared out everything?'

'They seemed upset but, yes, as far as I remember from Grandpop, everything had to go. Not the fine art, of course. All the statues and urns, and movable pictures, were snaffled by a specialist they knew. But Gramps took every stick that was left, once the art dealer finished pulling out treasures for himself. They had really nice stuff. Finials on everything. No missing legs. Inlays. We had so much to sell, our business took a proper upturn – though sales had to wait until we came back from Nuceria.'

I had long since dismissed any assumption that the clearance was a panic move when the first lapilli began falling, the kind of reaction that eyewitnesses to the eruption reported: pick up goods and run. Gellius and Lavinia had agreed they took household goods away with Secunda, suggesting she left because Primus had died.

To be quite certain, I double-checked with Crispus. 'All this definitely occurred *before* Mount Vesuvius exploded? Immediately before?'

'Oh, yes, it must have taken a week to empty a whole house. The stuff was just about listed and stored here when we felt tremors and had to evacuate.' Then Crispus must have realised, as I did, that his uncle had been more reticent. The young man became nervous.

'Relax, Crispus. Nobody will blame you for telling me specifics.' Crispus applied his particular lack of interest. 'All right. Just one other thing, if you happen to know. Who was the specialist dealer who acquired the fine art?'

That he did know. When he told me, I was only half surprised.

My third visit that day was to the dealer's house. With hindsight, I ought to have waited for Tiberius, but I wanted to dash ahead. Somehow wise choices never look tempting.

For once the art dealer was at home. A serving-woman answered my knock. She said the householder had been to a meeting but had just that moment come home. I was shown in. I recognised the man. He must have realised who I was.

'Greetings, Sea Captain.' I got in first. 'My name is Flavia Albia. You must be Dexiades.'

39

B^{*lue eyes.*}

B lue eyes.
I always notice. One or both of my unknown birth parents must have had blue, which I had inherited, though with more colour than the pirate's pale wash. It makes me instinctively wonder. My family might have been traders from overseas, not Britons.

I had expected the man, from Sardinia, to be swarthier. But the woman who admitted me had had pale eyes and, later, when I met his other people so did they. Their island lay at a crossroads in the ocean so there must have been a complex mix of types.

It threw me. In the Mediterranean, where dark hair and eyes dominate, this was not what I had learned to expect.

Informers need to resist prejudice. There was no point feeling caught out simply by looks. A pirate posed much worse dangers than that.

He was handsome. Fifty years of liking what he saw in a barber's blurry mirror had inevitably given him superabundant confidence. A strongly rectangular face. A direct, knowing stare from below pulled-down brows. Beard, trimmed. Teeth much in evidence. A tan, though if he had spent a lot of time hanging onto sailing ropes, the results were not extreme. It must have been some while since he was crew and had had to climb masts. If his current ship had a cabin, this captain would be in it – relaxing, as he counted up the enormous sums that can be made from profiteering in art. I was an auctioneer's daughter; I knew.

The black headdress he wore was neither the wound turban nor the bulky balloon that potentates flaunt in the Orient; it was more of a wrapped hat. Tight against his head, spare material fell backwards, not turning to the front like a Phrygian cap. For extra dash he had wound around the edge a twisted rope of other, multi-coloured material. Seagoing types don't want their headgear blown off by frisky winds.

Instinctively, I lifted the edge of my stole to cover my hair. I never usually did that for interviews.

I had read enough Greek novels and seen enough comic plays to know that if Dexiades was a pirate, the adventure I had stupidly walked into would mean rape, imprisonment, separation from my true love for many, many years . . . Any bad male author would condemn me to marry the pirate, a solution to the rape issue. Or a real stinker would condemn me to a career as a priestess in a remote temple.

You may think me weirdly fixated, but Dexiades was flashing his smile with the intent charm of a peckish shark that scented blood. 'To what do I owe the pleasure?' I had been alone in the presence of truly dangerous men before. I might emerge alive from it, but never quite untouched. My thoughts must have been apparent to him. 'You are looking as if you have heard that superstitious nonsense about piracy! Such slander people put about.'

Long practice gave me a veneer of bravado: 'Not at all. You are said to be a quiet seaman, who rarely comes ashore. Besides, it's import/export nowadays, surely? Be warned, however: if pirates exist, neither my husband nor my father would pay a ransom.' I tried not to let my bangles jingle. 'On principle!' I commented. 'Very Roman.'

Falco and Faustus did love me. But if someone sent a ransom note, I could hear my father exclaiming, 'Not to worry, she'll get herself out of it.'

'You are not Roman?' The pirate was paying attention.

'I come from the north.'

'Full of wild fighting women!' The gleam in his eyes was typical. His machismo found this idea *extremely* exciting.

I set my feet together neatly. 'No. Full of tired women who are left to muck out the horses while the men are drinking and boasting together.'

'Not so exotic! You like horses?'

'Not keen – and I can't stand overweight exhibitionists. *The Dying Gaul* makes a good statue, but that's all you can say for him. He needs to put a comb through his hair.'

'But a fine physical specimen of manhood, in his prime, with noble courage!' Dexiades naturally allied himself with men in their prime, especially those who displayed heroic nude torsos. 'Dying of his wounds, and yet somehow undefeated.'

I scoffed. 'Your sales-talk could ring truer.' Whatever the pirate had expected it was not this kind of sparring. 'Be accurate, Dexiades. For starters, that Gaul is a Galatian. He's not a victim of Julius Caesar. He's gone down with his torque and buckler to a bunch of Hellenistic Greeks in skirts. The original is on the acropolis at Pergamon. Far too many copies are around, my father would say. It debases the market.'

The pale eyes narrowed. 'Your father is an expert?'

'His name is Falco, Didius Falco. Art or pastiche, he knows his stuff – and his business will handle it.' I applied the wide-eyed look of a woman who was acting honest. 'I could say I dropped in today to thank you for renting your house to my husband, and that I hope we left it clean and tidy ...' I straightened, adjusting bangles briskly. 'But I had a business motive. My family are auctioneers. I have been told you deal in statuary, though I must say, I was unimpressed by the *Augustus* I saw here. Still, somebody will buy it – or have you offloaded the piece already? You have sources, clearly. I presume your trade mostly consists of excavated goods from the buried cities?'

'All legitimate. All open.' He was bluffing there. 'The team I use are very professional. It's systematic – they even leave signs saying "house dug" after they have explored a buried property.'

'The best pickings were taken some time ago, like the marble and statues from the Forum at Pompeii?'

'Yes, retrieved almost immediately. We would like to continue the search – there must be many more choice pieces to come up. I know there was a good line of Amazons in a basilica at Herculaneum, for example. The problem now is finding labour, especially where massive tunnelling would be involved. Diggers have been buried alive when excavations collapsed on them. People in this area are beginning to want normal lives. The catastrophe is over. They want to forget.'

'Why not sell new works? Tradition is on your side, I think. Capua was always a workshop for copies of ancient art. My father still takes pieces from there. Romans don't object to decent covers from the Greek. They like to be given a choice of materials and size. "Fit your niche" artisans do well ... Otherwise, what's wrong with import/export?' I sympathised. 'I presume it is you who ships wine from the Gabius estate to Rome, so tell me, when you go up to the city, do you ever carry, let us say, more solid materials?'

'Ballast!' Dexiades called it.

I chortled mildly. 'The old "recovered stonework" trick. "Oh, port official, this is only an honest load of lumps for new building foundations." Also called avoiding the sales tax.'

'Never!'

He might fib, but I was relentless. 'Bilges stuffed with pentelic marble, old stone that just happens to be beautifully carved . . . Don't worry, we've been in business a long time. We know all about what goes on.'

He was too wily to confess – he must have been informed that the man who briefly rented his home had been a Roman magistrate. Faustus could be taking an unwelcome interest, and for all Dexiades knew, this was a trick. I could be representing an excise enquiry.

'Rest easy.' I smiled. He wasn't the only one here who deployed brute charm as a tool. 'I haven't been sent as a honey trap.'

'No,' Dexiades replied in a long drawl, finally revealing menace. 'You have come because you are poking your nose into the affairs of my good friends the Curvidius family.'

We dropped the pretence. I stood my ground. 'My interest is warranted and has been welcomed.'

'Oxen's offal!'

'A search has been requested. Curvidius Fulvianus, being absent in Rome, specifically asked my husband and me to find the body of his missing brother. He wants to know what really happened to him.' I decided against saying it was the local magistrate who had commissioned me. In small towns news travels fast. The pirate might already have been told.

In small towns everyone knows everyone else. It might even have been Apuleius Innocentius who had informed him.

Dexiades placed one hand at his waist, where he could have been hiding a dagger under a wide, wound cummerbund that gripped his long tunic. There was no pleasantry now. 'And what is your verdict, little lady?'

Dear gods, I hate condescension. 'We found the body. Two people called Gellius and Lavinia then professed that Curvidius Primus had died in an accidental drowning. At home, in his bathtub.'

'You believe that?'

'Difficult to prove otherwise. He is reduced to bones. But it would make sense.'

'Better for everyone to know the truth then.'

'Absolutely . . .'

Dexiades inclined his head. I could see him evaluating me. How gullible would I prove to be, the not-quite-Roman interfering female? Of course, I was assessing him too – and I thought this piece of bombast was ready to lie through his Sardinian teeth.

I watched carefully. There are tell-tales that every interviewee needs to avoid. Do not blink too fast. Look up at your questioner. Prevent leg trembles. Resist giving a positive statement with a negative head shake. Never fold your arms defensively.

The pirate folded his arms. He was looking down as he said, 'If he drowned in his bath, it could have been self-inflicted.'

'Suicide?'

'He had suffered atrocious pain for many years.'

'Then wasn't he used to it?'

'The misery became worse.'

'Until he could no longer endure it?'

'I suggest so.'

'You reckon he decided to end it all . . . Was that in character? Did you know him?' I demanded.

'I knew his brother-in-law. We did much business. An admirable man.' That would be Gabius, the wine-producer. Suza's friend Blossia had told her there was nothing against him, though that was hardly a compelling recommendation. 'I was, and am, extremely attached to his sister.' Dexiades made no comment on Secunda's current distressed state.

I raised the issue: 'I met her. I am troubled about those who are caring for her. They dose her with unsuitable medicine, for one thing. Gellius and Lavinia have a lavish lifestyle. Where did that come from? It's open to question what their motives are, or have been in the past. The obvious answer is that they are preying on weaker members of this family. And why are they so keen to see the remains of Curvidius Primus cremated very fast, not waiting for his brother to attend the funeral?'

The pirate shrugged, abdicating responsibility. 'They are said to be nice people.'

'Ah, yes. And friends of the family!'

Dexiades had not so far admitted that he knew the Publilii. In fact 'said to be nice people' implied he did not. He must realise I was the crazy driver who nearly ran his carriage down on the Via Minerva. To me it was obvious where he had been going: he went to see the siblings, stayed with them, no doubt discussed Primus, chewed over what I had said, then loaned them his two-wheeler and the driver, Ergon, for their next-day visitation. I was now sure *he* had told the couple who my husband was, and the work we were known for. Perhaps it was Dexiades who urged them to change their original story into something that might sound more credible.

I dropped the issues around the Publilii, going up a generation. 'So you knew the vineyard couple, Gabius and Secunda. You knew them when he was still alive, and you still know her. What about her brother, Primus? Did you know him too – did you know him well?'

'Well enough.'

'Did you visit him?'

'On occasions.'

'Business or pleasure?'

'Business mainly.'

'Tell me, then,' I challenged suddenly, 'were you at his villa on that fatal occasion before dinner when he died?'

A very slight shadow that must imply deception moved in those light eyes. 'Oh, no!' His arms were still folded. He was still lying. 'No, I was not there that day. Primus would never have me to dine.'

'A pity. You could have helped me . . . Suicide, accident – or something worse?' I spoke the words lightly, then changed direction: 'What did you think of the man?'

Perhaps it sounded as if I had moved on. Dexiades unfolded his arms. He gave a description of Primus, assertively, a man who was used to controlling conversations. 'A sad case. An unhappy life. Roaring with ire, often for no reason. To be honest, Flavia Albia, Primus was the most unpleasant, aggravating nuisance. If he did commit suicide, part of his reason was to upset other people. He hated everyone around him. He loved causing problems.'

I replied, as if testing the theory, 'Even so, the Publilius siblings liked him, especially Gellius.'

235

'You have heard that?'

'I have been told, and not only by them, that Gellius and Primus were honestly good friends.' Dexiades pulled a face that said Gellius was a fool then. 'Supposedly friends of the family.' When he made no answer, I tried out, 'Or do you think they are always just friends to themselves?'

'I think you are a very wise lady!'

And I thought the pirate's opinion was worthless if he could not tell how badly I loathed his kind of meaningless flattery.

40

I wanted to get out of there. I prepared my move towards the door of the room. Although I felt he recognised my anxiety, the pirate made no attempt to stop me. Since we had briefly lived there, I knew the layout of the house. I would have to negotiate a narrow corridor, then wrestle with the front doors. I wondered how many other people were there. I wondered how long it would take me to run to the Two Scallops, and whether anyone I knew would be at the bar if I managed to reach it.

Stupid girl, Albia.

'I must go,' I stated decisively. 'I have arranged to meet my husband. He will be tapping his foot already ...' Time had gone by; that might even be true. Reaching the room door, I turned back – an old trick that never deceives villains. 'Another reason I called in, Dexiades, was to ask you about the valuables, the statues and artwork, that you handled when they stripped out the Curvidius villa.'

'I was happy to assist,' he answered.

'You removed all the high-value items?'

'I could advise on what fine art was worth.'

'And take a cut? ... Primus was dead, but would not have approved – not if, as you said, you were someone he never wanted to dine with.'

'His loss! He was a scratchy man. He often took against

people. But Fulvia Secunda was pleased for me to be around, to help at that difficult time.'

'I am trying to grasp the timescale, but I think it was after Primus had died?' Dexiades nodded. 'She was highly agitated but let the removal of chattels carry on around her? This can be difficult for dealers,' I sympathised, as if using knowledge from my father's work. 'The way this clearance happened could be seen as suspicious – though, of course, in your work you are accustomed to handling deceased persons' estates . . .'

'The house had to be closed up urgently. Poor Secunda – I am so fond of her – grew very anxious to leave. It had become, for her, such a tragic location. Her brother's accident aged her overnight.'

'Now you call it an accident, not suicide?'

'What does anyone else say?'

'Gellius and Lavinia insist it was an accident. No one else survives, unfortunately . . . When all the contents were sold up, did the Publilius siblings take an active part in that decision?'

'Understandably. Poor Secunda allowed them to take charge. They helped her with everything that needed doing,' Dexiades reassured me. 'They care for her devotedly to this day.'

'So they say!'

'They are very protective.' He said it almost grudgingly, as if they kept him out.

'I think she needs that. I am glad she has someone.' Softening, I went along with the idea of the siblings as guardians. 'But you see why I asked about property. Gellius and Lavinia claim they gained nothing from Primus's death – yet they assert that his will left them a legacy for being so "helpful" during his lifetime.'

238

'So?' asked the pirate, narrowly.

'According to his brother in Rome, Primus left no will. Of course, that is an issue for Fulvianus, if he chooses to raise it, though I shall certainly have to tell him what Gellius and Lavinia are claiming. He may wish to check how much they have taken from the estate, or whether they were entitled to anything at all. In his position, I know I would be very wary ... Tell me,' I sprang on him, 'to whom did you pay over the profits from the artworks?'

'Gellius and Lavinia,' replied Dexiades at once. 'Fulvia Secunda was in no condition to handle financial matters. I presume they passed the money over.'

'You saw no proof?'

'I would not expect to.'

'No, of course. Still, being fair, Primus may well have wished to assign gifts to them. Fulvianus may similarly choose to say thank you. In light of how much the young couple have done for his brother and his sister, rewarding them seems more than acceptable.' I sighed ruefully. Then I returned to it: 'But how much did they take for themselves, after Primus died? Nobody seems to have been looking at their actions. Did they appropriate too much? And had Primus accustomed them to receiving presents, in cash or in kind, while he was still living? It's clear that nowadays Fulvia Secunda has little say – and to me that is dangerous.'

Dexiades drew himself up like a cockerel about to crow. 'Do not,' he announced, 'fear for Fulvia Secunda! I am myself a very great friend of hers. The best friend she could ever have. Gellius and Lavinia know I am constantly watching what happens to her. They cannot move without me. I will always protect her interests.'

I was startled by his vehemence. I said I was relieved that someone with warm intentions was monitoring the guardians. Then I left.

No one prevented me. I was relieved to see those young boys who looked for stealable donkeys were loitering in the street outside as ever. They might not react to a scream, but afterwards friends of mine might quiz them . . .

Dexiades had followed me to the door. On the threshold he let slip that he knew we were refurnishing the villa. Would we like any decorative statues? He had a selection of pretty items that he would be delighted to show us.

I laughed gaily. Not if that meant his marble *Augustus*! In any case, my father would be horrified if we bought objects from anybody else. 'Family obligation.'

'Family discount?' chortled Dexiades.

I gave him a mysterious smile and once more suggested that he contact Falco if he had anything interesting to sell. My pa would be no pushover, I thought, not even for a pirate who acted as if he had a divine right to obfuscate.

I walked at a smart pace to the Two Scallops. A man I had never seen before, dressed in black with a dark headdress, materialised behind me. He walked all the way to that bar with a persistence informers recognise. He was following me.

41

I could see Hyro and Milo sitting outside the Two Scallops.
They were with a couple of other men, who also looked
paramilitary. Their size, their build, their manner were all clues.

I managed to gain speed as I neared the bar, mouthing a
silent plea. Hyro and Milo looked preoccupied, but they
stood up slowly, so my tail would see they were watching me
approach. I hoped they would not simply assume he was a
normal pest, a harasser who ignored wedding rings, the kind
of social fungus I could deal with myself.

Hyro called my name. The man behind stopped to scratch
his wide waist wrap, as if a hidden weapon was chafing him.
Then he swung around and walked off with swinging
nonchalance, back in the other direction. I skipped through
a hedge of wizened greenery into the oily, fishy aura of the
Two Scallops. Hyro and Milo sat down again, making space
on their bench for me.

I was safe, so I saw no reason to fuss. I noticed there were
empty beakers, but nobody was eating or drinking. Taking in
the sombre mood, I let my two friends introduce me. Their
companions, who also wore faded red tunics, were similar
wide-shouldered, twisty-scarred, shaven-headed fellows with
bunions peeping through their strappy boots. Like my two
they were members of the Seventh Cohort of Vigiles. 'Acer
and Antigonus.'

'Greetings, Antigonus and Acer. My contacts are closer with the Fourth, that shameless bunch of renegades,' I told them, as light conversation while I let them get used to me. 'Hyro and Milo call me the Girl from the Aventine. We worked together on the theatre-killer case.' Hard to tell whether the newbies were impressed, even though those gruesome murders had been recent and notorious.

For a moment we all sat there. Nobody was speaking, as if a previous conversation had been put on hold when I joined the group. A couple of travel packs leaned beside the newcomers' bench, so I looked down at the luggage and broke the spell. 'Have I interrupted something? Or aren't you able to tell?'

Hyro seemed embarrassed. 'We know we can say anything in front of you, Flavia.'

'Don't call her Flavia,' Milo intoned quietly.

I waved it away. 'What's up, my dears? Seventh having secrets?'

Antigonus shifted, which caused the bench to groan under the new boys' considerable heft. 'If she's safe, you'd better tell her.'

They all seemed shy. To help out, I put my palms flat on the table in front of me, straight-armed, then started a story for them. 'What can the explanation be? Red tunics don't take seaside holidays. If this is an expedition, I am surprised to see the Seventh operating so far from Rome. I am not even sure it's legal. Can I guess this has something to do with your high-life tribune?'

'You said it!' exclaimed Acer. He seemed relieved to unburden himself but disgusted by the problem. 'The big boy's done a flit. A whole century of us have been ordered to haul him home.'

'But,' hissed Milo, 'Albia – you haven't seen them!'

'Incognito?' I tried not to laugh. 'Yes, roaming about here openly might cause red faces. An officer is out on an unapproved spree? Risks a black mark on his career scroll, so his longed-for promo to the Praetorian Guard may be doomed? Seventy men and a knock-kneed centurion are dropped off the firefighting complement, to take a three-day march from Rome – bringing him a recall? This is strange stuff, my friends. Good grief, let's hope the Emperor doesn't notice the kerfuffle . . . Who sent you?'

'The Prefect of Vigiles.'

I was amazed. 'The top totty? Hang about! Caunus came on a formal operation. He is supposedly looking into corn imports, cluing up on granary logistics. If he's a little late with his findings, surely the prefect will give him an earful, but not call him a deserter?'

'This is looking serious!' Milo tried to quieten me, though there was nobody to overhear. Even the waiter was leaving us alone. Waiters know when to allow a 'business meeting' on their premises. They place their hope in calls for a huge drinks round, once the chat finishes.

I lowered my voice respectfully. 'Has something gone wrong?'

'Nobody knows where he is,' murmured Acer.

'Partying, we thought?'

'Nobody can find the party,' replied Antigonus.

'Last seen here, though? Didn't he promise to rendezvous with Hyro and Milo at the Two Scallops?'

'Should have crawled back to us by now,' Milo spelled out. 'He's been on the lam for two weeks. That's a very long party.'

'It's a party we might all wish we'd been invited to!' I stopped joshing and asked grimmer questions. 'What's the score? You boys told me he made friends with a seaman, who ferried him over from Puteoli. Milo, didn't you sail with them? Can you point out the vessel?'

'The boat's gone.'

'When did it leave?'

'Straight away,' said Hyro.

'What was its name?'

With hangdog looks, they admitted they did not know. Milo confessed, 'One evening it berthed at the port. We came down the gangplank. Next morning, the boat had vanished. We took no notice. We had been told Caunus was being taken somewhere for entertainment, some celebration squash that his crony had bigged up.'

'A brothel, presumably! He must have swallowed the old myth provincial swindlers use to entice dumb-looking tourists: "Come with us to a real fancy place, known only to the fun-loving." How could Caunus have fallen for a con like that? "There's a beautiful bar that only a local can find for you . . ." Who lured him? What's the name of his new pal?'

No joy there. Caunus must have called the fellow something. But when Caunus brought them with him, Milo and Hyro were only his escort and he was an officer who enjoyed being oblique. On board ship, Caunus and his playmate shared a flagon in the cabin, no doubt promising themselves it was the forerunner of many, served by slim, smiling girls in see-through skirts. The vigiles, who knew they would not be invited, had stood beside the ship's rail, gossiping about plays. Would they be shipwrecked and flung onto a rocky island where unfriendly fishermen would sell them into slavery? Now they thought that would have been a safer adventure than real life.

For me, it left one question. We were a long way from Rome. Caunus might be expected back in the office, bearing his report, but in normal bureaucracy two weeks of absence would be much too soon for anxiety. It was amazing that anyone in Rome had even noticed. Indeed, hard to think anybody cared.

I turned to Acer and Antigonus. 'This is all odd. Tell me, what are your orders?'

Acer tried to dodge. 'Only our centurion has seen the orders. Rufeius.'

'Is he any good?'

'Negative.'

'Typical! And not here.'

'Not yet. He's bringing the rest of the lads around the bay.'

'From where? How far away?'

'About half a day. We came on ahead. He fixed us a lift by donkey, after he was told the tribune had headed for Stabiae.'

I stayed patient. 'All right. What do we know? Your man with the swagger-stick, useless Rufeius, marched his century south, keeping the mission a secret. Did he report to anyone in Puteoli or Neapolis on arrival? What are his instructions – what are you men doing on a daily basis?'

Acer had given up in despair. He sat back to let Antigonus tell me. 'Two days ago, we marched in, at Puteoli. We came down the route of the new highway the Emperor is creating.'

'No new highway is built yet,' I challenged.

'In planning,' said Acer. 'Via Domitiana. Fast link to the Misenum fleet. It's due to follow an old route we came on – branches off the Appia then sneaks in via the Fiery Fields.'

I raised my eyebrows. 'The old road to Cumae? You really were travelling in secret?'

245

'Being discreet, our centurion's words,' Acer filled in. 'Slipping south like spirits. He didn't want a vigiles section being spotted on the Via Appia.'

'He thought you might be *watched*?' That seemed utterly unlikely. 'Humour me. You tiptoed in, avoiding crackpot spies en route, and . . .?'

'Began quietly searching house to house for Caunus.'

'Brothel to brothel and bar to bar, you mean?'

'Everywhere,' Antigonus insisted. 'Any building where a man could hide. Houses, shops, granaries, shacks. Up grassy tracks to farms. Down into cisterns. A cellar, well and roof-space search.'

'Theatres,' said Hyro, as if that clinched it.

'Some of the lads were sent one way, towards the trireme base at Cape Misenum, via Baiae. They took a report to show the fleet commander.' Acer groaned. 'He will have sailors going on board ships, and even looking in caves.' The fleet commander might be an ex-consul. If he knew about this, and had been roped in, it was no practice exercise.

'Bugger me!' cried Milo, to whom the use of sailors must have been news. 'If any marines turn up old Caunus while he's enjoying a very long crash-out in a cave full of naughty sea nymphs, he'll go crackers!'

Antigonus laughed. '*Morning, Tribune. Put your tackle away. Urgent recall from the prefect!*'

'*Get sober, get shaved,*' added Acer. '*Get scared of retribution . . .*' Although they were envious of the bender Caunus had fixed up for himself, they appeared tenderly proud of their tribune for his exploits. I sensed true worry that his unauthorised play-day was promising to land him in the proverbial mound of mule shit. Of course, if Caunus was court-martialled, they would be assigned a new man, which carried all the horror of the unknown. They needed to restore their own to favour.

'Somehow you heard he went to Stabiae?' I asked.

'Rufeius,' said Antigonus. 'He must have some special source of information.'

'A barmaid,' guessed Hyro.

'Well, she's too late. Caunus is a goner,' Hyro assessed it sadly. 'No general in a Medusa breastplate will fix another medal on his chest. This is the end of his rewards for valour. When he turns up, he's never going to talk his way out.'

'Hail and farewell, Gaius Caunus!' Milo pronounced, as if presiding at a funeral.

It was a measure of their low mood that when the Scallops' waiter put his head out, most of them held up their hands, refusing tuck and drink. Hyro called him back to ask for a beaker of Lactarii Mountains wholesome milk. Surprisingly, it was provided. 'You won't be wanting olives!' snarled the server. Hyro drained his cup in one long movement, then growled, no, he did not want fart-arse olives, thank you very much. He already had a broken heart and did not need herby oil spilled on his tunic.

This was the scene when a cart drew up, disgorging my husband. Tiberius peered at Hyro's beaker, surveyed the otherwise empty table, and nodded to the newcomers. I told him their names and century commander; he did not seem surprised. I said glumly, 'There's a bit of a stink, Faustus.'

Tiberius had the depressed air of a man to whom bureaucratic idiocy was always wearing, never new. 'Yes, I heard.'

The four vigiles sat up. They surveyed him as if he must have met a sphinx that spouted oracles.

I explained that Manlius Faustus was an oddball who believed in openness. He gave me a thoughtful look, then confirmed he believed people should be told what they were up against. This matter was too serious for furtively exchanging rumours during a pee in a public latrine.

'Now you're talking our language!' Acer cried admiringly.

Tiberius inclined his head shyly, then, being him, began at the start. He had been at a forge, talking to a man who had agreed to replicate his broken pipe fitment. 'He thinks we should get one in Capua – that's the best source for decent metalwork. I left the old part with him. He will organise a new one for us,' he told me, while the vigiles writhed with impatience.

'Let him unwind, lads. So, what happened, love?' I nudged gently, well used to his style of withholding.

'While I was telling him where to bring it, men with a warrant visited the forge.'

'Troops from Rome?'

'Locals. A posse of spare-time stevedores and shepherds. Armed, in so far as they were, with staves and sickles.'

'Urgent?'

'No, more like sauntering around with an air of puzzlement.'

Tiberius had charmed these characters. They revealed that Apuleius Innocentius, the duovir, had sent them out on an errand to look for somebody. Respecting that they were supposed to be discreet, Tiberius went to question the magistrate directly.

'Apuleius was delighted to see me. He wants my advice on what to do. He has received a disturbing missive from Rome – he thinks all the duoviri in Campania towns have been sent it. Took half a day to crack the cipher. Once he managed the code and saw what it said, he went into a blue funk. If he gets this wrong, it will be more than a smacked wrist from the Palatine. Whatever he tries, it's damned dangerous.'

'For whom?' I demanded.

'There's a missing tribune.' By now that was no surprise.

'It's Caunus! The rogue Hyro and Milo have to wait around for.'

Tiberius shook his head. 'Caunus may have intended to enjoy himself drinking and dancing, but we know he isn't doing so.' We all sat up straighter. 'Far from sleeping it off in a gutter, he has been kidnapped,' my husband announced.

'Kidnap?' the four vigiles all jerked and exclaimed.

Now he had started, Tiberius succinctly explained: 'Ransom demand sent to Rome – anonymous, of course. His rank is known, so his importance is realised. A large sum to free him has been specified, though so far with no delivery instructions.'

'Juno!' I muttered. 'What's being done about this?'

'Distress and outrage, followed by aimless pottering – the normal nonsense. Vigiles troops are on their way; locals are on alert to identify his location and whoever is holding him. Meanwhile, the kidnappers take the usual severe line: *Do anything official and we will throw him off a rock in Capreae.*'

'So Capreae is the last place he will be.' I snorted. 'Though the island is so full of massive imperial villas, he could be chained up in a cryptoporticus, pretty well anywhere. Manlius Faustus,' I used his formal name because of the listening vigiles, 'you see what this is. Historically, this kind of thing was organised by pirates.'

'Pirates like Dexiades?'

'I met him today, I need to tell you.'

'Flavia Albia!'

249

'Settle down. I emerged unscathed . . .' Tiberius dropped his head into his hands; the vigiles surveyed him with sympathy. I continued merrily: 'Dexiades would be an idiot to pull a stunt like this. Everyone knows what his trade is said to be so he would be a prime suspect. Seizing a public official for ransom would be madness too. He did not strike me as that kind of crazy.'

Tiberius replied gruffly that Apuleius Innocentius had already summonsed the pirate for an interview. That could be why Dexiades had been in Stabiae at his own house that morning, though of course he had not given me an explanation. Apuleius had said he stuck to the usual plea, that all his business was legitimate trading. There was no evidence otherwise: he produced a list of whereabouts for the time the tribune must have been taken. Apuleius had had to let him go with a caution.

'Apuleius has personal knowledge of him,' Tiberius told me with distaste. 'A connection we could do without. That statue of Augustus now lives in the duovir's garden. I saw it. Had to be the same one.'

'Did you say anything?'

'We were not discussing art. I leaned a rake in its hand to show our opinion of the purchase.'

'Good – assuming the duovir bought it fairly, and it's not a bribe . . . I don't like him and the pirate nuzzling.'

Tiberius agreed. 'Still, Rome's involvement may protect against local laxity. Apuleius fully understands that he and any actions he takes – or action he omits, come to that – are now under imperial scrutiny.'

'Down here, that may not worry him. He's a bonehead, you said.'

'He's a numbskull – but ambitious. If he bungles finding Caunus, he loses any hope of preferment from Domitian.'

At the Emperor's name, the vigiles became restless. They had to await orders from their centurion but Tiberius told them that, although he and I could offer little help, any resources we had would be available if wanted. We would leave them to await their comrades. We prepared to take our cart back up to the villa.

He summed up for them the gravity of the problem that faced the authorities. 'It's a horrible, complete mess. Caunus will certainly be kept well hidden. His life has been threatened – that has to be taken at face value so you must tread very carefully. But he needs to be found extremely fast. The longer this situation continues, the jumpier his captors will be, therefore the more chance they will slit his throat and we will never find his body.'

42

Tiberius drove. Suza had described my style.

As if bodies in future were not enough of a worry, past ones had also become relevant. 'By the way,' he said to me, as we began the journey, 'I learned that the duovir has Fulvianus staying with him. At his house. Just arrived from Rome. Wants to view whatever is left of his brother, then fix up a funeral. Apparently, he thinks it would be appropriate to hold the ceremonies at the villa.'

'*Our* villa?'

'Of course,' grumbled Tiberius, downheartedly.

This called for thought, knowing my husband's piety. 'I hope he's not asking you to let him erect a monument? Better take a stand: if he is planning a tomb, he has to buy back some ground from Uncle Tullius. *We* get to say where he can have it . . .' Roadside would be traditional. Once we allowed a burial, the land would be sanctified by the physical presence of bones and its eternal possession by the soul of Primus. Caretaking would not be our responsibility – unless we chose to pull out weeds – but we would be obliged to show respect and strangers would have a right to visit, in perpetuity.

Tiberius seemed to read my mind. 'The family must have a mausoleum somewhere. We haven't found one here.'

'That's true. No *Dear Passerby, stop and think kindly of me because I died too young.* No *This tomb of mine extends for one thousand paces side-to-side and three hundred front-to-back and the heirs may never sell up or permit encroachment.* Not even *Move along. Kindly don't piss or shit on me.*'

Tiberius gave a gleam in confirmation. He assured me, 'I am confident Uncle Tullius would reach an advantageous agreement.'

'Yes, but you are on the spot, dealing with it. You are a pious man and I don't want anyone taking advantage of your good nature.'

'I am impressed,' my husband told me, 'by how smoothly you have adopted the role of a strong-minded wife!'

I gave him a biff with fingertips and let the tomb issue drop. 'So Fulvianus knows the duovir?'

'Not really. Different generations, and he left for Rome too long ago. But he thinks it is a duovir's remit to play host to important visitors.'

'So he *is* taking advantage of someone!' I glimpsed how the family behaved locally. 'Curvidius has never held office as far as we know. He is unimportant, surely.'

'Relatively, but he's a local by birth, who has suffered a difficult bereavement, so diplomatic courtesy requires assistance.'

I scoffed. 'Clean sheets, big breakfast, a slave to clean his boots. He beats the slaves and has use of all the stationery? What does the duovir's wife say to that?'

'Not much. I met her, a pleasant woman doing her best to cope. When she saw me, I could hear her screeching silently, *And here's another dropping in to cause more panic and eat all the almond fancies.* You would like her. I never saw Curvidius, by the way. He had dumped his luggage on them, spent one night snoring so the roof joists trembled, then today had nipped out for lunch with an old friend.'

253

'He still has friends in this area?'

'Seemingly.'

Not us, I thought.

We continued in silence. A generous hostess would have started considering how this funeral could be organised. Curvidius had not even bothered to tell us he was here. I felt disinclined to view his event as my responsibility.

No escape. We were a respectable household. Almost certainly the task would end up with me.

At least I had a good steward, and he was here. Gratus would smoothly glide into action, never refusing to assist, never revealing his contempt for the parties involved. I could imagine him describing the nuisance afterwards with me: counting napkins, mopping vomit off children, placing seats for the infirm, making sure the ghastly group were all shunted out afterwards. Reminding them to take their bloody urn home with them! (Only, of course, if they were not setting up a tomb on our uncle's land.)

I tucked a hand through his arm and leaned against Tiberius slightly while he drove. As always, he was warm, solid and accommodating. Conscious that I was in thinking mode, he saw no need to interrupt.

My commission to uncover what had happened to Primus would be disrupted by the approaching funeral. It meant more than simply preparing for drunken aunties and stopping hired musicians stealing our bronze spoons. Now that his brother had arrived on the scene, I felt more pressure and urgency. We needed to be sure about any plot that had befallen the deceased. Ideally I would discover his true fate by the time his skeleton was eulogised.

In a just world, this funeral would be put on hold. One meeting with Curvidius Fulvianus had warned me that that would never happen. At dinner with Uncle Tullius, the man had been polite, but I was sure he would brush aside any request from me for time to provide clarity. He might just about let Tiberius take a stand on the matter – a man, and an ex-magistrate – but my commission from the duovir would be ignored.

Better get a grip. I had dealt with attempts at sidelining before. They never stopped me, even though the problem needed to be shoved out of my way. So where did things stand? What did I currently suspect?

As a whole, the Curvidius family had been locally disliked, while Primus attracted particular bad reviews. Depending on who was speaking, he had been awkward, unpleasant, aggressive, a brute and, towards the end, helplessly befuddled, perhaps by drugs and certainly by drink. Primus might have drowned in his bath, but I had doubts about what had led up to it and how it happened. My suspicions centred on the Publilius siblings.

The situation indisputably suited them. Gellius and Lavinia had acquired good, comfortable homes for more than ten years. They profited from their aunt's death, and admitted they had gained financially from Primus himself. A big question mark hung over that. They claimed he had left them a legacy, yet Curvidius Fulvianus had said no will had survived. He would need to clarify the position. If the Publilii were too grasping, he might need to retrieve what they had taken. That could make his own position awkward. He might have to justify his handling of the estate.

I had already been pondering how much the siblings had profited. Were they stealing while they lived with Primus? Was it ongoing? Could it be shown they were stealing from Secunda now? I would recommend that Fulvianus act by bringing in an auditor, and fast.

Time might have changed the situation. I did believe that when Gellius and Primus first became acquainted at the thermal springs, their friendship was natural and strong. But after the siblings moved up to live at the villa, maybe they took their position for granted. Was it possible that Primus became too fond of wine to cope with a situation that was growing murkier? Did he really take to drink after his wife died? Did Gellius and Lavinia then find they could peel off funds, steering him into over-reliance on them and abuse of himself, until a point came when it was easier simply to murder him?

The idea of them as killers grew stronger with me after I saw his sister's predicament. By all accounts she had once been a woman who stood up for herself. If Secunda knew there had been a murder it might explain her mental collapse. Perhaps she even witnessed the crime, then lived in a nightmare, knowing what had happened to her brother yet unable to do anything about it. She had little or no contact with Fulvianus in Rome. Her only connections seemed to be a dubious pirate who had known her late husband – and the Publilii.

Primus dying would be accepted. He had abused his body; he was always at risk; he might have fallen in his bath. People who failed to work out the timeline might believe the ash cloud from Vesuvius had contributed, but in any case his unfortunate end would seem sadly natural to outsiders. Face it: passing away from over-indulgence was relatively common.

I had to consider urgently that, with questions now being asked, it could threaten his sister's safety. I was unhappy about how Suza had observed Gellius and Lavinia 'looking after' Secunda. From what the apothecary had said about painkillers, drug abuse might have started with Primus. Was the same thing simply happening again?

No one would think twice if Secunda were also to die now. She was older, tremulous and fragile. Old ladies reach the end of their thread; they pass away; it's nothing odd.

Assume my fears were true. Assume the couple deliberately hid Secunda, telling the world she was traumatised, while they over-medicated her to keep her silent and passive. Would they take that wickedness to the ultimate? But if killing her was their plan, why had Gellius and Lavinia kept Fulvia Secunda alive for so long? Ten years? Well, there might be a reason: they might need her alive because, once she was gone, their free access to her resources would end. They had no ties of blood with her. She had family. On death, her estate would pass elsewhere.

In a classic fraud, the Publilii might persuade Secunda to write a will leaving them everything. But that might not be feasible. Families tie up their property so women cannot keep it. In particular, Secunda might have only a lifetime interest in what Gabius, her late husband, left behind. Perhaps he had other heirs, figures who were waiting for his widow to be gone. They might be very eager to inherit a prime vineyard. So long as Secunda remained alive, the property was vulnerable to predators. But if she went, it might well be that Gellius and Lavinia went as well: kicked out.

Why had any of this been allowed to happen? What had given Gellius and Lavinia such influence? Why had nobody restrained them? Was Secunda an unwanted problem? Were her own relatives happy to abdicate responsibility? Had her friends all died or had she been deliberately isolated?

Deeply concerned, I tried to imagine the siblings first taking hold. Had Primus ever challenged them? His temperament was volatile. Any realisation that he was being duped might have fired him up, especially against young people he had once welcomed into his home. I had some evidence that neighbours had viewed them askance; if he had complained, other people might have listened. He had had a sister and a brother alive, possibly more relatives. He had owned a house full of slaves too. In theory he could have rounded up protectors. That might have given Gellius and Lavinia a need to do away with him.

I could not grasp him or his predicament. He was too long gone. He was unreal to me.

His sister was different. I had seen her. Did Secunda have any understanding of the way she was being controlled? I grasped why she had been so swiftly extracted from the villa and whipped away to her own old estate a long way down the Surrentum peninsula. Fewer people would see her plight, if plight it was.

How must it feel to be trapped in your own home by people who say they have your interests at heart? If they are preying on you, what can you do? To others, they look smart, kindly and charitable. They seem completely innocent. They pretend to be grateful. They pretend *you* are grateful to *them*. Who will believe they are predators? Who would ever think that a self-willed woman, who once famously listened to nobody, could be ruthlessly exploited by nail-hard young charmers?

When Secunda ended up trapped by 'helpful guardians', was that why she stopped communicating? If outsiders believed in the devoted care she was supposedly receiving, what could she do? Things might go hard for her behind closed doors. Besides, any accusation she made would look like the ramblings of a confused elderly person.

Worse possibility: did she even begin to wonder whether she had mistaken the situation? Perhaps she felt that these lovely youngsters were genuine, that they simply could not be at fault. Perhaps she feared her mind had begun to fail her. Old age had slyly come upon her. Dementia was claiming her tired brain.

It could even be true. Had she, for natural reasons, now lost her memory, her character, her powers of reasoning? That would mean Gellius and Lavinia were in command of all they wanted.

'What have you been scheming?' asked Tiberius, as we neared the villa.

I summarised my thoughts. Now they were firmed up, it did not take long. 'I have been thinking that Fulvia Secunda is at risk. At her age, if she dies, who will ever look into it as a suspicious event?'

'You would.'

True. If anything happened while Gellius and Lavinia were in charge, I would investigate. Besides, her brother was in the district, so I would drag him into action for her.

After he had parked the cart, Tiberius jumped off first, then lifted me down. Hands on my waist, he said thoughtfully, 'I agree with all you say.'

'But?'

'You will need to check carefully whether you can prove any of this, Albia.'

Serenus had come forwards to unhitch and stable our beast for us. Nodding thanks, Tiberius and I walked together slowly towards the main house.

'I know,' I assured Tiberius. 'I cannot afford to get such an accusation wrong. A mistake could do more damage to

Secunda – assuming Gellius and Lavinia are really taking advantage of her.'

'Is there any doubt?'

Thinking about the old lady had germinated unexpected ideas. I stopped in my tracks and tried them out on Tiberius. 'We have heard that Fulvia Secunda once had as feisty a personality as her brother. Didn't Pescennius Neo, our neighbour, say the Curvidii were always quarrelling and fighting? Someone else told a story that they were all expelled from a school.'

Tiberius nodded. 'Weren't the words "Girls as well as boys"?'

'Exactly. We have definitely heard that Primus and Secunda never listened to each other, or if he ever shouted at her, she yelled straight back.'

'So?'

Tiberius opened the main doors for me to enter the atrium.

'What if,' I suggested, as the new idea gained strength, 'Gellius and Lavinia are not villains, but genuine kindly, caring people?'

'How come?'

'What if they are protecting Secunda? Conspiring yes – but conspiring to conceal a terrible secret. What if, for some reason that nobody has mentioned, the sister was so angry with her brother that she attacked him physically? What if it was Secunda who drowned Primus in his bath?'

43

Now my mind was racing. 'She lost her temper. She attacked him, he swallowed water and collapsed. Slaves burst in and dragged her off, then hauled him out of the tub. Afterwards Secunda had her breakdown, not because of some dreadful scene she had witnessed, but the terrible thing *she* had done.'

'Could be,' Tiberius mused thoughtfully. 'If it was a sudden tantrum, she might never have intended to kill her brother. In a sense, then, it could be called an accident.'

I jumped on something else: 'Gellius and Lavinia know what occurred. Perhaps they rushed in and found Secunda committing the crime. Let's presume she had done for him, they were too late, and nothing could help Primus.'

'It called for quick thinking. What options did they have?' Tiberius considered. 'There were no other family members to advise so they closed up the house, whipped Secunda away, and hid the fact that Primus had been murdered. However, they flinched from dealing with his remains. They left the corpse behind.'

I was now convinced. 'They saw Secunda's estate as a safe place. Now they nurse her, true guardians of her tragic secret. Ever since it happened, they really have been looking after her,' I concluded. 'All they say is true. They have held back only that she was responsible for her brother's death.'

Tiberius concurred. 'If this is right, they are foolish perhaps, but innocent. Through careful use of medicines, they keep the old lady sedated – but that is with the best of motives: to ensure she can never again do anything like that.'

'They are guarding her. They are defending her.'

'Utterly plausible,' Tiberius said. 'But now you will have to investigate whether this is actually true. The funeral,' he suggested, 'could be just what you need. Everyone with an interest will be gathered here. The occasion is public. It will be on our property, so we can take command. Then, Albia, you can interrogate witnesses and reach conclusions. Ascertain the facts and we can properly decide on justice.'

44

If this version applied, it also answered another question.

'The slaves!' I exclaimed. 'The three slaves who were left chained, in the hope they would die. Now I can understand why.'

Tiberius followed my meaning immediately. 'Porphyrus, Endymio, Myrtale. They probably witnessed whatever happened – fended off the sister, if she really was to blame. If it was murder, they knew. They might have lifted their master out of the bath and tried to revive him.'

'They were supposed to wait in the changing room. Even if the murder happened while they were outside,' I agreed, 'presumably they saw anyone who went in with Primus. Was it the Publilius siblings, or Secunda? Afterwards, the slaves became a threat,' I reasoned. 'Either they refused to keep quiet about the terrible event, or it was simply feared they would talk. My guess is that they wanted to. Perhaps Gellius and Lavinia, running the household, took no chances. The slaves were isolated under lock and key, then abandoned with the intention they would starve. If they survived until the eruption, it was pure chance that they were killed by the forces of nature.'

There were rules about slaves giving evidence, but during the crisis after Primus died, someone had had to prevent any threat those witnesses could pose. It did cast a horrible light on Gellius and Lavinia. Whoever killed Primus, it looked as if they were in command when the slaves were locked up.

It was hard to think of them, young, charming and well spoken, not even officially members of the family, yet somehow enforcing physical constraint on a trio of adult household staff. Perhaps their method was to place blame on the three slaves for killing Primus. Others then had to help round them up, push them into the shack and fix the chains. The rest may have gone along with the story in fear of being implicated in their master's death. In any case, if free people who ran a house decided to place slaves in chains, those chains would soon be bolted on. Reasons were not required.

Soon after the death, the eruption had started. It must have been hoped that all evidence would perish. The master's death could easily be passed off as part of the disaster. Probably no one had ever cared about the slaves.

At some point, maybe even before it was realised that Vesuvius was erupting, Primus's body must have been laid out. Perhaps he was left in a locked store so those who came to clear the house would not see the body.

It had to be remembered that until the great explosion of material was thrown up above the volcano, people throughout Campania were going about their lives as normal. If a sudden death had occurred, they were dealing with that too. It was easy now to view the eruption as an opportunity for the stricken Curvidius household, especially those in it who were guilty, yet at the time it must have been a complete coincidence. Primus would have died anyway. If it was murder, his loss would have been covered up, although perhaps the truth would have been realised earlier. Certainly, even without Vesuvius, the house and its valuable estate would have been given a new future.

would always be popular: cheery skeletons on beakers, who advised through grinning teeth, 'Drink, for we die tomorrow.'

They also imply, 'Those who were doomed died yesterday.' That is not us. For us, tomorrow will be another day. Don't waste your time worrying. Anything can happen tomorrow. May as well wait until it does.

Enough brooding. Left to myself, I was awash with sentimental philosophy, but suddenly had to pull out of it. I was still musing but had to apply a different mood: outward-looking, pleasant, generous, helpful. Arrangements for the funeral of Primus had to begin. His brother turned up to discuss it with us.

Still making the most of his rights as the duovir's house guest, Fulvianus arrived in a litter we recognised as belonging to Apuleius Innocentius. He had been sent alone. Apparently, there was some big political flap on, to which an outsider guest must not be privy. Tiberius and I were in the know, of course: clearly the kidnapped tribune had not yet been found.

Wherever Fulvianus had been for lunch with his local friend, they had made the most of it. Either they had a lot to catch up on, or maybe the anonymous friend thought the bereaved man needed bolstering. It was well into afternoon by the time he reached us, and on arrival the bearers who had brought him up from Stabiae had to wake him. When he fell out clumsily – his stiff joints had become more apparent than when we had met in Rome – his hair slanted forwards more untidily, and for a time his voice was troublesomely slurred.

We had not previously suspected he overindulged like his brother. If it was habitual, Uncle Tullius would have mentioned him having that kind of reputation among their business

269

crowd. However, this was not the same man who had carried his refills of Alban wine so easily that evening with us. Perhaps, Tiberius mused afterwards in his polite way, a return to the old family home after years away had inflicted on him the wrong type of nostalgia. I brought myself to say that it must have been very upsetting to inspect his brother's bones.

Tiberius had shown him the skeleton. They got it over with when Fulvianus first arrived. Tiberius and Larcius then took him briefly into the store where Primus had been found, though he did not want to linger. I noticed they gave no demonstration of the now fragmented cart.

We brought him indoors. We offered him time and full freedom to look around while he composed himself. He accepted, went off on a fast walkabout alone through parts of the villa, but soon returned to where we were waiting in the atrium. He did not seem particularly interested in the house. He had opened doors but only stared into rooms from the threshold. He never went upstairs. Nor can he have walked along as far as the bath suite, so he did not look at the tub where his brother had died. So far, we had not revealed the circumstances.

I handed him the ring that we believed had been his brother's seal. He glanced at the carving of Fortuna Redux, nodded confirmation and slipped it into a pouch on his belt. From the casual way he stowed it, he might have been pocketing his change for a takeaway flatbread.

I wondered what he would do with that signet. I could visualise it being tossed into a box of knickknacks, until it turned up years later amongst spills, toys and broken necklace hooks, when no one could even remember whose ring it had been. But perhaps he would inter it reverently with Primus.

In a small, quiet room we were intending as a study for Uncle Tullius, we told him about our concerns. We agreed it seemed clear his brother had drowned in his bathtub, as we had been told, although Tiberius and I were not convinced it was an accident. Neither did we countenance suicide. Carefully, we suggested foul play.

Fulvianus was aware of the Publilius siblings. I talked about the stranger aspects of their influence over Primus, and now their control of Secunda. I mentioned the possibility that they were not as devoted as they wished to appear but were lusting for financial gain. Tiberius warned quietly that they might have been stealing funds. It was, he said, a hard thing to suggest, but no one should ignore the possibility that Gellius and Lavinia had done away with Primus.

His brother showed no reaction.

Or, I pressed on, there might be an alternative premise: that someone else had caused the death, perhaps unintentionally. Gellius and Lavinia had simply been covering it up ever since. Immediately, Fulvianus himself piped up: 'You mean, my impossible sister did for our brother? She killed him?'

Yes, we agreed solemnly, that ought at least to be considered. 'Was your sister aggressive?'

'We come from a quarrelsome family.'

'Did she argue with Primus?'

'From birth.'

We waited for Fulvianus to reject the whole tricky conclusion, but he merely nodded. I reinforced the idea that, after his brother died, Gellius and Lavinia knew what had happened and had perhaps been looking after Secunda from the best of motives. I said there could possibly have been a witness to the drowning, although I had not yet managed to ascertain this. Fulvianus said, 'Find one and I'll speak to him.'

Almost as if he was annoyed by the pressure the situation placed upon him, Fulvianus exclaimed tartly, 'I shall have to go up the coast to my sister's place, take a look at her situation for myself.'

He was so brisk he seemed frigid. He had once told us, 'One has one's duties to family.' Aloof neutrality remained. He seemed neither shocked nor excited by anything we had told him. Most people would have responded in one way or the other. Then, unexpectedly, he thanked us for having done our best to discover the truth and for our tact in setting out our fears. Leave the matter to him. He would see to it.

Before his departure, he confirmed he would like to hold a funeral for Primus at the villa. 'If you can put up with it?' There would be no need for a tomb on our property because the family owned one, next to a road at Salernum, their place of origin; his brother's ashes would be taken there and placed with their ancestors. Until Fulvianus had seen his sister, he would defer a decision on timing. He had no intention of providing a show for gawping busybodies, so we need not expect many mourners. He had ordered a load of logs for the pyre. He might fix up a basic musician, just a flautist probably; he'd heard of one who worked locally. I promised that my steward would organise refreshments. His thanks were courteous.

Finally, Tiberius mentioned the three slaves. He gave their names and described the conditions in which we had found them. I explained why I thought they had been chained up.

'Never knew them. Not an issue, though. Thanks for mentioning. We can deal with the bones on the pyre. I'll draft an adequate plaque. Give me the names again?' Tiberius quietly repeated them.

Fulvianus was brisk. I disliked him ticking it off on his mental list with such cold use of 'deal with' and 'adequate'. Still, I knew that not all owners would give their slaves' spirits rest, so he was in his own way commendable.

There was no point in telling him a child had died too, because we had no idea who it was. Plenty of heartrending tombstones show grief for little children, but their names and ages, their sweetness and the joy they brought to their relatives have to be recorded. Tiberius and I cared for two little boys we might adopt, so that made us extra sensitive. But the child who had lost his life in that prison would always remain unknown.

Perhaps still affected by his luncheon, Fulvianus wanted to go on to the Gabius estate immediately. The duovir's litter-bearers refused to take him, claiming it was too late in the day. Too far as well, I suspected. Fulvianus made no fuss, which seemed to be his style. He climbed aboard the litter then set off back to Stabiae, saying he would make his way along the peninsula next day by sea. We offered that either Tiberius or I would accompany him, but he was brusque in saying he preferred to go alone.

He left. Whatever had happened to Primus, whatever was happening to Secunda, I could see matters being handled very decisively from now on. Any action would almost certainly be kept private within the family. A head of household would have powers, both by tradition and enshrined in law. Presumably Fulvianus would inform the duovir that anything untoward had been exposed and handled, so the authorities could relax. He would hardly demand compensation for his brother's murder, if it was the fault of their sister. If he wanted her punished, I doubted it would be via trial and exile.

Fulvianus had promised to let us know whatever he found out, and when the funeral was to be. Our role in any investigation seemed to be ending. After he had gone, we felt rather flat.

Everything livened up the next afternoon, when Fulvianus came by on the Via Minerva in transport he must have taken from the Gabius estate. Travelling back to Stabiae, he stayed with the vehicle but sent a slave running in to tell us he had not seen his sister. Fulvia Secunda had gone out on a fresh-air carriage drive, as Gellius and Lavinia sometimes arranged for a change of scene. The carriage never returned. Secunda had disappeared.

Oh, and by the way, the slave informed us, Fulvianus had decided that, whether or not his sister turned up again, the funeral would be held here regardless.

46

There seemed to be a flush of people disappearing. At that point I had no idea there would be another before everything was sorted. But if I had known, I doubt I would have done anything different.

My personal adventure began next day. Events started routinely enough. Not being needed at the villa, I rode Mercury down into Stabiae. I went to the second-hand furniture barn, intent on pursuing my theory that Criton, once a young slave at the villa, was a crucial witness. I had come to believe he knew how Curvidius Primus died, that he was probably present and may even have seen it happen.

No luck. The informer's curse: having become so keyed up to ask questions, I failed to achieve an interview. Criton's friend, Crispus, was there on his own again. He tried telling me Criton had gone out helping Septumius with a pick-up or delivery. I thought he was lying and could see he was worried. When cajoling failed, I threatened outright that if Criton was not produced, I would involve the authorities. 'I have friends from the Rome vigiles who are currently here in Stabiae. They specialise in finding runaway slaves.'

'He has not run away,' insisted Crispus.

'Well, it looks that way!' With Milo and Hyro handy, I really was prepared to instigate a hue and cry. 'He certainly escaped from his original owners. It may have been ten years ago, Crispus, but you never get an amnesty . . . The man whose property Criton is – in theory – has arrived in Stabiae. He wants to know how Primus died, and I shall have to warn him that your friend knows the proper story. He's very abrupt and will demand fast justice. Crispus, it isn't feasible to keep Criton's existence quiet now.'

'I know!' Crispus writhed. 'People are looking for him already. Someone came and shouted at my uncle.'

'Who did?'

'I don't know. Some men.'

'What men?'

'My uncle knew who they were. He didn't like them.'

'Is that why Septumius has taken Criton away?'

'I suppose so. We have a farm up in the hills. We don't use it much for agriculture but have a fig tree and some goats. Uncle uses the building as a spare store when we have too much stock to keep here. Criton will be safe out of sight.'

I played the professional wise-girl. 'That won't work. Your poor friend has been placed in worse danger. Your uncle too. Whoever those men were, they will find out and go after them.'

I may have been laying it on too thick. Instantly worried, Crispus asked what to do. Now that he saw me as a friend, it was easy to persuade him to give me directions to their upland property. I promised to warn Septumius and bring everyone back safely.

Crispus would not come with me; he had to remain in charge of the barn. People broke in and stole items if ever the place was unattended. He gave me directions. Still riding Merky, I set off alone up a steep track into the Lactarii Mountains.

This expedition, I concede, was not sensible.

Tiberius, busy on site, had barely noticed me leaving that morning. He had kissed me fondly, but had been abstracted. He had already sent Paris to learn of any progress in the search for the vigiles' tribune; that meant I had stolen out with no escort. Still, I was an informer. In Rome, I had spent more than ten years tripping through streets packed with dangers it was best never to think about. I had been trained by my father, the world's sneakiest scout, and mentored by my mother, an equally wise adviser. Neither would have approved of me going alone into precipitous hills that might have been packed with brigands. On the other hand, if told I was going there to fetch the only witness to a murder – in a case where I had a fee-paying remit – neither would have been surprised.

Falco might have grunted, 'Never go on a mission that involves breathtaking scenery and goats.' But he was a city-boy misery.

47

The scenery was indeed breathtaking. That was because I had to ride so high up through precipitous crags that the thinner mountain air literally took my breath. There were sheep and goats everywhere. When I felt thirsty, I thought about trying to milk one, but I could tell they were all half-wild mavericks who would never cooperate, even if I caught one. Alternatively, there were waterfalls. Icy cascades chattered over limestone rocks most prettily. For a thirsty woman who disliked heights, most were inaccessible.

The goats had made themselves trails that looked just like the real paths. Merky kept wanting to explore them. The directions Crispus had given me were unhelpful. I knew, from fairly early on, that I was going to get lost.

At least I could still see where I had come from – if I dared to look back and down. The Montes Lactarii, I discovered, were not only forbiddingly high, but composed of sheer drops and killer precipices. Their slopes might be clothed with beech, chestnut and pine forests, but if trees could cling by their roots to near-vertical rocks, they did so.

There were occasional terraces, from which I could gasp at the panorama. In between rest stops we climbed, then doggedly climbed further. I placed my trust in my donkey, which seemed sure-footed. Trails, occasionally passed off as roads, told us that people did come up here. Otherwise, the combination of thin air, cold spring water and silence, broken only by meandering bursts of sound from insects among herbs and heathers, made me feel I had lost contact with the real world. When we passed shacks or sheepfolds they looked as if they could be hundreds of years old. Originally they must have been.

I sometimes saw fine properties. In high summer, people of note would enjoy leisure there, an escape from the Mediterranean heat below; they could stuff themselves with tranquillity, staggering views and their sense of superiority. In many rural situations, you can glimpse such lavish bolt-holes, built as private retreats by the disgustingly rich. You wonder how they spend their time all day or, practically, how provisions ever reach them without obvious benefit of roads. Now I was riding right past places like that, though with no sign of life. In March, with white patches on the high peaks that might still be unmelted snowdrifts, all the wealthy owners were absent, their houses deserted. Nobody could give me directions.

From up here, the whole bay extended in my sight. If I went high enough, I would be able to see the entire length of the Surrentum peninsula, with all the far coast on the Neapolis side, Capri and other islands out to sea, and Vesuvius slumbering; below the precarious central ridge in the other direction the Paestanum Sinus would be gorgeously mapped, where tiny coastal villages clung to cliffs as they faced a completely different part of the ocean. No wonder this area produced poets, I thought grimly.

It grew colder. I was glad I had a good cloak. I wished I was wearing a second undertunic. I had seen none of the landmarks that Crispus had vaguely mentioned. His directions had sounded easy but now seemed pitiful. Was his explanation nonsense? I could not envisage how Septumius ever lugged large items of furniture up here to be stored. I began to wonder whether the young man had deliberately misled me. I should have forced him to come along as a guide.

I had lived half my life in Londinium and half in Rome, so I could take only a certain amount of twigs cracking, etiolated fungi and the smell of dank leaf litter. Frightening views of suicidal escarpments were beginning to pall too. We had crossed a wooden bridge some might have described as quaint, though it felt rotten and made my donkey querulous. The terrain varied between rocky grey outcrops, patches of cute alpine flowers or tangles of forest. In my head I could hear my father's voice jeering, 'Time to get out, Tiddles, before the bleating billy goats make your brain explode!'

How true. I was on the verge of taking his advice.

Then, finally, we hit a temple.

I had travelled around the eastern Mediterranean with my parents some years ago, so I was not surprised. I knew that, in the Greek and Roman world, if there was any hilltop pinnacle sensible citizens would regard as pointless and unreachable, mad people would stick a shrine on it. A lonely and godless spot? Give it a god for company. So there she was. Naturally a divinity had a temple up there. Picturesque sea views and beautiful mountain serenity? Just her kind of place.

She was Tyche, the goddess of chance and fortune. A complicated lady, whose oceanic connections by birth did not affect her other attributes: for some reason that must make sense in mythology, she represented the safety of cities. Mural crown and leaning on a rudder, normally, foot on the wheel of fortune to steady her. Associated with prosperity or, as a goddess of risk, she also presided over disappointment and loss. Do ask at her oracle what destiny awaits you, but that cornucopia of golden coins is never guaranteed to empty over your feet. *How's your luck?* as gamblers cry, when the dice are flying. It's usually satirical. You know what the score is going to be: you lost.

My luck followed those usual rules. I thought there would be a priestess; by rights she would advise me because I was a fellow-woman. Since temples give sanctuary, she might even be prevailed upon to allow Criton her protection.

Forget it, Albia! There ought to have been a priestess of the Tyche cult hanging around to conduct religious observations – but that afternoon she was out. She had gone home for nut fancies and a good long gossip with an old acquaintance.

Bitterly I wondered how it could be that in this wonder-land of panoramic effect and little else a lone priestess had managed to make a friend? I could not blame her, but for me it was inconvenient.

The priestess had, however, left her temple in the care of an attendant who had been ordered to clear leaves from the porch with a broom. Normally such a worker would have been pleased to see me because it meant he could pause in sweeping. This one had already stopped of his own accord. Sitting on the steps with his broom at his feet, as he took in the spectacular panorama, he was a pale, slender sprite in a more or less white tunic, with extremely hairy arms and legs. I put him in his thirties. He had dark brown eyes a fourteen-year-old might have fallen for, but lank hair that needed a good wash.

'No point living with scenery,' he said, as I hove into range, 'if you never pause to look.' He might have thought I expected him to jump up and look helpful. I knew better. I had visited rural shrines before.

I climbed from my donkey to sit on his steps with him. 'All right,' I agreed sceptically, gazing at the stunning vista. 'Nothing on earth beats this unbelievable view. I would love to give it the rapture it deserves, but unfortunately your luck is out. My mind is fraught. I am lost.'

'Luck?' asked the attendant. 'This is your place. We specialise in hazard. The inventor of dice gave his first ever set to Tyche, though she is not normally portrayed shaking a cup for a bet.'

This whimsical banter gave the impression he was happy in his life, though presumably he had no choice. Like many I meet in my work he was chatty, but if I wanted to squeeze information from him, I would have to tolerate his nonsense. Very few pilgrims came along, possibly because the temple was so high up and isolated. He was eager for conversation with someone other than a passing wood mouse, so he had me trapped.

'Greetings then. I am Albia, Flavia Albia. I act as a private investigator. What's your name, sunshine?'

'Quinctius Polydorus.'

'Sounds rather Greek?'

'Libertus,' he added proudly. In fact, with the most basic detective work, I had deduced he was an ex-slave.

'Congratulations on your manumission. How does a freedman end up here?'

'Duty to my patron, as was fiercely explained to me. Permanent show of gratitude in return for my new life. Otherwise, get my balls broken.'

'That's a tough patron!'

'Patroness. Quinctia, the priestess.'

'Forced you to dwell here with her among the solitary woods? Wouldn't you have rather set up for yourself as a shopkeeper?'

'I can live with this. I have light work and no bills to pay. I can kip in the cella and never have to wonder where the next meal is coming from.'

'So where is the ball-breaking Quinctia at the moment?'

'Her house.'

'When expected back?'

'Not tonight. We get a glorious golden twilight that settles like a quilt over the uplands – but she will skip that. Seen one, seen them all. Magical the first time, but gulping at the golden glow can become a chore. She may drop in tomorrow morning to conduct a few rites, if she's feeling up to it. She calls herself "long experienced". Frankly, that means past it. The other day, she accidentally set fire to some sacrificial wheat cakes. Anyway, I know the routines, so she left me to it.'

'Does she bunk off often?'

'No point usually. Some relative invited herself to stay. I suppose if a visitor comes all the way up the mountain, you must feel you have to make an effort. Those two are so decrepit that if they don't have a long natter now they may never get another chance. Their encounter will be like the Grey Sisters in the Perseus myth – only one eye and one tooth to share between them.'

To show he was trustworthy, Polydorus stood up and found a bucket of water for Mercury. He pulled her ears, which she accepted.

I chewed my thumb. 'Has Quinctia gone far? Where is her house? I don't want to disturb her but I think I need official help.'

'I am instructed to say she is on furlough.'

'Stretch a point?'

'More than my life's worth to disobey orders. Our priestess may be getting on, but I wasn't joking. She packed a fine right hook when she was younger. Trust me, she is totally off duty.'

'Oh, come, Polydorus, nobody gets a sabbatical from religious rites.'

'Tell her that! If someone turns up with a plea for a prophecy, they have to cross their legs and wait. She is gone, Flavia Albia, and you are stuck with it. This temple is not busy. While there is snow on the mountains, we regard it as out of season; we only provide a skeleton service for pilgrims, and the oracle is closed.'

'I can manage without the oracle. I need true facts. Here's the thing,' I pleaded desperately. 'I have a witness who may be in serious danger and I need to trace him urgently. I am looking for a man called Septumius. All I want is to find his farm.'

Polydorus inclined his head. 'We know Septumius. His goat had twins. He gave one to the temple for sacrifice.'

'Good! Is it possible he has recently brought a young man to seek sanctuary in your temple?'

'No. We never accept fugitives.'

'Criton?'

'Never heard of him.'

'So, they are not here?'

'Look for yourself if you want to.'

I looked. It was true. Septumius and Criton were not there.

Within the temple's dark interior, the cult statue gazed at me frostily. Tyche was a big-built, solid, silent woman, who sported a tall crown of heavily fortified city walls. She wore layers of flowing garments and managed to hold up, single-handed (in her left hand), a monster cornucopia that overflowed with luscious stone fruit.

I addressed her respectfully. 'Lady, I want only to find my witness and keep him safe.' As with so many people I interview, there was no response. Well, the goddess of fortune was a divinity of famously fickle flightiness. I left her to enjoy the silence, aloof in her incense-filled interior.

When I emerged from the dim cella, I was careful not to reel off-balance, dazzled again by the bright beauty of splendiferous views. My eyes were starting to ache at awe-striking vistas. I wanted to go home.

'Any luck?' asked Polydorus, politely.

'Not a sniff.'

'Sorry.'

'Polydorus, take pity on me. I have to find Septumius. He has a farm he uses more for storage than agriculture. One fig tree and a flock.'

'My workplace is fixed,' bemoaned Polydorus. 'I don't get out much.'

'What if I promise a temple donation?' I understood how shrines work. I had no money with me; Tyche would have to take the risk.

Money talks. Even though my cash was hypothetical, Polydorus began to weaken. 'A farm with storage? Hmm . . .'

That was when, finally, the temple attendant described a nearby property. He said he could not promise it was the right one. I must understand he worked for a goddess whose operations in the world were arbitrary and inconsistent. Still, he gave me directions.

I ought to have remembered that oracles in the wilderness are notorious for double-dealing. Still, I was stuck. I had to take what I could get.

I climbed aboard Merky and set off. As I looked back, I saw the freedman pick up what remained of the water in the bucket he had given to my donkey. He sluiced the last contents over the temple steps. I watched as he moved it around with his broom, using long slow swipes to clear away the wet, then working the bristles efficiently into the right-angles between the steps.

We followed his itinerary, until we found a small farm. A group of mules were tethered, implying people must be indoors. As promised, I saw a fig tree. A couple of goats looked over a hedge at me. A large, tall storehouse could well be housing old furniture.

An odd feeling came over me, nevertheless. I drew up at a distance, watching. Nothing occurred. The day was far gone, and I had no wish to be trapped up there in the mountains. Eventually I rode right to the farm building. I went carefully and quietly along the grassy track, but somebody heard me coming.

A door opened and a woman stepped out. She was swathed in dark garments, which she had tied around her in a way that looked foreign. Without bothering to speak to me she threw back her headscarved head and yelled. She must have been alerting unseen companions. Immediately, I knew for sure this was the wrong place.

48

I wondered whether Polydorus had sent me deliberately. Then why? Had Septumius gone to the temple before me, seeking aid in hiding Criton? Or was the freedman simply vague about local properties?

Before I had time to turn and retreat, three men came out from behind the woman. They were lean, mean brutes all dressed in black and accessorised with scars, weapons in wide belts and head wrappings. Whoever they were, I could tell their mood would not be friendly. As for their identity, I could make a guess. Their style matched Dexiades'.

They came right up. Hands grabbed my donkey's reins. I had rearranged my skirts quickly so less bare leg was showing, but when I felt shin-fondling I gave Merky a kick; the loyal beast swung her rump and knocked one man aside, but the effect could only be temporary.

They started speaking among themselves in a foreign language. Not to be outdone, I muttered a few words of Celtic, intermingled with plain gibberish. There was no hope of inter-barbarian sympathy, however.

I changed to a simple Roman matron. 'So sorry to bother you. I'm looking for a farm owned by Septumius. The second-hand furniture dealer.'

They looked suddenly interested. 'Where is that farm?' They could speak Latin when they wanted to.

'I have no idea. I am terribly afraid I must have taken a wrong turn. So silly of me!'

They had picked up on the name Septumius, which I could hear among the foreign argot. His son had told me men had come looking for Criton. These must be the men, and I didn't trust them any more than Septumius had.

'He told me he has a rather nice three-tier cupboard that I liked the sound of. He said it is in store up here somewhere. I want to take a look at it before I commit to purchasing . . .' Unsurprisingly they were not fooled.

'Name!' The one in the lead positively spat his question.

'Flavia Albia.' I saw no point in lying.

It caused even more excitement. Immediately I was seized and dragged down from my donkey. Someone standing behind me was holding me trapped. The leader looked me up and down, with obvious sexual threat. However, he asked the professional question: 'Rich husband?'

I scoffed. 'My husband is a builder. He is doing a job for his uncle, so he is not being paid.'

'Rich husband!' another man assured him. All the men sniggered.

'Pay me to get you back?' suggested the first man.

I was being groped by someone with serious body odour; I bucked and fought against it. 'Stop that! My man is very traditional. He will only pay up if he gets me intact!' I reinforced this with a backward kick. The groping stopped, or at least paused. After that I was only being pushed around, as was to be expected. One man grabbed hold of my arm and viciously yanked off a bangle. My yell of protest was as much because it hurt me, scraping skin. However, I knew why they wanted it.

'Husband knows this thing?'

'Husband gave it to me.' They laughed, tossing it between them and pointedly calling it a cheap gift. I knew it had not been. It was gold, though with plain aesthetics, which he and I liked. He would recognise it.

'Name of husband?' snapped the leader.

'Manlius Faustus. Please try not to upset him. Who are you?' I demanded. The mood of promised violence had faded slightly. My captors had an innocent respect for me as a usable hostage. If Tiberius sent a ransom, I would quite likely be raped before release, but for the time being I was valuable.

'Docetius,' answered my interrogator, which he weirdly followed with introductions: 'Surdinius, Bitho, Acatholos.' When mentioned, each gave a small bow. I acknowledged them, all I could manage while gripped by my captor. In any case, I curtsy to no one. Meanwhile Docetius was writing my husband's name on one side of a note-tablet. Not only could he write, but his hand moved with confidence and the lettering looked neat. 'And he lives . . .?'

'I can tell you have done this before.' He must have had a pro forma for ransom notes. 'Faustus can be found above Stabiae, at the old Curvidius villa.' There was a small silence, glances, then nodding. I let them see me sneer. 'Oh, of course you know where that is! You came onto the property and stole a pickaxe. We would like it back, if you've finished with it. The slave's nose isn't actually broken, you'll be glad to hear.'

Humourless, Docetius finished writing. 'You,' he told me, 'will stay here.'

I raised my chin. 'I understand. Well, if you are no trouble to me, I'll be no trouble to you!'

289

'You will be no trouble.' He made it ominous.

One of the men was leading away my donkey, taking her towards their mules. I shouted for him to bring her back. I said not only was Mercury a family pet, but when they were ready to return me to my people, they would need some way of transporting me all the way down the mountain from this eyrie. 'I do have to be sent back, you know. My husband is a Rome businessman. He will require an on-the-spot exchange. Proof of life, or no cash forthcoming. He will only give you the money in return for his wife.' Oddly enough they took the point. None was bright enough to think I might be asking for Merky to secure a ride to freedom, if I managed to escape.

That would be tricky. It seemed they would be keeping me in the big building I had first thought might be a furniture store. It was a solidly built cattle byre, which would be locked and guarded. I made a show of resistance as I was dragged over there and thrown inside. A long but narrow window, not big enough to climb through, gave just enough light so any animals who were kept there in winter would not live in the dark. Nor would brigands' captives.

Acatholos cried, 'Here's someone to entertain you!' before the door slammed shut behind me.

He said it to someone who was already there. He was seated at a small, rough-hewn table, glumly playing dice against himself. He was large and rugged, with the natural arrogance of an ex-soldier who had forced his way through the ranks. He gave me a fast look up and down, then rejected me as a bedmate, a gaming partner, or anything else.

'Who the flea's fart are you?'

I brushed myself down, straightening clothes. 'Flavia Albia, daughter of Falco, wife to Faustus, private informer

– and, to you, all-round menace. I've worked with your man Ursus. We last met in Rome beside Domitian's Odeum on the day of the bears. You won't remember me. Gaius Caunus, greetings.'

I had found the Seventh Cohort's missing tribune.

49

I looked around. It was a fast survey, squinting in dim light and ignoring a smell that was certainly not fresh laundry. I groaned, with an informer's traditional despair. Fate does not favour us. That goddess Tyche was so unfriendly she could lean on her damned rudder a long time now before I would make a donation to her mountain temple.

Caunus was living on a bare soil floor, equipped with a pallet to sleep on, a table and stool and a sanitation bucket. The byre must once have had an upper half-floor where the people who worked the farm might have slept above the warmth of their animals. It was cold now. That whole mezzanine platform, and any stalls or mangers, had been stripped out; I could see marks on the wall where they had once been, but now extra height was needed in the main space. Like Septumius, with his spare lock-up in the hills, Dexiades must also have had an overflow store for artworks he was hoping to sell.

We were sharing our captivity with an enormous statue. The monumental piece was apparently modelled on the Parthenon frieze, though fully three-dimensional. It comprised sets of writhing bodies caught in conflict: centaurs and lapiths, busily battling. Skill had been used on muscular torsos, delight taken in throttling, kneeing and eye-gouging. Fighting on both sides resembled the Olympic sport that has no rules, pancratium, but with added hoofs. 'At least it is not a dying Gaul!' That was lost on my companion. 'Did they pick you up as soon as you reached Stabiae? How long have you been living among this dusty statuary, Caunus?'

'Too long.'

I walked over and looked at the door.

'Don't bother,' advised Caunus. 'There's no getting through that.' I had once seen him use a pickpocketing gadget but, like the store where we had found Primus, the lock here only opened from outside. On principle I walked around checking walls and so forth. Caunus stopped giving me advice.

I told him that a full century from the Seventh had been detailed to march south to search for him, under secret orders from the Prefect of Vigiles. 'Gods alive, that's all I need! How did the fart-arse prefect get involved? Which bloody century? What bloody centurion?'

'Could it be Rufeius?'

'Tripe!'

'No good?' I asked demurely.

'Of course he's good. I trained him myself. But I never gave him lessons in extricating bandits' victims. Not a lot of that goes on around the Campus bloody Martius.' He was very unhappy. 'I'd like to see anyone nab a hostage on my watch!'

I tried to calm him. 'The ransom demand for you was sent to Rome. That was bound to cause a panic at high level. Hence the rescue squad. Your men are going house to house. The fleet commander is having trireme crews look among the mermaids in seaside caves.'

'Then the admiral is a pig's arse. Do I look as if I'm in a bloody cave?'

'Maybe they will think about the mountains in due course. I hope so. Is Dexiades behind this swindle, or are those men outside freelancing?'

'Dexiades controls it.'

'He is your party chum?' Caunus met my question with a filthy look. He must have accepted he had stupidly fallen for a well-worn criminal enterprise. Neither of us acknowledged that. He was embarrassed and I can be polite. (I know how, just never see much reason to do it.) 'In Stabiae he's known as the pirate,' I said. 'You and he failed to gel?'

'When his roughnecks jumped me,' if he was successfully jumped, Caunus could not have been sober at the time, 'I gave him a lecture on the penalties for piracy. He says he is King of the Bay and can do as he likes.'

'Then we'd better show him different. Maybe a dash of republicanism?'

There was a clash of ideologies. It was only to be expected. Caunus was now on his feet, pacing around angrily; since there was only one stool, I nipped over and pinched it.

'You look fit,' I mentioned, before he could splutter that I should leave what he undoubtedly saw as his throne of office. 'Not obviously knocked about. How do they treat you?'

The tribune said bitterly that he had been living a life of ease. It was a deliberate measure by his captors to keep him quiet and malleable. Wine and food were being supplied in decent quantities. He confided in me: he had been pouring half of the wine – well, a quarter – down a depression he had scraped in the floor behind the statue. It was a foul vintage and he intended to stay sober.

I tried to judge whether he was sober now. Probably not.

I said he was lucky with his soft regime; I described how Fulvia Secunda, for one, was kept subdued by addictive drugs. He said a woman would need it; women had no idea of rules. For his part, he had given his parole and would damn well be treated accordingly.

'Really?' I was sceptical. 'Or if anyone ever pays a ransom, won't you be cast off a plunging crag and left to rot among the scenery?'

To establish a connection with my new room-mate, I asked about his career. He recited the usual litany: footslogging in Spain, heatstroke in North Africa, lively moments in Moesia near the Dacian frontier. He had served his term, survived hostilities, come to Rome for a well-paid stint in the vigiles, and was lined up for a final posting in the Urban Cohorts or Praetorian Guards. Alternatively, he might retire. I thought being kidnapped while out on a jolly would not look too good on his personnel file. However, centurions have a way with words, when making excuses for their own behaviour. Despite being kidnapped on a binge, he might yet get away with it.

Caunus did not trouble to ask about my own career.

Time passed. I braced myself to endure a lot of passing time.

Eventually I saw for myself the tribune's soft life on parole. The door opened unexpectedly. The woman I had seen earlier came in and dumped a second sleeping mat for me and another stump of wood, carved by a woodcutter's apprentice, which passed as a seat. She turned back outside. Then, moments later, she heaved in a heavy refreshment tray. This she unloaded and piled with the previous empties. I asked meekly if she could supply me with a ewer and bowl for washing, though I did not push my luck by requesting a sponge and clean towel. Housekeeping requests met no response anyway.

Throughout, the woman was guarded by the man called Acatholos. To make sure we took him seriously, he had drawn his sword, the blade of which he thumbed suggestively. He drew blood, so he stopped posturing.

While the woman ministered, Caunus and I had to stand together on the far side of the room. She did not take the toilet bucket to be emptied. Neither she nor Acatholos spoke. If this had been a mansio on a travel route, I would have given it a one-star review.

After they had gone, Caunus enlightened me that the other men would have ridden off, but the young woman, whose name was Egloge, and Acatholos would be left here in charge of us. Acatholos should not be underestimated. The tribune assessed his weapon technically: the short, slightly curved sword was robust enough to cut through rigging ropes, slash leather sails, and even hack a path through undergrowth ashore. Its length meant it could be used in close-quarters combat, for instance when boarding a ship aggressively. 'Simplicity to use and they need no prior training. So do not try anything with him, young woman. Is that absolutely clear?'

'I hear you.'

'Don't,' emphasised Caunus, 'start kicking off like your damned father.'

The Seventh Cohort was stationed near our family auction house. Their tribune would have met Falco. Clearly he knew how all the Didius family reacted to stress – with furious cries of 'I'm not having that!'

Caunus was the usual standard of tribune, an idler when he could hide it, but efficient enough. I would take his advice and not try anything. What now? I had no idea how long I would be stuck there. I braced myself for a tedious daily routine.

Caunus and I sat down together, morosely eating. The diet supplied would not keep *me* quiet and malleable for long; it comprised only tough bread and all-you-can-eat goat's cheese. Egloge did not spoil us with garnishes of olives. When I tried the wine, it was a raw red throat-rasper. I made a note to request water, or possibly goat's milk.

After this, presumably the entertainment might be draughts. The tribune did not offer and neither did I. Instead, I announced that now there were two of us we must consider how to escape. We needed to do something, and if Caunus had ruled out Acatholos as a target, we would, I said, have to use the usual gambit.

'What bloody gambit?'

'The beautiful jailer's daughter trick.'

Now he knew what I meant. 'Stuff that.'

'Oh, come on, Tribune, this is all we have.'

'I am *not* schmoozing a bandit's ugly moll.'

'She's not that bad. We might have been stuck with a fat old fishwife with a hairy mole.' I had checked out Egloge, who was a straight-backed proud young woman with a good face, light eyes, gold hoops in her ears but no wedding ring.

'You have to do it,' I told Caunus. 'Even if she is of a Sapphic bent, she heard me talking about my husband, so she knows I am not a girl's girl. You are a tall, handsome Roman of military bearing.' Well, he was tall. 'You have the looks and I'm sure you have the skills . . .' Caunus was a tribune of vigiles: he had interviewed enough suspects to recognise brazen lies. Still, I kept going. 'Tomorrow you must talk to Egloge as if she is your heart's delight, win her around and get her to hold Acatholos down so we can make a run for it.'

'Absolutely not.'

'Tribune, there is no alternative. Come on, you know about acting. Hyro and Milo, by the way, are heartbroken over your plight. The diligent duo has been waiting for you at the Two Scallops, though Rufeius will probably take them under his warm wing, now they know you are unable to make the rendezvous.'

Rufeius, growled the tribune, was welcome to that barmy pair. I could tell he was filing me in the same pigeon-hole.

Bedtime was early since we had no oil lamp. Caunus moved his sleeping pallet as far as possible from mine. 'Stay over there. Don't try anything!' He seemed obsessed.

'Your virtue is safe with me,' I snapped back, making my tone equally nasty.

I knew I had only myself to blame for this. I was so tired I fell straight to sleep, or the mental recriminations would have been ugly.

50

Pulling off the jailer's daughter trick normally takes time. Jailers tend to tell their offspring not to be fooled by lies and sweet blandishments. Prisoners are necessarily only after one thing – and it isn't romance – so even if he writes yearning poetry, good daughters should avoid close contact with an unwashed, unshaven captive . . .

If Caunus was a secret poet, he hid it well. And he must have been unwashed and unshaven for at least a week, which dulled his natural magnetism. Egloge would need to be desperate. Of course, the theory behind the jailer's daughter trick reckons she generally is.

I was nervous. Even though I could rehearse the tribune in strategy, we had too little time. I feared the brigands might become apprehensive. If they heard that a paramilitary search had been mounted around the bay, they might abandon their ransom scheme. In that case they would need to dispose of us, for we could give evidence of not only how and where they operated but, crucially, their names and faces. Elimination was unlikely to mean setting us free among the wildflowers and woodland creatures in the scenic forests. It would probably include flying lessons, with a jumping-off point at a precipice.

Next morning the first thing that happened was that we heard hoofs: not rescue unfortunately, but the other bandits returning. Soon after, there were scuffling noises immediately outside, followed by banging against the building, then thumps in the roof space overhead. Although the mezzanine floor had been removed, there must still have been some form of loft above. I noticed a trapdoor in the ceiling, perhaps once used for depositing animal fodder from upper storage. It was too high for us to reach, even if we stood on the table, which was small, round, low and dangerously unstable. Yes, I tried it. Caunus watched dismissively.

Someone must have entered the roof space via a ladder outside. Thudding around above our room's ceiling, they made ham-fisted efforts to undo the trapdoor. It failed to budge. Angry voices sounded. After more footsteps and muttering, someone hit it hard and the hatch abruptly dropped open. One end fell and swung around, then was quickly pulled up again with a rope, until only a few inches remained open. The tie must have been hitched, to tether it in position. This increased the airflow, not much more. We heard a new voice, youthful, busily complaining. Nothing else happened.

Caunus growled that we were dealing with amateurs. He wondered what in Hades the fart-arse idiots were up to. I couldn't be bothered to supply matching repartee.

Outside, we heard retreating hoofs, the same as yesterday. If anyone had been left in the loft, he was having a nap.

All of a sudden, Acatholos and Egloge pulled off another sudden entry. To my surprise she was carrying a metal basin and a jug of water as I had asked her. I thought it unlikely she sympathised with my plight – perhaps keeping me sweet had been agreed as another means of captive-control.

And there was to be more. 'Music!' exclaimed Acatholos, dramatically. 'Entertainment for you!'

This made no sense until he walked over, stood beneath the partly open trapdoor and shouted loudly, 'Wake up and play, slave!'

'Stuff you, moron!' returned the young voice we had previously heard, very casually. His accent, to me, had a satisfying Roman timbre. Somebody had sent him to infant school, and I knew the kind of establishment: his teacher had worked out of doors in a back alley, somewhere like the Aventine. Pupils emerged from their education truculent and loud, though able to read, write, add and subtract. This one had even acquired spatial awareness: 'There's no room to swing a dead rat with all this junk.' We heard him pushing things around, presumably to make room for himself.

'Play prettily to amuse the people,' returned Acatholos, unmoved. Egloge was emptying the slop bucket by hurling the contents outside from the doorway.

The alleged slave had sounded rebellious, but he obeyed. Perhaps they were paying him. He started; we jumped. To our amazement, to pacify their captives, the bandits had brought along a flute player.

Caunus groaned, as he tuned up with gentle wootling notes. 'Tell him we do not want a concert party.'

'I had the idea from Milo and Hyro that that was exactly what you were looking for!'

'Not in a bloody byre, with a cocky blabbermouth for company.'

While we were distracted, Egloge banged down the bucket then jerked her head at Acatholos; they departed.

'Juno,' I groaned. 'When they come back it will be goat's cheese with instrumental accompaniment. Despair in Dorian mode.' But once he got going, the unseen musician struck me as quite good.

He must have been playing the twin-reeded double flute called the aulos or tibia. It can be used in a military context, though making it loud enough to hear above marching men takes serious blowing. Our artiste favoured a relaxed, laid-back salon style. Up in the hayloft, he must have been improvising; there can have been no light for him to see written notation, supposing he had even brought a knap-sack of compositions. Using the double pipes as a chanter and drone for lines that were sometimes cleverly separate or sometimes harmonically joined, he gave us reflective, meandering music, almost for his own pleasure. It was slow, temperate stuff whose soft sounds were genuinely calming. I sank into quiet nostalgia, remembering my wedding to Tiberius, when we had had an aulos serenade us during our procession.

Caunus kept up his petulant complaints. I told him he was a boor, who could never have listened to Egyptian bagpipes or he would be grateful for this.

After about an hour the player stopped and called, 'Sorry – need a comfort break!'

'Bring us a rope – and weapons!' bellowed Caunus. In the silence that ensued, he relieved his feelings by peeing so forcefully he seemed to want to drill a hole in the bucket. If it was a challenge, I could never match him, so I resumed making endless neat plaits in my hair. I knew how to be a ladylike prisoner.

I had not told the tribune that in my satchel, which the brigands had foolishly failed to remove from me, I carried a small but sharp blade that I called my fruit knife.

When the flautist returned, he changed style to show he was versatile.

'Oi, Orpheus!' I yelled up. 'Cut it out for a moment. We are trying to hone an escape plot down here.' Caunus looked furious that I had mentioned what we were doing, but I was full of confidence. 'Anyone would think,' I continued, raising my voice to the invisible player, 'you had been traipsing around Neapolis, impersonating a tribute combo, along with some look-alike Neronian harpist!'

At the sound of my voice and what I was saying, silence fell.

For final emphasis, I asked, 'Do you know "The Little Mess Tin Song"? It needs a marching beat, but the words are nicely scurrilous.' I started whistling the ditty; it was a party-piece of my father's and had been beloved of my first husband, Lentullus.

If the flute player knew it, my speculation about him would have been confirmed, but we were interrupted. Before the young man could respond, Egloge and her escort arrived again, this time with food. Above us, the music resumed, tweedling fugal variations on my father's army song. The two bandits failed to realise that communication was in hand.

I pretended to help Egloge unpack the new picnic, while whispering to her that she should be nice to the tribune because he had a crush on her. The bread had been toasted, which would disguise its antiquity, but it still came with goat's cheese. I expressed disappointment that the bandits had not brought in fresh breakfast rolls. And was there any chance of a bowl of oatmeal and almonds tomorrow?

After a glare at my silliness, Caunus slicked back his hair and prepared to use whatever charm he possessed. He was lying on his back on the floor, using his stool as a weight as he did pullover exercises. To have been a centurion he must have reached thirty, but I put him at closer to fifty now. He carried his age well; he probably felt he was still much younger. 'I'm so sorry that we are putting you to all this trouble,' he told Egloge, while effortlessly showing off his strength and how he could talk at the same time as swinging a lump of wood. In turn, she showed him how she could change over bowls while ignoring an idiot. 'You must lead a dreadful life in this isolated bolthole. Why don't you tell me all about it?' The man's chat-up lines were laughable.

Up above the music stopped.

Now that Caunus was dutifully working on his patter, my task was to distract Acatholos. I knew this would lead to trouble. I began by asking if he knew how much ransom had been demanded. He was eager to boast: half a million for the tribune, ten thousand for me. I could see Caunus listening in, looking proud of his superior value.

Moving on, I began perkily discussing military pay, which in the tribune's case might be relevant to our captors. Acatholos listened as if he was being told a nursery story, while I dragged out facts male relations had told me. The annual stipend of a legionary soldier had been raised to three hundred denarii by Domitian, although I pointed out that this would be before deductions for food, tent, uniform and, the hoary old standby, miscellaneous. Pay was only two hundred a year for the firefighting vigiles. I did not know the salary of a cohort tribune, but since he would be an elite ex-centurion, it jumped up into thousands. Gaius Caunus probably received as much in a year as the brigands were asking for me.

'And how do you fare, Acatholos? I have seen how Dexiades looks after himself – that's a truly lovely home he has! Is life as good among his crew?'

Acatholos finally recognised I was sowing dissent. Still, it was worth a try. Most workers harbour some level of grumbling unhappiness.

My taking an interest in him only gave the bandit one idea. I should have known. Well, I did, but there were few ways to keep his attention. He began hauling up his long tunic. 'Want it?' This was more of a threat than a question.

'No, thank you. I have a husband for that sort of thing.'

Rejection failed. They never listen. I was stuck with the old assumption that 'no' means 'yes'. He grabbed me; I had to fight back. Tiresome molestation ensued, a struggle that might have been modelled on the big statue of lapiths and centaurs. Acatholos had one lewd idea: mounting and rape. Mine was to employ elbows, knees, fists and fingers to stop him. He was stronger; I had been taught nastier tricks. I worked through his organs, punching hard to tenderise his liver and spleen, but he was enjoying the fight too much, so he barely felt my mortar-grinding of his gonads. Poking him hard in the eye worked. As he wiped away tears, I reached to find my knife from my satchel.

I felt sick. As an escape plan, this was a mess. I was failing, and Caunus had achieved even less. Even so, I gamely stuck my fruit knife into my assailant's body. I hit nothing vital but the sight of blood on his tunic gave him pause.

Caunus had put down the stool, one-handed; it was too near Egloge's foot and the young woman stamped viciously on his hand. Caunus yelled. He swung upright, with striking use of his core muscles. On his feet, he hit her. He would have called it a smack. She hit him back. She meant to crack his cheek.

Their patball might have continued, but just in time, someone else joined in with us. The hatch above swung open

305

fully. A foot in a toe-post sandal descended. The first leg was quickly joined by a second. Then, in one long movement, the whole flautist descended. He broke his fall by dropping right on top of Egloge.

'Does your mother know you jump on girls?' I asked. He blushed. 'Don't worry; I won't tell her.'

51

Our rescuer looked like a Greek philosopher. I knew he cultivated his image carefully. This was a particularly scruffy version.

Egloge had hit her head on the table and lay unconscious. The musician did not muck about. Somebody had taught him always to follow through. His precious flute was safely tucked into his wide leather belt; gripped under one arm, he had brought something bigger, dirtier and heavier. It was a pickaxe. Acatholos released me and rushed over. As he lifted his left foot to kick the young man in the guts, the flautist, two-handed, swung his weapon up. He was a strong lad, for a philosopher. He brought down the tool into the bandit's standing foot, which pinned Acatholos to the earth floor, blood pouring. He had driven the pickaxe through his right foot, boot and all. The result was hideous.

'Jupiter!' cried Caunus, as the victim screamed. An army man, he had not yet become used to the filthier morals and methods of big-city slums.

Egloge still had not come round. Acatholos was stuck, bent over, bleeding and unable to move as his assailant leaned down on the pick. 'Get going,' the flautist said to us cheerily. Caunus and I grabbed our meagre belongings and raced for the door.

'Bring the pickaxe. It's our property!' Our rescuer paused until we were outside. He grabbed a handful of goat's cheese, hauled out the pick and loped after us. Behind him he left even more blood surging from the bandit's boot, with more ghastly yelling. We locked the door. Caunus had the presence of mind to move the ladder that had been used to enter the upper store.

He and I surveyed the musician. He was short, stocky, pleasant-featured, impoverished, full of cheeky character, and not much more than twenty-five. Apart from meticulously battered sandals, his image as a thinker included a full-length trip-over tunic in a nasty shade of sludge, long dark corkscrews of hair and a thin, dishevelled beard. He had a small satchel slung cross-body, which had come from the same leather shop as mine.

'Whoever the fuck you are,' said the tribune, 'I must buy you a drink some time.'

'Falernian?'

'Don't push your luck, son.'

As the flautist guzzled goat's cheese, I performed an introduction. 'Gaius Caunus, Seventh Vigiles. This fighting intellectual is a stepson of Petronius Longus, retired from the Fourth. He brings up children to be tough. This one is currently cruising around Neapolis, Caunus, because Our Master in Rome doesn't favour free thinking. His mother tells everyone it's just a phase. She is my father's sister . . . Greetings, Marius!'

'*Io*, Flavia Albia!' returned my cousin, with the cracking grin all the men in the Didius family use.

'Good of you to drop in.'

'Seemed appropriate. You two were making a meal of it.'

'Cut the quickfire crap. Let's get out of here!' interrupted Caunus.

52

In a stable we found Mercury, who seemed pleased to see me, headbutting me to pull at her ears. One other animal was standing by, a skinny mule. I knew Caunus kept a prized beast in Rome that I had once annoyed him by borrowing. Once we had harnessed the beasts at the farm, therefore, he took this mule as of right; Marius had to double up behind me.

We beetled downhill as fast as we dared. The steep descent required care, and we were trepidatious about meeting other bandits coming back. Marius assured us they would not return, because he knew that they were going to a temple on an island, where arrangements had been made for the tribune's ransom.

'Official policy is never to pay!' Caunus growled. 'Only way or officers would be nabbed by barbarians every damned week. This must be a set-up. If it's an attempted trap, with Rufeius in charge, he has all the nous of a baffled gnat.'

'I thought you trained him?' I ventured.

'Untrainable. Trust me, someone's bright idea will go arse over tip.'

I said a local duovir had been involved, which made Caunus despair even more. Even reminding him that the fleet commander had taken a hand failed to improve the outlook.

I insisted we make for the villa. I was desperate to see Tiberius and reassure him. I wanted my cousin to come too: he had not only saved us so should be rewarded, but prior to that he was the flute player Suza had heard entertaining Fulvia Secunda at the Gabius estate. I intended to debrief him. Riding hard, it was impossible to talk further. My questions for Marius would have to wait.

Thinking about my capture, I felt oddly tremulous. Reaction was finally setting in. I could not envisage continuing my inquiry. Still, it must happen. Informers cannot abandon their caseload just because they have a personal misadventure.

We came down through the panoramic views, from the thin air to normality, without meeting anyone. We slowed once we hit the Via Minerva, then turned along the road. At the point where our track led off, two red-tunicked members of the Seventh Cohort were stationed, not men I had ever known. They looked startled to see Caunus, but saluted and allowed us through.

On arrival, there were cheers. Vigiles were everywhere; half the detachment had been assigned there in my absence. Despite its name, a century never numbers a hundred, more like four-fifths in practice, but that easily gave us thirty men, while Milo and Hyro had joined them at our property. They, with the builders and our household staff, rushed to greet us.

I slithered off the donkey, making a joke of the situation. 'No panic. Slight hold-up, but I had only nipped out to retrieve our pickaxe.'

Tiberius was holding me very tight by then. 'All right?'

'All good. You?'

'Better now!'

Over his shoulder I saw Marius make moves that looked to be from a military parade. He shouldered and presented the pickaxe as Larcius rushed forwards to receive the site tool. Marius apologised for the bandit's blood on it. Fondling his beloved piece, the clerk-of-works promised to treasure the stains as trophies. 'Any other stolen goods where you got this?'

'A bunch of big stucco scenes, cluttering up the loft they put me in. Labours of Hercules, prettified in plaster. I'm afraid I knocked a tusk off the snout of the Erymanthian Boar.'

'He's a lad!' commented the tribune.

'No piglet is safe with him around.' I performed introductions. 'Tiberius Manlius, Gaius Caunus.' I pretended we had properly deployed the jailer's daughter trick: 'Your tribune has turned into a hotshot lover. I taught him all he knows,' I told Milo and Hyro.

'No doubt he buggered it up?' returned Hyro naughtily.

'Cobnuts!' Caunus dismissed it. 'I had my own plan ready. I had been grooming the male guard, until that was overruled . . .'

Marius, an easy-going character, stood by saying nothing, but I made sure his crucial contribution became known.

The tribune had already ascertained that the absent half-century was on duty at a Temple of Hercules, the coastal location where his ransom would supposedly be paid. The temple stood on a tiny island of jutting limestone stacks, between Stabiae and what had once been the hamlet of Oplontis, at the mouth of the River Sarno. It lay about a stadium's length from shore, making a secure place for a handover. Laying an ambush on the island ought to work. However, the piratical bandits might escape by sea.

Caunus was all for riding off there himself. 'This needs someone efficient!' He stopped when a young woman rushed up from the house, carrying a very young baby. As they do, the child had a miserable cold. Goodness, the tribune had a partner. When she heard he had been captured, she had bravely made the journey all the way from Rome. I wondered if she would have come if someone had told her he had gone out partying.

'What were you hoping to achieve?' he grumbled, although while she cried with relief, he got on with wiping the baby's nose. He seemed not to need instructions.

'I could fling myself at their feet and plead?'

'Bloody daft idea!'

For once Caunus spoke mildly. He would know, as she might not, that his chances of returning to her had been slim. A key pointer was that if the bandits were expecting the ransom, they had made no move towards producing him at an exchange. *Proof of life or no cash forthcoming* . . .

Caunus sent a group of vigiles up the mountain to arrest Acatholos and Egloge; I said they should also search for Septumius and young Criton. 'If you find them bring them here. Don't stand for arguments. The lad is a crucial witness to murder.'

'Do it,' confirmed their tribune. It went against the grain to allow a female civilian to give orders to his men. 'I'm going to requisition carts from you, Aedile. That will take my lads up the mountain faster, and be useful for ferrying prisoners. One of the wounded will not be walking.'

Sparsus, eager for excitement, volunteered to drive. I told him to investigate the loft above the byre, then bring out any plaster plaques or other stolen goods. Dromo wanted to go. That was until we pointed out that the pickaxe had been stolen by the men in black who had hit him.

Caunus did not go back but nominated a deputy. Cohort tribunes steer their troops with a light hand, which they maintain allows trained men their independence. Or, if anything goes wrong, it won't be their fault. Besides, they have more important things to do.

Instead, Caunus and his wife, or girlfriend, were led off by Gratus for a reunion in private. Gratus must have assigned a room to them. The tribune had his arm around the young woman as they went, and I noticed it was him, now, carrying the baby. He even had his stubbly cheek against its tiny head.

That baby was already a favourite. Axilius, the jobbing carpenter, was busily making it a crib. Meanwhile, Fornix rushed away to prepare a grand reunion lunch. Tiberius sent Paris down to Stabiae to inform the duovir that the tribune and I had surfaced, and our safe location. Suza, sobbing, had kissed me, shrieked over my hair, and was gabbling about arrangements for freshening up. For that, I was informed, I had to wait. People had plans for me. In case I ever made it back, the workmen had mended the broken pipe, connected the water system, fired up the furnace and were heating a huge bronze boiler for hot water. Everyone was highly excited that I had returned in time to be the first into the rejuvenated bath suite.

I cooperated. Tiberius, smiling, encouraged me to be patient, as if this was a reward to our staff for dark fears after I had gone missing. Before racing off to set things up, Serenus gave me an unexpected hug. 'How has he coped?' I murmured.

'The chief? In bits. We never knew he had so many filthy swear words in his dictionary.'

Tiberius and I would have our own reunion, but not yet. We had hardly spoken to one another, but between us there was no need. I did murmur that I was sorry; he pulled a face

313

that acknowledged there was nothing he could do. I had come home safe. I had found the missing tribune. I had even brought a philosopher-musician to enhance our party.

While I waited for time by myself with a strigil and tooth stick, I sat with my husband, talking to young Marius. 'Where's your friend with the harp?'

Marius pulled a face. 'Girlfriend in Sinuessa. He says she's the one.'

'Will she keep him out of trouble?'

'That's what he wants, apparently.'

'Your mother and Petro will be happy we ran into each other . . . And what about you?'

'Working solo. I've put together a little lupin-round.'

Although he had come south as part of a duo, Marius had split from his partner as musicians do. Repertoire differences, he claimed, plus the Sinuessa beauty. He now spent his time travelling between big villas and offering not animal fodder, of course, but his services as a flautist. There was no call for his wisdom as a philosopher. 'Plutocrats hereabouts are carrying on as if the eruption never happened: boat parties, banquets, bathing spas, barbecues, drinks receptions, and – luckily for me – musical soirées. Next time there is a big festival, I am hoping to win one of the competitions. Prizes at the Isolympics, the Sebasta Games, are very generous, and then you get yourself a name.'

'Well, watch out for girlfriends who want to bleed you of your prize fund.'

'Oh, I avoid girlfriends!'

He said there was hardly a porticoed door he had not knocked upon. Then recently this lupin-round got him hired at the Gabius estate to play for Fulvia Secunda. Gellius and Lavinia had paid him well. Marius was observant: he felt there definitely was a story there – 'Something stinky?' He couldn't work out what had been going on, though most ideas I suggested to him seemed a plausible fit. The only thing he could not believe was that Secunda might have been behind the killing of her brother Primus. 'The old woman seemed a gentle soul – though I concede that stuff they dosed her with contributed.'

'You saw the medicine? I presume it had happened on other occasions, not only when my maid was watching?'

'Yes. I didn't know Suza belonged with you, by the way, Albia. By the time I found out you'd been there, you had left.'

'Dispatched for prying. Tell me, did Fulvia Secunda ever speak to you?'

'No – but I always felt she might have done.'

After I had left, Marius had also observed the subsequent visitation by Dexiades. 'It was fascinating, Albia. As soon as his carriage was heard trundling up, the couple had the old lady taken away. Blossia, the woman who looks after her, whisked her off to a neighbour's house. Very smooth exit – as if she had done it before. Dexiades was pressing for access to Secunda, but I could tell they never allowed it. According to him, he regularly visited to check up on her welfare.'

'Hmm! He assured me, too, that he looks after Secunda's interests, though I don't see him as the protective type.'

'Were the Publilii and Dexiades on good terms, Marius?' asked Tiberius, who was quietly sitting with us.

'Cool,' Marius replied. 'I had to be careful, but once I knew you featured, Albia, I kept eyes and ears open. Dexiades seems to have a mysterious hold. I felt Gellius and Lavinia were somehow obliged to put up with him, though it wasn't going smoothly. I did overhear him saying, "At this rate there will be no more payouts!" Gellius returned heavily, the choice would be up to Dexiades.'

'Blackmail?'

'Could be.'

'He was trying to control them? He lent them his carriage to come and see us next day.'

'Yes, he stayed over, and his carriage seemed to be something he pushed onto them.'

'We think he may have urged them to come, to make me swallow a good story,' I explained. Marius nodded. 'They don't like him?'

'Does anyone?'

'You didn't?' Tiberius queried.

Marius said no, especially since the siblings had ended his stint on hire, as if bullied into that by Dexiades. 'Whether it was his doing or not, they wanted me out of the house in a hurry.' After Gellius and Lavinia had driven off with Ergon, Dexiades was picked up by some of his men; he asked if Marius would like a job entertaining some prisoners. Marius agreed.

'What prisoners could be legitimate? Did you see working for him as ethical?' Tiberius knew my cousin less well than I did. Marius had played at our wedding but, having been struck by lightning, Tiberius had few memories of the occasion. He was now critical of how Marius squared working for Dexiades. 'Did you need money that badly?'

Marius answered calmly, 'I work or I starve, sir. I didn't even know one of his captives would be Albia. But I was curious. Albia's name had been mentioned and I could see she had posed questions that were badly received. I have been taught to jump into situations like that, Albia will tell you. If there seems to be mud, we stir it around with a big stick to see if anything jumps out. All of us in the Didius family love to intervene.'

Tiberius relaxed and laughed. 'That sounds familiar!'

Marius was reviewing his own memories. 'Manlius Faustus, the last time I saw you, you were prone on a pavement, gently smoking. We all thought Jupiter had topped you, and that Albia would go out of her mind.'

'She dragged me back to life.' Tiberius was brief, not one to sensationalise. Besides, it had always troubled him that he still had no recollection of the moment when that lightning felled him.

'Yes, around us even the gods tend to withdraw, quaking,' mused Marius. 'They give decrees and we just ignore them. Our family has no concept of fatalism.'

That was when I mentioned that the goddess of chance had in fact taken revenge. I explained how, up in the mountains, the attendant at the Temple of Tyche seemed to have misled me, leading to my kidnap.

'Not Polydorus!' my cousin exclaimed. 'Polydorus is all right. He would not have given you duff info deliberately.'

I was amazed. 'You know him?'

'I know virtually everyone. Around here is my lupin-round, remember. I sometimes have to play for ceremonies at that temple – though it's a detestable venue. The priestess is a real stinker.'

I might have wondered more about Polydorus, but people arrived to fetch me. Not only could I use the bath suite, now equipped with heated floors and warm water, but an extra treat was waiting. They had filled my tub for me.

317

53

When an adventure has shaken you, nothing beats silence and solitude. A comfortable bath is a good place for it. I had definitely been anxious while I was up in the mountains.

I made it clear there was no chance of an audience. Mixed bathing is permissible in private premises and I like to think I am not prudish, but parading nude before a whole lunch-eon party was not my style. Suza was allowed, but the others were firmly informed I would tell them all about the bath later. Lunch was to be held in the peristyle garden, so they could wait there. Someone should go and tell Fornix that today I would not want goat's cheese.

As I stripped off in the changing room – newly equipped with wooden clothes containers on the walls – I noticed a large old pair of men's bathhouse slippers. Backless, they had thick platform soles and heels for walking on roasting hot floors, with beaten-up brown leather uppers. Suza said the workmen had found them during the refit. I reckoned they might have belonged to Curvidius Primus. They were too big for me, certainly.

'Don't be long,' Suza instructed. 'The cook is going barmy, making lunch. Shall I wait?'

'No, just leave the clean clothes. I can manage.'

'I've put some necklaces out for you.'

Of course she had.

I went in alone to try out my tub. Suza had placed a mat alongside it, with oil lamps lit because the room had only dim natural light. Several unguent containers were positioned on the flat rim for me to choose from. I could guess at how carefully my girlie had pondered which to give me, and she had provided a big new sea sponge.

I stepped in cautiously. A bronze bath absorbs a lot of heat into its metal, so the water was warm, though not too hot. People had filled it moderately deep. I sank down into it, breathing slowly. Delicious. I dropped lower until my ears were covered, blotting out noise.

After a short soak, I washed all over, cleaned my hair, wrapped my head in a towel, then let a soothing trance take over. I was not even thinking much. I managed not to fall asleep.

Finally, I was ready to climb out. I began to rise, but suddenly fell back, splashing water wildly. The bath was too long for someone of my height. I had had to hold the sides to stop my legs floating and now I could not press my feet on its end to gain the right purchase before standing. It was too deep to gain a successful hold on the edge. It was too narrow to move around freely. I could not even turn over to kneel up and rise to my feet that way.

I realised I was helpless: I was stuck in the tub.

54

Hello, hello! I had not expected unplanned research.

I did not panic. This would be resolved, although it might entail embarrassment. Settling down in the water again, I imagined the possible final moments of Curvidius Primus. I was in no danger of drowning. For one thing, I could reach a hand down to the plug by my feet and remove it, letting out the water. However, the tub was a close fit. I could envisage how someone larger would find movement trickier.

He was big and unfocused. He would have been taller than me, so he could have pushed his feet against the end, yet his bulk would have prevented him reaching the plug. Lifting himself upright would have been difficult; someone had told me he always needed assistance to clamber out without falling. In this bath, a heavy man with a drinker's paunch could well have become wedged.

He had had slaves nearby. He was accustomed to calling out to demand things. He could have shouted for help.

'Suza!' I called, feeling shy about having become stuck. After a moment I roared more forcefully, 'Suza, I need you. Will you come in here?'

No answer. Either she was no longer there, playing with my jewellery, or with the thick bathhouse walls she could not hear me.

I took a new view of how Gellius and Lavinia had said they had been reading and sipping pre-dinner drinks out in the garden. If Primus had called for assistance, they could never have heard him. More importantly, when they claimed they noticed a commotion, they were lying.

Perhaps that was too harsh. Perhaps a slave ran out and shrieked to them that the 'accident' was happening.

I myself now heard someone in the corridor; unsure who, I simply called a hello. I was heard that time. My husband had come looking for me. I won't say I had been panicking but I was truly glad to see him.

'How's the bath?'

'Lovely, until you try to climb out. Don't laugh, I seem to be stuck, my darling. Did you hear me calling for help?'

'No! I've only just got you back safely – and now there's another alarm.'

'I'm sorry,' I said meekly.

Tiberius came alongside with towels over one arm. He assessed the situation and looked down at me, splishing like a sea nymph. He leered appreciatively. 'Nice! All clean and scented, just for me! I came in case you wanted me to dry your back.'

'Yes, please – but will you help extract me first?'

He reached down, I put my hands behind his neck, he pulled me half upright. I was slippery with unguents, lavishly applied. Unintentionally he dropped me. That was an interesting illustration of what might have happened ten years ago. Mind you, nobody had ever suggested Primus died during a seduction scene.

Tiberius grinned. I chortled. He wiped his hands on a towel, then tried again, wrapping another towel around my arm to stop me sliding; this time he hauled me up far enough, so I stood and stepped out. We ended up in a close marital crush, somewhat prolonging it.

Water had sloshed everywhere. Once again, Tiberius had acquired a wet tunic. He said he would tell Dromo to come and sweep around with a mop, though not right now. Staying close, we held one another for lengthy, loving, deeply enjoyable kisses.

I said that had been worth coming home for. He said there had better be more in the very near future. However, we should hold off, because otherwise, if we spent too much time in the bath suite and kept them waiting for lunch, everyone would know what we were up to.

He sauntered out, looking innocent. I quickly dressed, then walked through the corridor to the peristyle garden. During our meal, the master and I took opposite ends of a long table, smiling at each other down the line of platters in a way that must have told everybody exactly what was on our minds.

We had a good marriage and, although we did not care who knew, we rarely advertised it publicly.

'Tell me, Tiberius Manlius,' I asked him, in hearing of them all. 'Would you have paid the money the brigands were demanding for me?'

Putting him on the spot was a gentle tease. He paused, as if reluctant to reply.

'Policy,' Caunus reminded us. Tribunes have a natural bent for sniffing out lunch, so he and his little family had joined us. 'Ransoms should never be handed over.'

'Well, would you?' I repeated.

'I would,' Tiberius admitted. His voice croaked inadvertently. He was looking at me, but he meant everyone else to hear it. The last time I had heard him speak with such intensity, he had been making his marriage vows. 'This is how such criminals operate, of course. I had written to Uncle Tullius telling him to send funds. I would have paid what they asked, Albiola – and if I had had to, I would have paid more.'

He was famously proper, so his answer startled me. It had not been a condition of an afternoon in bed with him. All the same, when we took our siesta afterwards, this made our lovemaking together doubly sweet.

We forgot all about the 'cough mixture'. Even when we remembered, we were too lost in the situation to change anything the second time.

'That will be twins, then!' Tiberius prophesied.

I hoped the sphinx who gave oracles for him had gone off duty.

55

The Curvidius cremation was very nearly rained off. Fortunately, Larcius had looked at the sky, then stashed the necessary logs undercover. He had everything else either taken in or fastened down. All night, a heavy rainstorm battered hard. It had raced in down the peninsula, after picking up force over the Tyrrhenian Sea, then hurled its way overland in a straight line from Surrentum to the body of the Apennines. In the morning, everywhere was soaking wet, though a stiff drying wind helped. We woke to find that any visible trees were still leaning over in the storm's powerful tail. No ships or fishing boats could be seen out in the bay. Detritus of all kinds had been blown into corners, leaving a scene of mildly disturbing untidiness, as if some unknown danger had passed through while we were sleeping. Fortunately, after breakfast the weather died down.

Funerals can be such fun. People who hardly knew the deceased will trot up to pay respects, in the hope of eating a lot of spiced cake and watching family fisticuffs. If nobody storms off in a blind rage, vowing never to speak to some auntie again, the event counts as a failure. But this one looked promising.

I had rarely combined a funeral with an assembly of witnesses and suspects like this, and never with a murder victim actually burning in front of us. I felt optimistic. Once I am ready, I enjoy a good case finale. The risks of hysterical denials or an unexpected confession (true or fake) are usually high. Here, I was confident I had collected enough pointers to reach a conclusion. Some people, at least, would be surprised by what I knew and what else I had deduced. It would be intriguing to see how these people mourned. That might yet provide further clues.

Curvidius Fulvianus arrived around mid-morning, using the conveyance he had snaffled from the Gabius estate. He seemed oddly het up, perhaps because he was sharing his transport with a portable altar and a young live pig. Once the porker was extracted, wriggling and squealing loudly as if it knew it was to be sacrificed, we put it in the care of Larcius. I told him to make sure the vigiles didn't cook and eat it. Drax tried to make friends. The pig ran away so a wild chase followed. Sparsus eventually threw himself onto it in a fine tackle. The pig bit him. So did Drax, although that was an accident due to overexcitement.

Fulvianus said he had come early to field any awkward attendees. He had issued invitations for the afternoon, because there was no point in holding a torchlit procession, even under the massed starscape that blinks above Neapolis. Besides, the remains we had to place on the pyre would not take the normal long hours to be consumed. All the bones had already been subjected to intense heat; burning them again would merely be a signal to pacify any restless spirits. 'Afternoon avoids any need to supply lunch,' said Fulvianus, meanly. Then he confided, 'I am not looking forward to this. It could be the worst day of my life!'

That sounded unexpectedly human. Tiberius and I began a slight readjustment to our opinion of the man.

Another adjustment was needed too: Fulvianus had looked into the questions I had posed about the Publilius siblings.

325

'Did you bring in a specialist?'

'Waste of money. No need for forensic accountancy, I did a quick recce myself. My man in Rome has been handling various documents, since I took over as executor. He should have picked up anomalies. I've been back to the estate again and checked records. I found no impropriety regarding the vineyard. Nothing much was wrong with the domestic budget. My sister has little need for spending, of course. She may be loopy nowadays but – like others, I suspect – she's a mad old widow who's sitting on a healthy fortune. She is completely unaware. Even so, no one is pilfering. I can't call out the Publilii on any financial impropriety. The money my sister ought to have is all there, mouldering in bankboxes.'

That was a surprise. 'What about Gellius and Lavinia then?' Tiberius demanded. 'From appearances, they had been creaming off funds, and for a long time.'

'Apparently not.' Fulvianus had lost any previous dismay. 'They live in the house for free, of course, but that's reasonable. It is run like a quiet family home, no extravagance. The young man showed me invoices. All legit. I have no quibbles.'

'They couldn't have faked a set of figures to show you?'

'No. I saw the full bankboxes.'

'Where does their own cash come from, then?' I asked, puzzled by this turn-up. 'They must have a good income. They obviously spend liberally on personal adornment, for one thing.'

'That I don't know. So long as they don't raid our coffers, I don't much care. But I am grateful you raised the issue. My sister has disposable income that really should be made to work for us.'

I noted he said 'for us' not 'for her', but that was normal. If Fulvia Secunda was comfortable in her present life, and her brother oversaw things, even if he did it from Rome, nothing more should be said. Whatever happened would be his choice. Unlike the Publilii, he was legally his sister's head of household. He took note of what was brought to his attention and seemed to honour his responsibilities. Judging by his attitude to the funeral today, Fulvianus did what he ought, even when it felt burdensome. Few people can claim that.

I still wanted to know how Gellius and Lavinia managed to afford their coordinated fashionable clothes, big jewellery and life of indolence – not to mention what must lie behind those lotus-eaters' smug self-composure. 'Are the Publilius siblings expected today?' Since the reply was affirmative, I burnished my plans to challenge them.

'But what about your sister?' Tiberius asked, more urgently. 'Didn't you have a panic about her going missing on a carriage ride?'

'Yes – wasn't there a suggestion Fulvia Secunda has disappeared?' I joined in, pressing her brother. It was he, in fact, who had told us. We were startled he had not immediately assured us that he now knew where she was.

'Have you managed to see Fulvia Secunda, after all?' Tiberius demanded. 'Is she coming to send Primus on his way?'

'Oh, I saw her.' Fulvianus was oddly offhand. 'She will wave Primus away to the shades, even if she has no idea who is going or where to. That's the least of my worries.' Perhaps he could tell we thought his attitude strange, because he expanded: 'Secunda is safe. I wasn't telling anyone, but I had suggested a quiet move elsewhere for a few days. Out of the way of hangers-on.'

I could not leave it at that. 'I suppose even if your sister has no idea she is a rich woman, other people do know.'

'Exactly.' Fulvianus did not want to say more.

'There is that pirate,' Tiberius suggested, insisting on more detail. 'He has assured Albia he was close friends with your late brother-in-law and cares very much for your sister. We know he goes up to the estate, where even the Publilii don't entirely welcome him. Did they tell you that they send Secunda to a neighbour's house if he visits?'

Fulvianus nodded. 'The situation needs clarification, I agree. Dexiades tries to cosy up to her, eye on the fortune, undoubtedly. After she was widowed, I'm told he even spoke of marriage – a disaster! Our brother had to step in. Primus insisted Secunda move here with him, in order to keep Dexiades at arm's length.' Finally that explained how she had come to live at his villa.

'Did it work?' I asked drily.

'On and off. I had lunch with Dexiades recently. It was his idea – he does keep manoeuvring for contact with us – but I wanted to check him over. He kept harping on about his affection for my sister – for heaven's sake, have you seen her? He was trying to poison me with the notion that the Publilii are routinely stealing and abusing her. When he had drunk enough, he professed to want to rescue her from their clutches – *out of love*, if you believe it – then carry her off to what he called safety in Sardinia.'

'He's a pirate,' commented Tiberius. 'We have seen what he is up to, with the tribune and Albia. His idea of "safety" will be to rob or ransom Secunda.'

I agreed that an old lover in the looted-art world was some-one a frail widow ought to avoid.

'Well, I put her in a safe place until Dexiades is dealt with,'

Fulvianus asserted. 'That duovir has gone after him, I believe. He seems efficient enough, for a local man. Should be slapping Dexiades in custody any time now for his recent activities. Including your wife,' he added politely to Tiberius, who sat tight-lipped. He would not discuss the ordeal he had suffered while I was in captivity.

'I want to remind you, Fulvianus,' I said, 'your sister probably knows what happened when your brother died.' I decided not to suggest right now that she might have caused it.

Although Fulvianus did not rebuff me, he discouraged speculation. 'Does she really?'

'Knowledge could be dangerous. And whatever she saw that evening is supposed to have led to her breakdown.'

'I doubt that!' scoffed her brother. 'Something nasty in the bathhouse? No. More likely the barmy woman had been denied something she wanted, so she went into a sulk and has forgotten to come out of it. We shall see,' he concluded.

I found his response unsatisfactory but had to drop the argument because we received a noisy group of new visitors.

56

These next arrivals were vigiles. By chance two groups converged on us at almost the same time, each bringing sets of prisoners, who were being treated typically: with jibes, shoves and threats of beatings, which meant lashing with rope ends, since the noble fire brigade is not armed with weapons. As my uncle always said, the *spartoli*, or bucketeers, have enough weight to carry around, with their namesake heavy water pails, plus hooks, picks and mattocks, crowbars, axes, soaking quilts, smothering esparto mats, ladders – and, of course, hidden cudgels for when they feel like thrashing burglars during the night watch. That's without mentioning large bunches of keys they have collected, in case they need emergency access to locked accommodation. I don't mean a building where treasure is known to be kept, but some place where available women might be 'led to safety'.

Our property was now the base for the full century, which, after allowing for genuine sickness and skilful malingering, approached sixty burly men in faded red tunics, headed up by that fellow whose name had been bandied about: Rufeius, a breezy centurion. They immediately fell upon the two tents our workmen used, turfing out any remaining stores so they could establish a camp for themselves: thirty men intending to squash under each ridge pole in a tent meant for ten. It was best not to imagine how it would work.

Drax, our site watchdog, evacuated one tent where he had his water bowl and mat, then went racing around in circles, barking hysterically. He could not decide whether to bite first and ask questions afterwards – a tactic the vigiles would recognise – or to wag madly and hope friendly hands would pat him. Had these been soldiers, he could have found himself slobbering over marching-biscuit but, instead, the city-boy vigiles were soon demanding of me where they could find the nearest bar that served hot stews. There were none up here, and Fornix would be overwhelmed if expected to provide pottage for so many men. We managed to dissuade them from pulling apart the newly built pyre to make a bonfire to heat mess tins; spare cremation logs were waiting, so they pinched those. I soon realised why: there was no victuals problem because the group who had gone up the mountain had brought back a flock of goats.

Caunus emerged; he must have sniffed out that his men were making a barbecue in close proximity. Well, he heard and smelt the goats. At his appearance, the troops stopped cooking and assembled in wavery lines. 'Call that a salute? Smarten up, you slouchers. I will not ask who stole those bloody goats. Take a note, Rufeius. I want a prime cut on a warmed plate, with a nice sprig of rosemary – and give me a fresh glass of Lactarii milk to nourish a young lady who is a nursing mother.'

'Oh!' murmured Rufeius, with a happy-go-lucky grin. 'Charis found you, then?'

Caunus apparently suffered from deafness.

Once he had called his troops a hopeless shower enough times, he turned his ire onto the prisoners. His and my jailers from the farm had been picked up, though so far my quarries, Septumius and Criton, had not been discovered; men

331

had been left behind to search. The two ex-jailers were a sorry sight. Acatholos had lost a lot of blood; his foot was now wrapped in a dirty bandage. We offered to have it cleansed and salved properly but he refused. Infection was bound to claim the idiot soon. Having come so close to assault, I wasted no more pity on him. Egloge ought to have been in a better condition but had vomited and fitted during the journey down, so must be suffering from more than mild concussion. The other three captured bandits were men we recognised, Docetius, Surdinius and Bitho, picked up from the Temple of Hercules ransom exchange.

Rufeius told Caunus he had brought them so the tribune could confront them. 'Too bloody right, I will! I'll teach the slimeball cash-grabbers to capture me. Line them up and tell me how the crap you managed to lay hands on them.'

Rufeius gave a report, which he narrated with straightforward panache: that an ambush had been laid at the temple, using a chest with the supposed half-million sesterces ransom (a box of rocks), a couple of the more lightweight vigiles disguised as altar boys, and the centurion himself dressed as a priest, his head covered religiously. Three black-clad men had skidded up onshore on fast mules. They failed to notice it was a trap, even though the false priest had hobnailed boots under his robe. The rest of the lads jumped out from hiding, knocked the bandits to the ground, and seized their mules. Meanwhile, a ship slyly arrived beside the temple's rocky islet, presumably to take away kidnappers and loot. It turned tail, only to meet a line of triremes that had slid quietly into position under the fleet commander.

'The big prawn himself? Pass me a seaweed fritter! Would you believe it – a useful sailor! I do not see that hound Dexiades here?'

'Location unknown, I'm afraid, sir.'

'You may well be afraid, Rufeius! Redeem yourself or die hideously. I want every available man on alert to find him.'

Caunus demanded of the three bandits captured on the island whether they knew the pirate's current whereabouts; naturally, they denied it. He replied that the 'no comment' get-out was such a routine old ploy, it would not save them from him. He had a special cipher for it in his notebook: a downward dagger. If he was feeling artistic, he drew blood drops around the pictogram.

He and I knew them from the farm. We now knew Docetius, Surdinius and Bitho were also the intruders who had come onto our estate that night. They must have found the plaster plaques they had claimed to be looking for, which they hid at the farm; the artefacts had been kicked around the loft there by Marius but had now been rescued. While pinching the plaques, the three must have cracked open our water-distribution point and battered Dromo.

The bandits denied that too.

'Mighty Triton's arse!' commented Caunus, wearily. 'Don't you airheads own up to any damned thing?'

My husband used less metaphorical rhetoric, preferring facts: 'They were all seen on the premises. They were witnessed by my boy, Dromo, using our pickaxe to flood my uncle's property. One of them nearly broke Dromo's nose.'

Tiberius demanded an identity parade. Dromo, in his patched tunic, was summoned to the front, shuffling up with his usual guilty-looking stare. At first, he was too scared; he refused to cooperate. Tiberius and I drew next to him protectively. 'Dromo,' I explained, as if he were a shy five-year-old, kicked by bullies on his way home from school, 'one of these men attacked you and we need you to tell us which.'

'Whoever attacks my slave, attacks me!' Tiberius pronounced. 'Do not be afraid, Dromo. Tell me which one struck you in the face.'

Dromo looked from Tiberius to me, both of us reassuring. Perhaps he saw, for once, that he was fortunate. 'I let you down!' he gibbered. 'It is *my* job to protect *you*, Master.'

'And mine to look after you. Nobody will be allowed to hurt you again. Now look at those men carefully and show me.'

I wasn't so soft. 'Stop twisting around as if you need a toilet. Get a grip, Dromo!'

Dromo shrank against his master's side, away from me. He pointed to the bandit called Surdinius.

'Put that man in irons!' ordered Tiberius. It sounded commanding. Unfortunately, so far from their home station-house, the vigiles had no equipment with them.

Milo and Hyro intervened: they suggested the leg fetters that the Primus slaves had worn. 'Stick him in chains and forget him!' promised Milo, with glee.

'Let him rot!' jeered Hyro.

It had an interesting result. Unaware we had dismantled the hut, Surdinius let out a sudden yell. He screamed no, no, begging not to be left to die in the dark – in a prison, all by himself apart from long-dead bones and their angry spirits.

'Oh, that's a giveaway!' I exclaimed, rounding on him. 'How do you know some slaves were locked in here? How do you know they had been abandoned to die?'

Surdinius refused to say. Looks passed uneasily between him and the others; it was obvious they all knew. Had they been at the villa before, ten long years ago? Had *they* fettered and locked up the slaves?

334

Now other people began filtering down our drive for the funeral, so I would have to pursue the matter later. The bandits must have seen from my glare that I would.

We moved out our animals and secured all the captives in the stable. That meant they were out of sight and silenced temporarily, held in limbo until my gathering of witnesses. But Surdinius had given me a clue. In my mind a new lead had firmed up.

I was ready now.

57

In the next hour we were joined by various neighbours. Some I had never seen before, but among them were Bitus, the nosy turnip, still wearing his hat with the big hole; the pleasant old next-door couple, Heius and Favonilla; and the suave man who had lived in Rome, Pescennius Neo (togate). Word must have run around. Curvidius Fulvianus (also now togate) looked annoyed as he muttered to me that he had definitely not invited this crowd. His plan had been to avoid outsiders. I was sanguine. I don't always have scope to take minutes while I manipulate the end of an inquiry. Afterwards, when memories tend to fade, it helps extract my fee if clients can be reminded that a resolution did happen, and in public.

It can also be useful for people to find out about their neighbours. If they have learned exactly what behaviour caused the filthy-minded adulterer to be thrown out of his house, they will perhaps (if not already too late) keep their daughters away from him. If the confidence trickster's scheme has been exposed, then however nice a fellow they had always thought him, they might not put all their savings into that fraudster's greasy hands (well, not quite all). Or if a killer is being sent to the lions, they can book a ticket to watch.

Thinking about how I might proceed, I excused myself. There were arrangements I wanted to set up. For this, I brought in my loyal friends Milo and Hyro. 'You will like it, lads. This is going to be a neat piece of theatre.'

They were keen, even though they would need to use their muscle in setting out the props. I left them to seize on a suitable volunteer, teach him the script, and organise details. The action we were stage-managing would take place in the garden of the new wing, so until we were ready, no one else need be aware of it. 'Tell Gratus this should be where we lay out the mourners' buffet. Then . . . a grand revelation scene!'

Rites for Curvidius Primus would be taking place on the other side of the property. The pyre had been constructed in the old orchard area beside the entrance track. That meant a shorter journey for all the remains we had collected, as they were carefully brought out and laid together on the criss-crossed rectangle of logs. In lieu of a bier, our workmen had positioned a cover onto which, with surprisingly delicate actions, they hand-placed the various bones.

Further key players were assembling. A racket from four iron-shod wheels had signalled an enormous carriage, its size and domineering presence advertising that here came a personage of standing. Two wheezy white horses pulled the thing, straining to keep their feet on our rough track. A driver yelled nervously as the big vehicle rocked dangerously, threatening its axles. The carriage had curtained windows, a domed top with fringes, lamps for night driving and tiny statuettes of divinities to protect the occupants.

The owner was as impressive as her lacquered coachwork. She was helped out first, which she deemed her right. Stepping down onto the ashy patch of land where we parked vehicles, she screwed her mouth, gazing around in disbelief. A tall, imperious figure, ready to veil up, she was clad in black, in several heavy layers, though not enough to hide the jewellery she ported with the significance of commendatory medals. I put her at well over seventy; years had not mellowed her natural malevolence.

Curvidius Fulvianus moved forwards to greet her, a rocky path crunching under his shoes.

'Oh, there you are!' She presented her cheek, did not return his formal kiss and barely took breath. 'You haven't changed. You look as gormless as ever.' Pointedly, she surveyed what she could see of the villa. 'This place has gone badly downhill! The vines were never good for much, but the orchard's a loss, I suppose . . . Well, now I am here, let's get it over with.' At last, she paused. 'Are these the people you sold to? I suppose you had better introduce me.'

Agog, Tiberius and I were already preparing to be denounced. He had found his toga; I would pull up my stole at the right moment. Fulvianus made sure he named my husband as a magistrate. 'Manlius Faustus, an aedile from Rome, and his distinguished wife, Flavia Albia.'

'*Distinguished?*'

It was not the first time I had been summed up on sight as a rag-picker's by-blow. Since my origins remained unknown, she was possibly right but I would not cause upset by saying so. Mentioning Britannia was taboo as well, nor did I say I had been adopted by an informer. Tiberius took my hand in a firm, admonitory grip, although he knew Helena Justina had taught me never to start a fight until it became unavoidable. (Then punch your weight, with bells on.)

As a good hostess, properly taking my lead from my mild, polite husband, I returned quietly, 'My grandfather was a senator. So are both my mother's most noble brothers.'

The vision sniffed, unimpressed. 'I am Quinctia.' I had placed her already: this could only be the formidable

338

priestess of the Temple of Tyche. 'My position is extremely important.' Quinctia confirmed it. 'People have enormous respect for everything I do for the community.'

'I imagine so!' replied Tiberius. I hoped she missed his satirical tone.

'It is nothing to do with imagination, young man!' the priestess corrected him. She certainly lacked a sense of humour. 'My family are long-time sponsors of the temple. We practically own it. I myself have devoted my energy to its wellbeing for many, many years. My post demands the highest degree of service and self-sacrifice.' She performed a half-turn. 'Hurry up!'

Behind her came another, much frailer, old lady: Fulvia Secunda was being carefully extracted from the carriage by the temple assistant, Polydorus, and her maid, Blossia. Curvidius Fulvianus went across and kissed a papery cheek in the same way he had greeted the priestess. Secunda accepted it. She, too, gazed around vaguely as if failing to recognise her destination, even though she had been brought up on the estate and had returned later. At least bad memories were not visibly upsetting her.

Tiberius then stayed in control out of doors, while Curvidius Fulvianus and I escorted the two women into the villa to recover from travel. While Blossia and Suza renewed their acquaintance inside the atrium, I spoke in an undertone to Polydorus. 'You led me on a wild-goose chase, young man!'

He was unrepentant. 'I did my best. I told you I don't get out much.'

'Did you *know* you were sending me into the bandits' arms?'

'Certainly not, Domina. Septumius must have his farm in the same neck of the woods.'

'Don't talk about woods!' I snapped, shuddering at scenic memories. 'Well, he is hiding in some grove of beeches, and the boy with him. But we have men out on the crags to find them . . . Someone is here who also knows you.' I had seen Marius with a flatbread in one hand. I gestured, put the two together and instructed my cousin to keep Polydorus under close surveillance. 'Marius, I prefer you to pin him down with metaphysical reasoning, but if that doesn't work, just hit him.'

'That's mean, for a few inaccurate directions,' Polydorus objected.

I said misleading me implied he was up to no good. He would stay under guard until I found out why. Marius assumed his tough gladiator expression for emphasis. Tiberius had had Dromo give him a haircut and shave, but he was still in his Greek thinker's robes and sandals, so the master of the non-material merely looked slightly neatened up.

Polydorus nodded towards the priestess. 'I do what she tells me.'

'My patch – my rules!' I corrected him.

Following his glance, I recognised something.

The party indoors had been offered mild refreshments. Curvidius Fulvianus was lost in reflection: alone, arms folded, staring at a newly cleaned fresco but not seeing it. The flaky Fulvia Secunda hovered beside the atrium pool, sipping a tot of fruit juice that Blossia was holding for her. Meanwhile the priestess had also set herself apart from others, holding a small dainty from a platter Suza had offered, while staring at the décor in the same distant manner as her brother. Polydorus and I, with Marius, were standing in a doorway, looking on. From there I assessed the sight before me and resolved what had bothered me: I twigged who the dominant priestess was.

'At last I get it, Polydorus! Quinctia is not simply a venerated official whom Fulvianus placed in charge of his sister. She has a personal interest? Gods alive – she is another one of the family!'

Suddenly it seemed obvious. There were facial similarities, if you looked. Quinctia had not shrunk physically in the same way as Fulvia Secunda, who was older. Though stiff, she still carried herself tall, like Fulvianus. In posture and movement there was a family resemblance – and, most telling of all, that curt way of speaking and her irascible attitude.

It did not surprise me that Quinctia was the kind of sneak who had overheard what Polydorus and I were saying. I guessed she listened deliberately.

Since the game was up, she turned her aloof gaze on me. 'I,' announced the priestess, 'am the youngest daughter, Curvidia Quinctia. It has fallen to me to take over temporarily with Fulvia Secunda. She may be older in theory, but I am the one who counts.' The way she spoke called up a sudden memory of Fulvianus calling Secunda 'my ridiculous sister'. Clearly this one felt the same way. There must be a third: 'Our middle sister lives in Salernum and has declared she will not come today. Lending a hand while Secunda plays at being helpless is deemed too much for Curvidia Quartilla – and apparently she couldn't care less what happens to the bones of our poor brother.'

'Or want,' I suggested, 'to meet up with her siblings?'

'Oh, I don't blame her for avoiding that!' snorted the priestess, with a hoarse laugh. 'I'd have kept away myself, but someone capable has to be here.' I had received her attention for as long as she required; she turned away again.

341

'I missed the link,' I murmured to Marius and Polydorus. 'Curvidius Primus, the dead man, used a signet ring with the figure of Fortuna Redux. Of course, Fortuna is the Roman name for the Greek goddess Tyche, and the family are temple benefactors.'

Polydorus inclined his head in confirmation. 'Same goddess. Cornucopia, walled crown, globe . . .'

'Box of dodgy dice,' added Marius. 'A game girl, the lady of capricious chance.'

I said that if Fortuna/Tyche was scattering good luck on a whim today I hoped she would give some to me.

58

Curvidia Quinctia decided it was time we held the ceremony. Without a word, Fulvianus duly followed her. We
gathered up their sister and everyone else from the atrium,
then moved back outside to the pyre.

There, we found further additions to the mourning party.
The last vigiles members had arrived, bringing Septumius
and young Criton. They must have driven down in their
usual ox-cart and had not been secured as prisoners, although
troops were sticking close to them. When the pair caught my
eye, they looked shame-faced, but we did not exchange
remarks. There was no point in making Criton panic in
advance. The look on his face said he knew I had plans for
him, and there were other people whose presence might be
disturbing him. He would have been but a lad when they last
saw him, so they showed no sign of recognition yet.

Looking over to the parked vehicles, I saw the duovir's
litter. Apuleius Innocentius (togate) had already emerged
and was talking to Tiberius (togate with purple bands); I saw
Caunus (amazingly, also togate) being introduced. From
overheard snatches, they were comparing notes about yesterday's successful ambush of the bandits.

Alongside the litter, stood the pirate's carriage. Was he
here? A driver was giving nosebags of grain to the beasts, but
unusually he was not Ergon. Once the man had looked after

the animals, he went over to the litter-bearers. It was clear they all knew each other.

When I went to greet the duovir, I nodded towards the carriage. He grinned. 'Yes, I've just been telling your husband and the tribune: Dexiades stayed in town yesterday, well out of events at the Temple of Hercules.'

'No doubt he claims any kidnaps are nothing to do with him?' I retorted scornfully.

'But of course! Utterly innocent, dear lady, honest to god!' returned the duovir. 'I went to his house this morning, which he assumed was a friendly social call. He professed amazement when I told him what went down at the temple. I spelled out that the troops have taken three of his men, caught in the act, while the admiral of the fleet impounded a ship that Dexiades cannot deny is his. All the crew are in the hands of the marines. I've been told those who want to see their homelands again are beginning to talk.' Apuleius was enjoying himself as he told the story. 'Dexiades is there in his carriage, if he's needed. He fought to escape, but I had gone prepared with a posse. He and that reprobate who drives him around are firmly gagged and bound up like spit-ready pigs. Want to have a peek, Flavia Albia?'

'He can stay there and dread what's coming,' I decided. The danger of my experience as a hostage finally caught me. I felt sick momentarily, so I could not face seeing the pirate.

Tiberius, however, strode over to the carriage angrily. He leaned through the window and I heard him say, 'Expect to be dealt with severely! Flavia Albia had the wit and courage to escape your clutches, but you will answer to me. The tribune wants his reckoning too. He and I have been discussing what is appropriate, and I am looking forward to it. My wife,' uttered Tiberius, 'is not a tradeable commodity!'

Once I would have taken offence at him speaking for me. Somehow, during our short marriage, he had persuaded me to like it. We were bonded; today I was feeling how intensely close we were as a couple. It was by mutual choice we kept up a pretence that I was some kind of wild woodland bird, who might slip the domestic cage and fly away.

While he was speaking, a woman of around our age came out of the duovir's litter as if none too confident. She must be the duovir's wife, though he forgot to introduce her. I guessed she was eager to see what happened today, though perhaps unused to so many strangers. Smiling my well-mannered hostess smile, I marched up and shook hands. She looked as if she felt women of status should exchange air kisses, but I stayed well out of reach of that. 'Welcome. I am Flavia Albia.' I cannot imagine what she must have heard about me, for she blinked rapidly as she took her hand back defensively under her warm stole.

I can only be myself. Luckily there was no time to show anyone what that was because the last invited guests were here: Gellius and Lavinia.

They were brought in a nippy little two-wheeled gig, with a shy driver in a smart tunic. They wore beautifully tailored white funeral outfits, which to me looked brand new. Today they had no jewellery, since restraint at a ceremony like that is deemed to be more respectful. After all, they had always stressed how very much they cared for Fulvia Secunda – and how genuine had been the friendship between Gellius and the man whose funeral was now to be held.

As it definitely was. Curvidia Quinctia had chivvied up her brother to start.

59

If vagrant shades were watching us assemble in the cool afternoon sunlight, they flittered around invisibly, keeping to themselves. This kind of funeral was called 'The Roman Way'; it could be organised by professionals, but in private hands the celebrated Roman Way was rich with pitfalls.

'I suppose no one has provided a suitable beast for sacrifice to Ceres?' the priestess challenged. Her brother snapped back at her that he had one, one he had personally chosen; it was being kept calm in a pen. Undeterred, she changed tack; Curvidius Fulvianus had brought an altar for the rites too, but Quinctia dismissed his pathetic piece of marble, ordering Polydorus to produce hers, which she claimed was superior. Polydorus and Marius heaved a lump of stone from the big carriage's luggage rack, managing not to drop it on their toes; they began trying to stabilise it on the ground. Workmen went to help. Like most portable altars, it had a mind of its own: given a chance, it would fall over at a key moment.

Larcius hauled out the pig. Due to the lack of vegetation since the eruption, a decorative wreath had not been feasible, but Suza had stolen a ribbon from my room, which she and Sparsus had tied between its pointed ears. The pig had guessed the implications: it was a very unhappy animal.

Fornix had mixed up salt and flour for sprinkling to consecrate the sacrifice. Ceres must accept this gift so she would allow spirits' passage from the world of the living to the dark realms of the dead. As an aedile in Rome, Tiberius had had a close connection with Ceres, who presided over his work; he raised his arms in prayer, but it was the duovir who covered his head formally and conducted the sacrifice. Even Quinctia should have admired his dispatch. Not waiting for a ready audience, he nonchalantly stunned the young pig with a hammer then flipped the animal onto its back on the altar and slashed open its guts. Suza and Dromo, who had never stood so close to omen-taking before, let out shrieks and jumped back.

Quinctia shoved the duovir aside; she herself inspected the steaming organs. Only a very senior priestess would ever do this but, since her brother had failed to provide a professional augur, she considered herself entitled. Apparently, the prime offal was healthy enough to pass. She allowed the cremation to go ahead.

She then had to give way because Curvidius Fulvianus must act next. He was handed a lit torch by one of the vigiles, who were taking a keen interest in fire precautions. Fulvianus averted his face; as heir and head of the family, he tried to light the pyre. Although Larcius had covered the logs during the overnight storm, they must have become damp, so it was a struggle. Fulvianus was forced to look at what he was doing. He poked the torch around, then quickly looked away again. Still no result.

Men huddled in muttered discussion.

'Fling on some incense!' Apuleius encouraged, coughing. As a duovir, he must have had ample experience. He beckoned Pescennius Neo, correctly assuming the wealthy fellow had brought some. 'The resin will take.'

Incense was produced and flung. Flames choked. Finally, they whickered into life, somewhat.

I saw Tiberius nudge Fulvianus, who then remembered he had to speak. He gave a prepared eulogy. It took a standard form: we were celebrating the life of his dearest brother Publius Curvidius Fulvius Primus, eldest son of the family, son of Publius, pious and well deserving. 'Death took him too soon, though full of good report and worthiness, approved by his ancestors. His loss will be an endless sorrow to his relatives and friends.'

That was short; I liked it. It seemed Primus had never served in the army or held a civic post, so there were no public honours to list, nor mention of grieving parents, devoted wife or heartbroken children. His brother omitted tiresome anecdotes from their childhood, which their voluble sister was bound to complain about. No need for Pescennius Neo to reminisce about Primus standing for office against a victorious radish. Nor would it be tactful to recall that what most people remembered about Primus was his drinking.

As Fulvianus finished, my husband stepped up beside the pyre. People were surprised yet accepted his air of authority. Tiberius glanced my way; he was honouring a promise, so I raised a hand slightly in benediction. Then he, too, spoke, with more assurance and in a better voice than Fulvianus; he could have been on the rostra in the Forum and would have subdued even the rumbunctious Roman crowd.

'To the divine shades we send Porphyrus, Endymio, Myrtale and an unknown child, its sweet life ended all too soon. A violent fate took these souls, but their trouble is ended. They shall not be forgotten. Let them now sleep together, all without care.'

Marius began gently to play his double flute in melancholy funeral music. The flames took hold, while the slow spread of aromatic smokiness brought relaxation and reflection to those watching. The intense perfumes of myrrh and bdellium mingled with the green piney scent of galbanum, tangling in our clothes and hair. Against the outstanding background of the great Bay of Neapolis, with Vesuvius maintaining its sombre watch, we stood while the souls of the deceased began their final separation from our world.

After a decent passage of time, Tiberius and I invited the mourners to walk with us to the garden where they could partake of a funeral feast.

60

Everything had been laid out in the peristyle garden. Since we had first come to the villa, the ground had been tidied in this peaceful three-sided space, even though nothing as yet grew; columns had been straightened and cleaned; pots had appeared, though so far empty, and since our water supply had been restored a shell-shaped fountain burbled. Seating had been arranged to my direction, in rows. In the centre of what might one day be a topiarised knot garden, stood a substantial rectangular table, covered with a deeply overlapping cloth. Many platters and comports graced it. Fulvianus had paid for the occasion but as he had no staff in Campania we had lent him Fornix; our rotund chef had been preparing well, intent on turning out a spread to demonstrate his fanatical devotion to embellished finger-food.

Fornix generally hid in the background; he liked to be called out by satisfied diners at the end of a superb meal, then applauded. Instead, Hyro and Milo were on hand, with Gratus and Paris, both clearly in the know. I could see the black nose of Drax peeking out from beneath the tablecloth, but he only watched what was going on, hoping to catch any morsels that were dropped accidentally, or even on purpose if dog-lovers were kind.

Fornix had no time for a menu of dark and very heavily spiced items. His philosophy was to serve dishes that would be comforting to the bereaved – and easily managed. Cuts from the sacrificed pig would be brought to us shortly. Meanwhile there was as much meat as the cook had been able to lay hands on, some in cauldrons of stew with dunking rolls, or else easy-to-eat, elegant little pies and pasties. Everyone was encouraged to come to the table, where they were given bowls; either they could help themselves or my staff would serve the delicate or nervous. Breads were lavishly provided, both plain and flavoured, crunchy bannocks and moist must cakes, rich in cinnamon, nuts and raisins. When people took their seats, Paris and Gratus went around with trays of wine, water or Lactarii milk. I took goat's milk. I bore no grudge for my captivity in the mountains. I chose to be sober later.

I was biding my time. There was no point in even trying to begin my task while people were munching. Neighbours were absorbed in discreet conversations. The vigiles had stayed back from the rites at the pyre but they began to filter through to join us. Eventually, as I had previously instructed, they brought the captured pirates/brigands, including Dexiades and Ergon. The culprits had to sit on the ground; they were not given food. However, their gags were torn off, then Gratus grabbed each by the hair and poured water from a pitcher into his mouth. I often wondered about my steward's past. As he roughly doused the prisoners, he showed none of his normal suaveness.

Vigiles went up and cleared anything edible left on the table. At my signal, my own people whisked off all the paraphernalia: serving dishes and bowls, cups and cutlery were stashed nearby in a colonnade, very fast, before anyone might think it was a cue to begin leaving. Only the tablecloth was left. Sparsus dragged out the stubborn watchdog from his hiding place. I went and stood at the front, facing the audience.

Tiberius was seated, between the tribune, with his girl-friend, and the duovir, with his wife. Also along the front row were the Curvidius relatives; the Publilius siblings lurked just behind them. Taking a lead from my husband, any men who had worn togas discreetly shed the weight. We had neigh-bours, household staff, builders and vigiles, with sullen captives. I could see Milo and Hyro waiting by the corridor that led to the bathhouse, along with the two German paint-ers, Vindex and Dexter. I waved for them to stay put tempo-rarily, then held up my hands to attract attention. I heard the priestess exclaim irritably, 'Whatever does that girl think she is doing?' Silence was falling of its own accord. When people have had their emotions tweaked and are full of food, they can make a docile audience. One or two were still clinging to wine cups, though they sipped discreetly.

'Friends!' I called, then waited. The last shuffles and mutters died down. 'My name, for those who do not know, is Flavia Albia. I shall speak to you in my professional capacity. I work for families who have problems or questions they need me to investigate.' I paused, smiling. 'You have an air of expectancy as if you are hoping I will tell you a story!' Some looked surprised. Others seemed to know what was happen-ing. 'Well,' I said gently, my final ploy to force them to listen properly, 'I believe I have a curious one for you.'

Now they were all ears.

Let's be frank. I quite enjoy being in charge of a gathering like that. I learned it at the Saepta Julia, helping my father run auctions. I was dressed for the funeral today, which at least meant comfortable loose hair and plain shoes to go with my relaxed air of command. A gavel might have been useful, though once we started the re-enaction I would have nowhere to bang it. Otherwise, there was little difference in technique.

I began by stating formally that we had gathered today for the cremation of Curvidius Primus and his slaves. 'Here we are, with a distant aspect of the sea and Mount Vesuvius. It makes one understand the power of so many Greek theatres, carved into hillsides with a sense that the gods are closely watching. But this beautiful vista will always be resonant with sadness. Thousands of people died here in recent memory. We shall never know who many of them were, or what exactly happened to them. Thousands are missing, lost to posterity for ever. We have had to learn to live with our inability to find them. That does not mean that any extra death, not caused by the angry volcano, should be ignored.'

Once more I ceremoniously listed Primus and the slaves. I had been asked to work out, if possible, how and why they died. I said all their bodies had been discovered when my husband and his work team came to this villa to prepare it for a new owner. They appeared to have been there ever since the eruption. As far as we could tell, the slaves had been alive in their prison and died in the irresistible heat that rolled across Stabiae from the volcano. For me, at the very least it was tragic – and perhaps their imprisonment was criminal. 'I shall explore why it happened.' In my line of sight were the people I now believed were responsible, though they remained impassive; I gave no sign yet that I knew who they were.

'And what of Curvidius Primus himself?' I continued. 'His body had been left here, but we know that he was already dead when Vesuvius burst into life. He had died in his bath. People here at the time have given statements. Others who know the full truth have said nothing, but I hope to persuade them today. On the occasion of his funeral, isn't it right that we should finally make known just how he came to die?' Murmuring ensued. I let it fade. 'Various things might have happened. Did Primus commit suicide, because of the terrible pain he habitually suffered? Was he the victim of an accident? Did he slip and fall? Did he find himself wedged in the narrow confines of the tub and, because he was a large man, he could not escape? Or – and this is the worst scenario – did somebody else enter the room where his bath stood, with him lying in it, and for reasons that have never been mentioned, one or more people killed him?'

This time the murmurs were louder and more animated. Despite that, the noise settled quickly; they wanted to know where my argument would go. What I produced next must have been startling. 'I hope by the time I have finished, I can accuse whoever was responsible. But first, with the aid of some volunteers, I am going to show you how they did it.'

I signalled to Milo and Hyro. They came up, accompanied by the two painters. I stepped to one side so the audience would have a clear view. The two vigiles stationed themselves at either end of the emptied serving table. Grasping the top, tablecloth and all, they lifted and removed it. As they moved back, dragging the cloth after them, they revealed that the buffet had been formed using a large piece of elderly wooden door. It had been, in fact, the door to the slaves' prison. Nicely covered, no one would have known.

For support, it had been resting upon the bronze bathtub.

61

'This is a disgrace!' spluttered the priestess. 'You are reducing my brother's tragic demise to comedic farce!' Tiberius and those around him, the tribune and duovir, looked eager to see how I responded to this. If other people felt nervous, they hid it well.

With deft hands, Milo and Hyro quickly dressed our scene: sponges on the rim, the slippers found in the bath suite placed neatly together in front of the tub. No unguents, we had earlier agreed, because of the risk of breaking glass. They drew attention to these props with hand gestures. Hyro dipped fingers in, then sprinkled water off them with a dainty wave, to show that the bath had been filled.

I held up a palm for stillness. The stage management had already produced results: Fulvia Secunda broke away from her minders (Blossia and Suza had been heads together in conversation). Secunda wandered right up to the bath, where she picked up one of the battered old male slippers. I felt breathless. This might have been a moment when memory came back to the old lady. I knew it, and could see people who were sharing my hope. But Secunda only looked down into the water, then turned away again. She was still holding the slipper; she shook it as if waiting for something to fall out. Nothing happened, so she dropped it and lost interest.

Gellius and Lavinia left their seats and scurried up to her. For a brief beat of time, she recognised them. For once, she spoke. 'Medicine!' she quavered, pleading.

The priestess was on her feet. 'None of that!' snarled Quinctia. Then, rounding on the Publilii, 'See what you have done! I want it stopped. I want her weaned off that wicked stuff.'

Quinctia turned to their brother. Fulvianus nodded. Even though he seemed quelled by her anger, he made an open-handed gesture to signal his agreement to withdrawing the addictive drugs. Secunda was slowly brought back to sit down again. She took no further notice of proceedings. I could not help considering how she must once have been as forceful as her younger sister; the comparison with how Quinctia revelled in her power over others was tragic.

My assistants began their charade.

'We shall now demonstrate how Curvidius Primus was killed,' I said. 'Our brave volunteer will be Vindex.' We identified him: he was the red-haired one, who had more of a paunch. 'I hope people who knew Primus will confirm that this man is about the same size and weight.' There were nods.

Hyro and Milo told Vindex to remove his paint-stained clothes, which were handed to Dexter as wardrobe master. Dexter, the blonder of the two, already looked glad the victim wasn't him.

Vindex was shy. 'Don't worry, boyo,' Milo assured him kindly. 'There's nothing about your tackle to attract interest from anyone!' At once everyone stared at the relevant body part. Vindex hurriedly stepped over the side of the bathtub, and climbed in. Sinking down he let out a yell. Even if it had once been warm, during the feast the water must have cooled. Playing a stage clown to his heart's delight, Milo reprimanded the painter, saying the cold shock would be good for his circulation. Hyro relented, let out a whistle, then colleagues from the Seventh came running up, like the firemen they were, carrying more buckets, this time hot water to take off the chill. It also helped make the tub fuller.

'Try to drown yourself,' Hyro suggested to Vindex cheerily, as the water level rose. 'Pretend to commit suicide.'

Vindex splashed and sank, but floated back; his head and knees broke the surface.

'Can you get out?' asked Milo. 'Have a go.'

Vindex struggled madly, barely able to haul himself partway onto the side, though he must have been stronger than me, because he did almost manage it. 'Call for help, Vindex.'

'Help, help!' Then he fell back.

Dexter made as if to go to his assistance. 'Not yet!' chorused Hyro and Milo.

'Well, he's down again in the water,' Milo uttered, addressing the audience as if in a soliloquy. 'Unfortunately for Faustus and Flavia Albia, he is floating like a big fat lump of cork. He is still alive and will be back at their house to cause them stress with his hopeless painting. But now my handsome colleague will demonstrate the manner in which someone who wanted to be rid of him could do it.'

There was complete silence at this point.

'Imagine,' I said, 'Curvidius Primus, whom many of you knew, is enjoying his soak in this, his expensive private tub. His sister Secunda is reckoned to have been nearby in the steam room. Perhaps she was. On hand, too, waiting in the changing room with towels and clean clothes, attendants are where they can easily be called for. Two slaves, Porphyrus and Endymio, for the master, Myrtale for Secunda. Beyond the bath suite, out of doors, dinner guests are enjoying a quiet drink, here in this very peristyle garden, as they await their evening meal. Unbeknown to them, someone else enters and approaches the tub. "*Look out, Primus!*"'

My cry was melodramatic but served its purpose. There were gasps. Hyro sprang into action and stationed himself at one end of the bath; he pushed down Vindex by the shoulders. Vindex once more showed his strength and fought him off. Water splashed everywhere but Hyro gave up and stepped back. Vindex recovered his previous position in the bath. I fancied I heard German curses.

'You hopeless numbskull!' Milo reprimanded Hyro. You could tell the lads had watched a lot of plays featuring clowns. 'What are you thinking? It seems I have to show you what to do.'

Milo nipped nimbly to the other end of the bath. Hyro mimed disbelief that this would work. Milo mimed assurance. 'Hold your breath, Vindex!' Unexpectedly, Milo leaned in, grabbed Vindex by both ankles, and pulled his feet straight up in the air. Caught unawares, Vindex slipped bodily down in the bath. His head went under the water. He must have taken in a sudden gush. At a gesture from Milo, Hyro applied pressure to his chest with one hand, holding Vindex under.

'A few beats and lo! The subject is drowned,' announced Milo.

Tiberius jumped to his feet. 'Stop! He's not breathing! He's really done for!'

Realisation: Milo, Hyro and Dexter grabbed hold of the unlucky volunteer, now desperate to lift Vindex from the bath. Being naked and portly, he was slithery. Panic ensued. People milled in uncertainty. There was screaming. 'Pull out the plug!' yelled somebody. Members of the vigiles rushed up, grappled with the big German volunteer, took hold of his limbs, roughly hauled him out over the edge of the tub and laid him on the ground. The centurion, Rufeius, heaved Vindex over to turn him face down, pumping his back hard to bring the bathwater out of him. It took some time. His fellow painter was swearing as, finally, Vindex coughed his way back to life.

Helpers stood down.

'That,' I pronounced, 'shows how the dreadful deed must have been done. Sadly, any attendants failed to reach their master in time, while there was no convenient fire brigade leader, capable of reviving people who fall into the Tiber. Rufeius, thank you. Vindex, thank you too. Gratus is bringing you a restorative drink.' His comrade, Dexter, wrapped him up in towels. Hyro and Milo, hiding grins, kept well out of his reach.

I let the furore quieten then moved on: 'You have all now seen what must have happened. Note that for certainty it was better to have two perpetrators. If everyone takes their seats again, I shall discuss who those perpetrators must have been. However, it will make more sense if we consider first why they did it.'

62

My next task needed caution, but the bath experiment had prepared people. As I focused more closely on the evening Primus died, at last I was ready to call up a witness.

'The scene is set, Primus still alive and soaking, Gellius and Lavinia in the garden, slaves at the ready, Secunda also in the bath suite. However, there was one more person coming and going. His position in the household was minor so his role at bath time went unremarked. As another slave, and a very young one, he would be in effect invisible: Criton.' I called to him: 'Criton, I promise nothing bad will happen to you. I would like you to come here, please.'

Criton saw he had no choice. He and Septumius stood up behind the front row of the audience. The older man encouraged him, and Criton shambled to my side. I wondered if, since I'd last seen them, Septumius had given him a talking-to. At any rate, the lanky young man presented himself, though looking more shifty and unreliable than ever.

'You were a slave at this villa once?' He nodded. 'How old were you when you started?'

'Four.'

'And when you left?'

'About nine.'

'And when Curvidius Primus bathed in his tub, what was your job, Criton?'

'I brought extra buckets when he wanted more warm water.'

'And you were doing that on the day he died? Was it hard work? The buckets must have been heavy for you?'

Criton nodded. 'I had to go all the way round to the tank by the furnace. I couldn't really manage. It took me a long time and water often spilled out on the way back. He usually shouted at me. He'd say I took too long, and the bucket was only half full when I got there. It wasted the hot water.'

'He would be angry? Was that why you didn't like him?' A more subdued nod. 'But did you see him as your enemy? Surely you didn't hate him enough to murder him?'

'No! That was just how things were. Anyway,' the youth remarked, perking up to defend himself, 'I would never have dared to touch him, or what a beating would have been handed out! Kill him? You saw how difficult it would have been. I was a skinny little chap and, besides, I had a damaged shoulder. It still plays me up. Even if I had wanted to, I could never have managed it.'

I wondered if Septumius had talked him through and suggested answers. I did believe him, however. I took the obvious follow-on: 'The other slaves – Endymio and Porphyrus – might have helped you overpower him, I suppose. Did they hate Curvidius Primus?'

'They were older. They had learned to ignore it if he picked on them.'

'But a question may be asked,' I proposed. 'Were three slaves locked up in chains afterwards because they were responsible for killing their master?'

'No!' Criton readily spoke up for them. 'They never! By the time they heard all the noise, so they ran in, he was a goner. They dragged him out of the bath, but it was useless. They couldn't get him to breathe. They did not kill him and they could never have saved him.'

I lowered my voice. 'How do you know that? Let's be clear. You are describing what happened. So, you yourself were there?'

Criton was shaking his head vehemently. Our discussion was upsetting him, though he had not relapsed into complete panic. There was a clear sense that he wanted to make everything known this time. 'I never saw anything. I had come back with a new bucket of water but I stopped just outside. There wasn't room for me. Endymio and Porphyrus were in the room, shouting. She was there as well—'

'Who?'

'The sister.'

'Doing what?'

'Screaming, "No! no!" then "Stop it!" and—'

'Who was she telling to stop it?'

'I don't know. I couldn't see. She was also shouting, "My brother has been killed, O gods, this should never have happened." Myrtale ran up, I saw her, so she and Endymio squeezed in to drag the sister outside the room. I think Porphyrus was trying to help the master. They were all crying. I didn't look in. I was too frightened. I ran away to hide. Nobody seemed to notice me.' Criton seemed happier than I had seen him, divesting himself of a nightmare he had kept to himself for far too long.

'Afterwards, did somebody say the slaves had done it?'

'Yes, but they hadn't, and people must have known that. They were locked up,' Criton divulged, straightening

362

importantly, 'because they wanted to speak out and tell the truth. Endymio thought that otherwise the blame would be pinned on all of us. So they wouldn't back down. They had seen what happened. They saw our master being murdered.'

'And you, Criton?'

'I never saw it, Flavia Albia. You have to believe me.'

'Criton, I believe you.'

'I wasn't there,' he insisted. 'Not in the room. I took a long time to come back with the water. I was walking really slowly because I didn't want to go in there.'

'Why not, Criton?'

'I was too scared. I was a boy, and I was really frightened.'

'Criton, why?'

Criton hung his head. 'Because of the argument.'

Now at last we had it.

63

Everyone breathed.

I addressed him gently, though my gaze was firm. 'Who was arguing, Criton?'

'They were, the two of them. They went at it, yelling at each other over and over.'

'Who?'

'The master and his sister.'

'His sister Fulvia Secunda? She who lived in the house with him?'

'Her. He was in his bath and she kept storming around the little room, furious with him. He told her to get out and leave him in peace, but she refused to go.'

'What were they arguing about?'

'I don't know. I never listened to it. I was worrying about how I could creep in with the warm water bucket. I just tried to keep out of their way because they were so angry at each other, and I was so scared.'

'You never heard what they were saying or why they were so angry?'

'No.'

That was no use, then. And the three slaves who might have known were dead.

64

'She picked up his bath slipper,' Criton added, as an afterthought. 'He only wore them in the hot-room but he always had them beside the tub, the way they are now, because he used to take off any rings and bracelets he was wearing, and his Fortune amulet, all except his signet, which would never come off. He kept the rest in the left-hand shoe while he was bathing. Nobody was supposed to touch his things. While they were quarrelling, his sister picked up the right-hand shoe and hit him with it. But that never killed him. He just grabbed it back off her and hurled it across the room. That was when I made a run for it and went for water. Then they carried on yelling.'

We all gazed at Fulvia Secunda. The old lady sat, oblivious. She would have no throwing power now, even with a casual shoe. Her slave, Blossia, put an arm around her protectively. My Suza, never one to hold back, took one of Secunda's papery hands in hers, staring around defiantly. The impression they exuded was that this was a frail, delicate, sweet soul, who was utterly harmless.

'Yelling is one thing,' I commented, 'but it would be quite another matter to employ enough force to drown someone, if Secunda had attacked her brother.'

It was the duovir who laughed. 'Don't you believe it! She was famous. She had gone for him before.' He returned to the tale he had told us once, that his father had known the Curvidius siblings at school. 'When the teacher expelled them for fighting, it was because Secunda had hit Primus in the face so hard he lost those three front teeth. Well –' Apuleius rounded on Fulvianus and Quinctia, her relatives '– you were both there! She smashed him in the mouth with the teacher's stick. It's the truth, isn't it?'

Neither replied, but the priestess screwed up her face as if drinking neat vinegar, while the surviving brother folded his arms, gazing at the sky.

I told Criton to return to sit with Septumius. Quietly I reprised what this would mean. I explained that I had wondered whether Secunda had caused her brother's death. Suppose she really was prone to uncontrollable violence and, after a long and stubborn argument, she had turned on Primus fatally. Endymio, Porphyrus and perhaps Myrtale had seen her do it. 'But we have shown today that to drown a man like Primus two people would have been needed. Did somebody help Secunda? Even if that's true, who could it have been?'

People in the audience turned and muttered to their neighbours.

I interrupted the speculation. 'Then what happened afterwards? Assume for the moment that Primus had been murdered and Secunda was involved. It is clear Gellius and Lavinia took over the household because she was too hysterical. So, were they desperately covering up her crime? It appears the Publilii organised a hurried clearance of the house and took Fulvia Secunda a good distance away. Would that have been to hide her crime? If so, they have been guardians of the culprit and keepers of the terrible truth ever since.'

I turned to them and asked the question: was that the story? Neither would answer.

'I did also wonder whether in fact you two killed Primus,' I told them baldly. 'Out of greed. You have no known source for your life of luxury. But that's not it, is it? I think you do know what happened to Primus,' I challenged the pair. 'It wasn't you, nor was it Fulvia Secunda – but you saw who really did it. You are not nasty little predators on Primus and Secunda – I am prepared to believe you genuinely care about both of them – but nevertheless, you are determined blackmailers. You are taking money from the killer in return for your silence.'

'Rubbish!' said Gellius. 'This is libellous.'

'How could you?' wailed Lavinia.

'It's not difficult,' I rapped back. 'I believe the murderer has financed you ever since. That's the true secret. You are paid, and handsomely, to maintain your silence.'

'Prove it then,' answered Gellius.

'I will.'

He made the mistake of carrying on. 'All you have given us so far is the word of a slave. A slave cannot give evidence.'

I folded my hands at my waist. 'No. But there is somebody else who can. You told me, when I visited, that all of the slaves from the Primus household were transported to the Gabius estate. You claimed since then they have either died or it has been said that "they were dispersed". I first assumed "dispersed" meant they had been sold on the general market. That would mean you would probably have lost trace of them.'

Gellius and Lavinia were looking restless. They saw where I was heading.

'We are talking about a family,' I said. 'You must have reported that Primus had died, even if you kept the details a secret. Curvidius Fulvianus was away in Rome, but here in Campania were two sisters with their own households – Curvidia Quinctia has a home near the Temple of Tyche and I believe Quartilla lives in Salernum. Superfluous slaves could have been offered to them – and in most families they would have been. Did that happen?' I demanded of Quinctia, who nodded slowly. She was an intelligent woman; she had guessed what would now ensue.

'I shall call another witness,' I announced. 'Criton has told us his story. It is true that as a slave he can give formal testimony only under torture, which I have promised him will not happen. In any case, he never saw the moment when his master was killed. He cannot name the culprit. However, I believe somebody else was present. Quinctius Polydorus, freedman of Quinctia, please come to stand with me now and relate *your* story.'

65

The temple assistant looked much the same as when I had met him: pale and slender, his hairy arms and legs protruding from a poorly laundered tunic. A citizen in his thirties ought to know how to be better turned out for a formal occasion. Still he had cleaner hair, he had put on a belt and appeared to have shaved.

He was much more assured than Criton, but I helped him decide how to start. 'Your name is Quinctius Polydorus, *libertus*. As a free citizen, you may speak here and your testimony will stand. You know the rubric: you will give us the truth, the whole truth, and nothing but the truth. Polydorus, you are now an assistant at the Temple of Tyche. You hold a respected position, one of great trust. But, as a young man, you were once a slave in this villa. Curvidius Primus was your owner and master. Will you begin by explaining what your task was in his bathhouse?'

Polydorus gazed at me, as he worked out how I had come to know. It was more than merely supposing he had been passed around family households. I had remembered the scene at the temple when he sluiced down the steps, using long, slow swipes to clear away my donkey's undrunk water. He had manoeuvred his broom as if very familiar with the process. Smiling, he said, 'When there was excess water, I came along to make the bathhouse safe. I brushed flooding along to the drain covers so it would be sucked down.'

I smiled back. 'Now, tell us about that particular day, please.'

'Yes, I was there,' Polydorus told us. People shifted in their seats, understanding that we were about to hear the real truth.

'The master was taking his bath as always,' I prompted. 'Had he been drinking?'

'No more than normal. You wouldn't have known.'

'His sister went in to see him?'

'Certainly. She advanced on him, arguing like fury. When he flung the bath slipper back at her, he did it wildly and, like Criton said, water went everywhere. I stepped up as usual and cleared it. Criton had scarpered. They ignored me. It was obvious I might be needed again, so I hung around. Nobody took note of me. It was my job, I was doing it, I was part of the decoration. Even in the small space where the bath stands, I just dodged my brush around anyone who was standing there and shooed the water to the plughole.'

'Anyone else at the scene?'

'Endymio and Porphyrus were out in the changing room. With Myrtale. I'd been speaking to them earlier, but Primus used to splash around crazily so I had to keep watch. I saw little Criton scamper off with his bucket. I watched him go and I knew he would take his time because of the fight that was raging. People used to push him around unfairly. He was always very nervous.'

'You were older. Perhaps more curious? Did you listen to what the brother and sister were arguing about?'

'Oh, yes, it was fruity!'

'Really?'

'Unbelievable! She wanted to get married again and Primus was enraged. He yelled that, as her head of household, he utterly forbade it.'

'Are you sure, Polydorus? She must have been sixty.'

'Older! He said she had better accept he would never allow it. He even told her that what she wanted would be disrespectful to Gabius. She had fallen for looks and smooth talk, but the man didn't really want her. All he was after was the vineyard. It was nothing but a romance fraud. She was fooling herself. So her brother yelled at her to tell the fellow to take himself off. He was not getting his dinner here – he was not getting anything. Primus intended to stay in his bath until someone told him the beggar was gone.'

'Let us be clear, Polydorus. The unsuitable suitor Primus was insulting was here that evening, here in person at the villa?'

'Yes. Yes, he was.'

'As a guest?'

'No. Primus would never have anything to do with him, but he kept hanging around. He had come up that day to see Secunda. She was a grown woman, a respectable matron. Of course she could have her own visitors. She was very independent, a widow with all that can mean.'

I smiled. 'A force to be reckoned with! Was her paramour visiting on his own?'

'No. He was brought up from Stabiae by his driver.'

'Who waited for him outside?'

'No. Came right indoors and stayed close.'

'That sounds rather ominous.'

'To be honest, it felt that way, Flavia Albia, right from the start.'

'So! Primus knew the failed fiancé was there, but had not invited him and wanted him to leave?'

'Absolutely. Primus called him a cheap trader from a rock-bottom province, with the morals of a stoat.' Polydorus was enjoying himself. He liked an audience. Freed from restraint by the requirement to give his statement, he could be rude at will. 'Primus would not even discuss anything with him. He said the man was exploiting Secunda's stupidity so he just had to go.'

'And what then?'

'Secunda, crying, went to tell her fellow to leave.'

'Did he?'

'No. He rushed in on Primus. There was another loud argument. That time it didn't last long. He shouted, the driver burst out of nowhere and ran in too. Then they grappled with Primus in the way you showed us earlier. Pulled his feet up high and held him under. I remember I called out to my master to release the plug to let the water out, but he couldn't move, they were too strong for him and he must have swallowed water. I had bare feet and only an old stump of broom. I ran out to the corridor and yelled for Endymio and Porphyrus.'

'Did they try to help?'

'Yes, but the killers began knocking them about. Primus must have succumbed by then. Everyone struggled – there was hardly any room to move. It was chaos. Endymio and Porphyrus broke free. They pulled the master out onto the floor, but he was dead. The two killers just stood there grinning.'

'Was Secunda present?'

'She ran into the room and actually saw them as they were killing her brother. She was horrified. She screamed at them to stop, but they took no notice. She had no part in it. Once it was all over, she was utterly desolate. She must have thought what had happened was her fault. In the end she fainted. Myrtale and Lavinia hauled her away.'

'Lavinia was there?'

'Came in when Porphyrus was trying to revive the master.'

'What next, Polydorus?'

'Gellius came in. He tried to tackle the situation. Frankly, what he did was quite surprising. He was a young man in those days, but he had been good friends with Primus, so he was shocked, and I think very angry. I heard him say coldly, "This is a disaster!" The answer was brutal: that he should be careful, or the same thing would happen to him and Lavinia. Gellius must have been terrified but he hid it coolly and behaved like someone taking charge. "You had better come outside with me to discuss what can be done now." Then he and the pirate went off together.'

'The pirate?' I asked gently.

'Yes. The man who wanted to marry Secunda was him over there.' Polydorus pointed. 'Her brother was killed by Dexiades.'

66

To be certain, I made Polydorus state it formally: he had seen Dexiades and his driver, Ergon, murder Primus.

Not only that, the freedman said, with disgust, but as the driver left the room afterwards, he had shaken out rings and bangles that Primus kept in his bath slipper, and stolen the jewellery. Polydorus even saw Ergon try to screw the Fortuna Redux signet from his dead master's finger, but on fat flesh that was further swollen by immersion in water, it refused to budge.

Outrage rose at this detail. I released Polydorus and confronted Gellius. His consultation with Lavinia was rapid and silent but they were clearly re-evaluating their situation. I made him walk forwards so everyone could see him.

'Truth now!' I snarled. Then, finally, on my stern prompt, the story came out.

Gellius and Lavinia had gone to investigate a commotion; they found Dexiades and Ergon finishing off Primus in the way we had demonstrated with Vindex. Horrified, they watched the protesting slaves being beaten, until the pirates gave up and simply stood there jeering. Primus had succumbed, so the slaves were allowed to haul him out of the bath, too late. Porphyrus, with Gellius, tried to resuscitate him but nothing would work.

Everyone could tell Dexiades had woefully misjudged how Secunda would react. He expected her approval. She not only became hysterical, but remained so; she wanted nothing to do with him. Convinced he could control the situation, Dexiades made no move to leave the house. He brought in men armed with swords. Completely assured, he warned the Publilii that if they went to the authorities he would say they were the killers, acting from greed. He said it was in everyone's interest to cover up what had happened and carry on as normal – though, of course, this villa and its household were now controlled by armed men. Dexiades had his men chain up the three slaves who refused to cooperate. Gellius tried, but could not stop their imprisonment. Everyone else was too frightened to object. Primus had had a temper but was rarely physically cruel in ways like that, so such treatment only showed how dangerous the pirate and his henchmen were.

Gellius and Lavinia were young; they had been members of the family only through an aunt who had died and, with justice, they were physically terrified. They dared not call on the household slaves, because the slaves were equally petrified, while they themselves had never been very popular since they were seen as interlopers. Secunda was in dire straits. She had lost any belief in Dexiades yet he clung doggedly to his aim of controlling her and seizing her estate. She screamed if he approached. However, he brazenly stayed on the scene. All the time he behaved as if he had done nothing wrong.

'Had you no hope of help from the authorities?'

'Dexiades said he would blame us – and we felt our position was delicate.' Gellius made a helpless gesture. 'Flavia Albia, you have to understand how it was. The house had been rather badly run, while Primus was not entirely himself. All his relatives lived a distance away and were not on good terms with him anyway. Secunda was having a breakdown. Dexiades filled the villa with his own people; it looked as if he had been planning to invade all along. He pinched a great many valuables and fixed up for everything else to be taken from the house.'

Gellius was self-justifying, but less so than he might have been. 'When it became clear Secunda would not recover, I struck the best bargain I could. I negotiated with Dexiades that Lavinia and I could take Secunda to her own estate and care for her. Dexiades said he was still intending to marry her and take over her fortune. We have managed to fend him off and prevent him for a whole ten years,' stated Gellius. 'Lavinia and I can be proud of that.' I would not disagree. Many people present probably thought the same.

Lavinia herself now came and stood beside her brother. 'It has been at a high cost to Secunda,' she said. 'When it was clear she would continue to suffer such anxiety, we had to resort to wine and drugs to calm her.' She stared at the ground, admitting, 'Dexiades used to bring us the drugs.'

'We blackmailed him,' said Gellius, now standing stiffly, with an arm around his sister. 'We are not proud of that. We took as much from him as we could, in return for our silence. It seemed fair justice for our murdered friend.'

'Dexiades continued to visit on occasions,' I suggested. 'When I saw him that time, he was coming to hand over money and medication to you. After he heard about my enquiries did you all agree it was still in your interests that nobody learned the truth? You had no thought of admitting to me what had happened to Primus, no thought of allowing a fair resolution?'

'Lavinia and I were ready – Lavinia especially, in fairness to her – but Dexiades was adamant. He still harboured a hope that Secunda would recover. She was vulnerable. She no longer seemed to recognise him, or anybody, but we knew how he could have exploited her if he ever got his hands on her. I cannot even say she trusted us to protect her. She had no idea what we were doing. She would not have resisted, if he took control.'

'All for the Gabius estate?'

'Exactly.' Gellius looked rueful. He spelled out exactly the kind of fraud with which I had thought to charge him and his sister: 'Suppose Secunda remarried. After she died, her new husband would own everything. He could have made her write a will in his favour. For certain, she would not have lived for long.' Gellius hesitated. 'When her brother – Fulvianus – came last week, we did not tell him about Primus dying, but we did warn him what a danger Dexiades poses. Fulvianus sent Secunda to safe refuge with their sister at the Temple of Tyche.'

The priestess stood up. She had something in mind: as if taking a cue from her sister, Secunda also wavered to her feet. People hurried to support her. She looked at me. For the first and only time, she spoke to me. I hoped she had sensed I meant well towards her. 'I want to go home.'

Surprisingly her sister spoke to her quite gently: 'You shall. Your kindly guardians will take you back very soon. Everything will be the same as usual.' She shot Gellius and Lavinia a scathing look. 'Give them a stipend,' she commanded Fulvianus in a cold tone. 'They may as well keep on looking after her. You don't want her. I certainly don't want the bother, and neither will Quartilla. They call themselves friends of the family. She's not long for this world. Until she passes, you can pay them. Better you than the filthy pirate.'

She did not wait for his agreement. This was how a Curvidius sister expected to treat one of her brothers – and a Curvidius brother would generally go along with it. The only surprise was that ten years ago Primus had stopped his sister being taken in by the pirate.

Quinctia then stomped over to where Dexiades was still sitting among his crew, being guarded. I saw Fulvianus half rise from his seat, then he sank down. He was keeping out of this. The priestess told the vigiles to raise the pirate to his feet.

With a curl of her lip, she squared up. 'I remember you palling up with Gabius. He was an idiot – but even he knew not to let you best him. Then you homed in on his widow. You are a relentless pest! Do you admit what has been said about you?'

Dexiades stared at her, then spat. He aimed not at her directly, but onto the ground at her feet, so she was untouched but started back. She staggered momentarily. One of the vigiles offered a hand but, ever impatient, she rudely shook him off and regained her footing. Ramrod straight, she returned to her mission.

I had not bothered to question the pirate. I knew his kind. Some killers want to be known for their deeds; a few are relieved to be found out and stopped. Others will never admit, acknowledge, defend themselves, explain or repent. Dexiades would be one of those. He would stay silent until he died.

What he had done to this family would never now be in question. For a second more, Curvidia Quinctia glared, intending her brother's murderer to absorb her contempt. Then, to general astonishment, she stooped and picked up the water pitcher Gratus had previously used. It was made of heavy pottery. Drawing back her right arm then launching a long forward swing, Curvidia Quinctia whacked Dexiades with it, full across the face. He never saw it coming. Bound, he could not have dodged anyway.

She dropped the jug as if it were tainted by touching him. Covered with blood, he could be seen spitting out broken teeth. At the back of the audience I saw my cousin Marius stand up, clapping his hands above his head – though he did it silently.

As if socking men who offended her was a routine duty, the priestess of Tyche turned back to Fulvianus. 'Don't sit there like a ninny. We have overdue business. Get up, will you? Come to attend to our brother's ashes.'

She strode off back to the pyre while the rest of us followed, still wincing and muttering admiration for the punishment she had doled out.

At the pyre, shreds of grey smoke were wafting amid the final hints of incense. Curvidius Fulvianus once more veiled his head with his toga. Others hastily resumed formal garb. Marius began flute-playing again.

The priestess accused her brother of failing to bring a cremation urn. In fact, he had done so: a serviceable glass vessel with two handles and a pointed lid. In triumph, Quinctia rejected this. 'For heaven's sake, we can do better!'

Seizing his from him, she dashed it to the ground where it shattered on remaining hard tephra. Polydorus seemed willing to sweep up the dangerous splinters, but instead was sent running back once more to the enormous carriage; from it he carried a replacement that Quinctia deemed suitable. Who could say how she had got her hands on it. At my side I heard Tiberius snort under his breath. Fulvianus, henpecked and accepting, made no comment, although we two knew he must have seen it before. *Intolerable swine. I sent him a gift for his sixty-fifth birthday, never had back an acknowledgement, not one word of thanks.*

What was the gift? In case we find it?

Bloody great vase. Some Greek with a beard, putting his spear in. Cost me a packet . . .

The donor himself would finally put the birthday present to use.

Without complaint, Curvidius Fulvianus solemnly approached the pyre for his last duties as chief celebrant. He gathered up what he could of the meagre ashes, which he placed in the never-acknowledged gift. The very expensive Greek red-figure vase, with its fighting warrior, would be taken to the family tomb in Salernum. Inside it would be the pitiful remains we had managed to salvage: the cruelly drowned master, three slaves who had wanted to do right, a child, a decrepit horse and (I happened to know) a watch-dog. *Hail and farewell, Nibble . . .*

Into the depths of his vase, I saw Fulvianus drop his late brother's signet ring: Fortuna Redux, protector of cities, and personification of happy returns, the goddess of good and bad luck.

Everyone left soon afterwards. Gratus, my ever-useful steward, ran after the Curvidii with their funeral vase, reminding them to take it with them. Exhausted, I felt overjoyed to see the back of them. Neighbours and relatives of the dead man departed. Septumius seemed to hesitate, uncertain about Criton, who in theory remained a family slave. Curvidius Fulvianus covered that irritably: 'For heaven's sake, you take him. I never knew him when he was here, and I don't want him. Criton, you have by chance fallen among good people. Try to keep out of trouble. Lead a good life and sometimes think kindly of your old master.' Criton, as usual, looked unreliable.

Somebody asked Tiberius, 'Will you be staying longer, Aedile?'

'Not long.' He shook his head. 'No, we will have to go back for a family celebration soon. The Ides of April is Albia's birthday. My workmen must finish up our restoration here, so we can be in Rome by then.'

'Darling, you remembered!' With the tribune's girlfriend and the duovir's wife, I exchanged friendly, knowing smiles.

The vigiles hauled off the captives. The duovir was to deal locally with most of them – future sport for avid crowds at some sunlit arena on the bay. Caunus would take Dexiades to Rome. Milo and Hyro would be in charge of him, naked in a cage that the carpenter Axilius was to make to contain him on the journey. 'King of the Bay you may have been, but you belong to me now. I know that if you had received a ransom, I would have been murdered and dumped in a forest. The amphitheatre awaits!' Gaius Caunus was lipsmackingly keen on the idea. To murder a citizen is bad, but to kidnap a tribune is the worst possible crime – certainly to that tribune.

I did notice something as formalities were concluded: the tribune and the Stabian duovir shook hands surreptitiously on parting. I never asked either, but I have always wondered. Was there an unknown relationship between Caunus and Apuleius Innocentius?

Bunking off from his duties for days of degenerate party-ing seemed a rash risk for a tribune of incorruptible military speech and manner; a leading centurion who wanted to retain his huge retirement bonus; a man who was hung not only with combat medals but with Charis, of whom he spoke with respect, and that baby whose tiny nose he blew like a hands-on dedicated parent.

Could it be that the ambitious Apuleius had sought help from Rome for crimes that were beyond his local resources? Was it possible that a volunteer from the Seventh Cohort had been sent down south to assist him? Had this trip nothing to do with grain storage and management, but was Gaius Caunus in Stabiae officially looking for criminals under cover all along?

That evening it was too hard for my tired brain. Next morning we had other things to think about. We were hardly up and about when the sound of carriage wheels gave us nervous feelings. We went to see who could be arriving now, only to find that first out of the vehicle was my own precious dog. As Barley raced to greet me, hard on her heels came two small boys bursting with pent-up energy, rushing off to explore and look for danger. Seeing us, they veered around and ran upon Tiberius and me with happy screams of '*People!*' One each of Gaius and Lucius fell into our arms.

Behind them came their nurse. After Glaphyra stomped Uncle Tullius, come to inspect his new property and see what his nephew had done to it. He had already decided that he disliked the house, hated its position, would never enjoy country isolation and silence, and now he had seen it he suspected he had paid too much.

As he advanced across the stony ground that still covered what had been an orchard, now bare of trees, our clerk-of-works called us. The patch of ground where the pyre had stood yesterday had been cleaned up. Larcius was pointing.

'Is this a weed that's just cheekily popped out, or something more interesting, Chief?'

He knew what he was saying. There, forcing its way through the volcanic deposits, a small green sign of life was sprouting. An old tree's roots had somehow survived below ground, indefatigably tough. Everywhere in the wasteland around Vesuvius this might be happening, though perhaps not always encouraged by the warmth of funeral fires.

In the aftermath of tragedy, hope follows. The green sprout was an olive shoot.

AFTERWORD

Uncle Tullius quickly decided the villa he had purchased was much too large for his purposes and poorly located. If he had wanted to be up on the cliff, he would have bought something on the edge, with much better views. He sold the house and grounds to the tribune, as a retirement home. With feigned regret, he screwed out of Gaius Caunus a substantial profit, saying, 'I need to pay my nephew for all his team's restoration work.' Sharing out this profit seemed to work more in the uncle's favour than the nephew's. To me, that was no surprise.

Still wanting to invest in the Neapolis region, with supposed support for the local community, Tullius acquired a new-build townhouse down near the port in Stabiae. This he obtained at a cracking price, a real bargain, due to the felonious nature of its first owner. It had been confiscated as punishment for a capital crime. Tullius jumped in before the property was even put on the market by government commissioners; he always brushed aside our raucous accusations of insider trading.

When we visited our uncle's new townhouse the next summer, it had a room with finely stuccoed walls, which included plaques showing the Labours of Hercules. Tullius had brought them with him from the villa. He reckoned movable chattels were his; what Gaius Caunus did not know would not distress him. In any case they were slightly imperfect: the Erymanthian Boar was missing part of its snout.

Two years afterwards, my young cousin Marius won a substantial prize in the competition for auletes at the Isolympic Games in Naples. On the strength of this he came back to Rome, where I was aware that his concerts were often attended by one adoring fan: my maid, Suza.

Tullius Icilius bought a ship, which he kept for some years. According to him, this was useful for a man who engaged in the immortal traditions of import/export. When Tiberius demurred gently that the Icilii were warehouse owners not traders, he was told that nobody with any nous turns down the chance to acquire a sailing vessel that is going cheap because of a dodgy history. Now we could transport our own wines into Rome for family consumption. Tullius even joked that he could find space for any large pieces of ballast that my father needed to have carried up to auction from the flourishing Campanian art market. Whatever the ship had been called in the first place, he renamed it the *Fortuna Redux*.

The group statue of lapiths and centaurs ought to have been returned to its owner, but for some reason – perhaps he had died or gone away – this never happened. By coincidence, at an auction the following autumn my father sold similar pieces; they were smaller and much more manoeuvrable, as if someone had hacked them from a larger group to make them attract more bidders; they had a few dints, but Falco denied the pieces had fallen off a cart.

The other statue, *Augustus Looking Imperial,* was gifted to the town of Stabiae by Apuleius Innocentius, a local worthy, to celebrate some sign of favour bestowed on him by the Emperor. However, for what I hope are aesthetic reasons, it has never been installed.

As for the Curvidii, Fulvia Secunda soon passed away, as prophesied by the priestess. A will was discovered, which left all her estate, including the valuable vineyard, to Publilius Gellius and Publilia Lavinia. Since they had looked after her so well, this caused no comment. After all, they were friends of the family.

I have no knowledge of Curvidia Quinctia's fate; on summer holidays at the townhouse, we never went up to the Temple of Tyche. I am a city girl and share little of the Roman passion for finding solace in sea views and mountain scenery. I do know Polydorus put his foot down, so despite a freedman's duty to his patroness, he moved down into Stabiae town where he set up his own grocery; on our annual vacations, Fornix always filled our larder with provisions from his store.

I presume the unseen Quartilla remained at Salernum in charge of the family tomb.

I heard there had once been a third brother, Tertius, who had died young. People who knew me always forbade me to ask questions about how or why.

Curvidius Fulvianus was absorbed back into the business world in Rome and rarely heard of afterwards. I never found out what quarrel had caused him to leave Campania. As a father of four children, my husband knows about stress; he reckons members of that family should live as far from each other as possible. 'Otherwise,' says the wise Tiberius Manlius, 'there will be more bodies.'